Man In Black

Black Knights Inc: Reloaded

JULIE ANN WALKER

MAN IN BLACK
Copyright © 2024 by Julie Ann Walker

ISBN: 978-1-950100-18-7

Cover Art © 2024 by Erin Dameron-Hill

Interior Formatting: Bravia Books, LLC

Published in the United States of America
Limerence Publications LLC

To Alan.
Thanks for inviting me into your inner circle, taking care of my fur baby when I'm away, and always being game for a day of chasing waterfalls.

Nothing in the world happens by coincidence.

—Malcolm Nance

PROLOGUE

Black Knights Inc., Goose Island, Chicago, Illinois

Fisher Wakefield was blown away.

Not an entirely unexpected outcome given his chosen profession. As a decorated Delta Force grunt turned super-secret government defense contractor who ran missions so black they never received a code name or crossed the desk of some high-ranking official in the Department of Defense. On a good day his chances of getting turned into chunky salsa were hovering somewhere around fifty/fifty.

It wasn't an IED that took him out, however. Nor was it a 50-cal, a hand grenade, or a rocket launched from a bazooka.

It was a woman.

The woman.

She didn't end him with an arrow to his heart or a round to his brainpan, however. She ended him with a dress.

No, it's not a dress, he thought, feeling his heart rate kick up at the same time his breathing went shallow. *It's the pinnacle of dresses. The dress that every dress before it has tried to be and every dress after it will fail to be. The dress to end all dresses.*

Black satin. One of those necklines that looked like the top half of a heart. And a slit up one side that bordered on being indecent. Probably *was* labeled indecent in some of the more conservative parts of the state.

It held her breasts high when she appeared at the top of the stairs. Sighed open to reveal one mile-long leg as she placed her hand on the rail and stepped onto the first tread. And it moved with her like a second skin as she made her way down from the second floor of the old menthol cigarette factory that was headquarters for the custom motorcycle shop known to the world as Black Knights Inc.—and living quarters for the clandestine group of operators who worked out of it.

She walks in beauty like the night…

Lord Byron's famous line drifted through his head. He chastised himself for falling back on an old cliché when he had so many *other* gems to choose from.

Like Maya Angelou's… *I am woman. Phenomenally.* Or William Wordsworth's… *She was a phantom of delight when first she gleamed upon my sight.*

Both poems were appropriate. Both described the woman and her impact. But neither worked as well as Byron's. Because Byron's compared a lady to the night. And that fit her to a tee.

Her hair was as black as a moonless sky. Her skin was as pale and as bright as the stars. And when she smiled at him, particularly anytime she'd smiled at him lately, it was as hard and as sharp as a sickle moon.

"Careful. You'll be catching flies."

He realized he was gaping like a catfish trapped on a mudbank when Britt Rollins reached over and knuckle-bumped the bottom of his chin.

Britt was a former Army Ranger and an adrenaline junkie who liked jumping out of airplanes, climbing mountains, and racing dune buggies across the desert even when he *wasn't* on a mission.

Britt was also Fisher's best friend.

From the day they'd met inside a windowless basement room in the Pentagon—the day they'd been tasked with abandoning their military contracts and signing on to answer to none other than the president herself—they'd been cronies in crime. Bosom buddies. Or, as Britt liked to say, *wingmen for life.*

But where Fisher moved through the world with as much irreverence as possible, Britt seemed perpetually on the hunt for the next most-dangerous thing. Where Fisher was lucky to make a grilled cheese sandwich without setting the place on fire, Britt could whip up a crab boil or a bowl of shrimp and grits as easily as breathing. But most glaringly, where Fisher was deliberate and planned, Britt was haphazard and impulsive.

Their differences meant they made a good team. Where one was weak, the other was strong. And *that* had saved their asses more than a time or two.

Being teammates, best friends, and brothers by choice instead of blood, meant they *also* didn't bullshit each other.

Which is why Fisher didn't prevaricate when he answered, "Either I've died and gone to heaven…" He had to clear his throat. The hoarse grate of his voice reminded him of Humvee tires crunching over rough terrain. "Or I'm in hell."

"Gotta be the former." Britt's Lowcountry accent dropped the R sounds off the final word until it sounded more like *fahmah*. "Because only angels look like that." The ex-Ranger's voice was filled with awe as his eyes remained glued to the dress.

And the woman *in* the dress.

When something venomous and prickly legged unfurled in the center of Fisher's chest, he reminded himself Britt loved Eliza like a kid sister. Same as the rest of the Knights.

Er…same as everyone but me, he corrected, shifting his stance when his blood surged south in the normal reaction to seeing a beautiful woman wearing something that hugged every curve and slithered over every line.

Normal, but frustratingly unwelcome.

He and Britt had been working on their custom Harley choppers, Britt running a shammy over the chrome on his handlebars and Fisher finishing the job of changing out his headlight, when their office manager/live-in chef/and all-around girl Friday appeared on the upper landing. Now they stood motionless, mesmerized by the graceful sway of her hips as she carefully navigated the metal staircase in strappy, high-heeled shoes that showed off her fresh pedicure.

The paint on her toes was a sinful, ruby red. It matched the lipstick staining her mouth.

Fisher was amazed at how subtle a woman in seduction mode could be. No detail was too small. No element was overlooked. Everything was done for one purpose and one purpose only…to attract and hold the male gaze.

Sure as shit is holdin' mine.

Of course, she could be wearing a circus tent and rain boots and he'd still be unable to look away. Because Eliza Meadows was…

Well, the poem says it all. She's as beautiful as the night.

As mysterious, wondrous, and magical too.

Also…Britt was right. If anyone had earned their place beyond the pearly gates, it was Eliza with her soft heart and generous spirit. With her honesty and integrity and world-record patience when it came to working and living with a group of stubborn, arrogant, high-handed fighting men.

Too bad she's spent the last four months datin' the biggest bag of dicks this side of the Mississippi, he thought sourly.

All his softer sentiments were crushed beneath the weight of the venomous, prickly legged thing stretched to its full height inside him.

Eliza was the upper crust yin to his grits-and-gravy yang. She was a boarding school socialite. He'd grown up so poor he couldn't have jumped over a nickel to save a dime. She could look at the impressionist paintings in the Chicago Art Institute and tell the difference between a Monet and a Renoir. His idea of fine art was the faded, velvet picture of dogs playing poker that had been nailed to the wall behind the sofa in his cousin's house.

In short, he and Eliza had *nothing* in common.

Zip. Zero. Zilch.

Which meant she'd never been his. But, more importantly, never *would* be his. So there was no reason for him to be jealous of the high-haired son of Senator John McClean.

And yet, he thought, his breath getting trapped in his lungs when she stepped off the bottom tread and sashayed her way across the shop floor in his direction, *here I am. Jealous as a cock pigeon over his hen. And provin' the apple doesn't fall far from the tree.*

He blamed the venomous, prickly legged monster he'd inherited from his father for the sneer that spread across his face and the fact that the first words out of his mouth were caustic instead of complimentary.

"That man of yours ever consider takin' ya out for a scoop of ice cream? Why's he always makin' ya get all gussied up? What's he tryin' to prove?"

Her beautiful mouth, painted that scrotum-tightening red, flattened into a thin line. "Why do you insist on giving me grief for that?" She cocked a hip to give her balled-up fist something to perch on. The move caused the slit in her dress to slide open, revealing that one pale, perfect leg.

A leg that, in the wee hours of the morning—and sometimes right smack dab in the middle of the day—he imagined trailing his fingers over. Trailing his lips over. Trailing his *tongue* over.

"Maybe 'cause ya provide me with such a wealth of material on the matter." He grinned and then immediately reconsidered his words. Hitching his chin to her exposed leg, he slowly let his gaze travel up her hips and waist to settle on the mounds of flesh left bared by the dress's lowcut neckline. "Or, in the case of tonight's outfit, it's probably more fittin' to say such a decided *lack* of material."

Since his eyes were drinking in the lovely lines of her decolletage, he didn't miss the deep flush that stole up from her chest to stain her neck and cheeks. He followed the color until his gaze clashed with hers.

Her dark eyes, which she'd inherited from her Greek mother, slanted up at the corners to give her a slightly feline appearance. They were usually filled with a warm, inviting light. But right then, they were as hard and as cold as gunmetal.

Guilt whispered in his ear. He ignored it. And when she squared off against him like a prize fighter facing a big-fisted opponent, he thought for sure she was using her feminine appeal to drive him wild.

No way she doesn't know how sexy she is standing there like that. Nostrils flarin'. Purse clutched in a curled fist. Teeth bared in a snarl that makes a man want to fill her mouth with—

"Charlie can wear a pair of jeans and eat ice cream with the best of them." She cut into his thoughts.

Good thing. His thoughts hadn't been headed in a direction he was particularly proud of.

She glanced over his faded Levi's and standard-issue Hanes tee with a derisive sneer. Despite that, he felt the path of her gaze like a physical touch. Every inch of his skin heated in response.

"But he can also rock a tuxedo," she added, "eat caviar, and stand in a room full of this country's most powerful people with his head held high. Not too many can say *that*."

She punctuated the last word by tossing her dark hair over her shoulder. Most days she wore it slicked back in a bun or pulled tight in a ponytail. Tonight it was long and loose, falling in thick, shiny waves around her shoulders. Begging for the touch of a man's fingers.

To keep from reaching out, he shoved his hands deep in his pockets. The fingers on his right hand automatically curled around the cold steel of his favorite harmonica.

"I'd be more impressed if he'd accomplished all that on his own," he scoffed while waving a dismissive hand. "Given he was born with a silver spoon stickin' straight out of his mouth, it's a smidge less admirable."

"Oooh." The pulse in her neck beat fast in fury. "Why do you hate Charlie so much? Is it because he makes the world a better place through acts of charity instead of acts of violence?"

Like you.

She didn't say those last two words.

He heard them, nonetheless.

The truth was, he'd have traded places with Charles McClean in an instant. To have been raised by a powerful father who supported all his dreams and aspirations instead of an abusive asshole who'd ignored him in the best of times and emotionally and verbally abused him in the worst? To have been given the choice on what he wanted to do with his life instead of being forced into military service because the only other options for making a living in Nowhere, Louisianna, had been cooking meth or dealing cards on the riverboat casino?

To have Eliza?

To have been *worthy* of her?

He said none of this, of course. Instead, he barked a laugh that rang with cynicism. "That's a mighty high pedestal ya got him on, doll face. Careful. If he ever loses his balance, the fall will be long and the landin' will be hard."

"Annnnddd, I'm out." Having decided he wanted no part in their sparring, Britt vamoosed himself toward the back of the shop and busied himself with the V-twin engine sitting atop a bike lift.

When Fisher turned back from watching his best friend's cowardly retreat, it was to find Eliza's gaze still hard and cold on his face. The air around her seemed to vibrate with animosity.

It was sexy.

She was sexy.

But, more than that, she was smart and funny and kind, and he *liked* her. Like, *liked* her liked her. And it rankled more than he'd ever willingly admit that she'd never given him the time of day.

Well…that wasn't exactly true. There'd been a brief moment when he'd thought…maybe. But no.

"What makes you so sure he'll fall off?" she demanded. "Some people have no trouble balancing on those high pedestals because they *belong* up there. Also"—a muscle ticked in her jaw—"stop calling me doll face. You know I hate it."

Ignoring that last bit, he cocked his head and regarded her. "They always fall off. In the end."

"Sounds like projection to me." She bared her teeth in a snarl just as Peanut, the fat, notch-eared tomcat who was part mascot and part benevolent ruler at Black Knights Inc. padded over and began making figure eights around her bare ankles.

The act of rubbing his chubby body and crooked tail against her skin had the cat's motor turning over. And his purr was loud enough to compete with the rumbling engines of the custom bikes lined up like chrome-coated soldiers behind Fisher.

I get it, he thought. *I'd be purring too if I was lucky enough to be touching her.*

He'd purr. And then he'd growl. And then he'd sink his teeth into—

"Is that why you can't keep a woman around for more than a few days?" She ignored Peanut's antics. "Because you so quickly disabuse them of any misplaced notions you might actually want them for more than what they can offer you in the bedroom?"

She was baiting him. He knew it as surely as he knew those cliched stories about the rich girl falling for the guy from the wrong side of the tracks were only true in low-budget rom-coms and cheesy romance novels.

"Why would I care about findin' Mrs. Right when there are so many Miss Right Nows eager to take a ride on—"

"Stop." She lifted her hand, palm-out. For a brief moment their wills clashed right along with their eyes. Then her combative expression dissolved into one of weariness. "If all our conversations are going to end with us getting angry at each other, I think it's best if we stop talking altogether."

As much as he hated what'd become of their interactions, the thought of not talking to her at all filled him with sadness. And…*fear*?

But that was silly. How could he be afraid to lose something he'd never had to begin with?

"Easier said than done seein' as how we live and work together." He gestured around the old factory with its three-story ceiling, line of gleaming custom-made Harleys, and wide garage doors that they threw open when the weather was nice.

"It's a big space," she countered. "Plenty of room to avoid each other." With a saccharin smile that didn't reach her eyes, she added, "Let's start now."

Before he could get in another word, she bent to give Peanut's whiskered cheek a scratch. It was enough to have the cat's yellow eyes rolling back in his head. Then she straightened and breezed by him, heading for the front door.

The smells of too-strong coffee, grease guns, and metal shavings were momentarily replaced by the sweet scent of her perfume—spring rain on a bergamia tree. And his nostrils flared wide as he watched her straight back and heart-shaped ass with the still, silent concentration of a stalking cougar.

He searched his mind for a pithy retort but couldn't come up with anything that didn't sound childish. Left with no recourse, he was forced to let her have the last word.

After she gave the handle a twist, the large door opened with security-tight *beep* and a *hiss*. Then she was gone. A raven-haired siren disappearing into the hot summer night and leaving him feeling cold and desolate by contrast.

When the door swung shut behind her, he glowered at Peanut. "Why do ya always have to rub your kitty privileges in my face?" he asked under his breath.

The mangy feline slow-blinked in answer before flopping onto his side, lifting a leg behind his head, and dutifully going about the business of making sure his testicles were squeaky clean.

It was the kitty equivalent of a giant middle finger.

"Boy howdy, partner." Having recognized the skirmish had ended, Britt walked over to clap a hand on Fisher's shoulder. "You and Eliza been oil and water from the start. But now you're more like fire and kerosene. You can't seem to be in the same room without one or both of you blowing up."

It was true. Although…for a while there they'd found some common ground, pulled their punches, and called a truce. It'd been a short-lived thing though. Little more than a handful of days. And then Charles McClean had waltzed into the picture with his Ivy-League education and Gucci loafers, and everything had gone back to the way it'd been before.

No, Fisher silently corrected. *It's worse.*

Their previously good-natured ribbing had taken on a decidedly *caustic* turn. Where once they'd jabbed and jibbed, now they slashed and burned.

"Some folks just weren't meant to get along, I reckon," he told Britt, feigning an indifference he didn't feel.

"Mmph." The ex-Ranger tossed the shammy over his shoulder so he could cross his arms and regard Fisher with a curious cant of his head. "You think that's because she's shinier than a silver dollar and you're as country as a bowl of grits?"

"Nah. If that were true, she'd give *you* as much grief as she gives me. You're as country as I am."

"Not so." Britt lifted a contradictory finger. "I'm as *Southern* as you are. But not nearly as country. Charleston is a teeming metropolis compared to the mud bottom you grew up in."

Fisher couldn't argue. His place of birth was *literally* a one stoplight town. Little more than a wide patch in the road where everyone knew everyone, and the only difference from person to person was whether they attended the Baptist, Methodist, or Presbyterian church on Sunday morning.

"It's simple," he explained. "She's the closest thing we have to American royalty, and I was born so poor I couldn't even afford to pay attention. We're like two magnets with negative charges. We repel each other."

"Well, now." Britt scratched his chin, his fingernails *scritching* over his beard stubble. "You hear the contradiction in what you're saying, right?"

"No." Fisher shook his head at the same time he spied the television hung on the wall between the two large rolling garage doors. It was tuned to the security feed and displayed the scene playing out at the front gate.

He gritted his teeth hard enough to crack the enamel when Eliza slipped through the gap in the wrought-iron gate only to be caught up in Charles McClean's wide, waiting arms.

The man had parked his shiny gray Mercedes S-Class by the curb. Its chrome bumper and flawless paintjob *screamed* money. The generational kind. The trust fund and investment portfolio kind.

Fisher couldn't help thinking there was something profoundly wrong with anyone who would lay down that much cash on a car that could so easily be demolished by the next city bus.

Kinda like the six-figure motorcycle you ride?

The better angels of his nature always reared their ugly heads at the most inopportune times.

No, he silently argued with them. Which, yes, he realized meant he was actually arguing with himself. *It's different. First of all, Mardi Gras is a rolling advertisement for Becky's business.* Rebecca Knight, aka the loveable Becky, was the wunderkind motorcycle designer whose mechanical miracles kept the Black Knights' covers intact. *Second of all, I didn't pay for Mardi Gras. He's a benefit of the job. And third of all…*

Well, third of all, it was just *different*. He and Charles McClean were night and day, black and white, so opposite in all the ways that mattered he refused to hear words to the contrary. Even if those words were whispered inside his own head.

"In one breath you're saying you and Eliza couldn't be more different." Britt pulled him from his musings. "You know, her with her champagne taste and you with your beer pocketbook. In the next breath, you're claiming you're similarly charged magnets that can't help pushing each other's way. So which is it? You're so different you can't get along? Or are you so alike you can't get along? It can't be both."

Since Fisher had no way to contradict the logic of Britt's argument, and since he sure as shit wasn't going to admit the truth, which was that he found himself picking fights with Eliza to keep from sweeping her up and kissing the daylights out of her, he shrugged. "Don't know and don't care. All that matters is I have a night off. And since ya brought up my beer pocketbook, how d'ya feel 'bout joinin' me for a game of cornhole and a coupla Goose Islands?"

"I feel like you're putting a period on the conversation because you know I'm right. But I also feel like you're speaking my language when it comes to brews." Britt tossed the shammy over his chopper's handlebars. "And since arguing with you will get me nothing and drinking with you will get me drunk, I choose door number two. Lead the way."

Britt was hot on Fisher's heels when he made his way toward the short hall that led to the kitchen. His peripheral vision clocked the image of

Charles McClean—heretofore known as Captain Dickless—planting a long, lingering kiss on Eliza's mouth before she ducked into the Mercedes's passenger seat. And fantasies of ending the frat boy in bloody and painful ways danced through his head.

Some of what he was thinking must've been written across his face because Britt took one look at his profile and whistled. "Damn, man. Evil thoughts are like chickens. They come home to roost."

"You sayin' ya *like* the idea of our Eliza out with a man who's never turned a wrench or fired a weapon? A man who couldn't protect her from a rabid squirrel much less the kind of enemies we might have lurkin' 'round?"

Britt's expression turned censorious. "Don't piss on my boots and tell me it's raining. You don't dislike McClean because his hands are smooth or because his wallet is fat. There's something else going on with you. I can't put my finger on it precisely, but I got my suspicions."

Ignoring his best friend's conjectures, Fisher doubled down. "I'm just sayin' I think the world would be a better place with fewer rich, white, yacht-ridin' assholes like Captain Dickless."

If he'd known how prophetic his words would turn out to be, he would've kept them to himself.

CHAPTER 1

Senator McClean's residence, 2700 N. Lakeview Ave.

Eliza tasted blood. Hot. Salty. Iron-rich.

She *smelled* blood too. That thick, rusty aroma was unmistakable.

And when she blearily opened her eyes, all she saw was blood. A crimson sheet of it. As if someone had thrown a bucket into her face, coating her eyeballs in the stuff.

But whose blood?

Hers?

If so, she felt no lightheadedness. No wooziness. No pain.

Correction. Her cheek hurt and she could feel her heartbeat in her left temple. But it wasn't the kind of agony one would associate with that much blood loss.

But maybe that was how it worked when one was mortally wounded. Maybe the brain had a way of disconnecting from the body in the final moments so the person could pass in peace.

She waited for the fear to rise, that inevitable apprehension of the great transition and the unknown that watched from beyond. But it never came. Waited for the tears to fall, to feel the deep regret for all the things she'd wanted to do but hadn't yet. But they never fell. Waited for her heart to slow, for her thoughts to dim. But neither of those things happened either.

Thirty seconds became a minute. A minute turned into two. Finally, she was forced to admit that, despite the copious amounts of blood, she didn't appear to be dying.

Which left her only one course of action. *Take stock. Reevaluate. Try to make sense of the state of myself.*

She started with her toes, gave them a little wiggle, and found they worked. *Woohoo!* Moved on to her fingers and was delighted to discover they, too, functioned the way they were meant to. *Yippee!*

Ankles? Check.

Wrists? Check, check.

That's where her progress ended, unfortunately. When she tried to lift her legs, she couldn't. Same for her arms. They were pinned solidly against her sides.

She was almost certain she was lying face down with something on top of her. Something extraordinarily *heavy* that kept her body restrained and her cheek smashed tight into…

What? The floor? The ground? The foundation of a building that'd caved in on her?

Where am I?

She couldn't remember. Not where she was or why she was there. She couldn't even recall *when* it was. Day or night? Monday or Friday? April or October?

A black hole had taken up residence in the center of her brain. A deep void that sucked in every thought before she could latch onto it. Which was far more terrifying than the taste and smell and sight of blood. Because not knowing the who or how or why of what'd happened meant she hadn't the first clue how to save herself from the thing that held her immobile.

Or…maybe not *completely* immobile.

When she went to grab the locket she wore around her neck—a gesture so ingrained it was almost like breathing—her elbow bent. Just a little. But more than that, the weight pinning her shifted.

Or had it?

Had she imagined movement because that's what she so desperately wanted?

She'd never been claustrophobic. In fact, one of her favorite things as a teen had been to drag her best friend and boarding school roommate into the closet late at night so they could laugh and whisper and tell girlish secrets without the floor monitor knocking on their door and yelling at them to get to sleep so they'd be bright-eyed and bushy-tailed for class the next day.

Bright-eyed and bushy-tailed had been Ms. Stapelton's favorite phrase.

And when she was feeling particularly scared or overwhelmed by the danger her guys were in—that's how she thought of the Knights, as *her guys*—sometimes she'd crawl into bed and pull her weighted blanket up to her chin. Something about being closed-in and weighed down kept her mind from flying apart.

But now? Oh *now* she understood why people loathed tight spaces. She seriously wanted whatever was on top of her to *get the hell off!*

No. On second thought, it wasn't a want. It was a *need*.

Her bones ached from the pressure. Her lungs labored with the effort to draw breath. And her cheekbone felt like it might shatter if it stayed smashed against the hard surface beneath her for one more second. Not to mention, the terrible ache behind her left temple had grown into a throb so hard and steady, she was sure no medication could touch it.

Gritting her teeth, she tried moving her elbow again, angling it up from its straight position into something closer to ninety degrees.

It wasn't easy. But she was able to slowly, inch by inch, slip her left hand up until it was even with her shoulder. The liquid of life oozed hot against her palm, but she refused to think about the foulness of it. The absolute *horror* of it.

She completed the same maneuver with her right hand. Again, it took effort. And by the time she'd succeeded in getting her palm even with her shoulder, the urge to breathe deep was overwhelming.

But one, she *couldn't*. Not with her rib cage squeezed to the point of fracture. And two, breathing deeply would only pull the scent of blood farther into her lungs and… *No thank you.*

Panting like a dog instead, she willed the added oxygen to fuel her efforts. Then she pushed with all her might until her biceps burned, her shoulders strained, and the back of her head pressed hard against the thing pinning her down.

Her cheek inched away from the solid surface. Her neck and chest gained space too. But before she could scoot her knees up to aid in her endeavors, her muscles gave out on her and she lost all headway.

Her cheek smacked back into the pool of blood, sending pain radiating across her entire face. Blood filled her ear with a sickening squelching sound, filled her nose with its retched metallic scent.

The scream that tore from her throat then was one of frustration as much as it was one of pain or horror. It was forceful enough to flay her vocal cords raw and make her ears ring.

She was surprised to hear the sound echo out into a void.

A void?

She'd assumed she was walled in. *Caved* in. But her cry drifted off into the air before quickly dying out.

If she wasn't surrounded by whatever was holding her down, then if she could just get out from under the thing, she'd be free.

Free!

Desperation kicked in.

She wasn't sure where it'd been before. When one woke up covered in blood, missing all memory, and pinned beneath something rib-crushingly heavy, desperation was surely the *first* response.

Of course, wherever her desperation had been before didn't matter. Because it was with her now. Consumed her now. Flooded her bloodstream with that sweet, metabolic fuel known as adrenaline.

This time her cry was one of determination when she planted her hands on the flat surface and heaved upward. Her feet, which weren't as encumbered as the rest of her, scrabbled for purchase.

Come on! Come on! She silently screamed as she felt her hands begin to slip again.

Why didn't she use the gym in the outbuilding behind BKI? It was fully equipped with everything a person needed to get *shredded*—as Britt liked to call it. If she'd spent some of her downtown bench-pressing weights instead of baking cakes, maybe she'd be able to—

Her thoughts screeched to a stop when the weight atop her shifted. Slowly at first. Then all at once.

Whatever had been holding her down rolled to the side with a soft-sounding *shush* followed by a *thud* and—

She was free!

Free to rake in a deep breath.

Free to push into a seated position so she could use the backs of her hands to rub her eyes.

It didn't help. The blood just smeared. She reached down and lifted the edge of her…dress? She was wearing a dress? Why? Her usual uniform consisted of freshly pressed slacks and a prim button-down shirt.

Well, whatever, she thought, impatient now. Impatient to clear her vision and see what it was she'd gotten herself into. Impatient to figure out how to get herself *out*.

Her eyeballs stung from the vigorous scrubbing she gave them, but eventually her vision cleared enough for her to lift her head and look around.

The scene that met her fuzzy, searching gaze was…

Carnage.

That was the only word for it.

There were bodies. Blood. *Death.*

My guys! her anguished brain screamed.

But no sooner had the words echoed in her pounding skull than she knew her mistake.

The corpses strewn about didn't belong to the men she'd grown to know and love like family. This wasn't the floor of Black Knights Inc.

Relief rushed through her with enough strength to make her dizzy as she blinked at the awful scene. Blinked again. Blinked a third time because she couldn't fathom it. Couldn't wrap her head around the truth of the bloodbath even though she wasn't *un*familiar with the sight.

As the link between the Black Knights and the leader of the free world, she was often tasked with putting together mission reports that included images of gore and destruction. But it was one thing to see bloodshed shining out at her from a digital display. And another thing entirely to witness its reality.

With a macabre sort of fascination, she watched the pool of blood beneath a body ooze ever larger, heard the gruesome quiet that accompanied the end of life, smelled the stomach-turning scents of piss and shit. As if death wasn't demeaning enough, it had to go and make things worse by loosening the bladders and bowels of the people it'd come to claim.

"My god," she breathed, one shaky hand lifting to the locket around her neck. The feel of the cool metal acted as a catalyst, a cold, hard shock to her system. And, suddenly, it all came screaming back.

The cocktail party hosted by Charlie's father at his impressive Lincoln Park mansion. The milling around of a dozen smartly dressed people on the large flagstones covering the back patio. The soft sounds of jazz piped through the outdoor speakers.

The moment Charlie pulled her aside to propose. The sweaty chef who walked onto the patio carrying an evil-looking machine gun instead of a tray of tasty treats. The look of horror and determination on Charlie's face right before he'd launched himself at her.

Charlie!

Her head whipped around to find her worst fear realized.

He had been the thing pinning her to the ground. It'd been his big, strong body that'd shielded her from the gunman's murderous melee. Now he lay on his side, his baby-blue tie stained crimson with blood. His handsome face…gone.

Just…*gone.*

In its place was gristle and meat and—

Her gorge rose, but she swallowed it down as she scrambled over and pressed her fingers to the side of his neck despite knowing her efforts were futile. No one could live after losing that much blood. After losing that much of their *face.*

When no telltale *thud* rose up to meet her searching fingertips, she could no longer hold back the contents of her stomach.

She managed to crawl a few feet away before she retched convulsively onto the large, gray flagstones. Her vomit smelled of champagne and stomach bile. The instant the awful combination hit her nostrils, her gag reflex went full send.

She puked again.

And again.

Heaved until her throat ached and her stomach cramped.

Only when there was nothing left to bring up did she sit back on her heels, exhausted. Choking on her tears. Unable to catch her breath because her rib cage had become a vice around her lungs.

Oh, Charlie…

She couldn't comprehend that one second he'd been slipping a ring onto her finger and the next he'd been killed.

Murdered!

"Killed" implied it could've been an accident. Or a force of nature. Like, he'd crossed the street at the wrong time and been hit by a speeding taxicab, or he'd fallen off the sailboat he kept moored at Belmont Harbor and drowned in Lake Michigan.

But no. This was planned. This was intentional. This was…a massacre.

Charles Xavier McClean was dead. *Dead!*

How was it possible? How could something so awful happen to someone so good? Someone who had so much life left to live? Someone who'd wanted to share that life with her and—

Her thoughts crashed to a stop as a hard sob burst from her throat. For long minutes, all she could do was cry. Pull her legs to her chest and cry. Bury her face in her knees and cry.

Cry for the man who'd come to mean so much to her.

Cry for the sacrifice he'd made in saving her.

Cry for not being able to love him like he'd loved her.

Cry, cry, *cry.*

Charles McClean is dead.

Charles McClean is dead, she silently recited as she rocked against the flagstones. She didn't want Charlie's death to be like her mother's. She didn't want to relive the trauma of turning to tell him something only to remember too late he was gone—like she had a hundred times after her mother had been put in the ground. She didn't want to relive the agony of waking up in the morning having forgotten about her loss and then have reality slap her in the face and make her want to crawl back under the covers.

It was better to drill the truth into her brain now. To nail her new reality into her gray matter with a steel spike until there was no question of it.

Charles McClean is dead.

They're all *dead.*

Crawling back to Charlie's side, she was careful not to look at the gruesome mess that had once been his beautiful face. Pulling his large, well-manicured hand into her lap, she noted it seemed to be the only part of him that'd been spared the gunman's wrath. The rest of him was riddled with holes. The cream lining of his sport coat poked through the darker material like macabre flowers stained red with his blood.

She tried counting the rounds he'd taken and gave up when she passed a dozen.

"Charlie…" Her voice was hoarse with tears, harsh with pain.

He'd deserved so much better than this. Better than her and—

Her mind began running through all the if-onlys.

If only instead of freezing and blinking in confusion when she'd first seen the weapon, she'd grabbed his hand and pulled him around the side of the house, maybe they would have been able to outrun the gunman.

If only she'd had the wherewithal to snatch the canister of Mace from her clutch before Charlie tackled her perhaps she could have blinded the shooter and saved Charlie, saved the others.

If only she'd listened to her gut and declined the offer to attend tonight's gathering, perhaps Charlie would have stayed home too and maybe he'd still be alive.

If only…

They were the saddest two words in the English language.

She had no idea how much time passed as she sat beside Charlie's cooling body wishing she'd changed just one thing. Just one, teeny, tiny thing that might have made all the difference. But it was long enough for the blood staining her hands to turn ice cold. Long enough for her to squeeze out her last tear, leaving her as dry as the desert and as numb as a severed limb.

In the quiet that followed, her focus expanded.

She became aware of the warm summer wind whispering through the trees beyond the patio, making their leaves shiver and sigh. She noted how upbeat jazz still hummed lowly from the outdoor speakers—sounding macabre given the circumstances. And farther, beyond the large stone wall surrounding the senator's property, her ears picked up on the everyday sounds of the city. The *hum* of traffic. The *beep* of a horn. The *hiss* of a bus coming to a lumbering stop at a light.

A siren.

She sat up, waiting with bated breath for the authorities to arrive. But the high-low clamor didn't grow louder as it came closer. It grew fainter as the cop car drove off into the distance.

No one's coming to help, she realized.

No one had heard the awful *rat-a-tat-tat* of the weapon. The crashing of chairs and tables. The *screams*.

Oh, the screams… They were the last thing she remembered before Charlie jumped on top of her, sending her temple smacking into the flagstones so that she knew no more. Those horrible, awful, nightmarish screams.

Despite the warmth of the night, goose bumps peppered her skin as she gathered her courage in preparation for what must be done. She needed to get off her ass and find a phone. She needed to call in the authorities. But first, she needed to make sure the gunman was—

Oh my god! The gunman!

Why was she just now thinking of him?

Her heart had been in her throat since she'd regained consciousness. Now it swelled with terror, choking her, making her breaths wheezy as she quickly glanced around, allowing her gaze to skim over the gruesomeness of mass death in search of the perpetrator of it all.

Was he hiding somewhere waiting to finish off any survivors?

No. The man's body was splayed on the flagstones near the back door. The moment her gaze landed on him, she cried out in relief.

His chef's coat made him easily recognizable. But where once the garment had been white and pristine, now the front was splattered with blood, looking like the macabre canvas of a modern artist.

He still held the weapon in his hand. Although, it was no longer clenched in a tight fist. Now, it lay loose inside his grip. And it was impossible to know for sure, but it looked like he'd shot himself under the chin after he'd taken out everyone else.

Why? her mind cried. Why would anyone gun down a patio full of innocent people?

Unless…

Had it been politically motivated? Senator John McClean certainly hadn't been the sit back, raise his hand when it came time to vote, and collect his paycheck type of politician. Quite the contrary. John had been the loud, firebranding, anti-establishment kind.

A self-made billionaire, John had stepped down as CEO of the green energy company he'd built from the ground up only to take his talents to D.C. There he'd set about shaking things up and making enemies of the comfortable fat cats who paid mouth service to their constituents during election cycles only to turn around and vote against the interests of the people they'd sworn to represent once they were actually *in* office.

John had been a frequent flyer on the national news circuits, oftentimes lambasting his fellow senators for their apathy, hypocrisy, and outright treachery.

To say he'd been disliked by most of his peers was an understatement.

Did someone finally have enough? she wondered. *Did they decide he was too much of a liability?*

If so, why hadn't they just killed *him*? Why had they killed everyone else?

It was a question she couldn't answer. And honestly, she was too exhausted, too sad, too *horrified* by it all to try.

People got paid to find the answers to the question of *why*. It was time she called them in.

Pressing a kiss to the back of Charlie's hand, she silently thanked him and apologized to him in a single breath. Then she carefully placed his palm on the ground beside his body.

The mind was a strange place in times of trauma. It glossed over some details and focused on others. Like that Charlie's left shoelace was untied. Like that his socks were pink and printed with red and green watermelon slices—he'd had a thing for fun socks.

Like that she was already thinking of him in the past tense.

"Oh, Charlie," she whispered his name one final time and then slowly pushed to a stand.

The instant she was upright, her head spun and her stomach heaved. The throbbing behind her left eye radiated up and over the back of her head. And the ground beneath her feet felt like it went as soft and as soggy as a good tiramisu.

She grabbed the back of a nearby chair to steady herself. Only once she was assured she wasn't going to pass out did she tentatively press probing fingers to her head.

What she found had her wincing.

A knot the size of a golf ball bulged above her temple. When she gently palpated it, the pain nearly had her knees buckling.

Apparently, her temple had taken the worst of the fall when Charlie tackled her. That—her fingers moved to her cheek and she hissed—and her face.

"Hellfire and damnation." Fisher's favorite curse rolled off her tongue before she could stop it.

Fisher… She simultaneously wanted to scrub all thoughts of him from her head and call him to come get her.

Even though he'd always been a pain in her ass—more so recently—he was also as steady as they came. He'd phone in the authorities and then whisk her away to safety. He'd make all the decisions so she wouldn't have to.

"Stop it," she scolded herself. "You have this handled. You just need to find a phone and—"

A low, pain-filled moan sounded from somewhere nearby. Her head jerked up so fast she nearly fell over from the dizziness.

"Hello?" she called out, keeping both hands planted on the back of the chair lest she find herself face-first on the ground. *Again.*

"Help!" The cry was so faint, she wasn't sure she'd heard it. Then it came again. "Help us!"

"Where are you?" She pushed away from the chair so she could turn in a half circle, ignoring the pounding ache behind her eye and once more scanning the bodies in search of life.

She found none.

"Here!" On the opposite side of the patio, a blood-soaked hand appeared above the edge of an overturned table. It was small, feminine, and sporting an emerald the size of a baseball field.

"I see you!" she called. "I'm coming!"

Easier said than done, she silently added, disheartened at the distance to the table. In the space between lay dead people. And the thought of navigating her way through the sea of gore had her stomach threatening another revolt.

Thank goodness I have nothing left to bring up.

After raking in a deep breath—trying her best to ignore the smell of spilled champagne, blood, and…other things—she gingerly picked her way through the butchery.

She was halfway across the patio when her foot landed on an outstretched hand. She felt the soft give of flesh beneath her heel. Heard the crunch of bone.

"Oh god!" She glanced down and then immediately wished she hadn't.

The dark-eyed wife of a young congressman lay lifeless on the ground. A round had slammed into her left eye, taking the eyeball with it on its exit through the back of her skull. Gray matter lay in glistening, wet chunks around the woman's splayed brown hair. And the cream cocktail dress she'd been wearing, the one Eliza had so admired for its pretty lines and sweet, crocheted flowers, was ruined beyond recognition.

Except for one bloom.

One crisp, cream flower along the scooped neckline had managed to escape the carnage. But even as Eliza watched, it too began to fall victim to the gore.

Blood seeped from the surrounding material, slowly soaking into the delicate threads. It turned what was once innocent and pure-looking into something foul and corrupt.

The young congressman's wife—Eliza couldn't recall her name—had had a laugh so big and contagious that when Eliza had heard it from across the patio, she hadn't been able to stop herself from chuckling in response.

So much vitality, she thought sadly. *So much light and life. And now it's all gone.*

A snippet from an Emily Dickenson poem whispered through her head. *"Because I could not stop for Death, he kindly stopped for me."*

Obviously she spent too much time around Fisher when poetry sprung to mind at a time like this.

Fisher…

Why did she keep thinking of him? And *why* did every instinct in her body urge her to find a phone and call him?

Of course, the answer was simple.

When a person was suffering from shock and trauma, they automatically sought the comforting presence of loved ones.

And she loved Fisher Wakefield.

Despite his womanizing ways. Despite his irreverent sense of humor that so often rubbed her the wrong way. And despite the fact he'd never feel for her half of what she felt for him…

She loved him.

From the top of his curly, handsome head to the bottoms of his size thirteen feet.

Which was why she hadn't wanted to come tonight. She'd suspected Charlie was going to propose and she hadn't wanted to—

"Help!" The weak cry brought her back to the moment.

"I'm coming!" she called, continuing her journey across the patio.

She managed to reach the overturned table without stepping on any more body parts. But she'd waded though plenty of bodily *fluids*.

Don't think about that.

"I'm here," she whispered as she peeked over the edge of the table and took hope in what she saw.

An older woman with hair the color of bottled honey sat on the ground cradling a man's head in her lap.

"Senator Chastain," Eliza whispered.

The woman glanced up and gasped in alarm. It was then Eliza realized what a sight she must be, smeared with Charlie's blood.

Charlie…

Charles McClean is dead.

The words no longer sounded foreign. And there was a deep, abiding sadness in that.

"Are you hit?" Eliza asked the senator.

She'd met Bethany Chastain twice before. Once at the president's inaugural ball. And once while she'd been in Washington visiting her father. She'd been introduced to the woman's husband too. But for the life of her, she couldn't recall the man's name.

She blamed the bump on her head for the breach in her decorum. It felt like her brain had been scrambled.

"No." The senator's expression was vacant and tight with shock. "Bill, jumped on top of me and pulled the table down to shield us. But I think he's…" The senator trailed off, shaking her head helplessly.

Bill! That's right. Dr. William Chastain.

A professor for the Stritch School of Medicine at Loyola.

Eliza took in the deep, bloody furrow along one side of the professor's head and felt her heart sink. Head wounds were notoriously nasty. And a head wound from a bullet?

She hadn't known too many people who'd survived *that*.

"Is he…is he breathing?" Senator Chastain asked around a sob that sounded like it bubbled up from the back of her throat.

Eliza skirted the table to check the man's pulse. She was surprised when a steady beat met her touch.

"He's alive," she assured the woman, feeling urgency kick in. "But he needs an ambulance. Do you have your phone on you?"

The senator shook her head. "No…I…" She lifted a trembling hand to her temple. "I left my purse on the receiving table by the front door."

"And mine is…" Eliza stopped and cocked her head. *Mistake.* The move made it feel like her brain was sliding to one side of her skull.

Where *was* her phone?

Oh, right! She snapped imaginary fingers. In her clutch. And her clutch was…

Dread filled her as she stood and turned back to look at Charlie.

There. Under his leg.

"I'm going to get my cell phone, Senator." She placed a comforting hand on the woman's shoulder and grimaced at the bloody fingerprints it left behind.

"Why hasn't someone called this in?" The woman shook her head in bewilderment. "Surely someone heard that gunfire."

"This place is a fortress." Eliza gestured to the massive brick and concrete façade of the mansion. "It's got this entire block to itself. And even if it didn't, the firefight was likely drowned out by the city noise."

"There was no *fight* about it." The senator's voice shook with rough emotion. "It was a massacre."

"I know." Eliza refrained from comforting the senator further because one bloody handprint on the woman's shoulder was plenty.

Bethany Chastain shook her head, her bouffant of yellow hair—no doubt thanks to a talented stylist—still looking unbelievable tidy. "I can't believe it. John was right. This proves it."

Eliza frowned. "Right about what?"

The senator blinked up at her. "He didn't tell you?"

"Tell me what?" Apprehension had the hairs on the back of her neck standing at attention. What was the senator saying? What didn't she know that she was supposed to?

Senator Chastain opened her mouth to speak, but her husband moaned then, his eyelids fluttering rapidly and the fingers on his left hand twitching spasmodically.

The senator's cryptic words fell out of Eliza's head as urgency gripped her. Time was running out for the professor. "Just give me a minute, Senator, and I'll have help on the way."

The return journey across the patio was even more horrific than the initial trip.

A nearby streetlamp cast its light across the garish scene so that the wounds pocking the bodies stood out in harsh relief. The blood glistening on the ground looked darker, *wetter*. And already there was the smell of decay.

Bile crashed and burned up the back of Eliza's throat, igniting the length of her esophagus. Hot tears filled her eyes and left warm tracks down her cheeks. But she fought off the urge to go sit in a corner and scream at the senselessness of it all. At the *unfairness* of it all.

There was work to be done.

She was the only one who could do it.

Kneeling beside Charlie's body, she avoided looking at the mess that'd been made of him. Instead, she focused on the corner of her clutch peeking out from under his leg.

Gripping it with her thumb and forefinger, she tried yanking it free. It didn't budge. He was too heavy, and she couldn't get a good grip.

Closing her eyes, she blew out a shuddering breath. The thought of moving him, of watching all his once vibrant brawn and bulk shift lifelessly, filled her with dread. But there was no other way.

"Sorry, Charlie," she whispered, placing one hand on his hip and the other on his shoulder. After firmly planting her feet against the flagstones, she gave him a solid shove.

Just as she'd known would happen, his body flopped over, limbs loose as cooked noodles. The sound of his arm landing in a puddle of his own blood with a *splat* was something she'd relive in her nightmares.

But that was for Future Eliza to worry about. Current Eliza had more urgent things to accomplish.

She pulled her clutch into her lap. Her fingers were so sticky with blood that she struggled with the clasp. But eventually she was able to snap it open and pull her cell phone from the dark interior.

Autopilot had her pulling up her contacts list and her finger hovered over Fisher's name. But she scolded herself for the ridiculous impulse and instead quickly keyed in 9-1-1.

CHAPTER 2

Northwestern Memorial Hospital, 251 East Huron St.

"I think I'm going to throw up."

Just as Fisher reached for the kidney bean-shaped plastic container the nurse had left on the rolling tray beside the hospital bed, Eliza changed her mind.

"No. I think I'm going to pass out." She pressed a hand to her chest as if doing so could stop her lungs from working like bellows.

The top of her head was covered in dried blood. Except for the spot on one side of her face where the doctor had cleaned her up to assess the lump on her temple, she looked like something straight out of a horror film. *Carrie* on stage after the group of rival teens dumped the bucket of pig's blood on her.

And yet, to Fisher, she'd never looked more beautiful.

Beautiful because she's alive.

The thought of just how close she'd come to *not* being alive was enough to have his stomach souring. The two beers he'd had with Britt before she'd called to give them the dreadful news of what had happened to her sloshed around in the bottom of his belly like stagnant swamp water.

He nearly reached for the kidney bean container again. This time for *himself.*

"Why can't I catch my breath?" she asked desperately. The whites of her eyes stood out in harsh relief against the darkness of the blood on her forehead and cheeks. "I thought it was my head that was hurt. But maybe I breathed something into my lungs because—"

"It's the shock paired with the letdown of adrenaline," he reassured her, imagining the soles of his boots were glued to the floor so he wouldn't run to her side and pull her into his arms. Every instinct he had told him to cuddle her close, to wrap her up tight and make sure the world couldn't reach her.

But he wasn't sure she'd thank him for the effort. So he gave her the only thing he could. The advice of a man who'd lived through things like what she'd just lived through. Who'd seen death and destruction with his own eyes. Who knew what it was to watch someone he loved as they were taken from the world in the most brutal and barbaric of ways.

"If ya can force yourself to take slow, measured breaths," he instructed lowly, "the need to hyperventilate will pass."

"Right." She nodded, her lower lip trembling even as she squared her shoulders and made herself breathe slowly.

Within a minute, her chest rose and fell in even measures. And as soon as the crisis passed, all the starch went out of her.

He watched helplessly as her face crumbled. *And here comes the grief,* he thought. But, somehow, she valiantly held back a sob until the noise that popped out of her sounded more like a hiccup.

"I can't stop thinking about it." Her voice was a bare whisper, but he would swear her words ripped through the air inside the curtained-off section of the ER's triage room like a scream. "About *him.* Charlie, he—"

This time she had about as much luck holding back a sob as he'd have had holding back the muddy waters of the Mississippi.

Eliza Meadows was a tough nut. He'd never known what it would take to make her crack. And he couldn't say he was happy to discover that what'd finally shattered all her finishing school poise was being witness to her boyfriend's final moments and—

His eyes tracked down the huge diamond on her left hand. The facets of the stone caught the glaring florescent light and sparkled with so much fire he was tempted to shade his eyes.

Not boyfriend, he silently corrected himself. *Fiancé.*

Apparently, Eliza Meadows had agreed to become Mrs. Eliza McClean. And as much as he hated himself for it, he couldn't deny a sense of relief at knowing that would never come to pass.

The truth was, even though she was so far out of his league as to be playing on a whole other planet, and even though a woman like her was *dangerous* to a man like him, he wanted Eliza for himself.

Had *always* wanted her for himself.

The day she'd walked through BKI's front gates, he'd forgotten what life was like before her. And now he couldn't imagine what life would be like after her.

Some folks might try to say that was love. That he was *in* love with her.

But he knew the truth. He knew *himself.*

"God, Charlie." She pulled her knees to her chest and rocked atop the bed as too many tears to count trekked down her soft cheeks and dripped from her chin. They picked up blood along the way and left pink stains when they fell onto the thin hospital sheet draped over her legs.

His feet itched to inch closer. Every cell in his body strained toward her like he was made of metal and she was one big magnet. But somehow he managed to stay rooted to the spot beside her bed.

When he shoved his hands deep in his pockets, curling his fingers around the coolness of his harmonica, he waited for the comfort he usually felt in the gesture. The *grounding* he usually felt when the memories of the countless hours and countless lessons he'd been given drifted through his head like a puffy, pink cloud.

The familiar feeling of relief never came.

Instead, the hard metal reminded him of the cornerstone of Black Knights Inc., their rock, their pillar, their very *foundation* was hurting something fierce. And no matter how much he wished it weren't so, there was absolutely nothing he could do to help her.

Britt, who'd been standing in the curtained-off corner, walked over to prop a hip on the edge of the hospital bed. He pulled Eliza into a tight hug and then proceeded to do all the things Fisher wished *he* could do.

Like gently pushed her hair back from her face. Like rock her and shush her. Like smooth a gentle hand up and down her back.

The venomous, prickly legged thing inside Fisher tried to raise its ugly head. He beat it back with an imaginary stick and told himself he was grateful she was getting the support she needed. Even if that support wasn't coming from him.

Averting his eyes, he took an avid interest in the weave of the curtain material. It was light blue cotton. Faded from being washed in industrial-strength detergent. And a little ragged around the hem in one corner.

The triage room beyond was filled with the sounds of the ER. The soft moans of people in pain. The squeak of a wheel on a rolling IV stand. The pressed voices of doctors and nurses as they quickly tried to assess patients and get them either moved up to the appropriate floor of the hospital or treated and discharged.

There were the familiar smells as well. Antiseptic. Heavy-duty cleaner. Iodine. And, beneath it all, the faint whiff of fresh blood.

The aromas made his stomach cramp with the memory of his mother.

How many times had he gone with her to the emergency room because she'd needed a cut stitched or a bone set?

Too many to count. Until the day came when there'd been nothing the emergency department could do for her because her injuries had been enough to send her straight to the morgue.

He felt his expression turn dull. Hard. Implacable. But he didn't shove the old memories away. He needed them as reminders of where he'd come from—*who* he'd come from—and why he could never, *never* have Eliza even if she were suddenly to lose all sense of sanity and decide to give him a chance.

"It's okay, sugar." Britt's accent turned the last word into *sugah*. "I know it doesn't feel like it right now. But you'll get through this. We'll all help you get through this. The others are in the waiting room and they're eager to wrap you up and hold you close until you feel like you can breathe again."

The nurses had only allowed two visitors back into the treatment area. Graham, Hewitt, and Sam had all agreed to stay behind in the waiting room and let Britt and Fisher do the honors.

Well, it was probably more accurate to say they'd agreed to let *Britt* do the honors because Fisher hadn't even given them an option. As soon as the nurse had come out to greet them and tell them she'd let two come back to be with Eliza, he had jumped up from the row of chairs like his seat had been on fire.

"He's dead, Britt. Charlie's *dead*." Eliza's voice cracked in two around her fiancé's name. The sound was enough to crack Fisher's heart in two and he turned back in time to see her bury her face in the crook of Britt's shoulder. "They're *all* dead."

"Not all of them," the ex-Ranger reassured her. "Senator Chastain and her husband made it. *You* made it."

She pulled back in his embrace. Using a shaky hand, she shoved a lock of dark hair behind her ear. It crunched with dry blood.

"Thanks to Charlie." Her eyes were as round and shiny as new pennies when she flicked her gaze from Britt to Fisher and back again. "As soon as the gunman came out onto the patio, he threw himself on top of me."

Her trembling fingers automatically sought the large bump above her left temple. She winced when her probing revealed a particularly tender spot.

"He used his body to shield mine." Her dark eyes swam with fresh tears. "He took all the bullets meant for *me*."

Once again, she was caught up in Britt's fierce embrace. And once again, Fisher had to fight to keep the monster inside him from growling its displeasure.

When Britt looked over at him, he had the grace to grimace.

They were both remembering what he'd said about Charles McClean not being able to defend Eliza against a rabid squirrel. And they were both thinking just how wrong he'd been in his assessment.

Glancing at the ceiling, he offered up a silent apology to Charlie's ghost. Even though he didn't believe in an afterlife—he reckoned once a person was dead that was it. Poof! One second you're here, the next you're not—he still felt an obligation to acknowledge the man's sacrifice.

Sorry for callin' ya Captain Dickless. Turns out ya had big, clangin' brass balls.

While he was at it, he sent up a few words of gratitude too.

Thank you for lovin' her enough to forfeit your own life for hers. She's still got lots to offer this ol' world. And ya gave her the chance to see that through.

"I don't suppose any of those bullets were meant for you specifically," Britt reassured her. "From what you've said, it sounds like it was a hit on Senator McClean and the chef was just doing away with the witnesses."

Eliza used the backs of her hands to wipe the tears from her pale cheeks. The move smeared the wetness into the dried blood, turning it from rusty brown back into deep red.

Before she could respond, the doctor who'd been assigned her case parted the curtains and stepped into the small, enclosed space. "Knock, knock," he said in lieu of rapping his knuckles on an actual door.

Fisher felt every one of his thirty-four years when he looked at the ER physician. If the fresh-faced man in the white coat was much more than thirty, he'd happily eat his biker boots with a knife and fork.

How had he gotten to the age where *doctors* were younger than him? Where had the years gone? Where had his *life* gone?

Oh, right. It'd gone to Uncle Sam who'd been only too happy to waste his youth in far flung locales.

"We have the results of your scans back." In the way of all harried ER docs, the Doogie Howser lookalike wasted no time grabbing the rolling stool shoved into the corner and scooting it next to Eliza's bed.

Upon the physician's entry, Britt had gotten up to make room. And now the former Ranger stood next to Fisher. If the stillness of Britt's chest was anything to go by, he too was holding his breath as they waited to hear the doctor's assessment of Eliza's condition.

Head injuries were a tricky business. A person could seem perfectly fine one minute. And the next they could be dead on the floor from an intercranial bleed.

"There's no bruising or fractures." Doogie eyed the glowing image on his tablet's screen. "But you certainly have a concussion. Something between stage one and stage two."

When he glanced up, it was to see Eliza's dark eyebrows pulled into a V. He was quick to explain. "A stage one concussion has no loss of consciousness and no amnesia. Or the amnesia only lasts for less than thirty minutes. Stage two has a loss of consciousness, and/or the amnesia lasts from thirty minutes to twenty-four hours. You lost consciousness. So you're a little more than stage one. But you reported your memory loss only lasted a couple minutes. So you're not quite stage two."

In typical Eliza fashion, she wasn't satisfied with only a portion of the information. "You said there are three stages. What's the third?"

"That's the mack daddy. Characterized by a loss of consciousness for more than five minutes and a loss of memory for more than twenty-four hours."

"How awful." Eliza shuddered. "The couple of minutes I spent not knowing where I was or what had happened to me were terrifying. I couldn't imagine feeling that way for a whole day."

"Mmm." The doctor answered distractedly as he keyed something into his tablet. "Sometimes people are lucky to forget whatever trauma they've experienced."

When Eliza's eyes filled with tears, Fisher fought the urge to smack the medicine man on the ear. Some people's heads were hard-boiled, and it didn't matter how many fancy degrees they had or how many letters followed their names in the signature line of their emails.

Doogie realized the callousness of his remark when he saw the horror on Eliza's face. The look of contriteness that entered his eyes gave Fisher hope that, with experience, his bedside manner would improve.

"I'm so sorry, Miss Meadows. That was a thoughtless remark."

"It's okay." Her voice sounded as watery as her eyes looked. "You're right. There *can* be comfort in oblivion."

The doctor cleared his throat. "Yes. Well… I'm going to send you home with a concussion protocol."

Apprehension had Fisher speaking up. "You're not goin' to keep her overnight for observation?"

"No need." Doogie shook his head, causing his stick-straight hair to shift over his forehead. He pushed it back with impatient fingers. "She'll be better off recovering somewhere she can rest and relax."

"What's the concussion protocol?" Eliza prompted.

Right down to business. That was their girl Friday.

"Watch out for a worsening headache, nausea, vomiting, one pupil larger than the other, dizziness, slurred speech, confusion. If you experience any of these things, come back in immediately." Again, Doogie keyed something into his tablet. After he was finished, he stood and added, "No NSAIDs because they increase your risk of bleeding. If you need pain relief, stick with Tylenol. And rest. Rest is key. Rest is what your brain needs to heal."

"Am I supposed to stay awake for the first twenty-four hours?"

The doc shook his head. "That's old-school. New research shows sleep is beneficial. Just have someone check in on you every few hours. They need to make sure you don't have trouble waking up or answering some simple questions."

The physician's eyes noted the ring on her finger—it was hard to miss given the diamond was big enough to be seen from space—and pinged over to Britt. "I'm assuming you'll be more than happy to look after her?"

A yawning chasm opened up inside Fisher. The doctor automatically assumed *Britt* had been the one to give her that ring? *What am I? Chopper liver?* Then he reminded himself it'd been Britt hugging her tight when the sawbones had ducked into the little makeshift room. So Doogie had made a natural assumption.

Funny thing, though, even *with* that realization, Fisher couldn't seem to fill the void inside him. And even funnier still—funny strange, not funny ha-ha—was how *heavy* that emptiness felt.

It was like he'd just been given proof that the universe and everyone in it naturally assumed he wasn't fit to kiss Eliza's feet much less be the one to sweep her off them.

"We'll make sure she's looked after," Britt assured the white coat. "No worries, Doc."

Satisfied he'd done his duty by his patient, Doogie turned for the break in the curtain. But before he pushed through, he offered one final piece of information. "The nurses will come get you once they've processed your discharge forms. Hang tight until then."

Britt retook his seat on the edge of Eliza's bed and grabbed her hands. "We'll have you home in no time and—" He cut himself off, jerked his chin down to their clasped hands, and let his jaw fall open when he spied the ring on her finger. "Holy shit!"

Fisher wasn't sure *how* Britt hadn't noticed the damn thing before. Then again, Britt wasn't attuned to every little detail of Eliza's existence the way he was.

"McClean asked you to marry him?" Britt held up her hand so the overhead light blazed into the diamond and refracted a dazzling prism of colors around the curtains.

Hearing the words spoken aloud made Fisher's stomach rise and fall like it did when he hooked his parachute's static line to the plane's overhead steel cable before moving to the door to make a HALO jump.

No matter how many times he launched himself out of an airplane at altitudes high enough to require he suck on bottled oxygen, he never got used to it. Because even though his mind could understand the necessity for high-altitude-low-opening jumps to clandestinely arrive inside enemy territory, he could never convince his heart it was normal to hurl himself out of a perfectly good plane.

"He did." Eliza's voice was so small Fisher could barely hear it.

"And you said yes?"

Fisher lived through every circle of hell as he waited for her answer. When all she did was swallow convulsively and look like she was about to puke, he answered for her. "'Course she said yes. She's wearin' his ring, isn't she?"

Eliza glanced at him and there was…something in her expression. Something that made his heart skip a beat. But before he could ask her about it, the curtains parted.

He expected it to the be the duty nurse. But the two people who stepped into the little enclosure weren't medical professionals.

They were feds.

He knew them from their kicks. Because while anyone could wear a dark, non-descript suit, only FBI agents paired those dark, non-descript suits with lug-soled duty shoes.

Just when I thought this night couldn't get worse.

CHAPTER 3

"**O**h, joy. The fuckup fairies are here."

Agent Julia O'Toole blinked at the dark-haired man standing beside the hospital bed and wondered if his comment had been aimed at her and her partner or if they'd simply arrived in the middle of some curious conversation. It was impossible to tell from the man's blank face.

"Sorry to barge in like this." She kept her tone cool, professional. "I'm Agent O'Toole. This is my partner, Agent Douglas."

She gestured to Dillan who flashed his credentials and jerked his chin up in the *yo, what's up* way of all men who'd been blessed with an angular jaw and above-average height. She fought the urge to roll her eyes.

"Aren't you a little short for a fed?" The dark-haired man only spared Dillan a cursory glance before gluing his implacable stare to Julia's face. His Southern accent was as thick and slow as molasses, as potent as Tennessee whiskey.

Her knees threatened to wobble—she'd always been a sucker for a Southern drawl. But the set of the man's jaw, so superior and hostile, was enough to mitigate the effects of his deep voice.

Kneecaps firmly in place.

Donning her best Mark Hamill impression, she quipped, "My name is Luke Skywalker. I'm here to rescue you."

"Huh?" A line formed between his dark, slashing eyebrows, alluding to the sad fact that her wit was wasted on him.

"*Aren't you a little short for a stormtrooper?*" She made a gesture like she was swinging a light saber. When he only stared at her blankly, she waved a dismissive hand. "Never mind. Bad joke. Blame it on growing up with three older brothers who are all *Star Wars* fans. Anyway"—she turned to the woman in the bed— "my partner and I would like to ask you a few questions if that's all right, Miss Meadows."

"Y'all can't wait to do this later?" The dark-haired man's frown was severe. It would've been enough to turn a lesser person into pudding. But it only made Julia study him harder.

Worn jeans and a *Deadpool* T-shirt that read: Maximum effort! His hair was such a deep brown it looked almost black. And he had a tan. But not from recent sun exposure. It was one of those baked-on numbers. What happened to a man after having spent a lifetime in the sun.

He didn't have the chiseled features of the tall god standing next to him. In fact, if she were asked to describe his face, she'd say he was quintessentially a boy-next-door. Attractive in a pleasant sort of way, but nothing Hollywood would fall all over itself to splash across the silver screen.

Of course, the scar zigzagging its way across his right temple lent his otherwise amicable features a measure of interest and intrigue. And something about the way he stood gave her the distinct impression that, despite his perfectly pleasant face, his nature tended toward the dark and dangerous.

And that was all before she got to his eyes…

Crystal blue. Shrewd. Assessing. When he stared hard at her, waiting for her response, she would swear the air around her thinned.

"Wish we could wait until later. But the human mind is notoriously unreliable." Stepping toward the bed, she finished with, "The sooner we can get in an interview with Miss Meadows, the better."

"Better for whom? Not better for Eliza." Blue Eyes gestured impatiently. "She's been through hell and y'all want her to paint you a picture of it."

"Never mind Britt," Miss Meadows interjected. Julia clocked the woman's accent. Posh. Studied. Definitely East Coast. "He's feeling particularly protective tonight."

The diamond on Miss Meadows's left hand glinted when she absently picked at a loose thread on the hospital blanket. Julia wondered if Blue Eyes had been the one to put it there.

Speaking of…

"Britt what?" She regarded the man expectantly.

"Rollins," he was quick to reply. "Sergeant Britt Rollins, 75th Ranger Regiment. Retired."

Aw, that explains the edge of danger. Plus, he has the perfect posture of a military man.

"And I'm Fisher Wakefield." The lighter-haired giant who'd been silently taking in the exchange stepped forward to shake her hand. His big mitt engulfed hers. His palm was warm and dry, hard with calluses.

He worked with his hands. That much was obvious. And the eagle feather tattoo peeking from the bottom of his short-sleeve T-shirt matched the one Sergeant Rollins sported.

Were they in the same regiment? Is the tattoo a symbol of their unit?

Julia filed the information away for later. She never knew what might be important. Something that seemed insignificant in the moment could be the thing that solved the case, or bagged the suspect, or turned out to be the piece of evidence to sway a jury.

Giving into propriety, Sergeant Rollins followed the giant's example and stepped forward to shake. Although he offered his hand to Dillan before he offered it to her.

A calculated slight? Her eyes narrowed in consideration.

All thoughts zapped right out of her head, however, the instant his fingers curled around hers. Literally. Static buildup had a tiny lightning bolt arching between their palms.

Simple physics, she told herself, noting the thickness of his palm inside her own, the strength of his grip.

A brief image of what it would feel like if he ran his hand up her arm to gently cup her cheeks flashed through her head, shocking her with its vividness. And its inappropriateness.

Did he notice how quickly she dropped his hand?

Oh, he noticed.

The slow smirk that spread across his face told her as much.

She hated that smirk. She hated it worse that it suited him. And what she hated most? That she was thinking about him at all.

She should be concentrating on the case. On this interview.

Blaming her recent dating dry spell on her lapse, she gave herself a silent pep talk. *Tell your hormones to hit the road and focus on the work, Jules.*

"I promise we won't take up too much of your time tonight, Miss Meadows," she said at the same instant Dillan stepped forward and announced, "We just need to ask you some questions about what happened at the senator's house while the answers are still fresh in your mind."

What's that crunching sound?

Oh, right. Those were Julia's back molars.

Dillan Douglas hadn't kept it a secret that he'd been displeased when she'd been promoted over him. In fact, he'd thrown a *man fit*. Which was like a toddler fit when it came to the amount of pouting but differed in the amount of ear-blistering curse words involved.

He'd managed to get his emotions under control in the two days since her new position had been announced. He no longer shot her venomous looks or sneeringly referred to her as *Oh Captain, My Captain*. But she suffered no illusions that he would not try his best to take over this case from her.

It wasn't even that he thought she couldn't do the job. It was simply that, despite her stellar track record as a junior agent, he assumed he could do it better.

Perhaps his confidence came from having an Ivy League degree. Or maybe it came from spending his entire life being treated like the king of the world simply because he'd been gifted with good looks and a Greek statue's physique. Or, more likely, it came from being a legacy hire—his father and grandfather had been feds before him.

She'd heard him say more than once, *"Being a good agent runs in my blood."* And, of course, the notion that *she*, the daughter of a Southside fireman and a graduate from Western Illinois University, might actually be better than him at…well…*anything* had never crossed his mind.

She *was* better than him, just FYI. She could outshoot him, outscore him on their fitness exams, and it was no secret she was the better interviewer.

Dillan was too arrogant. Too brash. Too *pushy*. It put witnesses and potential suspects off.

But the problem with having been born blond and female, not to mention having topped out a whopping five-feet-one-inch in height, was that people assumed her IQ must be something close to her shoe size. She'd spent her whole life being underestimated.

She was determined to prove to everyone that she deserved this promotion. That she deserved this headline-grabbing case.

Pulling her cell from the inside pocket of her suit jacket, she smiled faintly at the woman in the hospital bed. Eliza Meadows looked small and wide-eyed with shock. But there was a determined cant to her chin that Julia respected.

"You mind if I record our conversation?" She wiggled her phone in emphasis.

Miss Meadows shook her head.

Ah. A cooperating witness. So far, so good.

Angling the phone's microphone toward the bed, she started with the obvious. "Why were you at Senator McClean's house tonight, Miss Meadows?"

"I'm dating Charlie." The woman's face contorted with anguish in the instant before she corrected herself. "I mean…I *was* dating Charlie."

So…Sergeant Rollins is what? A brother? Friend? Coworker?

Even as the questions flew through her head, Julia imagined taking out her service weapon and shooting them down.

It didn't matter to her *what* Rollins's relationship with her witness was. Or, at least, it *shouldn't* until it impacted the case.

"That would be Senator McClean's son?" she clarified for the record.

"Yes." Miss Meadows nodded slowly.

Julia allowed her gaze to drop to the rock that probably cost more than she made in five years. Miss Meadows followed the path of her eyes and Julia watched as the woman's face tried to cave in on itself.

Covering the giant diamond with her opposite hand, Miss Meadows whispered hoarsely, "Charlie asked me to marry him tonight."

Interesting, Julia thought.

"I'm very sorry for your loss." Her words were sincere although she hadn't delivered them with as much warmth as she would have had she not been on the job. She had to be twice as aloof and authoritative to get half the amount of respect people naturally afforded Dillan. It wasn't fair. It wasn't *right*. But it was the way of the world. "And I'm sorry we can't give you the privacy you deserve to grieve in peace. But what my partner said is right. It's better if we get this initial interview over and done with while your memories are still fresh."

"I understand." Miss Meadows nodded weakly, and Julia noticed how she began to absently twist the engagement ring on her finger like she wasn't comfortable with its presence there.

"Is that what this gathering was for?" Julia asked. "An engagement celebration?"

"No." Miss Meadows shook her head and then stopped and looked momentarily confused. "I mean, I don't think so. Senator McClean wouldn't have invited his colleagues if that was the case, right? He'd have invited Charlie's friends?"

Instead of answering, Julia posed another question. "So what was tonight's gathering in celebration of?"

Miss Meadows's forehead wrinkled, making the blood that was dried there crack and flake. "I don't know. I got the impression it was an impromptu thing. Charlie invited me only this morning."

"Was it usual for Senator McClean to have his fellow politicians over to his house?" Dillan piped up.

Julia bit the inside of her cheek to keep from biting Dillan's head off. He *knew* better than to butt in before she'd given him the nod that it was his turn.

There was an art to interviews. And despite what Hollywood would have people believe, it didn't involve two interviewers constantly tag-teaming a witness.

"If it was, I never knew of it. But that's not saying much. Charlie and I didn't really socialize with his dad. Not because there was any animosity there or anything," Miss Meadows was quick to explain. "It's just that the senator is a very busy man." Miss Meadows frowned and corrected herself. "*Was* a very busy man."

"One who wasn't well-liked by his peers," Dillan interjected. "Which makes tonight's gathering all the more suspicious."

Now Julia fought the urge to whack him on the back of the head like she did with her brothers when they'd done something stupid—which happened more times than she'd like to admit. The first rule of any interview was never to lead the witness.

Instead of resorting to violence, however, she continued along Dillan's line of questioning. *If you can't beat 'em, join 'em.*

"Do you think it's odd the senator invited over people from both houses of the legislature? I was under the impression senators don't usually consort with lowly congressmen."

The wounded woman's brow furrowed. "Now that you mention it, yes. But I'm sure Senator McClean had his reasons. Charlie always said his father never did anything without a reason."

"But you weren't privy to his reasons?" Dillan asked.

"Like I said, Charlie and I didn't spend much time with his dad. In fact, tonight was only the third time I'd ever been to Senator McClean's house."

John McClean threw an impromptu party with his son, his son's new fiancée, and half a dozen government officials plus their spouses, Julia mused. *What's the connection between all these players?*

The investigator in her knew if she could find the answer to that question, she'd probably find the answer to *why* the chef had tried his level best to permanently deprive them all of oxygen.

And on the subject of the chef...

"Were you introduced to Peter Sullivan?"

"Who?" Miss Meadows canted her head and frowned.

"The chef."

"No." The wounded woman grimaced. "The first time I saw him was when he stepped onto the patio and started spraying bullets." Her frown deepened. "Why bullets?"

Julia blinked. "What do you mean?"

"I mean, he was a chef, right? If he wanted to kill us all, why didn't he use the tools of his trade and poison our drinks and our food?"

It was a good question. One Julia had already contemplated. "In a situation like this, poison is risky. How could he be sure everyone ate and drank? And even if he somehow *could* ensure that, he couldn't be sure they'd imbibe enough of the poison to kill them. If a perp is hoping to make absolutely certain no one walks away unscathed, bullets are the best bet."

"But I'm living proof even bullets aren't a sure thing."

Indeed you are, Julia thought. Aloud she said, "You were very lucky, Miss Meadows."

She then spent the next ten minutes asking the usual questions and was a little disappointed with the answers she received. Eliza Meadows had no clue why she'd been invited to a spontaneous party peopled with Washington D.C. glitterati.

Or at least she *appeared* not to know.

Julia never took anyone's word at face value. She always made sure to confirm the stories she heard. And she had every intention to corroborate Miss Meadows's statements because it might just be good luck, or it might mean something else entirely that the woman had survived when nearly everyone else at the party—including the shooter—hadn't.

Nearly everyone else. There were two other survivors. And Julia needed to interview the one who wasn't currently sprawled on an operating table.

Maybe the good senator could shine some light on why John McClean had called together that particular group, and why his personal chef—a man who'd been in his employ for three solid years—had suddenly turned on him and everyone in his vicinity.

After thanking Miss Meadows for her cooperation, she reached into her pocket and pulled out a business card. "If you think of anything else"—she stepped forward to hand over the card—"please don't hesitate to reach out."

It wasn't the wide-eyed woman who took her information. It was Sergeant Rollins.

Again, a spark sizzled between them when their fingers briefly touched. And again, she blamed it on physics.

He's got to be wearing wool socks or something.

Her gaze automatically pinged down to take in his biker boots. They were the steel-toed kind, big and black and clunky.

There'd been a time during her brief Goth era when those boots would have been enough to send her into a swoon. All they did now was make her eager to get her *own* boots upstairs and in front of Senator Chastain.

Dillan led the way, sliding through the slit in the curtains. She was halfway through herself when she felt a large, warm hand encircle her wrist.

She didn't have to turn back to know who was touching her. The blood raging in her veins, primitive and strong, told her it was none other than Ol' Blue Eyes himself.

She'd done her best to ignore it. And when she hadn't been able to ignore it, she'd done her best to explain it away. But she prided herself on being honest. And that meant admitting the truth.

She was attracted to Sergeant Rollins.

Like…*attracted* attracted. The hot-nights-and-sweaty-sheets kind of attracted. The spend-three-days-in-bed-and-only-leave-it-for-food kind of attracted.

She might know nothing about him as a person. She had absolutely *no* idea if they had anything in common. But the feral, animal part of her recognized the feral, animal part of him as a potential mate.

As Dad always likes to say, when it comes down to it we're all just a bunch of monkeys.

Bracing herself and making sure none of what she was thinking showed on her face, she turned and was greeted by the most amazing pair of icy-blue eyes and the most lickable-looking five-o'clock shadow.

"I don't know if it matters, Agent O'Toole." His deep voice and soft drawl swirled in her ear like a wet tongue. She struggled not to shiver. "And I'm sure you'd make the connection yourself soon enough. But Eliza Meadows is Leonard Meadows's daughter."

Her mind blanked. Then recognition had an imaginary lightbulb blinking to life. "Leonard Meadows, as in the chief of staff to the president of the United States?"

"One and the same." Rollins nodded, and now her heart pounded for a whole new reason.

This case wasn't just going to be headline-grabbing. It was going to be career-making.

Or career-breaking, a little voice whispered from the farthest corner of her brain.

She cocked her head and eyed him curiously. "So what's a former Ranger and the chief of staff's daughter doing here in Chicago?"

"Building custom Harley choppers," he answered unhesitatingly. "We work at Black Knights Inc."

"Ah." She nodded. "I've heard of you guys."

She thought she saw something dart across his face. But it was there and gone so quickly, she couldn't be certain.

"I work with Grace Jackson," she clarified. "She's married to one of your coworkers, correct?"

"She is." His eyes narrowed ever so slightly. "Are you friends with Grace?"

"Mmm." She shook her head. "She works in the counterterrorism division. I'm on the criminal investigation side of things. But we've exchanged a hello or two around the coffeepot." She lifted a finger. "Wait a minute. Doesn't the starting pitcher for the White Sox ride one of your creations?"

Some kids were baptized Catholic. Southside Chicago kids were baptized Sox fans. It wasn't an option.

Again, something briefly crossed his face. Something that resembled relief. But it was gone in the blink of an eye, leaving her wondering if it'd ever been there at all.

"Indeed he does." His chin jerked down briefly. "And the point guard for the Bulls too."

From Ranger to rider, from military man to motorcycle man. She didn't *want* to be intrigued by Sergeant Britt Rollins. But there she was, completely captivated by his cowlick, forehead scar, and the way his T-shirt clung to the hard balls of his biceps when he crossed his arms.

Oh, that is so inconvenient.

Despite her better judgment—and the pressing need to get upstairs and interview the other witness—she heard herself say, "Grease-monkeying has to be less stressful than volunteering as government grist in some faraway land."

"Pays a whole helluva lot better too." He offered her a genuine smile and a wink. The unrepentant sexuality contained in the latter lit her on fire.

Really inconvenient, she thought as she turned and hurriedly caught up to her partner.

CHAPTER 4

Black Knights Inc.

The steam that rose around Eliza was so heavy and thick she could barely see the shampoo bottle in the steel caddy hanging from the showerhead. The clouds of water pressed in on her like hot, wet hands, sticking their waterlogged fingers down her throat and filling her lungs with their stifling humidity.

She didn't reach for the faucet to adjust the temperature, however.

She *needed* the heat. Needed it to seep into her bones because she couldn't shake the cold that'd settled in her core. Needed it to scour Charlie's blood from her skin, from her hair, from the inside of her nose because it was all she'd been able to smell since regaining consciousness. Needed it to steam away the memories…the *guilt*.

That last part was wishful thinking, of course.

There wasn't enough water in all of Chicago to purge the horror she'd witnessed. Wasn't enough on the whole *planet* to wash her clean of her regret and remorse.

She didn't know where her tears ended and the water pouring over her head began as she dully watched the red whirlpool circle the drain. Figured it didn't matter in the grand scheme of things since both were getting the job done.

With the help of her bodywash and a good scrubbing with her loofah, it wasn't long before the spiraling pool at her feet ran clean, all the evidence of the night's tragedy on its way to the city's sewer system.

Just that easy.

She laughed humorlessly.

Nothing about this was easy. Nothing was going to be the same. *She* wasn't going to be the same.

Like water when it became ice, she'd retain the same molecular structure she'd had before, but she'd be irrevocably altered. *Changed.*

She could already feel herself growing harder. *Colder.*

Cold in places the blistering water and searing steam couldn't touch.

Lathering her hair with shampoo, she winced when her fingers hit the lump on her temple. Pain rolled around the sides of her head and radiated into the back of her skull. And maybe she was a glutton for punishment because, after leaving the swelling behind, her hand automatically sought out the bruise on her cheek.

The instant her probing fingertips landed on the contusion, she cried out. Even the slightest pressure made her eye socket feel like it was ready to explode and send her eyeball blasting out of her head like a cannonball.

"Stop it," she scolded herself. "You're crying because your head hurts? Because your face hurts? Imagine what *Charlie* must've endured. What he must've…" Her voice broke. "What he must've *suffered*," she finished, her brain conjuring up the image of his bullet-riddled body, the obliteration of his beautiful face.

The grief that slammed into her then was enough to drive her to her knees. She had no idea how long she stayed that way, a supplicant to the sorrow that blew through her as fierce and as cold as the Nor'easters that came down from Canada in the winter and turned the city into a block of ice. All she knew was that by the time her tears dried up, her fingertips were wrinkled like raisins.

Enough, she scolded herself. Although, it was her father's voice she heard in her head when she continued. *You're being self-indulgent. Get it together. Pick yourself up.*

Her first attempt at standing ended with her knees giving out on her, forcing her to pitch forward. For a few moments, she remained that way, letting her head hang between her shoulders, letting the harsh spray beat down on her hips and legs. Then she took a deep breath and tried again.

With the help of the edge of the tub, she managed to shove to her feet. But it felt like her muscles were made of mashed potatoes.

Closing her eyes, she mustered what energy she could to rinse the shampoo from her hair. *Nope. It's a mistake to shut my eyes,* she thought when the image of Charlie's smiling face as he'd slipped the ring on her finger projected itself onto the backs of her eyelids.

Would he have proposed had he known what was in her heart? And if he'd known what was in her heart, would he still have chosen to take the bullets meant for her?

She'd never know the answers. The only man who could give them to her was growing stiff in the city morgue. And it was all so senseless. So useless. So…*awful.*

The guilt rose inside her like a knife that sliced through bone and viscera. It tried to drive her to her knees again. But she gathered the last of her reserves and switched off the spray.

With one towel wrapped around her body and another curled around her head, she shuffled across the cool tile before stopping in front of the sink. The mirror was foggy. She swiped a hand over the glass and then immediately wished she hadn't.

Her reflection showed the bruise on her cheek was a deep purple that faded to angry-looking red around the edges. The swelling at her temple was still the size of a golf ball. And the look in her eyes was one she'd never seen on herself.

She'd seen it on her guys a time or two. When they'd come home from a particularly harrowing mission.

"The thousand-yard stare," Fisher had explained when she'd commented on the phenomenon. *"The look of a man who's seen too much."*

Her gaze skittered away from the mirror. Not because she couldn't stand the sight of the swelling or the bruises. But because of that look.

As much as the cold that'd settled in her center, that look told her there was no coming back from this. There was the Eliza who'd existed before this night. And there'd be the Eliza who existed after.

As soon as she stuck her electric toothbrush into her mouth, she knew the endeavor was a no-go. The *buzz* was too much for her throbbing head. She had to switch off the device and do things the old-fashioned way.

Nothing but elbow grease.

Which was fine. There was something comforting in the repetitive motion. Something reassuring about completing such a mundane, everyday task.

She concentrated on scrubbing each tooth one by one until she'd gotten them all. And by the time she rinsed her toothbrush she felt almost…well… not normal. *What even* is *normal now?* But she no longer felt like she might shatter into a million pieces if someone breathed too hard in her direction.

The locket her mother had given her caught her eye. It was her most prized possession and lay curled in the crystal soap dish she used to hold it while she showered. Instead of gleaming bright and pure, however, the links of the chain were caked with blood. The delicate filigree etched into the face of the locket acted as tiny channels that'd collected the awful stuff.

It felt like an affront to see something so precious fouled by the terrible evidence of the night's brutality. She set about scrubbing the necklace with a vigor she wouldn't have thought possible given her mashed potato muscles.

Only once she was satisfied not a speck of blood remained did she carefully dry the necklace and then slowly open the locket. The instant she saw her mother's face, she experienced a pang of familiar longing.

She pined for the support of the woman who'd nursed her through childhood illnesses. Yearned for the kind of guidance that could only come from someone who'd known her her whole life—knew her better, perhaps, than she even knew herself.

But that's not true, is it? she thought joylessly.

Her mother *hadn't* known her her whole life. In fact, her mother hadn't even known her a quarter of it.

Athena Meadows had died two days after Eliza's seventh birthday.

Thirty-one…

That's how old her mother had been when her private jet suffered a catastrophic failure and crashed into the Atlantic Ocean off Cape Cod.

Thirty-one…

That's how old *Eliza* would be in just five short months.

Her eyes roamed lovingly over the tiny photo held secure in the locket. She analyzed features she knew as well as her own.

Some of them *were* her own.

She had her mother's tilted eyes and wide mouth. They shared the same black hair and slightly lopsided grin. But where her mother's nose had been short and pert, Eliza's was long and straight. Where her mother's face had been round and smooth, Eliza had inherited her father's square jaw and cut-glass cheekbones.

Eliza was pretty. That wasn't a humble-brag. It was simply the truth. She had symmetric features and a thorough skincare routine. But Athena Meadows? Oh, Athena Meadows had been drop-dead gorgeous.

The snippet of the Wordsworth poem Fisher had quoted the first time she'd shown him her mother's picture rang in her head.

"Her eyes as stars of twilight fair; like twilight's, too, her dusky hair."

The man couldn't boil a pot of water without it bubbling over or make himself toast without burning it to a crisp. But he could quote Plath and Whitman as easily as if he were reciting his own social security number.

She loved that about him. Loved *most* things about him if she was being honest.

Not that he was perfect by any means.

He had no sense of fashion. His wardrobe consisted of well-worn Levi's and a revolving assortment of plain black T-shirts. He had the palate of a thirteen-year-old boy, his favorite foods being chicken fingers, Hot Pockets, and Uncrustables. And he had this weird habit of pronouncing Wednesday phonetically...*wed-nes-day.*

No, he wasn't perfect. He was a human and therefore flawed.

But he's perfect for me, she thought dejectedly. And knowing he'd never choose her was a singular sort of heartache she'd have happily gone her whole life without experiencing.

As if thinking of him conjured him up, a gentle rap on her bedroom door was followed by the sound of his deep, warm voice. "Ya doin' okay in there, Liza?"

Liza...

He rarely used her nickname. A shame since it sounded so right in his mouth.

Gritting her teeth, she fitted the locket around her neck and then peeled the towel from her body before giving her hair a quick dry. Slipping on the fluffy lavender bathrobe she kept on a hook behind the door, she cinched the belt tight while padding across her bedroom.

With her hand on the doorknob, she took a deep breath.

It was difficult hiding her feelings from Fisher when she was in full control of her faculties. It was going to be nearly impossible now that every nerve ending in her body felt raw and exposed.

The memory of the day they met crystallized in her mind.

She'd walked through the front gates of Black Knights Inc. filled with nervous jitters and with her father's words ringing in her ear. *"You're the president's eyes and ears with this crew. Don't let her down. Don't let* me *down."*

Of course, every thought had fallen straight out her head when she'd spied the man pacing in front of the garage doors.

His hair had looked light brown until he'd stood in direct sunlight. Then the rays had glinted off the lighter strands and turned him into a blond god. His long legs had been encased in denim that'd showcased the muscles in his thighs and the high, tight curve of his ass. And his mouth…

She'd been struck dumb by the remarkable beauty of his mouth and had since determined it was the mouth of Tom Hardy and Brad Pitt's love child. So firm and full and perfect. With a cupid's bow that looked like it'd been carved into his face by a master sculptor and a plump bottom pad that invited the nip of her teeth and the lick of her tongue.

He'd been humming softly to the baby in his arms. And the smile he'd flashed her when she'd stopped next to him had been so bright and blinding, she'd simply stood there and blinked.

He'd introduced himself and little Hazel, the daughter of Boss and Becky Knight, and his deep, Southern drawl had sounded like a song she knew was going to be her favorite from then on. Oh, and something magical had happened in her stomach.

There'd been a fluttering sensation, both delightful and sickening.

Butterflies, she'd realized with a start. She'd never truly experienced the sensation until that day.

She'd been experiencing it every day since.

Each time he smiled at her.

Each time he bickered with her.

Each time she had to pretend to be annoyed with him when the truth was she yearned for him like she'd never yearned for anything or anyone in her entire life.

"You're not passed out on the floor with a brain bleed, are ya? Do I need to bust down the door?"

The sound of his voice, so close, had her jumping and quickly turning the knob to throw open the door. The hallway light blazed into her room, causing his tall shadow to fall over her.

There they are. Right on cue. Those damned butterflies.

"I'm okay," she assured him. "Thanks for checking."

His hazel eyes looked brown in the artificial light, but she knew they flashed pirate's gold in the sun. And like a pirate, he'd stolen her heart.

His daring and bravery and uncompromising dedication to his teammates had been unlike anything she'd known before. And if that'd been all there was to him, she probably would've grown to admire and respect him just like she'd grown to admire and respect the rest of her guys.

What'd made her heart go pitter-pat, and what'd ultimately allowed him to abduct the damn organ completely, was his wit and whimsy. The way he could be equal parts strong and soft. How he never made her feel small or less-than, because even when he was teasing and tormenting her there was always an undercurrent of good-hearted admiration in his words.

In short, Fisher was generous and genuine, steadfast and true. The best example of a legitimately *good* person that she'd ever had the honor to meet.

Now, she watched his eyes as they tracked over her face, lingering on the swelling at her temple and then fixing on the bruise on her cheek.

"I know." She gave him a baleful glance. "It looks awful. And believe me when I tell you, it feels worse than it looks."

The string of curse words that tumbled out of his mouth were so scorching she wouldn't have been surprised to turn around and find her curtains had spontaneously combusted. He finished the litany with, "Welp, there's only one thing to do then."

She lifted the eyebrow on the eye that *didn't* feel like it had its own heartbeat.

"Get ya tucked in," he finished. His Southern drawl somehow drew out the four syllables into about six or seven. "Like that wet-behind-the-ears doctor said, sleep is the best thing for ya."

When he stepped over the threshold, she stumbled back. And when he cupped a hand around her elbow to steer her toward the bed, it was enough to send those silly butterflies into a frenzy.

Four years.

They'd been colleagues for four years. Working together. Living together.

And certainly arguing together—their arguing was legendary at BKI. But in all that time, he'd never stepped foot inside her bedroom.

Sure, he'd leaned a shoulder against the doorjamb to talk to her on a handful of occasions. Sure, he liked to drive her wild by grabbing the top of her doorframe and leaning into her room to wish her a good night—the move always made the hem of his T-shirt ride up so she got a nipple-tightening glimpse of his love trail. And sure, he'd sat outside her closed door to keep her company the time she'd come down with the flu two days before they'd been scheduled to fly out on an important assignment.

Quarantining herself had been the only sane thing to do. When she got sick, it was an inconvenience. When *they* got sick in the middle of a mission? It could mean the difference between life and death.

But now he was here. In her sanctuary. The place where she'd held her breath and listened for the slightest sound he made. The smallest cough or the quietest snore.

Had she mentioned his bedroom was right next door?

For four years, she'd roomed next to the man who'd won her over a little at a time and then all at once. For four years she'd slept with her head only a few feet from his because their beds backed up against the same wall. And for four years she'd sat in the velvet armchair pushed into the corner anytime she heard him playing his harmonica.

She could always guess his mood from whichever song drifted in through the thick, brick wall. If he was sad, he went for the blues, Billie Holiday or Eric Clapton. If he was happy, it was Taylor Swift. Every time. And when she heard him break into "The New Romantics" or "Lover," she couldn't help smiling to herself.

There was something endearing about a big, bad, fighting man being a Swiftie.

"You're in my room." The words tumbled out of her mouth without her permission.

"Is that okay?" There was hesitation in his face. He hastily dropped his hand from her elbow, and his touch left behind a warm spot that she wanted to cover with her fingers and hold onto forever. "Looked like ya were 'bout to fall down. I reckoned the closer we were to your bed, the better."

Bed.

He was in her room and he'd said *bed*.

Worse, his eyes drifted over to the bed in question, and she wondered if he could sense the fantasies she'd had about him while lying *right there*. Were there psychic vibrations left over from all the times she'd quietly pleasured herself while thinking of him as he lay in his own bed only a few feet away?

To distract him—and herself—from the way the air around them seemed to thicken, she glanced at the drink in his hand. "Hot chocolate? In July?"

He passed her the mug. She realized her fingers were blocks of ice when the warmth seeping through the clay made her frozen bones ache.

"Shock chills ya to the bone," he said. "It's a kind of cold no one can understand unless they've experienced it themselves."

He knows about the ice in my core.

Well, of course he did. He was Fisher Wakefield. A big, bad fighting man with a heart of gold and enough empathy to fill an Olympic-sized swimming pool.

That was *another* thing she loved about him. His work all these years hadn't hardened him. He wasn't quiet or stoic like Graham or Hewitt. He was still softhearted. *Sensitive.*

When a lump formed in her throat, she forced herself to swallow it down. She couldn't let him know how vulnerable she was. If she did, he'd take her in his arms. And once she was there, she'd never want to leave.

Self-preservation had her falling back on their tried-and-true method of communication.

"Did you make this or…" She curled her top lip and eyed the hot chocolate with suspicion.

His frown was severe. When he crossed his arms, the sleeves of his plain black T-shirt stretched tight around his biceps. "No. That's Britt's handywork. And stop lookin' so relieved. I can make hot chocolate."

She'd brought the mug halfway to her lips, but that had her lowering it again. "Um, correct me if I'm wrong. But didn't you dump half a bottle of vanilla extract into the pan the last time you tried to make my recipe?"

"Your recipe didn't say how much vanilla extract to add. It just said *vanilla extract*." He made air quotes. "So I measured with my heart."

She rolled in her lips to keep from laughing—the stuff had been undrinkable. In the next instant, however, her conscience reminded her of the man who'd wanted to be her husband had died saving her life. Which meant she had no business laughing.

Once again guilt slammed into her. It was more than her mashed potato muscles could take. They threatened to give up on her entirely.

"Whoa." Fisher cupped both her elbows when she wobbled. He carefully lowered her to the side of bed and then took the steaming cup of hot chocolate from her to set it on her nightstand.

When he sat down beside her, the mattress depressed under his weight. She slid toward him until they were shoulder to shoulder, thigh to thigh.

They'd never been the touchy-feely sort of coworkers. Or maybe it was more accurate to say she'd never been particularly touchy-feely with *him*. The truth was, touching him a little only made her want to touch him *more*.

There'd been a brief period, however, after he'd shared a painful truth about a mission in South America, when they'd expanded the boundaries of their relationship and shifted from being simply coworkers and sparring partners to being…well…*friends*.

During that time, he'd taken to throwing an arm around her shoulders or nudging her chin with his knuckle. But it'd all come to a stop as quickly as it'd started.

Had he regretted telling her what had happened on that fateful mission? Had he decided he preferred her feigned animosity to her friendship? Had she said or done something to make him change his mind about the amended nature of their association?

It was a mystery she'd never solved.

But as she felt his body heat seeping into her, warming parts of her the hot shower hadn't been able to touch, she admitted she'd *missed* being close to him.

When she leaned her head on his shoulder, he stiffened and she feared he'd pull away. But to her relief, his heavy arm came around her shoulders and his fingertips left five perfect indents in the soft material of her robe when he squeezed her tight to his side.

She hadn't realized how much she needed a hug until it happened. And despite thinking she'd cried out all the tears she had, more spilled over and ran down her cheeks.

"Sorry," she whispered, using her sleeve to mop up the mess.

"Nothin' to be sorry 'bout." He squeezed her shoulder again. "Given all you've been through tonight, all you've lost, I'm gobsmacked you're not a puddle on the ground."

"Gobsmacked." She sniffed pitifully. "Does everyone from Louisiana talk like you?"

"Nah." He shook his head. "The Cajuns mix in all this funny-soundin' French. Folks from New Orleans have this weird accent that's all citified, like they were raised somewhere up around Boston. And don't get me started on the Creoles." He hooked a thumb toward his chest. "But folks from my neck of the woods sound like our neighbors to the north and east, like people from Arkansas or Mississippi. *Country* to our cores."

"I've always liked it," she admitted quietly, squinting at the light given off by her bedside lamp. Even its low glow felt too bright for her concussed brain. "It's very charming."

"Good lord." He grabbed his chest like his heart might try to escape the confines of his rib cage. "Was that a compliment?"

She rolled her eyes. "Don't act like it's the first time."

He gave her the side-eye. "Name one nice thing you've *ever* said about me."

You're thoughtful. You're quick-witted. You're the most gorgeous man I've ever laid eyes on.

"You play a mean harmonica." She mentally patted herself on the back for coming up with that answer so quickly.

Her sense of accomplishment was short-lived when he rolled his eyes. "Pfft. That's not much of a compliment since I'm the only harmonica player you've ever known."

"You never forget to put your dishes in the dishwasher. Unlike Sam. I swear that man thinks a dish fairy lives in the cupboards and it's her sole job to wash his dirty dinner plates."

"Big whoop. So I clean up after myself. What a mean feat for an adult." His voice dripped with sarcasm. "Where's my gold medal?"

"Okay." She scowled at him. "You have excellent taste in poetry and an amazing ability to find the perfect line or stanza for just about every situation."

"Wish I could say I started learnin' poetry 'cause I love it. But once I joined the Special Forces, I was surrounded by guys who had fancy degrees.

Seein' as how I managed to graduate high school on a wing and a prayer, I figured if I didn't want to get handed all the grunt work, I had to trick my teammates into thinkin' I had more than two brain cells to rub together. No one thinks you're dumb when you're quotin' Whitman."

She blinked at him. "Lack of education doesn't mean lack of IQ, Fish. You're one of the smartest people I know."

His eyebrows arched up his forehead. "Comin' from a woman with a whole bunch of fancy degrees, that's sayin' something. Thanks, doll face. *That* felt like a compliment." He slid her a sly grin. "I'm assumin' the knock to your noggin' is to blame for this sudden change in personality."

She chuckled and then immediately remembered that *nothing* should be funny.

A sob caught in her throat and she blinked up at the ceiling, trying to stop the tears before they could start. Or…*re*start.

It was a useless endeavor. They spilled over and landed on the lapels of her robe.

"Wish like hell there was a way I could take this pain from ya." His voice was low and rumbling.

Later, she would blame shock and exhaustion for what happened. But in that moment, all she could think was that she needed him.

Needed his strength.

Needed his comfort.

Needed to feel something other than horror and guilt.

Throwing her arms around his neck, she pulled him close. So close she could feel the heavy beat of his heart against her breast. So close she nearly crawled into his lap.

She wanted to crawl into his *skin*. Maybe if she was sharing his skin, she'd be warm again. Be strong again. Be able to go five minutes without dissolving into a blubbering mess.

He hesitated. Just for a second. Then both arms came around her and nothing had ever felt so right.

"Tighter," she whispered, her tears making her throat sound full. "Hold me tighter, Fish. Hold me as tight as you can so I don't break apart."

"I got ya." His lips moved close to her ear. She could feel his warm breath blowing the damp strands of her hair. "And I know it doesn't feel like it right now. But you're goin' to get through this."

"It's not fair. Why am *I* the one who's alive? What did I do to deserve to be here when the others aren't? When *Charlie* isn't?"

"Survivor's guilt is a thing. That's why we have a name for it. But a mind full of guilt is a mind full of spiders. I wouldn't wish their bite on anyone. So ya got to let 'em go. There's no shame in bein' alive. There's *never* any shame in bein' alive."

"But Charlie…" Her voice broke on the name. "He was such a *good* man. He should be the one here now and—"

"Nope." He squeezed her tighter. But not to keep her from breaking apart. He did it to stop her from talking. "I won't hear another word like that. You're the kindest, bravest, smartest woman I know. Charlie was lucky to have ya. And that ring on your finger says he knew it as well as I do."

She screwed tight her eyes, heedless of how it made her bruised cheek hurt. "If you'd known Charlie, you'd know he deserved—"

She couldn't say the rest out loud. So she only *thought* it.

He deserved so much more than me.

"It's not about who deserves what. There's no rhyme or reason for who fate chooses to take or spare."

"He's dead." Even though she'd repeated the phrase dozens of times in her own head, it was the first time she'd said the words out loud. "Charlie's dead."

"I'm sorry as I can be for your loss." He ran his hands up and down her back. Up and down in a hypnotic rhythm that turned her bones gelatinous.

Jell-O bones to match my mashed potato muscles, she thought a little deliriously.

His aftershave had worn off since he'd applied it that morning. But she could still detect subtle hints of it. It was masculine and earthy, with smoky notes like a fine Scotch.

Up and down. Up and down. His palms were wide enough to span her waist. His calluses occasionally snag on the terry cloth of her robe and her mind automatically conjured up fantasies of what it would be like to feel those big, worn hands running over her bare skin.

Had he heard the way she suddenly gasped?

Did he feel her heart pick up tempo?

Could he tell she was turning to liquid in his arms?

She used the excuse of having to tighten her belt as a reason to push out of his embrace. She spent longer than necessary getting the job done. Not because her hands were shaking—although they were—but because she needed the extra seconds to school her features. To wipe the hunger from her expression.

If she had thought she felt bad about laughing at a time like this, that was nothing compared to how truly awful she felt for experiencing desire.

She knew she must look a fright, because when she finally worked up the nerve to look at him, Fisher winced. "I should've brought up a steak for that bruise." His finger moved over her injured cheek. His touch was so light she felt no pain.

"Are you saying you want to put your meat on my face, Fish?" The words were out of her mouth before she could stop them.

One slashing eyebrow arched over his forehead, and she was suddenly glad for the bruise. It helped hide the blush that crept into her cheeks.

"How much pain medicine did they give ya at the hospital?"

"None." She grimaced. "I'm raw dogging this concussion."

"So then it's just your scrambled gray matter that's got ya throwin' sexual innuendos my way?"

"It was a joke. That's what we do. We joke."

"That's what we *used* to do," he corrected with a raised finger. "Recently we've been bickerin' more than jestin'."

"And whose fault it that?" She was too tired to question how unwise it was to travel down this particular lane of conversation. "One minute I thought we were becoming besties. You'd chuck me under the chin or throw your arm around me. The next minute you were all irascible and irritating. And you treated me like I was a plague carrier, always staying five feet back."

He tilted his head and regarded her with a look she couldn't name. "And ya got no idea why that is?" His voice had dropped an octave, so she felt the rumble of it low in her belly.

"No." She shook her head, trying not to let him see how that bedroom voice of his affected her. She was glad for the long sleeves on the robe that hid the goose bumps peppering her arms. "Please. Enlighten me."

"*So dawn goes down to day. Nothing gold can stay,*" he quoted. And then, as he always did, he credited the poet. "Robert Frost."

She frowned. "Meaning what? Everything is fleeting? Including our camaraderie?"

"Somethin' like that." He turned to retrieve the mug of hot chocolate. "Drink up. Doctor Britt's orders."

"You know that thing I said about you having the perfect line or stanza for just about every situation? I take it back. That last quote was irritatingly unsatisfying."

"Drink, Eliza." He nudged the mug in her hand toward her mouth.

"Why do I get the feeling you're changing the subject?"

"Probably same reason you're avoidin' takin' a drink of that there hot chocolate. Because we're both stubborn as mules and neither one of us likes being backed into a corner or told what to do."

To prove him wrong, she haughtily took a large sip.

The hot chocolate wasn't hot anymore. At least not temperature-wise. Taste-wise? Oh, taste-wise it was *straight fire* as Hannah Blue, the purple-haired girlfriend of their resident sharpshooter, would say.

Eliza gulped down half the mug's contents before sighing and wiping the back of her hand over her mouth. She hadn't realized how dehydrated she was. Crying was thirsty work.

"Britt added a dash of cinnamon." The sweet, rich liquid had soothed her throat. She no longer felt like her larynx had been scoured with a bottle brush.

"Did he?" Fisher stole the mug and took a tentative sip.

Her gaze was automatically drawn to the spot where his lips wrapped around the rim. She wanted to place her mouth there the next time she had a drink. It was probably the closest she'd ever come to kissing him.

"Tastes the same to me," he said with a shrug.

"Says the man who thinks margarine and butter are interchangeable."

He took another sip and a drop of liquid clung to the line delineating his plump bottom lip. She couldn't stop her eyes from tracking down to that drop. And it took all her self-restraint not to lean forward and lick it off.

When his tongue darted out to do the job for her, she stopped herself from groaning by dropping her eyes to her duvet cover and picking at a piece of lint.

"Fisher, I—"

What? What had she started to say?

That he was the reason she'd felt only sadness when Charlie had gotten down on one knee? That he was the first thing she thought of when she woke up in the morning and the last thing she thought of after laying her head on the pillow at night?

That she loved him?

Talk about the cherry on top of this craptastic sundae, she thought with no small measure of misery. *I've already witnessed a massacre and the brutal murder of the man who wanted to marry me. Why not add in a little rejection too?*

Fisher *would* reject her.

She knew it as surely as she knew her father would have his assistant send her yet another silk Ferragamo scarf for Christmas.

When it came to sexual congress, Fisher had made it abundantly clear he'd be more than happy to be her huckleberry. How many times had he offered her *"some horizontal refreshment"* or jokingly assured her he'd like to *"add his banana to her fruit salad."*

But when it came to love?

Oh, when it came to love, he'd sooner cut off his own balls.

He intended to Hugh Heffner his way through the decades. *"I'm goin' to die old and robed while happily bouncin' some bird on my lap,"* he liked to say.

"Hey." He bumped a knuckle under her chin. "What is it?"

She hated it when he looked at her like that. She worried he'd be able to see inside her most secret self. See the truth of her. The truth she'd managed to keep from him for four long years.

"I just wanted to ask you how you do it." She clung to the first excuse that came to mind.

"Do what?"

"Keep going after witnessing such—" She couldn't find the right word.

Horror? Tragedy? Atrocity? None of them came close to describing the scope of the slaughter.

She didn't need to finish. He knew what she was asking.

"Ya want the depressin' answer? Or the flippant one?"

"I'll take the flippant one," she decided quickly. "I can't manage any more bad news tonight."

"When life's chewed ya up and shit ya out, ya just got to persevere. Like a piece of corn."

She blinked. Then she blinked again and shook her head. "I miss the time before I ever heard that sparkling bit of wisdom. You couldn't have come up with a pithy poem about *just hanging on* instead?"

His wide grin drew her gaze to his mouth—that wonderful, kissable mouth. And it wasn't just her gaze that was mutinying. It was her lungs too. When he tucked a strand of damp hair behind her ear, she sucked in a soft breath.

"Eliza?" His low, rich voice reached out to her as surely as his hand did. He used his thumb and forefinger to grip her chin and force her eyes to his face. "Do ya want to talk about it? Would it help?"

No. Talking about it wouldn't help. *Thinking* about it wouldn't help. What would help was *forgetting* about it. What would help was if he made love to her so passionately and so thoroughly that there was no room for thoughts in her head because her entire focus would be on her body.

"I—" The ring of her cell phone made her jump guiltily.

Saved by the bell.

CHAPTER 5

"I'm sorry I haven't had time to call. I was rushed to the ER and then, as soon as I got home, I jumped in the shower because I was covered in blood."

Fisher watched Eliza's fingers instinctively curl around the locket that held her mother's photograph. He'd noticed she reached for the piece anytime she got nervous—which she did every time she spoke to her father.

Not that he blamed her. Leanord Meadows was as sharp as a tack and as gruff as a grizzly bear hungry from hibernation. It was an intimidating combination.

"No, no." He watched her press a hand to her forehead. "I don't want you to fly me to D.C. I'd rather stay here."

Even through the phone's small speaker, her father's voice was low and commanding. Fisher couldn't make out everything the man said, but he was pretty sure he caught the phrase *safer here with me.*

"Safer?" Eliza scrunched up her face and then quickly wiped the expression clean as if the movement hurt.

It probably did. The swelling near her temple would dissipate in a day or two. But the bruise on her cheek? *That* was going to last for weeks.

He'd learned many things in Delta Force. How to assess an injury was one of them. The bruise she'd sustained from having her face slammed into the ground when Charles McClean dove on top of her was a doozy.

Ol' Charlie boy hadn't exactly been a small man. What he'd lacked in height—Fisher would've guessed he topped out at about 5'11"—he'd more than made up for with muscle.

That's what fine food and expensive personal trainers will do for a man, he mused resentfully and then reminded himself of two things. One, there was no longer any reason to be jealous of Charles McClean. And two, instead of disparaging the man's lifestyle, he should be thanking the guy for saving the only woman Fisher had ever…

What?

What *was* it Fisher felt for Eliza?

Unfortunately, he knew the answer. It was possessiveness. The caveman kind where he wanted to throw her over his shoulder, cart her off to his lair, and then guard her from any comers who might think to cut even so much as a look her way.

Which sounded nice to the moon-eyed girls who went gah-gah over the heroes in those teeny-bopper books about sparkling vampires and bare-chested werewolves. But anyone with an ounce of intelligence knew possessiveness was about as far from *nice* as a person could get.

Possession was about ownership. Love was about freedom.

Sadly, Fisher didn't know how to love. He had a hard, cold stone where his heart should have been. He'd inherited the damn thing from his father right along with the prickly legged monster.

"You know the security here is top-notch." Eliza's words dragged him from his unwelcome thoughts. "And what could be safer for me than being surrounded by a bunch of black ops soldiers? Besides," she finished with a sticky-sounding swallow, "the danger to me is over. The shooter is dead."

The *physical* danger might have passed. But Fisher knew emotional danger still loomed.

She was in shock. As soon as it dissipated, she was going to crash and crash *hard*.

His eyes tracked once again to the ring on her finger, a ring he couldn't have afforded even on his best day. He didn't envy her the coming hours and days when the reality of her situation set in. When it finally hit her, *truly* hit her that the man she loved was dead.

When the prickly legged beast snarled, venom dripping from its fangs, he mentally squashed it with his boot and forced himself to take stock of his surroundings.

He'd peeked into her room dozens of times over the years. But he'd been careful never to step foot inside. For one thing, living and working with folks meant there was very little privacy to be had. And what privacy any of them *could* find was held sacrosanct. For another thing, when he was inside her room he couldn't escape her smell.

Her perfume lingered. That clean, crisp scent that always made him think of spring and the promise of something beautiful after a storm. And anytime he smelled it he wanted. He yearned. He wished for things that could never be and that just made him…well…*sad.*

Her bed was black metal. The blanket thrown over it was one of those cream, fluffy things that was basically a big pillowcase. And the painting hanging above her headboard was a blurry, nighttime cityscape—Chicago as seen through a rain-soaked windowpane.

The chair pushed into the corner was large and plush and blush colored. It matched some of the threads in the thick rug on the floor. There was one of those standing, full-length mirrors beside her dresser that reflected the two of them on the bed.

He looked large and hard and menacing.

She looked feminine and soft and…*broken.*

He wanted so badly to pull her back into his embrace. In fact, now that he knew what it was to hold her, to feel her heart beat in time with his own and appreciate how perfectly her head fit into the crook of his shoulder, he wondered how he'd ever lived his life *without* holding her.

And there it is again. That toxic need to conquer and claim.

To distract himself from his shortcomings, he let his gaze swing around her room one more time. He clocked how the pattern on the curtains matched the fabric covering the little pillow tossed into the armchair. How the jewelry stand on her dresser held only a few delicate pieces even though he knew she could probably afford to buy out half of Tiffany's. How the large wax candle in the glass hurricane holder on the occasional table by the door was half-melted and scented the air with the faintest tinge of vanilla.

Her room was sophisticated and inviting, just like the woman herself. A warm little sanctuary inside the cold, industrial expanse of the old menthol cigarette factory. And a far cry from the sparce furnishings and threadbare quilt that filled his own room.

If he'd ever needed more proof of their differences, all he had to do was compare the small squares of space they'd carved out for themselves there at BKI.

Where she was soft and refined, he was hard and coarse. Where she was tasteful and stylish, he was boorish and uncivilized. But, most importantly, where she was used to the finer things in life, he'd gotten used to making do with the bare necessities.

The society girl and the boy from the wrong side of the tracks indeed.

"Dad, please." Her tone had grown exasperated, and he was sorely tempted to rip the phone from her hand and tell her father to fuck off. The last thing she needed was to get on a plane and fly halfway across the country. "I'm exhausted. My head is killing me. All I want is sleep."

He watched as a line appeared between her eyebrows. Then she shook her head. "No. I *don't* know why Senator McClean invited me over tonight. I mean, I guess I assumed he was just giving Charlie a chance to rub elbows with some D.C. dealmakers. You know Charlie was always looking for support when it came to funding his charities."

Ah, yes. Charles McClean, the ultimate do-gooder.

The prickly legged thing blinked open an eye but Fisher shoved an imaginary finger over its eyelid and told it to go back to sleep.

"Yes." Eliza nodded. "I got a chance to talk to the senator. Just for a few minutes before he was called away by a colleague. But, Dad? Why does any of this matter? It's not like you can solve the case from the Oval Office. Let the FBI agents do their job. And let *me* get some sleep. I'll call you in the morning when I can think straight and then you can ask me anything you want, okay? I promise I'll be better at answering questions then."

He didn't hear what Meadows said next. He wondered if the man said anything at all, because Eliza sighed deeply and then simply thumbed off her phone.

"He's worried about ya," he assured her.

Leonard Meadows was a hard man, a *harried* man, always in a rush. But Fisher didn't doubt the guy loved his daughter. He'd seen it in the old codger's eyes the one and only time the chief of staff had made a clandestine trip to BKI with Madam President to check out the men they'd hired to do their dirty work.

Or, as Eliza liked to call it, their *red tape and dossier-averse work*. Because the only authority the Knights reported to was the commander in chief and the only mission reports they put together went straight to the top, stamped with the directive: *burn after reading*.

"I know." She nodded slowly, her expression hidden from him by a curtain of dark, damp hair. "He just has a terrible way of showing it."

There was a note of misery in her voice. It was nearly hidden beneath the more glaring note of longing.

He knew what it was to seek the approval of a parent incapable of giving that very thing. Unlike her, though, he'd stopped searching at a very young age.

Easy to do when your dad is none other than the notorious Nash Wakefield.

He wanted to tuck her hair behind her ear so he could see her face. But he knew better than to tempt fate. It was one thing for *her* to instigate physicality between them. But another thing entirely for *him* to do it.

If *he* did it, he'd want to do it again. And again. And *again* until all he was doing was touching her every chance he got.

Then he thought… *fuck it.*

Careful of her injuries, he gently brushed her hair over her shoulder and anchored the front strands behind the delicate shell of her ear.

Like the rest of her, her ear was pale and perfect. His fingers lingered longer than he'd intended, his thumb and forefinger following the curve of cartilage and then lightly squeezing her earlobe.

Soft.

What other parts of her are this soft? he wondered before quickly dropping his hand and calling himself every dirty name in the book.

She didn't need his desire; she needed his support. She didn't need his passion; she needed his friendship.

Or did she?

When she turned to look at him, her heavy-lidded eyes—those bedroom eyes of hers that were seductive without meaning to be—showed more than simple sadness. More than pain or grief or even vulnerability. They showed…*hunger?*

He'd been with enough women to recognize when one wanted him. Except…

That can't be right.

She'd spent four years batting away his every advance and rolling her eyes at his every offer of getting her naked and horizontal. And surely, tonight of all nights, she wouldn't suddenly decide to change her mind on the matter.

The lamps on her bedside tables had those old-fashioned Edison bulbs screwed into them. They gave off a golden glow that bathed her in sepia-toned warmth and apparently had his eyes playing tricks on him.

That's it. It's those damn fancy bulbs that have me seein' things that aren't there.

Even so, his tongue felt tacky. Like it couldn't unstick itself from the roof of his mouth. His blood ran hot, rising to the surface of his skin to warm him all over. Then there was the dull ache low in his belly, the one that told him—

That's my cue to leave.

"Welp." He slapped his knees. "Reckon I better adios myself next door."

"Wait." When her cool hand curled around his wrist, his heated brain conjured up an image of how good it would look, how good it would *feel*, curled around something else entirely. "Don't go. I—"

She swallowed and shook her head. It caused her hair to fall over her shoulder again and conjured up a quick, feverish fantasy of what it would feel like to have that long, dark hair brushing over his chest. His belly.

"You need sleep." He'd trained his heart to remain steady even when bullets were buzzing and bombs were bursting. But all it took was feeling her hand on him and it beat forcefully against his ribs, making them ache.

"I don't want to be alone, Fish." Her pretty mouth thinned. Her unpainted lips were usually a soft pink. But now they were so pale they faded into the skin over her face. "When I'm alone, I can't stop the memories."

She wasn't asking for Britt or Graham or any of the others. She was asking *him* to stay, to be the one to help keep her demons at bay.

The feeling that rose up inside him felt like happiness. But he'd experienced so little of the emotion, he couldn't be sure.

"Probably not a very good idea," he managed through a throat that had gone as dry as the Sakhir Desert that time he and the Knights had been tasked with doing business in Bahrain.

"Why?" Her expression showed confusion.

'Cause I won't be able to stop myself from touchin' ya.

The words made it as far as the back of his throat before he closed his teeth on them. She tilted her head and there was a plea in her eyes, a request that spoke without words.

He couldn't deny her.

He'd never been able to deny her.

"I'll stay until ya fall asleep," he relented.

The smile she gave him then, that sweet smile that was quintessentially Eliza and just a little lopsided, winged across the space between them and hooked into his heart.

Well, the hard, cold stone that acts as my heart, he silently corrected.

"Let me put on pajamas."

She was off the bed in a flash. Too quick for her scrambled gray matter, because she wobbled and threw out a hand to steady herself.

He instinctively caught her fingers and rose to support her elbow. "No sudden moves with a concussion," he warned. "Sends the room spinnin' like you've had too much wine."

She bit her lip and the sight nearly drove him to his knees. How many times had *he* wanted to do exactly that? Catch that plump bottom pad between his teeth and give it a quick nip before soothing the sting with his tongue?

She made a face. "Something tells me *this* hangover is going to kick my ass."

He winced. "Wish I could tell ya otherwise, but experience says you're probably right."

"Great," she muttered and let go of his hand to walk over to her dresser. She fished her pajamas from the top drawer and then disappeared into the bathroom.

Curling his fingers around the space where her fingers had been, he sank down on the mattress.

What the hell are ya doin', Fish? You should be callin' in Britt or Hewitt. Yeah, Hewitt's perfect for this job. He'll slouch over there in the chair and read until she falls asleep.

Just about the only time Hewitt Burch *didn't* have his nose pressed between the pages of a book was when he was at the controls of a helicopter or sitting atop the black marvel that was his custom Harley.

Fisher was about to go search for the former Night Stalker—the nickname given to those in the 160th Special Operations Aviation Regiment—when the bathroom door opened.

One look at Eliza and he knew he wasn't going anywhere.

Staying with her was dangerous.

Leaving her was impossible.

CHAPTER 6

Northwestern Memorial Hospital

"That sorry sonofabitch left survivors."

Yang grunted his agreement as he sat in the lobby of the large hospital building and watched people shuffle in and out of the automatic exit doors. There were those who wore smiles and carried flowers, no doubt headed to the maternity ward to congratulate someone on a new arrival. Others wore the haggard, downtrodden expression of loving someone who was desperately ill or actively dying.

Most people loathed hospitals. Loathed the idea of disease and death. Not Yang.

Disease and death were as common as birth and life. As *inevitable* too. Which meant they were nothing to fear. Plus, he didn't know of another place where one could witness the full gamut of human emotions—from the highest of highs to the lowest of lows. And for someone who'd made a career of studying people, it was a bit of an academic experience.

"He was not a professional," he said matter-of-factly. His eyes narrowed on the petite, blond FBI agent when she stepped from one of the four elevators. He knew she was FBI from the way she carried herself, with an air of authority.

Others probably looked at her and saw little more than her long ponytail and lack of height. But Yang knew better than to judge a book by its cover. He recognized the expression in the lady agent's eyes. It was one of whip-sharp intelligence.

The square-jawed man who towered next to her had the *look* of a federal agent. But Yang would bet his next ticket to China that Blondie had the brains of one.

I had hoped to beat them here.

"He was paid to do a job." The voice on the other end of the call was filled with derision. "Or at least his *family* will be paid. And payment *made* him a professional."

Yang—that wasn't his real name; it was simply the codename he used on this side of the world—didn't argue. There was no point. Besides, he had work to do.

"I assume you want me to finish what he started?"

"I think you'd better. Just in case," Bishop's tone had gone from disgusted to tired.

Bishop wasn't the man's real name either. But it was the only name Yang had ever called him.

"Just so you are aware," he warned, "the feds beat me here."

A grunt sounded through the phone. "No surprise there. Four members of Congress are dead along with various and sundry of their family members. The bodies probably hadn't even begun to cool before the local branch had their best team investigating."

"From what I can glean, Professor Chastain has not regained consciousness. But I am sure Senator Chastain was only too happy to answer their questions."

"And that's the crux of the issue, isn't it?" Bishop sighed heavily. "Because we have no idea what answers she might have given."

"Mmm." Yang pretended to study his shoes, but his eyes tracked the agents as they exited through the automatic doors. "But your source who is overseeing the investigation will no doubt make his report soon enough. And *then* you will know."

"I'll know if it's not too late. I'll know if I haven't been outed."

"You have not been outed," Yang assured Bishop. "Sullivan called and said as much. He said Senator McClean had not had a chance to tell the group why he had gathered them together."

"Sullivan said he hadn't heard McClean make any sort of announcement. That doesn't mean the bastard hadn't gotten the chance to pull people aside and share his suspicions one-on-one."

"So then we simply do what we must." Yang turned toward the lobby when the glass doors slid shut behind the FBI agents.

"Right." There was determination in Bishop's voice. "We finish the job Sullivan started, frame that kiddy-loving sonofabitch from Indiana, and hope John McClean didn't have time to share his suspicions about me with Eliza or either of the Chastains."

"Precisely," Bishop agreed.

For a handful of seconds, there was quiet on the other end of the call. Then, Bishop cursed. "Damnit! You just know that two more suspicious deaths are going to sharpen the feds' focus and make things more difficult for us."

"Only two more?" Yang's tone didn't change. But he knew, if anyone could see inside the dark shadow cast by the brim of his pulled-low baseball cap, they would find curiosity in his eyes.

"Eliza Meadows and Black Knights Inc. are a far more complicated issue. I need to think about how to handle them."

CHAPTER 7

"**S**nug as a bug in a rug." Fisher tucked the fluffy blanket tight around Eliza's arms and legs. Not so much because he thought she'd appreciate the gesture. More because he needed her covered head to toe.

Her pajamas were…well…probably *not* meant to be overtly seductive. But on Eliza they might as well have been a lace teddy. The bottoms were long and shiny and slunk around her hips and ass when she walked, emphasizing every delicious jiggle. And the top? Oh, the top was pure fantasy.

Spaghetti straps.

Silky purple material.

Thin enough to cling to her nipples and show him their exact size and shape.

H-h-holy shit.

It had taken everything he had to lift the comforter and watch her crawl into bed without joining her there. And then he used what was left of his fraying control to stalk over to the armchair. When he sat, he curled his fingers so tightly around the armrests it was a wonder he didn't rip the upholstery clean off the batting.

She looked so youthful with her face scrubbed clean of makeup and her usually tidy hair spread across the pillow in disarray. But her eyes were those of a woman when she whispered. "Come lay next to me."

She pulled an arm from beneath the covers to pat the empty space beside her.

His heart made a flying leap into his throat at the same time his stomach tried to exit his ass.

"Not gonna happen." He shook his head, although the urge to strip naked and cannonball into bed as quickly as humanly possible was intense.

"Why not? I don't have cooties. It's okay if you accidently touch me."

"It should be obvious by now, Eliza, that when I touch ya, it's never by accident."

She frowned. "Guess that explains why you do it so rarely. Especially lately."

Now his lungs had joined his heart in their attempt to fly out of his mouth. "Are ya sayin' ya wish I did it more?"

Despite the bruising and swelling, he could see the petulance on her face. "Well not if you don't *want* to."

She crossed her arms and the move made the tops of her breasts swell above the neckline of her pajama top.

He shifted into a more comfortable position in the chair. Then shifted again when that didn't bring him any relief. Then gave up when he realized the only comfortable position to be found when sporting a giant hard-on would require he get naked.

"Doll face, I've wanted to touch you since the moment I saw you." He watched her swallow convulsively. "Ya made it clear ya weren't interested."

"I wasn't interested in being another notch on your bedpost," she said with a flick of her wrist.

Hellfire and damnation!

What was she saying? That if he'd tried to court her instead of simply trying to bed her then she might have been interested?

Nah, that can't be right. Rich girl and boy from the wrong side of the tracks, remember?

He must have misunderstood.

"Right. You didn't want to be a notch on my bedpost because you are you"—he waved around the room to indicate its sophistication—"and I am me."

Her eyes narrowed. "What's that supposed to mean?"

"It means you're smart and rich and refined. And I'm…*not*. You're not into slummin' it. I get it. No harm, no foul."

She narrowed her eyes. "We've already established that education does not equal intelligence. As for the money, I can assure you it doesn't buy a person happiness. And *refined*? Pfft. I sneak your Unscrustables when you're not looking."

"Thief!" He pointed to her nose. "I kept blamin' Ozzie!"

She shrugged and then sighed. "Look, I haven't been turning you down for four years for any other reason than it'd set me back years in therapy."

That made his chin jerk back. "How so, doll face?"

"It'd reactivate my abandonment issues," she answered easily. Before he could question her further, she plowed ahead. "And anyway, we weren't talking about you coming over here to plow me into a sex coma. We were talking about you coming over here and lying next to me *as a friend*. You do realize sex isn't the only way two people can be physical. There's such a thing as platonic affection."

He snorted. "What I feel for ya is *never* goin' to be platonic. There. Is that better, darlin'?"

Her bedroom eyes looked particularly dark and inviting in the golden lamplight. But her tone was as prickly as a porcupine. "Which part? The part where you're incapable of having a relationship with a woman that doesn't involve sex? Or the part where you changed your pet name for me from doll face to darlin'?"

"I'm capable of havin' relationships with women. I love Becky, Michelle, Penni, Samantha." He ticked off the wives of the OG Black Knights on his fingers. "And I can guaran-damn-tee ya I'm not havin' sex with any of them."

Her expression flattened Kermit the Frog-style. "Only because Boss, Snake, Dan, and Ozzie would beat you to a sticky pulp if you tried."

"True." He shrugged and bit the inside of his cheek when her expression showed sheer exasperation. "Look," he told her, "I'm stayin' over here *because* I want to be a good friend. If I came over there." He hitched his chin in her direction. "My hormones are likely to overcome my good intentions."

Her voice was low and small, and she picked at a thread on the edge of the comforter. "Maybe that would be okay."

"Huh?" He leaned forward, placing his elbows on his knees. He *couldn't* have heard her correctly.

"I mean, if I'm fending off your advances, I won't be thinking about…" She swallowed and turned her face away. Even so, there was no mistaking the little sound of misery that escaped her throat.

All the teasing and temptation in him melted away, leaving only empathy. "I wish I'd been there, Liza. Wish I'd seen the things ya saw, shared in your pain. Maybe then the horror of it would be halved."

She shook her head before turning back to him. "How do you do that? How do you make me want to strangle you one minute and bear-hug the life out of you the next?"

He shrugged and offered her a grin he hoped would lighten the mood. "It's a gift."

For long seconds, she searched his eyes. He wasn't sure what she was looking for. And he wasn't sure if she found it. But eventually she said, "I like it when you call me Liza."

He lifted an eyebrow. "I reckoned ya might think I was bein' too informal."

The look she gave him was incredulous. "We share a wall, Fish. I know when you take a shower and flush the toilet. I think we left formal behind years ago."

He chuckled. "Liza it is then."

A small smile played at the corner of her mouth. He couldn't help but feel a burst of pride that he'd been the one to put it there.

All he wanted was to see her smile. To ease what pain he could.

That's all you want? The better angels of his nature challenged.

Fine. That wasn't *all* he wanted. But it was enough.

He'd make it be enough.

"It starts with a little grin just like that." He pointed to her face.

"What does?" A line appeared between her eyebrows.

"Healin'. It starts with a small smile that becomes a little laugh. And then, before ya know it, the hurt no longer feels like it's killin' ya from the inside out."

Folks said the eyes were the windows to the soul. And the expression in Eliza's told him her soul was battered and bruised. Be he hoped like hell it wasn't broken.

She patted the space beside her again. "Come lie next to me, Fish. I trust in your ability to restrain yourself. Besides, feeling someone near me is the only way I'll be able to relax enough to fall asleep."

"Liza—"

"I won't beg," she interrupted. "I respect myself too much for that. Besides, I don't want your sympathy unless it's freely offered."

He understood the basic human need for human contact after suffering trauma. And he couldn't deny the answering ache in his chest.

This is going to be hell, he silently admitted even as he stood and took the first of three steps that brought him to the side of the bed.

"Thank you," she whispered and then went and made everything so much worse by throwing the covers back and indicating he should crawl in beside her.

Is she tryin' *to kill me?*

Sitting on the edge of the bed, he unlaced his boots and kicked them off. By the time he slid between the cool sheets, blood pounded in his ears.

"Thank you," she said again as she dropped the covers atop his chest. And then…

Oh, and *then* he felt her slim, cool fingers slip inside his hand.

For a while, neither of them moved. He struggled just to breathe. And his mind was a mess of swirling thoughts, so he was startled when her voice suddenly cut through his internal chaos.

"What happened to make you stop touching me? Do you regret telling me what happened in South America?"

He'd managed to avoid her question earlier by quoting Robert Frost. There was no way to do so a second time without making his avoidance obvious. And so…he was left with the truth.

"Charles McClean happened."

She turned her head to look at him. "I don't understand."

"It was one thing to flirt and carry on when you were single, but it felt wrong when you were seriously datin' someone." He realized how that made him sound and was quick to explain. "Not that I was anglin' to be more than friends with ya." He stopped and grinned. "Or at least that wasn't my *sole* intent. But it was more like if I'd kept carryin' on like I had been, I'd have found myself even *more* jealous of ol' Charlie than I already was. Keepin' my grubby mitts to myself was a kind of self-preservation."

"You were jealous of Charlie? Why?"

"'Cause he had ya when I wanted ya."

She turned back to stare at the ceiling. For the span of a couple heartbeats, she stayed silent. And when she finally spoke, her voice was whisper-soft. "Wanted me for a night or two, you mean."

She kept coming back to that. Did that mean she hadn't been shoving aside his advances because she was a rich debutante and he was the boy from the wrong side of the tracks? That she'd been shoving them aside because she wanted more from him than he could ever give her?

A part of him reveled in the notion that the great Eliza Meadows might actually want him the way he wanted her. But a bigger part of him admitted that her want of him, and particularly her want of something more than he could offer, would make everything worse.

"I wish I were capable of wantin' more," he admitted hoarsely. "But wantin' more for a guy like me is dangerous."

Now he was staring at the ceiling, but he could feel her turn to him when she asked, "Why?"

"'Cause of who I am."

"And who are you?"

"Someone who's only good for a night or two."

"Why?"

He forced a grin and met her confused gaze. "You're soundin' like a broken record."

She countered immediately. "And you're being frustratingly obtuse."

He sighed and turned back to stare at the ceiling. It was impossible to hold her gaze when she was so close. When she was so open and revealing.

"Just take my word for it when I tell ya that if ya were to ever give me a chance, you'd be *happy* all I can offer is a night or two."

She snorted. "You're making it sound like you're a bad lover. But you forget I've seen the satisfied faces of women the morning after you've taken them to bed."

"That's not what I'm sayin' at all," he assured her. "I'm sayin' I don't have what it takes to be a good a partner in the long run. And if I tried, I'd just wind up hurtin' whichever unlucky lady decided to take a chance on me. That's the last thing I want."

For a long while after that pronouncement, silence filled the room. He counted his heartbeats. Counted her breaths. Counted the rows of bricks on the wall across the way as he waited for her response.

He could tell she wanted to press him further—Eliza had the curiosity of a cat—but eventually she relented and changed the subject. "Tell me about your mother."

The request, seemingly coming out of left field, caught him unawares. "Wh-what?" he sputtered. "Why?"

"Because you've thrown up a *road closed* sign on our previous route. But I still need a distraction from the horror movie that flashes across the backs of my eyelids anytime I close my eyes. Besides"—her fingers tightened around his, causing his jaw to tighten in response—"I've always been interested in the woman who raised you. I know there's no love lost between you and your father. But what about your mom? What was she like?"

"No love lost?" He snorted. "That's one way of sayin' I hate the bastard from the top of his head to the tips of his toes."

"Why?" The inquisitiveness in her tone wasn't the voyeuristic, meddlesome kind. It was the *genuine* kind. The kind that said she was asking because she truly cared, truly wanted to understand what made him tick.

It was the only reason he answered. Although later he'd want to kick his own ass for the bluntness of his delivery. "Because he killed my mother."

"What?" She gasped and sat up in bed. The sudden movement made her wobble and he found himself sitting up beside her to steady her with a hand on each shoulder.

Warm. Her skin was so damn warm.

Smooth too. Like a baby's bottom. Although his mind certainly wasn't conjuring up images of an infant.

Even though his eyes wanted to track down to what he knew would be her nipples poking against the silky fabric, he managed to keep his attention focused on her lovely—albeit bruised and swollen—face.

"What did I tell ya 'bout movin' too quickly?"

She ignored him. "*That's* why he's in prison?"

"Doing life without parole in Pollack Penitentiary." He nodded. "The bastard deserved the death sentence. But because it was considered a *crime of passion*"—he made derisive air quotes—"he was only found guilty of second-degree murder."

Thinking of how his old man was still drawing breath when his mother was nearly two decades in the ground made him grind his teeth so hard his molars ached. "If ya ask me, the world would be a better place if he'd had a needle shoved in his arm years ago. But I don't make the laws. Or the sentencin' guidelines."

He watched her throat work over a swallow. The skin there looked as pale and warm as the skin on her shoulders. His fingers itched to touch her again. Which is why he busied them—and himself—with turning toward the lamp on his side of the bed and switching off the knob.

The light in the room was instantly halved.

Good.

He didn't want her seeing how deeply he could hate. How easily it would've been for him to beat and strangle his father the way his father had beaten and strangled his mother.

How much like him I truly am.

Settling back against the pillow, he refused to meet Eliza's gaze as she stared down at him.

Either she realized he needed the illusion of privacy if he was going to finish telling his tale, or she didn't like what little she could still see of his expression. Because she switched off her own lamp. To his relief, the room was plunged into darkness.

His eyes were instantly drawn to the large window and the night sky beyond.

In the city, there was no such thing as pitch blackness. Light pollution dulled the brilliance of the moon and diminished the twinkling of the stars. So much so that when he was home in Chicago he forgot what it was like to look up and see the Milky Way spread out above him like a blanket of confetti.

He realized it wasn't the city's glow affecting his ability to count the constellations now, though. It was a quickly approaching storm. A large, dark cloud rolled across the moon, obscuring its silver face.

Menacing was the word that drifted through his head as he stared at the stygian sky. That thought was quickly followed up by something else. Something that made the hairs on his arms lift. *Portentous.*

Dark nights were meant for dark deeds. For the stalking of demons. For...*death.*

He scolded himself for his foolishness. Having been raised in the backwoods of Louisiana, he'd grown up with tales of haints and the fifolet and skin-walkers bent on mayhem and murder. So it was easy to sometimes forget that all the evil in the world was perpetuated by man and not some shadowy, faceless monster that crawled through the night.

He felt her settle back against her own pillow. Felt her snuggle beneath the covers. And then he had to hold back a sigh of relief when he felt her little fingers once again interlace with his own.

After what he'd revealed, he wouldn't have been surprised if she never wanted to touch him again.

The sins of the father and all that jazz.

Her voice was as thick as the darkness in the room when she whispered, "I'm so sorry, Fisher. How old were you?"

"It was three weeks before my sixteenth birthday. I spent the last two years of high school bouncin' from couch to couch. And as soon as I got my diploma, I was out of there. Gone. Adiosed from anyone who knew about the stain on my family name, about what my daddy had done to my momma."

For a while after that, she was quiet. And when he heard her breaths go from shallow to deep, from thready to steady, he thought maybe she'd fallen asleep. But her voice didn't hold even a hint of sleepiness when she finally asked, "Why'd he do it? Kill her, I mean. Did you ever find out?"

Of all the questions she could ask, that was the easiest to answer. "Because Nash Wakefield never should've fallen in his version of love. Because all he was truly capable of was obsession. Because he was possessive and controlling and jealous. Because he *could*."

He heard her long, windy exhalation and expected a follow-up question. It never came.

Into the silence he said, "He got off work early one day and saw her talkin' to a man outside the Quickie Stop. Not flirtin' or touchin' or anything like that. Just talkin'." His stomach roiled as he relived what he knew of the events. He'd heard all the witness testimony at trial, had seen all the gas station security footage that'd been played for the jury. "He didn't even give them time to react or explain that they were strangers who were talkin' 'bout how hot the weather had turned. He just reached beneath the seat of his truck for his pistol, shot that nice man in the head, and then dragged Momma home where he beat her and raped her and finally strangled her to death."

He didn't mention the part where he'd come home from school to find his mother on the floor, her face bloody and bruised, her sundress bunched up around her waist, all while his father rutted away between her thighs. He didn't tell her how he'd jumped onto his father's back, screaming for the bastard to stop. And he didn't say how his father had flung him off with such fury that his temple had smacked the side of the coffee table and he'd gone out like a light.

Well, not exactly like a light.

It'd taken a few seconds for the darkness to completely suck him under. And the last thing his dimming eyes had witnessed was the degradation and resignation on his mother's bruised and bloodied face.

When he'd come to, it was to find her dead and his father on the run. Luckily, it'd only taken the authorities thirty-six hours to catch up with Nash Wakefield. And after that, life had become more about surviving for Fisher than actual living.

He'd been surviving ever since.

"Fish." Her throat sounded full, like she was holding back tears. "I don't have any words. I don't know if there *are* any words for something like that. I'm so sorry for you, for your mother. I—"

"I'm sorry too," he cut in. "You've been through hell tonight and here I am pilin' on with my sad-sack tale and—"

"No." He couldn't see her, but he felt her shaking her head. Heard the raspy sound her hair made as it rubbed against the cotton pillowcase. "I asked and you answered. And honestly—and this probably sounds awful— but seeing how you've come back from such a tragedy gives me hope I'll bounce back too. Maybe someday I'll be able to feel like what happened is a chapter in my life instead of the whole damn book."

He desperately wanted to pull her into his arms. Just roll onto his side and curl himself around her until every bit of him was holding every bit of her.

Instead, he satisfied himself with a gentle squeeze of her hand. "It's a sad day when ya realize the person you need the most has just taught ya that ya really don't need anyone at all. I thought I wouldn't make it without Mom. But I did. And you'll make it without Charlie too. I'm not sayin' it'll be easy. I'm just sayin' it'll get done."

Her swallow was sticky-sounding. But she didn't continue with that line of conversation. Instead she whispered again, "Tell me about your mother. Not the awful way she ended, but how she lived. Who was she?"

If it'd been anyone but Eliza asking, he would have waved away the question and changed the subject. Talking about his mother wasn't something he did. Not because she'd been ugly and awful to him. But because she *hadn't* been.

She'd been fun and loving and supportive and so, so…

Broken.

He hadn't known it back then. He'd been too young and ignorant to the ways of the world and to wholesome, healthy relationships. But he knew it now.

What he'd suspected in theory before he'd joined Black Knights Inc., he'd since come to understand as fact. Having watched the original Knights with their partners, he could see how completely toxic his parents' love had been.

Love. He snorted silently. *More like a noxious blend of delusion, narcissism, and codependence.*

"She was beautiful and smart." He started quietly, but his voice grew stronger as he went on. "She had this big smile and an even bigger voice. The kind of voice that raised the roof of the church when she sang in the choir. She loved yellow, wore it all the time. Loved feedin' bread to the ducks at the pond. And she always acted like she accidentally let the bananas get overripe. But I knew she did it on purpose. 'Cause I loved banana bread."

He closed his eyes and the image of his mother sitting on the park bench, a bag of stale Wonder Bread in hand, flashed through his head.

"She's the one who taught me to play harmonica. She'd been taught by her daddy who'd been taught by his daddy before him. She was small-town royalty. Her father was the local plastics manufacturer, and she grew up with the silver spoon and all the Southern charm you could ever want. I'm sure her old man did about a hundred somersaults in his grave when she took up with my old man."

"Your grandfather died when she was young?" She unconsciously ran her thumb along the side of his. Alternatively, he was *very* conscious of the way her soft touch made his stomach muscles tighten.

Platonic my ass, he thought before answering.

"Her senior year in high school. I think maybe that's how my father got his hooks in her. 'Cause she was hurtin' and vulnerable. Anyhow, her older brother took over the plastics business and after she married my dad, she kinda lost touch with her family. Or, more like, my father isolated her and kept her all to himself. But she named me after them. Her family, I mean. Their surname was Fisher. And so even though I've never known any of them more than in passin', I still carry around a piece of them."

"How does a smart, beautiful, wealthy woman find herself tying the knot with an abusive, murderous man?" If he'd been able to see Eliza, he knew he'd find her sleek, dark eyebrows pulled together over her nose.

"It wasn't like Dad started out that way." He blinked contemplatively into the darkness. "Momma said he was the cock of walk, all good looks and charm and pockets full of money from the tips he got dealing cards on the riverboat. He seduced her with little gifts and honeyed words. In fact, he could sweet-talk her like nothin' you've ever seen. Even when he'd go out of his mind with jealousy because she'd opened the door to the mailman instead of letting the letters be dropped in the box or waved at the neighbor man mowing his yard, he'd always tell her it was because he loved her so much. Because he knew she was too good for him and so he lived in constant fear she'd leave him."

"She believed him?"

"For years." He nodded. "She had stars in her eyes when it came to Dad. Thought he hung the moon even when he slapped a bruise on her face or grabbed her wrist so hard he broke her bones." He sighed heavily. "She mistook his jealousy for love, made excuses for him by sayin' it wasn't his fault he'd been raised rough. And I think she honestly believed she could change him if she just loved him hard enough for long enough."

"How awful," she murmured. "And how sad."

He hummed his agreement. "It only got worse once he got caught skimmin' money on the riverboat and lost his job. He'd been usin' his position there to draw in tourists and locals alike to illegal, backroom poker tournaments. So when he lost his position on the boat, he lost his side-hustle too. And that was the beginnin' of the end. He got angrier and angrier about life. And that made him meaner and meaner to me, but especially to Momma. She was just beginnin' to see through all his bullshit, just beginnin' to realize his good looks and charm covered up a heart as cold and as hard as stone when he killed her. That was probably *why* he killed her, actually. Because, for the first time, she truly *might* have gotten around to leavin' him."

Her inhalation sounded shaky. "Why do the most horrible things happen to the best people?"

"Because the universe is a sadist. It likes to see us suffer."

Her voice was so quiet he barely heard her. "I hope that's not true."

Guilt whispered in his ear. What was he doing being all doom and gloom when he was supposed to be making her feel better?

"Want me to play ya a song?" It was trite and trivial, but it was the only thing he could think of to change the subject. Even though she liked to tease him about his "countrified" choice of musical instruments, he knew she enjoyed hearing him play. "Unless it'll hurt your head," he was quick to add.

"My head hurts regardless," she assured him. "So go on. Play something. But not the blues. I'm blue enough already. Play me something sweet. Play me something to remind me that things aren't all bad all the time."

He pondered his options for a few moments and then pulled his harmonica from his pocket. The metal was warm from his body heat when he placed the instrument against his lips. And he'd barely played the first handful of notes when he heard her chuckle.

It was sweeter music than what was coming out of his mouth harp.

"Invisible String," she whispered into the dark. "That's a good one."

Pleased she'd accurately picked out the Taylor Swift tune, he continued to play, careful to keep the volume low in deference to her aching head. By the time he finished, he thought again she might've fallen asleep. Her breaths were deep and steady.

Shoving his harmonica back inside his pocket, he went to slink out of the bed and leave her to her rest. But she stopped him with a hand on his arm.

"Do you think there really are invisible strings tying people together? Like, fate or kismet or whatever?"

"I think when it comes to love and fate, people have it all wrong."

"What do you mean?" He could hear the frown in her voice.

"I mean, lots of folks put stock in that whole *fated* lovers thing as if it's the most romantic notion ever. But I think it's just about the *least* romantic idea there is."

For a while, she said nothing. Then, "I hate to sound like a broken record, but what do you mean?"

"I mean, if we have no choice over what happens to us, if the universe is pullin' all the strings, then that means if ya fall in love with someone, it was preordained. *You* had nothin' to do with it. And I just can't reckon how anyone could think that's the ideal." He cocked his head as he considered his next words. "What *is* romantic is the idea that out of four million men, you would *choose* one."

He could almost hear the wheels turning inside her head. "So then what happens when the one you choose doesn't choose you back? What happens when the one you choose—"

He knew what she was driving at. And he made sure to stop her in her tracks. "You've loved once. You'll love again. You've got too much of the stuff inside ya not to share it with someone."

The catching of her breath told him he'd hit the nail on the head. And despite his best intentions, he'd gone and made her cry. *Again.*

Not knowing what else to do, he went against his better judgment and every ounce of self-preservation he had and folded his body around hers, big spoon and little spoon. Like lovers.

Except…all they'd ever be is friends. Especially now that he knew she might have once considered the idea of letting them be more.

CHAPTER 8

"What a bitch."

"Excuse me?" Julia took her eyes off the traffic on Lake Shore Drive long enough to glance over at her partner.

I should've taken State Street up to Division. There's a boatload of traffic lights, but at least that route isn't bumper-to-bumper this time of night, she thought as she slammed on the brakes to keep from rearending the car in front of her. It had stopped on a dime when a bolt of lightning spread its electric fingers across the sky, followed immediately by a crashing *boom* of thunder.

Midwesterners were supposed to be used to thunderstorms. But you couldn't tell it from the way everyone started driving like they were eighty years old with cataracts and automatic braking.

"Bethany Chastain," Dillan sneered. Then he added, "Excuse me. *Senator* Chastain."

It was true the senator had been…less than cooperative. In fact, there'd been times she'd seemed almost hostile. But Julia gave the woman the benefit of the doubt.

"She's been through hell tonight. And her husband just came out of surgery. I think she's allowed to be a little contrary."

She took one hand off the steering wheel to wave it dismissively. It was the hand Sergeant Rollins had grabbed. And maybe it was fanciful thinking, but she would swear if she concentrated really hard, she could still feel the warmth left behind by his touch.

"Contrary?" Dillan snorted. "That's just a nice way of saying she was a bitch."

Julia sighed. "Is it *all* women you dislike or just women in positions of power?"

Shit.

She'd always prided herself on how good she was at biting her tongue around Dillan. Not just good. *Great!* Like if Guinness was handing out awards for *Woman Most Capable of Holding Back When a Man Should Be Put in His Place*, she would surely take home the prize.

Intrusive thoughts of Ol' Blue Eyes had been popping into her head since she'd left Miss Meadows in the ER. She blamed those for her outburst. Well, those and the fact that she was dog-tired.

Tired of *Dillan* mostly, if she was being honest. Because the more uncooperative the senator had become, the more hostile and authoritative *he* had become. Eventually, she'd been forced to end the interview early and drag him out of the ICU waiting room lest they completely burn bridges with the senator and turn her from a slightly contrary witness into an openly hostile one.

To her relief—since if she couldn't keep her shit together and find a way to work *with* him then her boss was likely to pull her off the case—Dillan didn't seem to take offense to her slip of the tongue. In fact, he chuckled.

"I like women just fine. Better than fine. They're some of my favorite people. But I calls 'em as I sees 'em," he mimicked an old-timey accent. "And I say the senator is a bitch."

She slid him a look that was packed with disgust just as the sky opened up and traffic ground to a halt. She switched on the windshield wipers and watched as they tried—and failed—to keep up with the deluge.

"Women are some of your favorite people?" she challenged. "Name three women you actually *like*."

"Easy." He ticked off the list on his fingers. "My mom, my sister, and my other sister."

Why am I not surprised?

"Name three women who *aren't* family who you actually like."

The grin he shot her was shit-eating. "Scarlett Johanson, Gigi Hadid, and Taylor Swift."

She resisted the urge to reach over and punch him in the dick. "So…a beautiful actress, a beautiful model, and a beautiful singer-songwriter. Wow, Dillan. Whatever could it be about these smart, successful, talented women that you admire?"

He made it clear he didn't give a rat's ass what she thought of him when he shrugged carelessly. "Don't ask the questions if you're not going to like the answers."

Deciding there was no winning with him, and choosing her sanity over his ruthless arrogance, she changed the subject. "What do you think she meant when she said she couldn't trust us?"

He snorted, easily shifting gears alongside her. "Politicians are always watching out for their own asses. She probably thought we'd put something in our report that might be less than complimentary."

"You mean something less complimentary than she refused to cooperate with our federal investigation?"

"I mean…yeah." He nodded. "Who knows the mind of a career crook?"

That made Julia frown. "What makes you think she's crooked?"

"They all are."

And…there it is. The unraveling of my last thread of patience.

"Wow, Dillan. Maybe it's time you stopped watching Newsmax and got off Truth Social."

He snorted again. "Just because they float right-wing conspiracies doesn't mean they're wrong."

"I think, by the definition of *conspiracy*, that's exactly what it means. And that's before you add in all the propaganda and fear-mongering. Those platforms prey on people. Please tell me you're joking, and you haven't really fallen victim to their disinformation."

"I'm joking and I haven't really fallen victim to their disinformation." He parroted her word-for-word. "I mean, who has time to follow any of that anyway? I get my news from Facebook or TikTok in sixty-second clips."

She wanted to scream. But she managed to keep her voice even when she gritted, "That's not any better."

"Meh. To each their own." He turned on the radio and left her to her thoughts.

Fine by her. At least her thoughts didn't make her feel violently homicidal.

As the lead singer of Green Day told the world he refused to be an "American Idiot" *–ha! Appropriate. And the irony probably flew right over Dillan's head—*she replayed her interview questions and the senator's answers in her head.

"Why were you at Senator McClean's house tonight, Senator Chastain?"

"Because he invited me."

"And why'd he invite you?"

"Because we're colleagues who work on committees together. And because we live in the same city when we're not in D.C."

"Are…were…you and Senator McClean close?"

"Like I said, we were colleagues."

And so on and so forth. The senator had answered her questions without really giving her anything helpful at all.

It wasn't until Julia had asked Bethany Chastain if she had any idea why John McClean's cook would've turned on him that things got interesting.

"John wasn't exactly well liked by most people. Especially powerful people in Washington."

"So you suspect someone paid *the chef to kill him? But then why try to kill everyone else? Why not just kill McClean?"*

That's when Chastain had clammed up and claimed she couldn't trust the FBI. Not that she couldn't trust Julia and Dillan, but that she couldn't trust the entire *bureau.*

Curiouser and curiouser.

Green Day came to a crashing end and a commercial for the latest *Star Wars* series to hit Disney Plus played on the radio. Julia was instantly reminded of her whole *I'm Luke Skywalker; I'm here to rescue you* gaffe back in the ER. She cringed.

He must think I am the biggest nerd to ever walk on two legs.

Then she scolded herself for caring about what some stranger she'd met only once and whom she might never meet again thought of her.

A dark, delicious, slow-talking stranger with the prettiest eyes and the most intriguing scar and—

Gah! Really, *really* inconvenient!

CHAPTER 9

Black Knights Inc.

Fisher called himself ten kinds of fool for making Eliza cry again. And he wished there was something more he could do for her than simply hold her close and whisper reassuring words in her ear.

Every ragged sigh broke something inside him. Every soft whimper made him want to find that gunman and kill the bastard all over again for what he'd put her through. Every tear that dampened her pillow made him wish for powers of resurrection. He'd use them to give her back the man she loved.

"I didn't say yes." Her voice slipped to him through the darkness, low and soggy-sounding.

"Didn't say yes to what?" With his face nestled into the back of her head, the sweet, clean scent of her shampoo slid inside his nose.

"To Charlie."

He pushed up on his elbow to stare down at her. He could barely see the outline of her profile in the darkness. Then lightning flashed—the storm was fully upon them now—and he noted the wet tracks her tears had left on her cheek.

With a gentle thumb, he brushed the salty impressions away and marveled at the softness of the skin beneath. For such a lanky woman, she was soft in all the right spots. Her breasts were well-formed and heavy. Her ass was plump and peach-shaped. And she had the most delicious little curve in her lower belly. The perfect place to fit the palm of a man's hand.

It'd certainly been the perfect perch for *his* palm as he'd spooned her. And with his dick snuggled up tight against her ass, it'd taken herculean effort to keep the sorry sonofabitch from giving her a full salute.

He probably wouldn't have managed it had it not been for her tears. Her sorrow had been just enough to take the edge off and convince him that even though he was a horny asshole, at least he wasn't *that* much of a horny asshole.

"I'm sorry," he said now with a confused frown. "I'm still not followin'."

"When he asked me to marry him, I didn't say yes." She turned onto her back just as another lightning bolt hit the top of a nearby building. Its electric flash strobed into the room, momentarily highlighting the misery in her eyes.

Something stilled inside him. He thought maybe it was his heart.

With a gentle finger, he brushed some hair back from her brow. He made sure to keep his voice softly supportive even though his curiosity was a rabid dog eating at him. "Why? I thought y'all were a match made in heaven."

She laughed, but there was no humor in it. After taking a deep breath, she admitted in an anguished tone, "I didn't love him. I *should* have loved him. He was smart, sweet, and funny. He was handsome, generous, and… most importantly…*kind*."

The prickly legged thing that lived in Fisher lifted its head and snarled as she listed McClean's redeeming qualities. He imagined stomping on it with the hard heel of his biker boot until it was nothing more than a shiny, black oil slick.

Unfortunately, it wouldn't stay dead for long.

No matter how many times he'd vanquished the vile creature, it always returned.

I mean, who in their right mind is jealous of a dead man?

Oh, right. Me. Nash Wakefield's son.

"And on paper we *were* a match made in heaven," she continued. "We both came from political families. We both chose jobs we hoped would help make the world a better place, a *safer* place. We had similar tastes in music and literature and—" She stopped and shook her head. "But I didn't love him."

Her confession sounded like music to Fisher's ears. Which annoyed him further. He shouldn't care one way or another because all he could ever offer her was a brief physical fling and the things she was talking about were far broader and deeper than that.

He *shouldn't* care. And yet…he did.

Why?

If he'd been anyone else, anyone besides Nash Wakefield's son, he might've thought he'd fallen in love. But because he *was* Nash Wakefield's son, because he'd seen firsthand what obsession and jealousy looked like, he knew the score.

He couldn't have Eliza, but he didn't want anyone else to have her either.

How sick and twisted is that?

An anguished little moan slipped out of her, and he couldn't stand not being able to see her face. Even though Eliza wasn't terribly emotive—a trick she'd either learned from her stoney-faced father or from all those hoity-toity boarding schools she'd attended—he could still tell what her carefully chosen words were hiding when he could read what was in her eyes.

Her dark, sparkling eyes always gave her away.

Thumbing on the lamp, he blinked when the golden glow washed around the room. It was briefly overtaken by another flash of lightning. The accompanying *crack* had Eliza squeaking like a mouse with a stomped-on tail.

When he looked at her, it wasn't pain or guilt or grief he saw on her face. It was horror. *Fear.*

And *that* he understood. All too well.

He had loved thunderstorms as a kid. Loved the awe he felt when Mother Nature unleashed her power. Loved the patter of raindrops on a tin roof. Loved the way the air smelled clean and fresh once the storm moved on.

But now? He dreaded them. Dreaded the sound and fury. Dreaded the dazzling brightness of an arcing lightning bolt and the heart-wrenching *crack* and *boom* of thunder.

It was especially hard at night.

When he was sleeping, it was impossible to tell the difference between a thunderclap and the sonic snap of a bullet as it left a barrel. When he was unconscious, he couldn't differentiate between the sudden flash of lightning and radiating flames of an exploding bomb.

Too many nights he'd sprung awake, covered in sweat, and gripping the pistol he kept under his pillow. Too many nights he was faced with the terrible truth that, like every other fighting man he knew, he hadn't escaped this career without psychological scars.

Now Eliza is scarred too.

He hated that for her.

"It's okay," he said reassuringly, but his smile was close-lipped and grim. "After what you've seen and heard tonight, loud noises are bound to be triggerin'."

She licked her lips and he tried—and failed—not to focus on the tempting pink tip of her tongue. "You've seen and heard worse. And *you* aren't jumping out of your skin."

"Only 'cause I've had more practice at keepin' calm and carryin' on. Thunderstorms are hell. Fireworks are worse."

"PTSD." She grimaced.

"In our line of work, it's inevitable." He shrugged one shoulder. But he didn't feel half as indifferent as he acted.

"Great." Her voice flattened right along with her mouth. "Guess that means I need to find a good psychiatrist. My last one lives in New York, and I stopped seeing her when I moved here."

He twisted his lips and broke the unwelcome news. "Problem with our current situation is we can't exactly talk about anything we do, even to a professional."

"True." She stared off into the distance as if she was considering her options—or lack thereof. Then she drew back and looked at him. "You've thought about this, haven't you?"

"'Course I have. I'm not an idiot. I reckon I'll spend years on a shrink's couch once I retire." He used the subject matter to return them to something she'd said earlier about therapy. "Why do ya have abandonment issues?"

She blinked rapidly, momentarily discombobulated by the change in topic. But she recovered quickly enough. "According to my old therapist, it's because my mom died suddenly and then my dad shipped me off to boarding school before I had time to mourn. I needed to cry on his shoulder, but he couldn't be bothered." The lamplight showed her lips thin. "It's like you said, the one person I needed the most was the one person who taught me I didn't really need anyone."

Fisher had never been a huge fan of Leonard Meadows. But hearing her talk of needing her father only to be rejected by the man made him want to find the chief of staff and knock some sense into the old fart's head.

With a baseball bat.

Before he could respond, however, she took a page from his book and switched subjects. "Aren't you curious *why* I couldn't fall in love with Charlie?"

He had to take a moment to think about his answer. Eventually, he shrugged. "Just reckoned you were smart." When her chin jerked back, he quoted A.E. Housman. "When I was one-and-twenty, I heard a wise man say, 'Give crowns and pounds and guineas, but not your heart away.'"

She studied him in the golden lamplight. Again, he wasn't sure what she was looking for. But just as he opened his mouth to ask, she said, "So what? You think falling in love is foolish?"

"Not foolish. But it can be dangerous for some people."

People like me.

Although, in the still of the night, the dark, private part of himself admitted the truth. That he'd give anything to fall in love. To feel *safe* to fall in love.

He'd recently seen a social media post where someone said they didn't want to be crazy in love. They wanted to be calm in love, understood in love, happy and patient in love. And he'd thought to himself…*because that's real love. Not the desperate, frantic, addictive feeling that is infatuation and obsession, but the comforting, secure,* healthy *feeling that is true love.*

"That's the second time you've used that word. *Dangerous.* Why?" She dragged his mind back to the conversation. "Because there's a chance you'll get your heart broken?" He started to tell her some folks just weren't built for the emotion. Leastways not the healthy kind. But she plowed ahead. "But there's also a chance you *won't.* And when it's right, it's so, *so* right. I mean, just look at the men who lived here before you, who still work here now. Have you ever seen anything more beautiful than the love they have for their partners?"

It seemed she was full of rhetorical questions because, again, she jumped ahead before letting him answer. "I didn't know what true love looked like, what true *partnership* looked like, until I came to work here. And now that I know, I won't settle for less."

He opened his mouth, but she wasn't finished. "That's why I didn't say yes to Charlie's proposal. Because he never looked at me the way Boss looks at Becky. Because he never dragged me into a dark corner to kiss me cross-eyed like Ozzie is always doing with Samantha. Because I had no desire to text him two hundred memes and TikToks and funny anecdotes a day the way Michelle does with Snake because she wants to be connected to him even when she's not near him."

Whether she knew it or not, she was putting into words all his thoughts.

The original Black Knights were the reason he knew *crazy in love* wasn't the golden ticket, that *calm in love, patient in love, and understood in love* was where it was truly at. And he wished…*oh* how he wished he was capable of those things.

The ache in the cold, hard pebble that was his heart was so intense his voice came out hoarse. "So why are ya wearin' his ring?"

She looked down at the massive diamond that caught the glow of the lamp and refracted sparks of fiery light around the room. "Because he slipped it on my finger before I had a chance to answer. And the next second the gunman stepped onto the patio."

He watched breathlessly as she pulled the giant stone off her finger and leaned over to gently place it inside the top drawer of her nightstand.

When she laid back against her pillow, staring at the ceiling and the strange shadows that danced across it thanks to the rain running in rivulets down the windowpane, her expression reflected the self-flagellation of her thoughts. "Would he have sacrificed himself for me if he'd known what my answer would be?"

Her lower lip trembled and tears once more gathered in her eyes. He wasn't sure it was wise. Hell, he was pretty positive *none* of his decisions this night had been wise. But he pulled her back into his arms.

She came willingly. Eagerly, even. And that pleased him in ways he didn't dare examine.

"I feel so guilty, Fish." Her breath was hot against his neck. When her tears fell on his skin, they were hotter still. "I feel like I deceived him or—"

"Ya did no such thing." He was quick to cut her off. "McClean sacrificing himself had nothin' to do with what he thought ya felt for him and everything to do with how he felt about you."

For the span of half a dozen heartbeats, she was quiet. Then, she admitted hoarsely, "Honestly, I don't know if that makes it better or worse."

"It makes it so all you should ever feel is grateful." He brushed a hand over the back of her head, marveling at the silky softness of her hair. It had mostly dried and was only damp near her scalp. "I feel so grateful to him." And then, before he could stop them, words he had no intention of ever uttering popped right out of his mouth. "I can't imagine a world without you in it. I can't imagine *my* world without you in it."

He felt her stiffen in his embrace. Heard her breath hitch.

He'd said too much. *Revealed* too much.

She scooted back so her nose was no longer pressed against his neck. Her dark eyes narrowed as she rubbed a shaky hand over the wetness on her cheeks.

Even with the swelling and the bruise, she was beautiful. *More* beautiful because, without the mask of cat-eye mascara and her usual fire-engine-red lipstick, he could see *her*. The *real* her. The young, sad, *hurting* her.

He wasn't sure what he expected her response to be to his ill-timed admission, but it certainly wasn't her asking, "Will you kiss me, Fish?"

The request blew through him with the force of an H-bomb. His lungs collapsed. His head exploded. And he wouldn't have been surprised to feel his heart stop beating.

Before he had time to respond, she continued, "Will you make me forget all this death and remind me what it means to be alive?"

She wants you! The posh, sophisticated Eliza Meadows wants you, *a lowly Louisiana boy who barely has a pot to piss in. Quick! Kiss her before she changes her mind!*

Had he mentioned that along with the better angels of his nature he sometimes dealt with the worser devils who also inhabited his psyche? They'd been bigger influences in his life when he'd been younger. Age and wisdom had taught him to ignore them. *Mostly.*

He should ignore them now.

Lordy, he didn't want to. He'd been waiting four long years for her to ask him that exact question.

Luckily, his better angels chose that moment to pipe up. *Isn't this a curious about-face? She's always assured you she'd rather eat mud than take you up on your myriad offers to get her naked. So what's changed?*

He knew the answer, of course. It was as plain to see as the nose on his face.

She'd been witness to a massacre. She'd lost a man she liked and respected, even if she hadn't loved him. She was suffering under a mountain of survivor's guilt. And this was her reaction to all of that.

Which meant…if he did as she asked, she'd probably regret things in the morning.

So what if she does? That's on her. She's a grown-ass woman free to make her own decisions.

Okay, so that was a good point.

Don't do it. She's raw, exposed. You'll be takin' advantage of her vulnerability. And that's a line that can't be uncrossed.

Damnit, that was a good point too.

"Eliza, I…" His voice trailed off as he struggled to find the right words. He was torn between what he wanted—what he'd *been* wanting since the moment he clapped eyes on her—and what he believed was right.

In the end, there was a clear winner in the war the angels and devils waged within him, and he found himself squaring his shoulders and blowing out an unsteady breath.

She wouldn't welcome what he had to say, but it was better to deny her in her hour of need than be the sonofabitch who took advantage of the situation.

"I've wanted to kiss ya since the first moment I saw ya, doll f—I mean *darlin'.*" He chose his words carefully. "But now that you've opened the door on the possibility, I just can't make myself step through. It wouldn't be right."

She blinked as if she couldn't believe her ears. He couldn't blame her. He was having trouble believing he'd actually said the words.

Damn you, better angels! He shook an imaginary fist in the air.

"Why not?" Her voice was soft and full of confusion.

"'Cause I don't know if you'll regret it in the mornin'. And all the reasons you've had for keepin' me at arm's length for the last four years are still there. Ya said it yourself. Ya want what the others here have. True love. True partnership. And when it comes to those things, I'm not the one, so…."

He let the sentence dangle, punctuating its end with a shrug of his shoulder.

Something flickered in her eyes. Something that had him narrowing his. But it was there and gone in a flash.

"I'm not looking for love, Fish," she assured him with a sad-sounding chuckle. "At least not tonight. Tonight I just want to forget. Won't you do a gal a solid and help her forget?"

Her request hung in the air, a palpable force that tugged at something deep inside him. It was something that whispered in his ear, telling him he might be different. Something that promised him there might be hope for him yet. Something that…*lied*.

A muscle ticked in his jaw, a physical representation of the conflict inside him. "What happened to ya sayin' ya didn't want to be just another notch on my bedpost?"

"I'm not asking you to *sleep* with me." Her tone was matter-of-fact. So reasonable. So rational sounding. "Just kiss me, Fish."

Could it be that simple?

Could he kiss her and offer her a little comfort? A little distraction? A little *reprieve* from all the horror she'd witnessed without it being any more than that? Without it *meaning* any more than that?

At the hospital he'd thought there was nothing he could do to help her. But he could do this. Couldn't he?

What's a little kiss between friends? the devils whispered. And the angels? Oh, the angels had gone suspiciously quiet.

Without their grounding influence, there was nothing to stop him from cupping her face. Nothing to stop him from gently brushing a thumb over the bruise on her check.

Ya can't give her the great Black Knights Inc. love affair she wants. But you can give her this.

"Ya sure?" he asked through a throat that was raw with emotion.

She nodded slowly and the pleading in her eyes broke through the last of his resolve.

"If we do this, it's just this," he warned. "I don't do hearts and flowers. And I definitely don't do love."

"I told you, I'm not asking for any of that." Her warm breath whispered across his eager lips. It smelled of hot chocolate, dark and sweet.

"Promise me ya won't regret this in the mornin'."

"If I regret it, I'll have no one to blame but myself."

That did it, just decimated the last of his restraint because she'd absolved him of all responsibility, of any future guilt. He leaned down, intent on brushing his lips against hers. But before he could, her cell phone jangled to life.

CHAPTER 10

Eliza could feel the flames of frustration burning bright in her cheeks when Fisher pulled back and said, "Ya need to get that?"

"No?"

One corner of his decadent mouth—a mouth she'd been *millimeters* away from kissing—

quirked. "Was that a statement or a question?"

"Damnit!" She reluctantly pulled out of his arms, threw off the duvet cover, and sat on the edge of the bed. She'd slipped her phone into the drawer of her nightstand after her father's call. And she seriously considered smashing the device to bits instead of answering it when she pulled it out.

Of course, the instant she saw the name on the screen, all her ire was replaced by curiosity. And a hint of alarm.

Fisher, who was looking over her shoulder, made a sound of disbelief. "You have Senator Chastain's number?"

"Mmm," she hummed distractedly. *Why in the world would she be calling me?* "She gave it to me at the inaugural ball. She said since she represented my district here in Chicago that I should feel free to call her with any policy concerns." She glanced over her shoulder to find one eyebrow arched high on his tanned forehead.

"Yeah." She made a face. "I know. Nepotism. But blame the game not the player."

He sucked on his teeth but didn't press the issue further. Instead, he asked, "What do ya think she wants?"

She shook her head as she stared down at her screen. "I have no idea."

"Only one way to find out then." He hitched his chin toward the phone and she hastily thumbed on the device before it could send the call to voicemail.

"Senator Chastain?" She hoped her tone sounded cool and professional and *not* like she'd been seconds away from finally, *finally* kissing Fisher Wakefield. Seconds away from having his perfect lips moving over hers. Seconds away from tasting the sweetness of his breath on her tongue.

And sure, asking him to kiss her had probably been a foolhardy request. Kissing him would only make her want to do *more* than kiss him. And doing *more* than kissing him would ultimately end in him leaving her like he left every other woman who warmed his bed. Which would absolutely demolish her already bruised and battered heart.

But she figured that was a problem for Future Eliza to deal with. Current Eliza just wanted to feel something other than guilt and horror and sorrow. Current Eliza was determined to experience one small intimacy with him so she could take it out and relive it on all those cold, lonely nights that stretched out as far as her eye could see. Current Eliza… didn't give a damn about the regrets or recriminations come the light of day, because if this night had taught her anything, it was that she wasn't assured a tomorrow.

"Have you spoken with the FBI?" Bethany Chastain's voice rang with the same authoritative tone she used when she badgered witnesses at senate inquests.

Eliza was instantly on guard. And now that she wasn't distracted by Fisher, her face reminded her that it had its own heartbeat, and her head reminded her that it was concussed. "Yes. Why?" She rubbed two fingers against the ache centered behind her browbone.

"What did you tell them?"

"The…the truth," she answered hesitantly, wincing and gingerly touching the knot near her temple when it suddenly felt like someone had shoved a knife through the side of her skull. The swelling seemed to be going down some. Or maybe that was just wishful thinking. "What else would I tell them?"

There was a brief pause from the other end of the call. Then, "And what *is* the truth, Eliza?"

"I'm sorry." She glanced over her shoulder to find Fisher frowning fiercely. His expression said he could hear everything the senator was saying, and the look in his eyes asked *what the fuck?* All she could do was shrug, because…*what the fuck, indeed.* "I don't know what you mean, Senator," she said into the phone.

"Why did John invite you tonight?"

She was beginning to feel a bit like an interrogee. "I don't think Senator McClean *did* invite me. I think he invited his son and I happened to be Charlie's plus-one."

Again, a pause. And then, "How odd."

The sounds of distant voices and an announcement over an intercom system echoed through the phone. Eliza recognized the cacophony of a hospital. "Senator, are you okay? How's Professor Chastain?"

"Out of surgery but still hasn't regained consciousness." It was the first time in the conversation the woman's iron-lady mask slipped. A tremor entered her voice. Eliza could hear her sniffle before the sound of rustling tissue paper rasped over the connection.

"I'm so sorry for everything you're going through, Senator," she said sincerely. "I can't imagine how—"

"I don't have time for your sympathies." Bethany Chastain cut her off, and Eliza lifted an eyebrow. She should be used to arrogant, high-handed politicians by now. After all, she'd been raised by one. But sometimes their pompous attitudes still caught her off guard. "I called to tell you to be careful of who you trust. Careful of who you talk to."

Eliza was growing more alarmed by the minute. "I don't know what you mean, Senator."

"It's good you don't. Stay not knowing."

"Senator—"

"I have to go. I just came down to get a coffee that doesn't come from a vending machine, and to take the opportunity to call you. But I see now I needn't have bothered about that second thing. So I'll get upstairs to be with Bill. Take care."

"Senator, I—" Before Eliza could say more than that, the line went dead.

Was it *all* politicians who cut off calls without so much as a goodbye? Or was it only politicians of a certain age who felt their advanced years gave them the freedom to be rude?

She'd have to ask her father the next time she spoke with him.

"What was that about?" Fisher asked.

She blinked and shook her head. "I have absolutely no idea."

A muscle twitched in Fisher's cheek. "Should you call the feds or..." He grimaced like his next suggestion rubbed him the wrong way. "Or your dad?"

Fisher was like the rest of the Knights. They admired and respected her father for the work he did. But they didn't really *like* him.

In point of fact, Eliza wasn't sure *anyone* actually *liked* her father. He was too hard, too cold, too...*ruthless* when it came to trying to push through policy.

Except for maybe President Stevens.

Yes, Sandra J. Stevens seemed to get along with the mighty Leonard Meadows just fine. Which was a good thing since the chief of staff was the second most powerful person in Washington and it *behooved* him to be well-liked by the first most powerful person.

Lots of folks thought it was the VP or even the majority leader of the senate who ran the race with the commander in chief. But nope. It was the chief of staff.

"Eliza?" Fisher pulled her away from her thoughts. "Do ya need to inform someone of the senator's call?"

Maybe? But she was so tired. And her head was back to throbbing dully. And no doubt everything, all these problems and questions, would be waiting for her in the morning.

"Does it make me a terrible person to want a few hours where I *don't* have to think about what happened tonight? To want a few hours to forget?"

"Yup," he answered unhesitatingly. "You're definitely a terrible person."

She blinked and then realized he was teasing her.

"You're an ass." She smiled and shook her head.

"Oh, for sure." He was quick to agree. "But I made ya smile. And tonight that's my one true ambition."

"Your one true ambition, huh?" She side-eyed him. "You, sir, need loftier goals."

"No I don't."

She chuckled and he shot a fist in the air. "And now I've gone and made ya laugh! I just keep on winnin'!"

"But *I* want to be the winner," she said with an exaggerated wiggle of her eyebrows. "Weren't we doing something important before we were interrupted?"

"Were we?" He feigned ignorance. "I can't remember."

She grabbed her chest as if he'd stabbed her in the heart. "Ouch. Way to wound a woman's pride."

His hair was longing for a cut and curled invitingly around his ears. When he grinned that Fisher grin of his, the one that was all charm and teeth, she couldn't help grinning back.

Of course, in the next moment, she remembered the sound of gunfire, remembered the state of Charlie's body, and her expression crumbled.

"Ah, hell." He pulled her close and she burrowed into his chest, taking comfort in the warm, delicious smell of his fabric softener, in the reassuring feel of his heart setting a strong, steady beat against her cheek.

"It'll be like this for a while," he whispered as he smoothed a hand over her hair.

"What will?"

"The grief. It'll come in waves. Tsunamis to start. And then breakers. And finally, after a while, they'll just be little swells. And all ya can do is ride 'em out. Each and every one of 'em until eventually ya won't even notice that they rock your boat."

CHAPTER 11

Having stolen a white lab coat and a paper surgical mask, Yang slipped through the security doors of the ICU behind a nurse who was too busy balancing a tray of bandages and salves to pay attention to the man hot on her heels.

After speed-walking past the nurse's station—the coat and the mask meant those there barely spared him a glance—he made his way down the long hall in search of the unfortunate professor. He'd learned if he acted like he belonged somewhere, people naturally assumed he did.

What is it the Americans like to say? If it walks like a duck and quacks like a duck, it must be a duck? Or, in my case, a doctor.

The first room showed an old woman with tubes sticking out of every visible orifice. Her chest rose and fell in a mechanical way that told him she was on full life support.

The next room held a young man of indeterminant ethnicity. His dark skin and black hair said his ancestors came from somewhere with a warmer climate. But because his face was fully bandaged, Yang had no idea about the shape of his features.

Gunshot wound? he wondered. *Some horrible facial deformity?*

The third room was empty. But there were sheets on the bed and the various detritus of a long hospital stay: cards pinned to the wall, flowers sitting in the windowsill, a handmade quilt that someone had obviously brought from home. Either the patient was out having tests run or, more likely, since this was the intensive care unit, they'd died and the family had yet to come collect their things.

The fourth room was another no-go. So was the fifth. As Yang approached the middle of the hall, he avoided looking directly at the security camera mounted in the far corner. There was no way to avoid being caught on camera in the modern age—especially in a high-tech hospital. But it was possible to keep oneself from being *recognized* by knowing how to hide identifying features.

Hence the mask. Plus, his hair was dyed a dull carroty red. And he'd donned prosthetics on his ears, nose, and brow ridge. It was probably a bit of overkill, but…

Better safe than sorry.

It was any good operative's motto and Yang wasn't just a good operative. He was a great one. That he'd survived twenty years in the business was a testament to that fact.

As he continued down the long hall, the glass doorways showed him people in various stages of illness, injury, and dying. Dozens of machines *shushed* and *beeped.* The smell of antiseptic was strong. And every once in a while, one of the patients grunted or moaned. But for the most part, there was silence.

Individuals who found themselves in the ICU were usually either sedated or had naturally entered a state of semi-consciousness. And it was strange to think that the most serious floor of the hospital was also the most peaceful one.

Ah. There you are.

The room was empty save for the patient. And even though he'd known the senator would be absent—he had waited to make his move until he had seen her crossing the lobby downstairs—there had always been the chance that a doctor or nurse would be in the room.

He would have continued on his way if there had been. But as luck would have it, the coast was clear.

All the same, he had to work quickly. Senator Chastain had been on the phone when he had seen her. But she had not looked like she was setting in to talk for long.

Reaching into his pocket, he pulled out the tiny spray canister of cyanide and ducked into the professor's room.

Introducing cyanide into the respiratory system resulted in death in under three minutes. The symptoms mimicked those of a heart attack. Which meant unless someone went looking for the poison, it was unlikely it'd ever be discovered.

Considering the professor was a man of a certain age who'd suffered a major head injury followed by cranial surgery, Yang figured no one would go looking.

At least not initially.

Whether people knew it or not, they tended to fall back on Occam's razor, the simplest answer being the correct one. He had used that human inclination to his advantage in the field for nearly two decades.

How many of his kills had been attributed to bad luck or natural causes? Twenty? Thirty? Truth was, he'd lost count. Enough to make this feel like little more than a walk in the park.

He could've simply slit the professor's throat, he supposed. Easy as pie and a piece of cake, as the Americans liked to say. But that route would put the FBI on high alert. And the last thing he needed was for them to whisk Senator Chastain away to a safe house.

Not that he could not get to her while she was under federal protection. He had done it before. He could most definitely do it again. But if they put her under lock and key, it would certainly make things more challenging.

If his long career had taught him anything, it was that life was far more enjoyable if he found ways to make less work for himself.

He made a cursory study of his mark. The professor was nearly unrecognizable with his head swathed in bandages and his face swollen like an over-ripe melon. But the name on the door and the mole on the man's cheek just below his left eye assured Yang he had the correct victim.

"Through the triumph of your death, may you benefit all other beings, living or dead," he whispered as he gently removed the oxygen mask from the man's face.

He had left behind the teachings of Buddha, his mother's religion, not long after government soldiers had come to his village to take him away for training. But whenever he killed, the prayer for the dead still naturally fell from his lips.

Careful not to breathe in any of the poison droplets, he sprayed the mist into the mask before quickly fixing it back over the professor's face. Then he pocketed the empty canister and turned for the door.

He need not wait to see if the cyanide worked. It would. He'd used it many times before.

The return trip past the nurse's station was as uneventful as his initial journey had been. The four blue-scrubbed individuals checking charts and keying in information didn't even look up from their activities.

He was through the security door and standing in the outer hall waiting for the elevator when an alarm sounded in the ICU. The blaring *meep, meep, meep* told him Professor Chastain's blood pressure, heart rate, and respiration had all fallen below safe levels.

You work fast, my friend. He patted the canister in his pocket and then tried not to react when the elevator doors opened and he was presented with Senator Chastain's haggard expression.

For a moment, he considered pulling the small knife from his pocket and shoving it into her jugular. But just like the professor, that route would be too obvious. If he could, he wanted to avoid being obvious until Bishop had decided how he wanted to handle Eliza Meadows.

Nodding, he stepped back to let the elderly woman exit the elevator. Then he watched what blood remained in her pale face drain away when she heard the commotion coming from beyond the doors to the intensive care unit.

"Bill!" she gasped, darting past him to run down the hall, her kitten heels *click-clacking* on the cold tiles.

Stepping into the elevator, he covertly peeked at the camera in the corner. He knew the fish-eyed lens would see a short man with orange hair and a prominent brow ridge. His nose prosthesis made a large bulge in the mask over his face. But it would be a completely *different*-looking man who exited the hospital. And by the time the big, silver box hit the ground floor, his next moves were planned out precisely.

Stay in the security camera blind spot. Check. He'd already determined one of the cameras by the front desk was malfunctioning.

Dispose of lab coat and nose. Check, check. He dropped the stolen coat, mask, and fake nose into a steel trash can on his way toward the automatic doors.

Put on baseball cap. Triple check.

He was on the wet street and heading toward the lake when he pulled his disposable cell phone from his pocket. As he waited for Bishop to answer, he ducked from awning to awning to avoid the worst of the rain. But truly, it was of little use. The deluge was such that all it took was a couple seconds of exposure and he was soaked.

The hairs on the back of his neck lifted a heartbeat before a bolt of lightning zigzagged across the sky and connected to the rod atop the tall, trapezoidal building known as the John Hancock. A split second later, thunder clapped so loudly his ears popped.

Electricity was such an awe-inspiring force. It had the ability to kill in an instant. And yet, it was also used to sustain life. Think defibrillators and pacemakers.

Wait a minute. That gives me an idea.

"Well?" Bishop was never one for niceties. Yang could appreciate a man who got right down to business.

"One down," he reported into the phone. "One to go."

"You know how you'll do it?"

"I know how it *should* be done. But I will need a computer hacker. Do you have someone I can use?"

For awhile there was silence on the other end of the call. Then, "You killed my hacker six months ago."

Yang thought back to their last job together, taking down the power grid in Texas. Not only had they failed to reach their objective—thanks to Black Knights Inc. and a nosy dark web surfer who worked for the Department of Defense. But also Yang had been forced to get rid of the hacker he and Bishop had hired for the job.

Yang had finished off poor Vincent Romano in a similar fashion to how he had just finished off the good professor. After sneaking into Romano's hospital room, he had injected potassium chloride into the man's IV.

"Not to worry," he assured Bishop now. "I will make contact with my handler. He will find someone for the job."

After all, half the population of my country are hackers.

"Very good." Bishop sounded relieved.

Before Bishop could cut the call, Yang informed him, "I overhead Senator Chastain talking on the phone to Eliza Meadows."

There was a brief pause followed by a full-throated, "*Fuck!*" Then, "Did you hear what she had to say? Was it about John McClean's suspicions?"

"I could not wait around to listen in. I had to use the opportunity to visit the professor's room. But I thought you should know."

"Fuck, fuck, *fuck*." Bishop rarely lost his composure. But when he did, the F-word was his favorite expletive. "I guess that forces our hand then. We have to assume anyone who was at McClean's party might be privy to his information."

"But surely Eliza would have told your source who is following the case if that were true. And surely your source would have informed the president. Has she received any phone calls? Read any emails? Been pulled aside by the Secret Service?"

"No. She went to bed with a headache an hour ago."

"So it is safe to say that if Senator Chastain *was* privy to John McClean's suspicions and then passed those suspicions on to Eliza, that Eliza has yet to share that information with anyone else."

"Why would she hold off?"

Bishop used his favorite curse word. "Fuck if I know. But I'll feel better once she's dead. Just like the others. Just in case. And in the meantime I have work to do moving money from our patsy's account into the offshore account set up in Mrs. Sullivan's name." A growl of annoyance sounded over the connection. "Jesus, this night has been a pain in my balls."

Yang agreed. Not about the night being a pain in his balls—it was actually more like par for the course for him. But about needing Eliza Meadows to stop drawing breath. The original plan had been to get rid of everyone at the party. And he was a big believer in sticking with the plan. "Thoughts on how you would like me to end her?"

Bishop hissed impatiently, "Not yet. Take care of the senator. And in the meantime I'll work on a way to take out Eliza."

CHAPTER 12

Sullivan Residence, 5652 North Glenwood Ave.

"Pete was taking a lot of medication. M-Maybe that's why he did it. Maybe some of it messed with his h-head or something."

Debra Sullivan sat on the edge of the sofa. She wore a well-loved terry-cloth robe that had bleach spots on the sleeves. Her brown hair was secured in big, foam rollers. Her eyes were puffy from crying. And when she spoke, she did so haltingly, as if she had trouble talking around the lump lodged firmly in the center of her throat.

Julia and her partner had tried for ten minutes to convince the woman her husband had murdered his boss and the majority of the guests at the cocktail party. But Debra had refused to believe them. She'd kept shaking her head and insisting, *"Pete is a pacifist. He voted for Bernie Sanders. He believes in commonsense gun laws. He would never."*

They'd finally resorted to turning on the television and tuning it to a local news source that was reporting on the situation. Then they'd showed her the Facebook post that had gone live on her husband's profile an hour earlier. It wasn't some long, self-aggrandizing manifesto à la Patrick Wood Crusius. It'd simply been a heartfelt apology to his wife.

Dear Deb, it had read. *I know you'll never understand what's happened. And I know you'll never forgive me. But please believe me when I say this was the only way for me to make sure you're all taken care of. And we both know all I did was hasten the inevitable. I'm sorry I couldn't stay with you longer. I'm sorry I won't see the wonderful men you'll raise our boys to be. I'm so, so sorry and I'll love you for eternity. ~Pete*

At that point, Debra had broken down into chest-heaving, face-mottling sobs that had made further questioning impossible. Julia had left Dillan in the living room with the devastated woman while she'd made her way to the kitchen to get the poor thing a glass of cold water.

She'd taken her time on the journey.

One, she prided herself on being cool, calm, and collected on the job. But her tender heart—the one that made her a two-time foster dog failure and a sucker for every cookie-selling Girl Scout in the neighborhood— couldn't stand seeing anyone cry. She invariably ended up crying herself. And two, she wanted to study the family photos hanging on the wall in the hallway leading to the kitchen.

She'd only seen Peter Sullivan post-mortem. And death was the great eraser on the chalkboard of life. Whatever mien or demeanor Peter had maintained while breathing had been obliterated the moment the Grim Reaper touched him with his scythe.

The photographs, however, gave her a better idea of who the perp was. A man who had doted on his wife and two small boys. A man who wasn't afraid to be silly and wear matching pajamas for Halloween and Christmas. A man with a genuine smile and a lightness in his eyes that made it truly difficult to imagine him committing the night's dark deeds.

And yet, he did…

"Why was he taking so much medication, Mrs. Sullivan?" Julia asked Debra now, briefly glancing at her phone to make sure it was still recording the conversation.

"He had cancer." Debra Sullivan's hand shook as she reached for the glass Julia had placed atop the coaster on the steel and glass coffee table.

The Sullivans had juxtaposed the ornate architecture of their home with minimalistic furnishings and decorations. It looked very classy and chic. But Julia had always thought old Victorian homes should be whimsical, stuffed with tchotchkes and clutches of drying herbs and overstuffed, well-worn furniture.

"What sort of cancer?" she asked.

"P-pancreatic," Debra answered haltingly as if saying the word aloud left a foul taste in her mouth.

"That's a death sentence, right?" This from Dillan. "Which explains the line in his post where he said he hastened the end."

Every time he opened his mouth, Julia wanted to scream. He was about as subtle as a sledgehammer. And Debra Sullivan was on the verge of breaking down again.

The last thing they needed was another fifteen minutes of time wasted while they waited for the poor woman to regain enough composure to finish answering their questions. With each ticking of the second hand on the clock, the pressure to come up with a lead or a motivation or some iota of an explanation weighed heavier on Julia's shoulders.

She needed to do well on this first case. She *had* to do well. And not just to prove her metal to her supervisors and anyone who'd ever doubted that a pipsqueak of a Southsider could rise through the ranks of the FBI. But to drag into the light exactly what had happened at the senator's house—and *why* it'd happened—before some bored, basement dweller who spent way too much time on the internet started circulating conspiracy theories.

The World Wide Web was a wonder in that it allowed everyone equal access to any information they might seek. But it'd also proved just how gullible and idiotic humans truly were because most people chose to seek the most titillating, scandalous, and far-fetched information out there.

It was Julia's responsibility to focus the narrative before the flat-earthers and Holocaust-deniers got their Cheeto-dusted fingers on it. But to do that, she had to have actionable facts. Hard evidence. *Believable* motivation.

There was nothing worse than going to the press with bad intel and then having to recant that message later. It would make her look incompetent. Make her bosses look ineffectual. Make the *bureau* look bush league. And that was the quickest way to get knocked down to the mailroom.

Huge tears slipped down Debra's cheeks and landed on the lapel of her robe. But she managed to keep from dissolving completely.

Julia and Dillan were seated in the two armchairs facing the sofa. The tissue box was on the little occasional table between them, and Julia hastily pulled out two tissues and passed them across to the woman all while shooting Dillan a look that said, *Could you* be *any more of a dick?*

His expression of *What did I do?* was emphasized by the shrug he gave her.

Sigh.

Julia's father liked to say everyone had their cross to bear. Julia's cross was 6'3" and went by the name of Dillan Douglas.

"We told his oncologist we didn't want to hear about the odds. Pete didn't believe in them anyway. But…" Debra bit her lip and looked out the bay window. The glass was split into panes by mullions. And the raindrops drifted and collided into one another, leaving wide, watery trails in their wake. "But he'd been losing weight lately. And when he wasn't at work, he was sleeping a lot," she finished hoarsely.

So Peter had been nearing his end, Julia silently mused before continuing to ask the pertinent questions.

Had Mr. Sullivan ever had any problems with his boss, Senator McClean? Had Mr. Sullivan mentioned anything about buying the weapon he'd used in the massacre? Had Mr. Sullivan seemed out of sorts before leaving for the McClean residence that morning?

Debra's answers to all were no.

Which left Julie wondering, *Is she right? Is there nothing more to this case than a dying man on heaps of medication losing his shit?*

It was a possibility. But it felt too pat.

Four members of Congress were dead. If Senator Chastain hadn't survived, it would've been five. And anytime government officials were involved, she had to suspect political motivation.

"I know Pete was worried about what we'd do for money if he ever—" Debra swallowed. "If he ever succumbed to the cancer. He didn't have life insurance. And after he was diagnosed, no one would insure him."

"Is it possible Senator McClean had written your husband into his will? I mean, Peter's post to you mentioned it was the only way for him to make sure you and your boys were taken care of. Is there money coming your way?"

Debra blinked myopically. Her head shake was resolute. "No way. Pete and the senator weren't that close. I mean…Pete *respected* the senator. He always said John McClean was a statesman and not a politician, an old-school guy who took the job because he actually wanted to make this country better as opposed to taking the job for its power and prestige. But

Pete didn't exactly *like* the senator. He said the man was hard-assed and uncompromising. So it's not like they were sharing brandies after dinner or smoking cigars together."

"Then what do you suppose your husband meant by it was the only way to make sure you and your boys were taken care of?"

"I have no idea." Debra covered her face with her hands as her shoulders shook with fresh sobs. "Oh, Pete."

Julia knew a dead end when she saw one. Debra Sullivan had no clue why her husband had done what he'd done. She'd had no indication that he was planning anything. She had nothing further to offer the investigation.

At least not right now.

"Thank you for your time, Mrs. Sullivan." Julia slid her business card across the coffee table. "If you can think of anything else, please don't hesitate to reach out. And I'm so sorry for your loss."

Debra blinked at her uncomprehendingly and Julia understood. The woman still hadn't accepted the reality of her husband's death. And if she *could* accept that reality, it meant he'd perpetrated an act of such evil that she couldn't believe anyone would offer her condolences.

Julia had seen it a dozen times on the faces of the family and friends of offenders. Her soft, squishy heart made her add, "You're going to be put through hell in the coming weeks and months. I hate that for you and your boys. But remember, there's no such thing as guilt by association. At least not in circumstances like this. *You* haven't done anything wrong."

Debra's chin trembled. But before Julia could pull out two more preemptive tissues, her phone blared to life.

Because the noise at a crime scene was usually at stadium concert levels, she'd turned the volume on the device up as high as it would go. She'd since forgotten to turn it down and the double *brrrring-brrrring* was loud enough to wake the dead.

It was certainly loud enough to wake the two Sullivan boys who'd managed to remain asleep and tucked up safe in their beds while their mother had been given the awful news of what their father had done.

"Sorry. God, I'm *so* sorry." Julia immediately thumbed on the device, and then winced when she heard little feet hitting the floor above her. Not three seconds later, one of the Sullivan boys called from the top of the stairs. "Momma? Who's here?"

Sorry Julia mouthed again.

Debra didn't respond. She simply rubbed the wetness from her eyes with the cuff of her sleeve, stood from the sofa, and headed for the staircase.

"Nice work," Dillan whispered from the side of his mouth.

"Me?" she hissed and shot him a poisonous glance. "You have the bedside manner of an executioner."

He gave her another indifferent shrug—it seemed to be his standard reaction to most things she said. And she rolled her eyes before saying into the phone, "This is Agent O'Toole. Sorry to keep you waiting."

"Agent O'Toole, this is Nurse Benson at Northwestern Memorial. You told me to call you if there was a change in Mr. Chastain's status."

"Yes?" Julia motioned for Dillan to get up and head toward the door. "How is he? Is he awake?"

"I'm afraid he's dead, Agent O'Toole."

Julia, who was in lockstep behind Dillan, stopped in her tracks. "Excuse me?"

"He coded ten minutes ago and we weren't able to get him back."

"Sonofabitch," she hissed.

Now it was Nurse Benson's turn to say, "Excuse me?"

"Sorry." She was quick to apologize. "That wasn't meant for you. Thank you for your call."

She thumbed off the phone and found Dillan eyeing her expectantly. "Professor Chastain is dead," she informed him. A dull headache was beginning to throb behind her right eye.

Dillan's ridiculously handsome—and annoyingly dimpled—chin jerked back. "How?"

"Don't know." She shoved her phone into the breast pocket of her suitcoat. "Let's go find out."

CHAPTER 13

Black Knights Inc.

The spicy scent of Fisher's aftershave lingered in Eliza's nose as she paced at the end of the bed. Her father's voice boomed through her cell's speaker as he once again attempted to browbeat her into flying to Washington.

"Dad," she interrupted line-item number six on his ongoing list of reasons why she needed to pack up and leave Black Knights Inc. behind until the mystery of the shooting at the cocktail party was solved. "I'm sorry Professor Chastain died." She wasn't surprised her father had heard the news mere minutes after it'd happened. No doubt he'd told his contacts in the bureau to phone him with any and all new information regarding the case. "But that changes nothing. I'm safer here than I would be anywhere."

Fisher tossed off the covers and sat on the edge of the bed. Without sparing her a glance, he began pulling on his biker boots.

First there'd been Senator Chastain's cryptic phone call. Then she'd had another mini-emotional breakdown. And now her father had called.

Three strikes and you're out!

Her opportunity to do something terribly wonderful—or terribly foolish—looked like it was about to walk out the door. A tension that matched the roiling chaos of the storm clouds outside took hold of her.

She needed to get off the call with her father. Now. Before Fisher could leave and the moment was lost. Maybe forever.

"Surely you don't suspect foul play," she said hastily into the phone. "I mean, the man was shot in the head and then spent an hour in surgery having his skull cracked open. At his age, is it any wonder he had a heart attack?"

"I don't discount *any* possibility. And neither should you." She detected notes of concern and weariness beneath her father's usual bombast.

It was the weariness that stopped her pacing and had her forgetting Fisher—or at least deprioritizing him—to give her father her full attention. Leonard Meadows was such a larger-than-life figure that sometimes she forgot he was also seventy-one years old and saddled with one of the most stressful jobs in the world.

"How about we revisit this discussion in the morning, once I've gotten some sleep?" she offered placatingly.

He didn't answer her immediately. Instead, she heard him shuffling paperwork and knew he was still at his desk in the anteroom off the Oval Office.

Glancing at the clock on her bedside table, she noted the time. It was nearly one in the morning in Chicago. Which meant it was almost two AM on the East Coast.

"You should get some sleep too, Dad," she added quietly. "Weren't you the one who always said things are clearer in the light of day?"

"No." He harrumphed. "That was your mother. I always say why put off to tomorrow what can be done today. I *also* always say better safe than sorry." She opened her mouth, sure she would have to argue her case further. But she snapped her jaws shut when she heard him sigh heavily. "But you're right. You need rest."

"So do you, Dad," she told him softly.

"I'll sleep when I'm dead."

"You keep burning the candle at both ends like this, and that's likely to happen sooner rather than later."

Silence greeted her pronouncement. She blinked at her own audacity and instinctively curled her fingers around her locket.

She and her father didn't have the type of relationship where she could *say* things like that. In fact, she wasn't sure they had much of a "relationship" at all.

As a child, she'd always felt like she was simply another task he needed to complete. Head up a campaign? Check. Outline policy for the next candidate he'd decided to put his substantial political clout behind? Check, check. Make sure to pay his daughter's boarding school tuition? Triple check. And once she'd become an adult, their interactions had evolved into something she'd describe as more of a "professional partnership."

"I'm going to assume it's the bump on your head that's making you sassy." His voice was gruff, but she thought she heard a note of affection. At least, she *hoped* so.

She desperately wanted—nay, *needed*—to end the conversation before Fisher took off. But she felt obliged to ask, "Are you well acquainted with Senator Chastain?"

"Bethany?" Her father's tone sharpened. And even though she couldn't see him, she knew his gaze had sharpened as well. "We find ourselves on the same side of most issues and so we work together often enough. Why?"

"She called me a little bit ago to ask me what I told the FBI."

Silence met her announcement. And then, slowly, "Why would she do that?"

"That's the thing. I have no idea."

"Tell me exactly what was said, Eliza. Word-for-word."

Senator Chastain's words drifted through her head. *"I called to tell you to be careful of who you trust. Careful of who you talk to."*

But the senator couldn't have been talking about her father.

She relayed the conversation as best as she could remember and ended with, "I think she thinks tonight's bloodbath was politically motivated. I think she thinks one of her colleagues had had enough of Senator McClean's fire-branding tactics and decided to take him out."

"And attempt to kill everyone else too, just so there'd be no witnesses?"

Eliza shrugged. "Stranger things have happened."

"Mmm," her father hummed noncommittally, and she could tell his wheels were turning. Instead of sharing what he was thinking, he simply said, "I'll wish you a good night, Eliza. Please call me the moment you wake up."

"I will, Dad. I promise."

He grunted his approval and then, as usual, ended the call without saying goodbye.

She felt better having told her father about Chastain's call. If anyone could make heads or tails of it, it was certainly him. In fact, she wouldn't be surprised if he was phoning up the senator at that very moment to demand she tell him what she knew or, leastways, *suspected.*

After carefully setting her phone on her dresser, she gave herself time to make sure she'd removed the heavier notes of disappointment from her voice before turning to Fisher. He stood beside the bed, and one look at his face told her all she needed to know about his intentions.

"I take it this is goodbye?" She managed to hold off her frown of defeat and turn it into a wry twist of her lips.

He shoved his hands deep in the front pockets of his jeans. She didn't notice how the move made the tendons in his forearms pop.

Okay, so maybe she *did* notice. She'd always been a sucker for a good pair of forearms. And Fisher had some of the nicest she'd ever seen.

"Like ya told your pops, everything will look clearer in the morning. How 'bout we revisit *our* conversation then too?"

She rubbed at the unending ache behind her browbone. An ache that she could only partially blame on her concussion. "I'm beginning to think it's my lot in life to be railroaded by stubborn men."

"I just want to make sure it's *you* doin' the askin' and not your concussion."

She lifted her hands and let them fall in frustration. "Why does everyone think my head injury is making my decisions for me?" She realized he hadn't heard her father's comment and clarified. "Just because I have a golf ball growing from my temple"—she pointed to the swelling—"that doesn't mean I've lost the ability to think for myself."

"We're all just tryin' to do what's best for ya, doll f—" He stopped himself and finished with, "Darlin'. That should make ya feel good."

It did. She felt very protected and cared for and *coddled.* But she worried if she waited until the morning to revisit the subject of kissing him, she'd lose her courage to ask for what she wanted. Or, more likely, lose her ability to forget all the reasons why she *shouldn't* ask for what she wanted.

Plus, there'd undoubtedly be more chaos, more turmoil. Surely Agent O'Toole planned to drag her down to the local FBI office to give a formal statement. And just because she'd been witness to a massacre, that didn't mean life stopped. The Knights still had work to do. *She* still had work to do in supporting them.

So if it was going to happen, it needed to be tonight. *Now.*

"I've told you what would make me feel good," she declared with a challenging cant of her jaw.

He scrubbed a hand over his face. When he dropped his hand, his expression was the picture of indecision.

Okay, fine, she thought. *Let him stand there and vacillate. As for me? I know what I want.*

The first step she took in his direction had his chin jerking back. The second had him shuffling backward. The third saw the backs of his legs hitting her nightstand, effectively ending his retreat. And the fourth brought her within six inches of him.

Close enough to hear his subtle growl of unease. Close enough to feel his body heat radiating out to tease and tantalize. Close enough to hook one finger into the waistband of his jeans and give him a little tug.

It wasn't hard enough to move him. But her eyes were level with his strong, tan throat. So she didn't miss the jerky bob of his Adam's apple.

It was the most gratifying sight she'd ever seen. She decided she quite *liked* turning the tables on him. Being the one who was propositioning, who was…*pursuing.*

Gone was his confident swagger. Gone was his practiced charm. In their places stood a man who wasn't quite sure what to do with the determined woman in front of him.

But Eliza knew exactly what to do.

Framing his face with her hands, she went up on tiptoe.

"Liza, I—"

She placed a finger over his perfect lips. Goose bumps lifted the hairs on her arms when his warm breath bathed the digit. "Shut up and kiss me, Fish."

When he opened his mouth to protest, she silenced him by leaning forward and pressing her mouth to his.

The instant she made contact, she smiled. His gorgeous lips were just as she'd imagined, simultaneously soft and firm. And yet it was all better than she'd imagined. Because his breath was wonderfully warm and tasted of hot chocolate, and his beard stubble was deliciously raspy against her palms.

Humming her pleasure, she tipped her head slightly and softly ran the tip of her tongue along the seem of his lips. Just a quick caress. Just a delicate taste.

And…that's when her courage failed her.

The movies made it seem like that's all it took. Just one small kiss from the heroine and the hero was overcome with passion, crushing her to him, ravaging her silly. But that was fantasy and this was reality. And in reality, all Fisher did was go stalk-still and stiff as a board.

She was tempted to step back and drop her hands. To chalk the entire experience up to one massive failure and an exercise in abject embarrassment.

Maybe if I slink away now, I'll be able to salvage an infinitesimal amount of my pride. Because despite all his propositions and suggestive words, he's obviously not into this.

Then again, if she slunk away, if she left things as they were and didn't try to press her advantage, she'd probably never work up the nerve to try again.

This is it. It's now or never. Make *him lose his reservations.*

Right. *Right!* But how was she supposed to do that?

She had no idea how to play the temptress. The handful of men she'd been with over the years had been the eager, excitable sort. All too willing to take the reins and ride off into the sexual sunset without waiting for her to do much in the way of persuasion or even participation—Charlie included.

Not only had that proved to be terribly unsatisfying, but it also meant she'd never been given the opportunity to practice her skills of seduction.

For all intents and purposes, she was a novice. Which shouldn't have mattered because *he* was supposed to be the professional when it came to this stuff. *Ugh!*

She was about to raise the white flag when a thought occurred…

She *had* recently gotten hooked on a series of alien romance novels—thanks to Hannah Blue. And the books were nothing if not…well… *educational.*

Racking her brain, she recalled how the heroines of the series seduced the big, blue aliens when the latter were being stubborn or recalcitrant. As she replayed the titillating scenes in her head, she noticed a pattern.

A pattern that was easily repeatable.

Let's just hope it works on big, reluctant humans as well as it seems to work on big, blue aliens.

First step, lessen the distance between their bodies.

According to the books, the aliens with the vibrating penises—*if only that existed in real life*—couldn't resist the feel of breasts pressed against their hard, muscled chests.

She closed the gap separating her from Fisher until not an inch remained. Until her breasts flattened against his pecs. Until her hips pressed into his pelvis. Until she could feel the shape of him through the denim of his jeans and—

Wow. Okay. So…he's a big man all over.

Second step was to rub herself against him. *All* of herself, lips and boobs and pubic bone.

The lips were easy enough. She moved hers across his, delicately testing the texture of his amazing mouth and gently taking another taste by flicking out the tip of her tongue.

He groaned and the sound had delight fizzing up her spine like champagne bubbles.

It's working. My master plan to seduce the shit out of Fisher Wakefield is working!

Who knew reading alien erotica would come in so handy?

The boobs were a little more difficult when it came to knowing what to do with them. Was she supposed to do a side-to-side motion? Up and down? The books lacked specificity in this area, so she was left to go with her gut.

When she did, it was *her* doing the moaning. The silk of her pajama top combined with the hardness of his chest to create the most delicious friction. Her nipples instantly hardened, becoming achy, needy points. And she was no longer thinking about how she should be moving. She worked on instinct, undulating in any way that produced the most pleasure.

Her hips naturally followed suit, gently rolling, softly pressing. And to her unfettered delight she felt him respond.

He hadn't been soft to begin with. But he grew hard as a rock against her.

The feel of that long, thick column of *maleness* had an answering wetness slicking the insides of her thighs. She couldn't help but whimper.

A low, guttural growl sounded at the back of his throat in response. And finally, *finally* his arms came around her. Crushing her to him.

One big hand splayed across the middle of her back and the other curled possessively around her hip to help her in her bump and grind.

Thank goodness. She needed all the help she could get. She'd stopped being able to think coherently the minute she felt him swell and harden.

Now, he'll ravish me like they do in the movies.

Except, when his lips parted hers, he didn't shove his tongue inside her mouth to dart and devour. Quite the opposite. His kiss was slow and thorough. Gentle, tender, and so profound she found her emotions rising right along with her passion.

Seconds passed. Minutes. Hours. *Years?*

She lost track of time, lost track of herself, lost track of everything but the motion of his tongue, the nip of his teeth, the slow suction of his mouth.

This is so much better than the movies, she thought a little deliriously. Because he wasn't simply kissing her. He was making love to her mouth. Learning all its tastes and textures.

She'd been kissed before. Quite a bit over the years, in fact. Her first tongue tango had occurred at the tender age of thirteen when she'd bowed to peer pressure and joined a game of spin the bottle at Tara Turlington's birthday party. She'd enjoyed the experience enough to repeat it often.

But she'd *never* been kissed like this. Kissed as if her mouth was the most fascinating landscape he'd ever explored, and he was determined to map every inch of it. Kissed as if the secrets to the universe existed somewhere on her lips and tongue and he wasn't going to stop investigating until he'd uncovered each one.

Part of her wanted to blame the novelty of the experience on having never been kissed by a man she loved. But she knew that was taking credit away from where credit was due.

Fisher Wakefield simply knew what he was doing. He knew how to leisurely lick and suck and stroke until her eyes crossed and her toes curled, until her heart—the heart that had always been his—beat feverishly against her breastbone in a desperate bid to get closer to him.

"Liza." Her name rumbled from his mouth into hers. It was the most delicious thing she'd ever tasted.

She moaned in response and that seemed to be all he'd been waiting for, because he redoubled his efforts.

I love him so much, she thought desperately. She loved him and now that she knew what it was to be held by him, to be *kissed* by him, nothing else would ever do.

She was doomed. Doomed to pine for a man who wanted nothing more than this. Doomed to long for a love he wouldn't…or *couldn't* give. Doomed to always fantasize about a life that would never be hers.

The futility of her situation mixed with her already frayed nerves to have tears burning behind her eyes. But she refused to give into them. Refused to ruin this singular, shining moment.

Her hands fell from his face to grip his shoulders, seeking an anchor as the storm of her emotions swirled around her as surely as the storm outside swirled around the factory building. The taste of her unshed tears mixed with the chocolaty goodness of his breath to create a bittersweet symphony of flavors on her tongue.

"Fisher," she breathed against his lips, desperately wanting him to experience what she was experiencing. To admit that what they shared was so much more than passion.

Couldn't he feel how special it was between them? Couldn't he feel how much her heart ached for him and the tenderness he showed her?

"Lord, you're sexy," he growled.

She should've been flattered. But that wasn't the declaration she was after. Those weren't the three little words she so longed to hear.

The hand that'd been splayed against her back slid down to cup her ass. He used the other to grip the back of her knee and bend her leg up until the part of her that was hot and needy pressed tight against the part of him that was hard and ready.

Her arms went around his neck and she was lost to the sensation of his lips and tongue, to the ferocious desperation that gripped her body, to the carnal way he rubbed against her.

After twirling her around so he could lay her down on the bed, his hips found the welcoming space between her legs. Despite their clothing separating them, she gloried in the feel of him nestled tight against the part of her that needed him the most. Gloried in the feel of his weight pressing her down into the mattress. Gloried in locking her heels together behind his ass to aid him in his movements.

Unfortunately, the moment she settled into the age-old rhythm of bump and grind, the quiet voice that lived in the back of her head began screaming a warning.

Too far! Too fast!

This was more than a kiss. And if she let it continue, there was only one place it would end.

She didn't want to sleep with him.

Well…she did. She'd wanted to sleep with him pretty much since the moment she'd laid eyes on him. But that hadn't been what she'd asked for.

She'd asked for a kiss. A taste. A brief glimpse of what might have been had she been the kind of woman who could make love to the man who'd stolen her heart without the act simultaneously breaking the fragile organ wide open. Or had he been the kind of man willing to offer more than just his body.

Stop him! the voice screamed. *Stop this!*

Before she could take heed, however, Fisher released her mouth to leave a trail of warm, wet kisses down her jaw. The instant he wrapped his talented mouth around the pulse-point on her neck, sucking rhythmically to the beat of her own heart, she lost touch with each and every one of her reservations.

All her internal warnings faded away as she gave in to the undeniable *physicality* that was Fisher Wakefield in seduction mode. He was so hot she wondered how the bedsheets didn't burst into flames. So skilled she understood the dreamy expressions on the faces of the women who'd been lucky enough to share his bed.

It was that last thought that had reality and all its harshness crashing back in.

"Fish." She threaded her fingers into his hair. The strands were silky and cool, a stark contrast to the warmth of his scalp.

"Mmm," he hummed against her throat, laving her pulse point with his tongue before catching her earlobe between his teeth and sucking the delicate skin so gently her eyes crossed and she considered throwing caution to the wind and simply allowing him to make love to her even though it would undoubtedly prove to be her ultimate undoing.

No! Stop this right now! the voice of reason demanded.

"Fisher." This time her tone was forceful. She fisted her hands in his hair and pulled his mouth away from her.

"Yes, darlin'?" The smile he gave her was as sweet as angels, but his eyes were the devil's own when his gaze fell to her kiss-swollen lips. "What can I do for ya?"

"We have to—" It sounded like someone had shoved a wad of uncooked sourdough down her throat. She had to swallow and try again. "We have to stop."

"We do?" One thick eyebrow winged up his forehead. "Why?" Concern suddenly clouded his eyes. "Is it your head?"

It's my heart! she wanted to scream.

"I asked you to kiss me." He was still positioned perfectly between her legs, still moving subtly and creating a mind-melting friction. "I asked you to help me forget for just a moment. And you've done that."

His hips stopped their delicious movement. Even though it was for the best, she wanted to cry out with disappointment.

His expression turned broody in the low glow of the bedside lamp. But his tone was neutral when he said, "Ya sure that's *all* ya want?"

No! I want everything! All of you! All the things you've sworn you can never give me!

Aloud, she admitted, "Like I said, I won't be just another notch on your bedpost. And you won't consider letting me be anything else. So we're at an impasse."

He blinked and went so still she thought he'd stopped breathing. His voice had been deep with passion. Now it was full of something different. "Do ya *want* to be somethin' else?"

Here was her chance. She could tell him everything. Tell him how much she loved him. How much she dreamed of building a life with him. How much she wanted to spend each and every day waking up to him in the morning and lying beside him at night.

But what good would that do her?

He didn't feel the same. He'd *never* feel the same. He'd made that abundantly clear. And so…she lied.

"No." She shook her head.

Something flickered behind his eyes. Something that made her want to grab his cheeks and force him to look at her so she could study it. But he pushed himself off her and stood beside the bed with his hands on his hips.

His hair was wild and wavy from her fingers. His full mouth was blushed red from her kisses. And the evidence of his desire was starkly outlined against the fly of jeans.

He looked like *man* personified. *Sex* personified. And it took everything she had not to pull him back on top of her…screw the consequences and screw that screaming voice of reason.

He made a face of misery before reaching down to adjust himself.

The sight of his long, tan fingers curling around the length of his erection was so erotic she felt her womb contract. And his utter lack of self-consciousness shocked her when he said, "Alrighty. I reckon I better head next door to take care of this myself, then. Ya want me to call in one of the others to come sit with ya 'til ya fall asleep?"

The prim and proper lady she'd been raised to be tried to make her blush bashfully. But the wanton woman he'd awoken in her responded in kind. "No. I need to take care of some business myself."

CHAPTER 14

A paper cup of vending machine coffee steamed between Julia's hands. She'd yet to take a sip. Even though she needed the caffeine—this long night was growing longer by the minute—she knew the stuff would taste like swill.

She was a bit of a coffee snob. Espresso machine at home. Peet's Coffee if she was out and about.

But beggars can't be choosers.

"They said his heart gave out. That the trauma of the bullet wound and the subsequent surgery was just too much for him."

Bethany Chastain still wore her cocktail dress. It was one of those matronly numbers, emerald green, long-sleeved, and form-fitting without being revealing. At one point, it'd probably looked elegant and festive. Now, stained with blood and frayed at one seam, it just seemed sad and macabre.

Of course, most things in an ICU waiting room seemed sad and macabre, even when they weren't damaged or bloodstained.

"But *I'm* the one with the bad heart," the senator continued, her voice hoarse from the tears she'd shed over her dead husband, tears that'd left trails in her makeup. Senator Chastain didn't look a day over fifty and

Julia gave silent kudos to the woman's plastic surgeon. "Bill had the heart of racehorse and the blood pressure of an Olympian," she insisted. "I just can't…"

She shook her head and glanced forlornly at the glass door leading to the hallway. It looked like she hoped a doctor would come in and tell her it'd all been a giant misunderstanding. That Professor Chastain *wasn't* dead. That she hadn't lost her husband of forty years.

"I'm so sorry for your loss, Senator," Julia said quietly. "And I can assure you, Agent Douglas and I are doing everything we can to figure out exactly what happened tonight and why."

Dillan took that as his cue to interject. "Did the chef appear agitated or otherwise out of sorts to you, Senator?"

Bethany Chastain blinked uncomprehendingly, and Julia took a hasty swig of the scalding-hot, bitter-has-hell coffee to keep from saying, *Duh, Dillan. The man went on a murder spree. Of course he appeared agitated.*

"You mean while he was spraying bullets around the patio?" the senator scoffed and then spoke Julia's own thoughts out loud. "Yes. He appeared agitated."

"You had no contact with him *before* he came onto the patio?" Dillan persisted.

Senator Chastain hadn't exactly been slouching. Years spent in front of reporters and having to present a strong, confident façade to her constituents meant she had near perfect posture. But her shoulders had been drooping. Now she straightened them.

"What are you implying? That I make a habit of sculking around my host's kitchen?" Her keen gaze narrowed as she turned from Dillan to Julia and back again. "Or that *I* am under suspicion here? Do you think I had something to do with tonight's—"

"Not at all, Senator," Julia was quick to cut the woman off. She didn't like the deep flush that stole up the senator's chest and neck. "We've just learned some interesting information about the suspect and—"

"He isn't a *suspect*," Senator Chastain said with a snarl as she shoved to a stand. "He's a *murderer*. An *assassin*." Her voice rose as she began to pace angrily around the room. "And I wish he was still alive so I could kill him myself!"

"Please, Senator." Julia set aside her coffee so she could guide the senator back to her chair. Bethany Chastain had worked herself into a tizzy. Her chest rose and fell with harsh breaths. She was running her hands through her blond hair until it stood out from her head in frantic tuffs. "Come sit back down and let's—"

"I don't want to sit." The senator skewered Julia with a killing look. "I want to *rage!* I want to drag God down from Heaven and scream into his face for letting this happen. I want to—"

Senator Chastain stopped and blinked myopically. Then she grabbed her chest and stumbled forward.

"Senator Chastain?" Julia squeaked in alarm as she caught the woman by her forearms. "Dillan! Help!" she cried when the senator's full body weight crashed into her.

Bethany Chastain wasn't a large woman. But she was larger than Julia. And even though Julia worked out regularly, she wasn't up to the task of holding up another human being who seemed hellbent on crumbling to the floor.

Dillan, forever slow on the uptake, didn't manage to gain his feet before Julia was forced to her knees, trying her best to control the senator's descent.

"What the hell?" Dillan asked when he *finally* made it to Julia's side and was able to catch the senator by the waist.

"I think she fainted," Julia grunted. "Help me get her on her back."

With the senator safely on the floor, Julia was able to get a look at the woman. She immediately knew it wasn't a simple fainting spell.

Something was terribly wrong.

The skin over the senator's face was mottled and waxy looking. Her eyes were open, but she stared unseeingly at the acoustic tiles on the ceiling. And the way her mouth opened and closed reminded Julia of a fish out of water.

Fear and adrenaline spiked through Julia's bloodstream to have her raising her voice higher than was necessary in the quiet emptiness of the waiting room. "Go get a doctor, Dillan! I think she's having a heart attack!"

She didn't wait to see if Dillan did as ordered. Instead she grabbed the senator's hand and reassuringly patted bones that felt as fragile as snowflakes. Glancing down at their clasped palms, she noted the senator's liver spots, snarled veins, and enlarged knuckles.

Plastic surgeons had yet to find a good way to address hands. And that's where Bethany Chastain showed her age.

"Hang on, Senator." Julie did her best to instill confidence in her voice. "The doctors are coming. You're going to be fine."

The senator's eyes shifted from the ceiling tiles to Julia's face. In the weeks to come, Julia would recall the fear in the woman's gaze, the way the senator seemed to beg her without words to *do* something.

But there was nothing to be done. And Julia watched helplessly as the senator dragged in one final breath and then let it out in a slow wheeze.

"Oh, god. Oh, no." She used two fingers against the senator's throat to check for a pulse. "Don't do this to me, Senator. Come on!"

When only a thready flutter met her searching fingertips, she got ready to do chest compressions. But she was saved the effort when two medical professionals burst into the room with flapping stethoscopes and a rattling crash cart.

She stumbled out of the way, tentatively settling onto the edge of her chair as the nurses went to work checking the senator's vitals.

The nurse with curly black hair and a five-o'clock shadow yelled, "We have V-fib!"

Julia realized Dillan had followed the hospital staff into the room when he dropped into the chair next to her. His voice was a bare whisper, meant only for her ears. "What are the odds?"

She cut him a questioning glance.

"That two of the three eyewitnesses would croak within a few hours of the shooting," he clarified.

"Senator Chastain isn't dead," she hissed in disgust at his lack of feeling for the drama playing out in front of them.

"Looks that way to me," he muttered, and she turned back in time to watch the nurse with the long, blond ponytail take a pair of scissors to the bodice on the senator's dress.

There was no such thing as modesty in a medical emergency. And after the bodice was flayed open, the senator's bra was sliced in two without a second thought.

Julia felt like a voyeur. But she couldn't look away as the curly-headed nurse fitted an oxygen mask attached to a bellows-like device over the senator's face and proceeded to blow air into the senator's unresponsive body. A small, plastic case was placed on the ground next to the prone woman and Julia recognized it immediately for what it was.

Defibrillator.

"We have a pacemaker here!" Nurse Ponytail yelled and she was careful to avoid the device as she placed the defibrillator's sticky paddles on the senator's chest.

A pacemaker. So that's *what the senator meant when she said she was the one with the bad heart.*

"Clear!" cried Nurse Ponytail and Julia watched as the two medical professionals pulled away from the senator.

The defibrillator delivered its jolt of lifesaving electricity. But the movies got it all wrong. The device didn't make a loud *kathunk.* Nor did Senator Chastain's back arch off the floor. Instead, there was an eerie silence as the senator simply…*stiffened.*

Julia's own heart thundered in her chest as she watched Nurse Curly Hair go back to pumping oxygen into the senator's lungs. At the same time, Nurse Ponytail checked the senator's pulse.

"Still in V-fib. I'm increasing the joules," Ponytail declared.

A doctor—or, at least, Julia *assumed* the woman with the cropped brown hair and lab coat was a doctor—hurried into the room and dropped to her knees.

"What have we got?" she asked, her tone calm and efficient.

Nurse Curly Hair gave her the scoop using medical terms Julia had only heard on *Grey's Anatomy.* The doctor nodded and pulled out a tray from the crash cart.

"Administering epi," she declared with a clenched jaw as she shoved a needle into the senator's arm.

Whatever the syringe carried didn't work. Because the senator was shocked twice more.

"Damnit!" Ponytail snarled after the final try. "We've lost her. Starting chest compressions."

Julia sat helplessly. All she could do was numbly watch as the hospital staff valiantly attempted to save the senator's life. And after what felt like an eternity, but could only have been a handful of minutes, the doctor sat back on her heels and blew out a shaky breath.

"Stop." She placed a hand on Ponytail's shoulder. "She's gone." Glancing at the large analogue clock that hung on the wall above the doorway, she added, "Time of death 3:04 AM."

"Like I said," Dillan murmured beside Julia.

She shot him a censorious look.

"What?" He lifted a hand. "I was right, wasn't I?"

CHAPTER 15

Black Knights Inc.

Britt Rollins quietly slipped out the front door of the old menthol cigarette factory. When he turned to shut it behind him, he had to awkwardly balance the two mugs of hot chocolate he carried.

He couldn't sleep. Which was usually the case when he got a middle-of-the-night call from his older brother.

Knox had been on the outside for little more than two weeks following his second stint in the big house. And even though Knox had promised Britt he was keeping his nose clean, Britt had recognized the fast, excited way his brother was talking.

Knox was on the trail of a new con. Britt was sure of it. And like an addict who'd just taken a hit, Knox was high on the excitement.

In a way, Knox *was* an addict, Britt supposed. His big brother didn't crave the oblivion of booze or the zest of cocaine, but he lived for the euphoria of the next big score. And the quest for easy money meant Knox had spent the majority of his adult life behind bars.

If Knox got caught this time, he'd spend the *rest* of his adult life there. There'd be no more five-year stints. The long arm of the law believed in second chances. But it didn't believe in third ones.

Britt couldn't help but feel responsible.

Not in any *direct* way. He wasn't pushing his brother toward illegal activity. Quite the opposite. He did his best to encourage Knox to steer clear of such nonsense and make a life for himself he could be proud of.

But Britt was responsible in an *indirect* way. Because Knox Rollins's life had taken a sharp turn onto its current twisted and illicit road when their father died, and Britt had become Knox's responsibility.

Had nineteen-year-old Knox not taken on the burden of raising thirteen-year-old Britt, had he not been forced into some less-than-legal dealings to keep a roof over their heads and food on their plates, had he been allowed to stay in college and finish his degree, things might have been different.

Knox might have been different.

Or maybe not…

The Rollins boys were both thrill-seekers, both hedonists by nature. Britt fed his cravings for excitement and adventure by skydiving and rock climbing and surfing Maui's big waves. But who was to say Knox wouldn't have always found a way to feed his cravings through unlawful enterprise?

Were crooks born or made? Britt had always assumed it was the second, that horrible luck and impossible choices were the reasons most people turned to a life of crime. But perhaps that wasn't the case for everyone. Maybe for some people, the thrill and stimulation they got from illicit activity was stamped into the very fabric of their souls.

It was a depressing thought.

Sighing heavily, he made his way across the grounds toward the gatehouse. The asphalt expanse had been recently seal-coated, and the chemical smell of the stuff, like a mixture of sulfur and crude oil, lingered in the damp air.

The storm had moved on, but it had left behind dark puddles that gathered the moonlight and reflected it back into the night sky like mirrors.

Off in the distance a siren wailed. The Chicago River lapped leisurely at the banks on the backside of the property. And closer in clashed the discordant notes of a jazz band.

Manus Connelly, one of the four native Chicagoans who'd been taking round-the-clock shifts guarding the gate at BKI, had terrible taste in music. He was an excellent conversationalist, though.

And that's what Britt needed.

Some conversation. Some amusement. Some *distraction* from his swirling thoughts.

All the Connelly brothers were good for a rowdy and raucous good time. They had personalities as big as their statures and as many jokes as they had freckles. But Manus was the true wordsmith, a genius when it came to exchanging quips and matching wits.

When Britt got within five feet of the wrought iron gate, it began to slide open, rattling on its track as it went. The guardhouse had monitors showing footage from the security cameras around the property. No doubt Manus had seen the moment Britt exited the building and had been waiting for him to cross the grounds.

After Britt slipped through the opening in the gate, Manus's big head with its giant bush of red hair poked through the access window on the side of the little building. His thick, Chicago accent mixed with the humidity of the air until Britt felt enveloped in all that was Chi-Town. "What's up, my man? Can't sleep?"

"Not a wink." Britt passed a mug through the window and Manus accepted it gratefully.

"Damn." Britt waved a hand in front of his face when he was hit by the noxious cloud that wafted out of the guardhouse. "It smells like a camel's ass crack in here. What the hell have you been eating?"

"Sausage and sourcrout." Manus gave him a toothy grin. "And don't knock it 'til you try it."

"I'll pass." Britt leaned his elbow on the windowsill. "Is Birgit German?" he asked, referring to Manus's pretty wife. "I didn't know that. Although I probably should've guessed given her name."

"Mmm." Manus nodded. "First-generation German American. Her folks came over in the late seventies."

"Huh. A second-generation Irish American and a first-generation German American. Did y'all meet over a pint of beer?" He smirked at his own joke since both cultures were known for their love of the hop juice.

"As a matter of fact, we did. First time I saw her was at the St. Patty's Day parade. We drank green beer until we puked. By the time Octoberfest rolled around, I'd put a ring on her finger."

Britt laughed and shook his head. "A Windy City romance made in heaven."

"True enough." Manus saluted him with a self-satisfied grin before sniffing the contents of his mug. "Hot chocolate? In July?"

"Made it for Eliza. You know how shock and trauma have a way of chilling you down to the marrow of your bones."

Manus chuffed distastefully. "Wish I didn't. But I do."

Having worked at Black Knights Inc. for nearly a decade, he and his brothers had born witness to some high-stakes action that would've had your everyday security guard shitting his shorts. The Connelly boys were as tough as old cow hide, though. *Thankfully.*

"Eliza's recipe?" Manus asked before taking a tentative sip of the steaming liquid.

"Mmm." Britt nodded, drinking from his own mug. "With just a dash of cinnamon tossed in for good luck."

Manus nodded appreciatively. "And how is our girl?"

One corner of Britt's mouth quirked. "She kicked Fisher out of her room a while ago. So I'd say she's fine as a fiddle, back to her regularly scheduled programming." He paused and shook his head. "It astounds me how two people I love like family can be so different. But they're like fire and ice."

"If you ask me, they're more like fire and gasoline."

Britt snorted his agreement since he'd said something very similar earlier that evening.

They lapsed into silence as they enjoyed their drinks. Manus went back to eyeing the security footage. And Britt sighed deeply as he watched the owner of the bagel shop pull into the empty lot.

The place opened at six AM. Which meant the bagels started baking hours before.

Britt had never been much of a morning person. But there was something appealing about the simplicity of running a business like the one across the street.

No middle-of-the-night flights to the other side of the world. No one attempting to put a period on the end of his life. No bombs or bullets or illicit assignations with fellow operatives in the back rooms of bars. Just early mornings.

Early mornings. And monotonous days. And weeks that drifted into months…

Britt wouldn't last a minute in a job like that. But he wished, *oh* how he wished he could. Because then he could invite Knox to come live and work with him.

As it was, Knox couldn't be trusted to know the truth of Black Knights Inc. Knox couldn't be trusted with much of anything, come to think of it. And that's what bothered Britt the most.

The brother he'd so loved and admired growing up, the brother who'd sacrificed his future so Britt could have one, had lost himself somewhere along the way. And the man who showed up in his place?

Well…Britt barely recognized that guy.

A slight breeze blew an empty plastic bag down the street. He lifted his face to catch the notes on the wind: wet concrete, the faint fishy scent of the river, and the ever-present tinge of car exhaust.

Over the years, he'd grown to appreciate Chicago. Appreciate the hustle and bustle, the way Midwesterners were a no-nonsense bunch, and how seriously they took their deep-dish pizza and Italian beef sandwiches. But he'd never loved the City of Big Shoulders the way he loved his hometown.

Unlike Chicago, there was very little hustle and bustle in Charleston, South Carolina. Southerners didn't do much of anything quickly, and he figured that was because they spent eight months out of the year trying not to sweat their asses off. Whereas a Midwesterner would come right to the point, a Southerner preferred to meander around a bit, believing part of the fun was in the conversational journey.

The people living in the two cities had one thing in common, though. They both took their local cuisine seriously. Except in Charleston it was all about the she crab soup and the shrimp and grits.

It'd been a little over five years since Britt had been home. Five years since he'd walked along the battery or heard the bells chime at the Cathedral of St. John the Baptist. Five years since he'd sat in a courtroom to hear a judge sentence his brother to hard time.

Taking another sip of hot chocolate, he wondered how long it'd be before he was sitting in another courtroom, listening to another judge tell his brother he was going in for the long-haul.

Manus had turned down the volume on his radio, but a particularly discordant *clash* of cymbals brought Britt's mind back to the present. He frowned at the redheaded behemoth. "You know, I've always prided myself on being polyjamorous."

Manus lifted one bushy orange eyebrow. "I'm not here to kink shame anyone."

"Poly-*jam*-orous," Britt emphasized. "Meaning I listen to almost all music. Rock, pop, country, blues. But I have never understood the appeal of jazz. It sounds like a bunch of noise and—"

"Hold that thought," Manus cut him off. "We have company."

Britt pushed away from the window's ledge and watched a large, black SUV slink up the empty street like a stalking cougar. Government plates were pinned to the front bumper and a telltale tint filmed the windows.

Bulletproof, he thought. Then he clarified. *Well, bullet* resistant. *There's no such thing as true bulletproof glass.*

"Possible they're just passing through?" Manus asked when the SUV pulled past the guardhouse and the driveway that led into the compound.

"Unlikely seeing as how blondie there in the driver's seat is the one who came to the hospital to interview Eliza."

"Middle of the night visits from the feds can only mean one thing," Manus muttered. "Bad news," the two of them said in unison.

Manus chuckled. "Pinch, poke, you owe me a Coke."

Britt shot him a flat-mouthed look. "What are you? Seven?"

"Nope." Manus shook his head. "But that's how old the twins are. Just celebrated their birthday last weekend. And their throw-back witticisms are contagious."

Britt harrumphed. "And here I was giving you credit for being the cleverest of all the Connelly brothers."

"You were? When?"

"On my walk out here."

"Well, at least you were right about one thing." Manus gestured with his chin toward the SUV. It had pulled a uey and was headed back their way.

When the vehicle rolled to a stop beside the curb, tension crackled along Britt's nerve endings like static on a dry day. Anticipation sharpened his senses when the engine shut off.

It was an understatement to say the little female agent was easy on the eyes. There was no mistaking the pert perfection of her nose, the generous proportions of her mouth, or the way she filled out her utilitarian pantsuit like a dream.

Add that to what seemed to be a razor-sharp mind and a charming sense of humor—he'd been so caught off guard by her *Star Wars* reference, he'd completely whiffed it—and it was safe to say he was intrigued by her.

Then there'd been the moment when he'd *literally* felt sparks as they touched.

Seriously, is she wearing wool socks with those lug-soled duty shoes?

It didn't seem likely in July. But it was the only explanation he could think of.

When the SUV's front doors opened, he gulped down the last of his hot chocolate in hopes it would settle his jittery stomach.

I can disarm an assailant in two moves, fast-rope out of helicopters into enemy territory, and hump forty pounds of C4 through the desert without breaking a sweat. But put a smart, sexy blond in my path and I'm completely knocked off my game.

He blamed part of his edginess on his natural aversion to authority figures. From the first time the local five-oh had knocked on his front door looking for his brother to this moment right here where he worked for an off-the-books defense firm, having to deal with anyone who *worked forces*—as the incomparable Rage Against the Machine once sang—made his asshole pucker.

Agent Douglas was the first to exit the vehicle and Britt noted the man's perfect haircut and expensive suit. He was good at reading people, and he pegged Douglas for an arrogant sonofabitch who enjoyed the power and prestige of his position more than he enjoyed the actual job.

Then there was Agent O'Toole…*Julia.* As she rounded the front of the vehicle and stepped onto the curb, he noticed she looked a little worse for wear. Her blond ponytail had slipped down to the nape of her neck. There was a stain on her white button-down shirt. *Coffee?* And deep lines had carved themselves into the skin beside her mouth. Yet…

The keen, almost zealous light in her eyes told him she *loved* being a fed. Loved it for the intellectual challenge of solving a mystery. Loved it for the satisfaction that came from putting the guilty behind bars. Loved it for the all the right reasons and none of the wrong ones.

If all authorities were like her, he'd probably be less likely to curl his lip in disgust anytime he saw a badge.

"You're out late," he observed blandly.

"We're on a case." Julia mirrored his expression. "What's your excuse?"

He shrugged noncommittally. "Night owl."

"Now why doesn't that surprise me?"

Britt hooked his thumb in a belt loop. "Probably because not much does." When she frowned, he clarified. "Surprise you, I mean. You strike me as the observant sort, not prone to being caught off guard."

She feigned a put-upon sigh. "Blame it on being raised by blue-collar Southsiders. I think *observant* gets stamped on our foreheads the minute we exit the birth canal. Well, that and the White Sox logo."

Damnit. He liked her.

He didn't want to, but he did.

"So what brings you here this time of night? Or…morning?"

She squinted toward the east where the sun would rise over the cerulean waters of Lake Michigan in a couple hours. "I'm tired. I'd like to say what I've come to say only once. And that's going to require Miss Meadows's presence. Can we come inside?"

Britt heard Manus grumble his disapproval. It was the man's job to protect Black Knights Inc. and all its secrets. It stood to reason he didn't much like the idea of the FBI breaching the sanctity of the walls.

Britt didn't like it either. But making the agents stand on the curb while he ran upstairs to fetch Eliza would be even more suspicious than taking them inside and letting them get a gander at the setup.

"Follow me." He waved and felt the moment Agent O'Toole fell into step behind him. He *sensed* her in a way he couldn't explain. It was as if the electricity he'd felt in the hospital had followed her here.

As if on cue, the hairs on his arms lifted. If the thunderstorm had still been raging overhead, he'd have blamed it on that. Instead, he had to admit the real culprit was the woman herself.

Does she moonlight as Ms. Marvel? Sheesh.

As they neared the door, Agent Douglas whistled. "You guys sure have a lot of security."

"Most of Becky's bikes sell for six figures," Britt was quick to explain. "And some of the truly custom jobs go for a cool half mil. Then there's all the money in equipment and tools. So…yeah. We have a lot of security."

"And Becky is?" Agent O'Toole's warm, husky voice traveled up his spine like tickling fingers.

"She's our crackerjack designer. We wouldn't be in business if it weren't for her." He turned slightly to hook a thumb toward his chest. "The rest of us who work here? We're just grease monkeys. Becky's the one with the talent and the vision."

His cell buzzed in his pocket. He didn't need to pull it out to know it was Knox.

He should answer.

He didn't want to. He didn't want to hear that frenetic excitement again. And he certainly didn't want to hear any more lies.

No one ever talked about how love could be a blade that twists inside a person. How it can make a guy bleed out in places nobody can see.

"You're not the only night owl, I see." Agent O'Toole's voice pulled at the knots in his tangled mind.

When he frowned in confusion, she hitched her chin toward his noisy pocket. "When someone phones me at four o'clock in the morning, I figure they're either a night owl or there's an emergency. You need to get that?"

"It can wait," he assured her and opened the large front door.

The shop floor was dark. But he remedied that by throwing on the four switches that had the huge overhead lights mounted three stories above blazing to life.

Agent Douglas whistled again as the row of custom choppers blazed into sight. Paint glistened. Chrome gleamed. Hand-tooled leather seats glinted dully.

"Wow." Agent O'Toole walked over to the last bike in the row. It was Britt's ride. But she couldn't know that. "Now I understand the need for the razor wire and all the security cameras. These aren't motorcycles. These are works of art."

When she ran her hand over the leather seat, Britt felt like she was touching him. Chills skipped up his spine.

His voice was gruff when he said, "Y'all feel free to look at our stock while I go wake everyone."

"Everyone?" Agent O'Toole lifted one eyebrow.

"We're more like family than coworkers," he explained. "We'll all want to hear what you have to say."

He didn't wait for a response before heading upstairs. Five minutes later, he was leading the crew—who sported various degrees of dishabille—back down to the shop floor.

Introductions were made and Julia blinked myopically at the gathered group of men.

Of the six active-duty Knights, only Hunter was missing. He and his wife, Grace, had recently moved out of the old factory building and into a small condo in the Streeterville neighborhood. But everyone else was present and accounted for.

There was Sam Harwood, whose SpongeBob SquarePants pajama bottoms had been a Christmas gift from Hannah, his purple-haired girlfriend. Fisher, who'd been naked as a jaybird when Britt slipped through the open door into his dark bedroom, had thankfully redonned his jeans and T-shirt from the day before. Hewitt Birch wore plaid Joe Boxer briefs and a white tank top. But it was Graham Colburn who caught Agent O'Toole's eye.

Not that Britt could blame her for gaping.

For one thing, Graham was six-and-a-half feet tall. For another thing, Graham hadn't bothered to throw a shirt on top of his gray sweatpants, so his John Cena muscles bulged and gleamed in the overhead light. And lastly, Graham wore an expression that said he ate small children and puppies for breakfast.

Inexplicably, Britt felt a frisson of jealousy. He had to bite his tongue to keep from telling Graham to go put a shirt on.

"Well." Agent O'Toole cleared her throat. "Seems the gang's all here."

"The gang's always here," Fisher informed her. "It's one of the perks of livin' and workin' in the same buildin'."

The little agent's brow furrowed. "Not too many jobs offer onsite living quarters nowadays."

Fisher shrugged. "It's either let us live here or double our salaries. And since this place has the space." He gestured around the cavernous shop. "It's pretty much a no-brainer which one Boss and Becky chose."

"Boss and Becky are the owners?" Agent O'Toole hadn't taken out her phone to record their conversation, but Britt knew she was filing away information, nonetheless.

"That'd be them," he told her and felt the instant her eyes landed on him.

He hadn't been able to discern their exact color in the hospital. But the bright glow of the shop lights showed they were the warmest brown that melted into gold near her pupils.

Fox eyes, he thought. *And something tells me she's just as cunning.*

She gestured to an empty bike lift and the various stools scattered around the shop. "Mind if we head over to that table thingie and grab some seats? I've been on my feet since eight AM yesterday, and my dogs are barking."

He gestured for everyone to pull up a seat around the stainless-steel bike lift.

The way the little blond dropped onto her stool told him she hadn't been joking about her dogs. He felt his mouth twitch at the same time he resisted the urge to pull up a stool behind her so he could massage her tense shoulders.

The smell of grease guns, metal shavings, and fresh paint was strong. And beneath all that was the ever-present aroma of the high-octane coffee the crew lived on.

Agent O'Toole looked like she could use a cup. But this wasn't a social call, so no one made the offer.

Once everyone was situated, Eliza asked the question that was on all their minds. "What brings you out here so early in the morning? Have you made progress on the case?"

"Is it early?" Agent O'Toole rubbed her brow. "It feels awfully late to me."

"Poe-tay-toe, poe-tah-toe," Sam said gruffly.

Sam had been in a foul mood ever since the D.O.D had asked Hannah to work on a two-week project in Washington. Britt was anxious for Sam's better half to return so maybe they'd have their good-natured sharpshooter back.

"I suppose that's true," Agent O'Toole conceded. Then she asked Eliza how she was "holding up."

"Still in shock if I'm being honest," their girl Friday admitted with a watery sniff. "I keep having to tell myself that Senator McClean and all his lovely guests are dead. That *Charlie's* dead. That it wasn't all some terrible nightmare I can't seem to wake up from."

Fisher, who'd placed his stool next to Eliza's, lifted his hand like he wanted to offer comfort. Then he hesitated as if he wasn't sure he should. Finally, he reached over and grabbed her hand. When her fingers curled around his tight enough to make her knuckles turn white, Fisher's shoulders slumped in relief.

Well, Britt thought. *What have we here? Have these two finally called a truce?*

It appeared so. And all it'd taken was a concussion, a mass murder, and one dead fiancé.

"I'm so sorry for everything you've endured tonight," Agent O'Toole said. And they weren't just pretty words. Britt could tell she actually meant them. "And I'm especially sorry that Agent Douglas and I dragged you out of bed when you're recovering from a head injury." The pretty agent cocked her head and asked, "How *is* your head, by the way?"

Eliza wiped away a tear that had escaped down her cheek. "Feels like every city worker in Chicago is operating a jackhammer inside my skull. But other than that?" She flapped a hand. "I'll live."

Even though Eliza was slender, Britt had never thought of her as a small woman. She was taller than average. And she often emphasized her height by donning heels. But she looked tiny wrapped up in her fluffy, terry-cloth robe with her bare toes curled around the middle rung of her stool.

"That's good to hear." O'Toole nodded. "And we'd like to make sure that continues, so we're suggesting you come with us to a safe house."

Every eye in the room was suddenly glued to the little FBI agent's face.

A lesser person might have shied away from all that attention. Especially considering that attention came from men who towered over her and had miens that'd made many an enemy quake in their combat boots. But Julia O'Toole appeared unfazed.

"What's happened?" Fisher asked. He'd scooted—perhaps unconsciously?—closer to Eliza, and he dropped her hand so he could put an arm around her shoulders.

Huh. Will wonders never cease?

Fisher hadn't exactly kept it a secret he found Eliza attractive. How many times had Britt heard Fish proposition the poor woman? He'd lost count. But Britt had never taken Fish seriously.

In a group of men who never suffered from lack of female companionship, Fisher was the playboy amongst playboys. The guy propositioned every eligible woman he met. And quite a few of them took him up on his offers because he looked like one of those dudes from the high-end cologne commercials.

Maybe Britt *should* have taken Fish's invitations seriously though. Maybe all this time Fish had been harboring a little thing for Eliza.

As Fisher's anointed *wingman for life*, Britt approved.

He hadn't considered it before, but the two made a good match. Eliza tended to be too serious, and Fisher was playful and flippant. Eliza liked to cook, and Fish would likely die of starvation if left to his own devices. They both liked Taylor Swift and while Eliza watched medical dramas and Fisher preferred streaming Canadian sitcoms like *Trailer Park Boys* and *Letterkenny*, Britt had walked past the TV room plenty of times to find them sharing a giant bowl of popcorn and enjoying each other's shows.

This could be good, he thought. *This could be really good.*

"Senator Chastain and Professor Chastain are both dead," Agent O'Toole announced and Britt was yanked back to the topic at hand hard enough to suffer mental whiplash.

"How'd the senator die?" Fisher asked, and Agent O'Toole cocked her head, having homed in on how Fisher didn't ask after how the professor died because he already knew.

Sharp, Britt thought admiringly. *Nothing gets by her.*

"Eliza's father called and told us about the professor, but this is the first we're hearin' of the senator," Fish explained.

"Ah." Agent O'Toole nodded. "Having the chief of staff as a father has its perks."

"Dad's worried about me," Eliza was quick to clarify. "That's why he told us about the professor. He wants me to come to D.C. so he can look after me until you get to the bottom of…" She trailed off and then shrugged helplessly. "Well, whatever this is."

"Might not be such a bad idea," Agent O'Toole allowed. "The Secret Service can probably offer you as much protection as we can. And no doubt you'd like to be with your father at a time like this."

"You suspect foul play." This from Hewitt.

The man rarely spoke. He was usually too preoccupied with whatever book he held in his hands. But when he did open his mouth, it was almost always with a definitive.

"I never discount anything." O'Toole wore a troubled look. "And given two of the three surviving witnesses to tonight's massacre ended up dead within hours of the event, we thought it better to be safe than sorry."

"*You* thought it better to be safe than sorry," her partner declared, shooting O'Toole an exasperated look. "I think they were both septuagenarians who suffered injury and trauma and their deaths were a natural consequence of those things."

Only because Britt was watching closely did he catch the flicker of irritation in the little agent's eyes. Her tone was completely professional when she told the gathered group, "My partner might be right. He probably *is* right. But I tend to get itchy when there are one too many coincidences. And Senator Chastain's untimely end was the one that did it for me."

Eliza nodded as the information set in. Then she shook her head. "But wait. How *did* the senator die?"

"Heart attack," Douglas declared. "Happened right in front of us."

Eliza frowned. "If you witnessed her death and know it was natural, why are you worried—"

"We'll know more after both bodies are autopsied," O'Toole insisted in that quintessential, no-nonsense way Britt had described earlier. "In the meantime, I want to make sure you're safe. So which would you prefer? A safe house with us?" She waggled a thumb between herself and her partner. "Or the White House with your father?"

Eliza blew out a blustery breath. "I'll tell you what I told Dad. I'm safe here." She gestured around the shop. "The place has enough security to be a supermax."

O'Toole glanced around and Britt followed her gaze, gritting his teeth when he saw the rolling Craftsman toolbox—the one that usually hid the large red button on the wall which activated the opening to the Bat Cave—had been shoved to the side. The red button was in full fucking view, and it might as well have been a blinking neon sign that said, *This opens the super-secret doorway to the tunnel that's dug under the Chicago River.*

Why would a bunch of greasy motorcycle mechanics *need* a super-secret entrance/exit to their compound?

That was a great question. One none of them were ready to answer.

He breathed a covert sigh of relief when the blond finished her perusal without seeming to focus on the button. And he was suddenly *glad* for the long hours she'd pulled because he suspected she wouldn't have missed that detail if she hadn't been running on fumes.

"You're right," O'Toole said. "This place might as well be Fort Knox." Hearing her speak his brother's name, even though she hadn't meant it that way, had Britt jumping. He covered up his reaction by coughing covertly into his closed fist. "But if you're going to stay here, my advice would be to confine yourself within the compound walls until Agent Douglas and I can figure out what's happened."

Eliza nodded and looked relieved. "I'll stay here until you tell me it's safe to leave. But, if you don't mind me asking, how long do you think that'll be?" She made a face. "Not that I'm super social as a general rule. And given everything that's happened, I certainly have no desire to be out and about. Then, of course, there's this." She pointed to her bruised and swollen face. "But are we talking days? Weeks? *Months?*"

"Hopefully it'll only be a couple of days. The coroner has promised she's moved the senator and Professor Chastain to the top of her list. We should know very soon whether they died of natural causes or…" O'Toole frowned before finishing, "Or *not.*"

"That's good news." Eliza nodded. Then she grunted like someone had punched her in the stomach.

He realized why when Peanut's head appeared above the edge of the bike lift. The cat hopped up on the tabletop and proceeded to bump his head beneath Eliza's chin while his crooked tail cut a sinuous path through the air.

"Oh, look at the pretty kitty," Agent O'Toole cooed.

"This is Peanut," Eliza announced.

Upon hearing another female voice, Peanut had looked across the lift. With a slow blink and an even slower strut—truly, the furry little fuck was putting on his best show—he made his way over to Agent O'Toole and then set about seducing her by flopping onto his side so she could pet his rotund little belly while he made biscuits in the air.

The blond agent praised him for being a good boy and a handsome boy. And, for the first time in his life, Britt found himself jealous of a cat.

"You might need to go see your optometrist," he told the pretty fed, watching her slim fingers run through the cat's fur and imagining what it would feel like for her to touch *him* like that. "Peanut is *far* from handsome. Note the notched ear, crooked tail, and battle scars from when he fancied himself a badass alley cat."

"In case no one ever told you, Sergeant Rollins, scars are *very* handsome. They give a face character." She bent down to rub her nose against Peanut's and continued in a baby voice, "Don't they, big guy? Yes, they do."

Britt had to fist his hands in his lap to keep from reaching up to trace the jagged scar that zigzagged across his temple.

Had she meant that comment for him? Or was that simply what he *wanted* to think?

"Careful," Agent Douglas said to the group. "She'll steal him away from you and add him to her menagerie." He crossed his arms and regarded his partner with a superior-looking smirk. Britt decided the tall, well-built agent had a very punchable face. "How many rescues are you up to now, O'Toole?"

When the blond sat up, Peanut chirped his disappointment. "Two dogs, one cat, and a foulmouthed African grey parrot," she admitted with a self-deprecating shrug that Britt found absolutely charming.

Despite himself, he felt his mouth pulling into a grin. "Foulmouthed?" he asked.

O'Toole rolled her eyes. "For fifteen years Gunpowder's cage was in the office of a weapons dealer. So you can imagine the language he grew up hearing. His favorite phrases are *sugar tits* and *dick breath*." Her sigh was put-upon, but he could tell by the twinkle in her eyes she secretly delighted in the humor of the situation. "My older brothers have banned my nieces and nephews from coming to my house because they claim the kids come home with curse words hot enough to blister their ears. Considering my brothers are firefighters and not known for having very clean mouths, that's saying something."

"Gunpowder? Weapons dealer?" He bit the inside of his cheek, loving that he was getting a glimpse past the badge to the woman herself. "That's a little on-the-nose, don't you think?"

"I *do* think," she agreed with a nod. "I would've gone with Long John Silver since he's grey. Or Marty McFly since he's a bird. Which are still on-the-nose, but far superior choices. But his previous owner named him Gunpowder, and who am I to come along and change it after fifteen years?"

Damnit! He liked her. Like *really* liked her.

"Anyway..." She pushed up from the table but sat down heavily again when Eliza said, "Did Senator Chastain tell you her suspicions before she died?"

Britt remained expressionless but his gaze—and every gaze in the room, for that matter—landed hard on Eliza.

Their girl Friday rubbed at her head. "She called me before she died. She told me to be careful who I trust and—" She dropped her hand to snap her fingers. "And I'm just now remembering what she said to me after I regained consciousness and found her and Professor Chastain hiding behind an overturned table."

The only thing that kept Agent O'Toole from scooting forward eagerly was the bike lift. Even still, she leaned toward Eliza while continuing to absently pet Peanut. "And what's that?"

"She said, 'John was right.'"

"Right about what?"

"I don't know." Eliza shook her head. "I didn't ask. I had to go find my phone to call help. But I have to think it means Senator McClean was right about all the people…" She shook her head and rephrased. "I mean, all the *politicians* he called out for being crooked. Do you think all of this was politically motivated? Like, was he killed to shut him up and everyone else was collateral damage?"

"We're certainly looking into anyone and everyone who might have considered themselves an…*enemy*…of the senator's," O'Toole assured her.

"But what do you think Senator Chastain meant when she told me to be careful who I trust?"

Agent O'Toole shrugged. "Either she was simply paranoid, or John McClean found out something about someone high in the government and Bethany Chastain was worried this person, whoever they are, had enough clout to do her harm and maybe you too because of your relationship to your father." She made a face of disgust. "If you want the truth, I think this whole case stinks to high heaven. And even though I haven't pinpointed where the stench is coming from, believe me, I will."

"Those aren't just fine words." This from Agent Douglas. "O'Toole is like a dog with a bone once she's on the trail of something big."

Agent O'Toole shot her partner a surprised look.

"What?" He gave her a laconic shrug. "I never said you're a bad agent. I've just always said I'm a better one."

"And that's our cue to leave you good folks to get some rest." O'Toole pushed up from her stool.

Peanut tried to entice her back by rolling onto his back and meowing at her. But she simply rubbed his potbelly one last time and complimented him again on being *such a handsome boy.*

Hands were shaken. Goodbyes were said. Two minutes later, Britt found himself escorting the feds across the grounds toward their waiting vehicle. As they made their way over the asphalt, the sounds of a waking city met their ears.

Early-morning commuter trains rumbled in the distance. Taxi cabs idled on corners, waiting for executives to come down out of their condos and hail a ride to work. And streetsweepers *hissed* and *growled* as they finished up their shifts.

It would be an hour before the sun was up. But the sky to the east was no longer as black as pitch. It had lightened to a faint, muddy-looking gray.

"So what's the red button for?"

Holy shit!

Julia O'Toole had a way of blurting out her questions that made Britt's ass clench. He had a shooting pain at the base of his spine to prove it.

To give himself time to think, he played dumb. "Pardon?"

"In the shop there's this red button on the brick wall. What's it do?"

He nearly shot a victorious fist in the air when a plausible explanation came to him. "It starts the fire mitigation system. When we're working, we use blowtorches and metal grinders and all manner of machines that employ immense amounts of heat or throw off sparks. And there's a lot of flammable shit…uh…*stuff* in the shop. There are situations where if we had to wait for smoke to set off the sprinkler system, it'd be too late and the whole building would go up."

She grunted. "Who knew building motorcycles could be so dangerous?"

He breathed a covert sigh of relief when he didn't detect any skepticism in her voice.

If being a clandestine operative teaches a guy anything, it's how to lie with a straight face.

Although, he wasn't sure that was a good thing.

"It's not chasing down bad guys, but it has its moments," he told her with a friendly wink that, in retrospect, wasn't all that friendly. More like *flirty.*

A soft blush stole into her cheeks. She tucked a stray lock of hair behind her ear and quickly turned her gaze toward the gate as it rattled open on its track.

Well…how about that?

Fisher might be the playboy amongst playboys, but Britt had been with his fair share of women—*more* than his fair share, some might say—and so he recognized the signs. The flushing skin, the nervous grooming, the inability to maintain eye contact.

Little Miss Federal Agent wasn't immune to his charms.

Now the question was, what did he want to do about that?

Nothing, he staunchly told himself. Because one, he couldn't tell her the true nature of his job, and so was there any point in starting something that would be based on a lie? And two, with his convict brother looking like he was about to dive headfirst into something undoubtedly illegal, did Britt really want to be involved with someone who carried a badge?

No. To both questions.

When they were past the gate and standing on the sidewalk next to the SUV, he offered his hand to Agent Douglas before tentatively doing the same to Agent O'Toole.

Tentatively because he was expecting another jolt of electricity.

When their hands met this time, however, all he felt was the softness of her palm, the delicateness of her fingers, and the firmness of her handshake.

"What's the eagle feather for?" she asked after dropping his hand. He curled his fingers, trying to hold on to the feel of her.

"Huh?" Her ability to switch conversational gears was truly astonishing.

She pointed to his tattoo. "You all have identical tattoos. In the hospital, I thought maybe it was a symbol of your unit or something. But I did some digging on you and your coworkers. You're all former military. But none of you served together."

Of course she did some digging. And probably ran into enough black holes to be curious.

When he and the others had signed on to Black Knights Inc. their service records had been redacted out the wazoo. Anyone looking would know the basics. But the specifics had been edited until their military resumes looked like swiss cheese.

"Boss and Becky run a sort of halfway house for former spec-ops soldiers." He waved a hand back at the three-story brick factory building.

"Boss was a SEAL, you see. And he knows how difficult it can be for guys like us to reacclimate to civilian life. BKI is sort of a soft place to land. And this?" He rolled up his sleeve to reveal the entirety of the eagle feather. "This represents strength and the dualities of life. Those of us who've made a home here get the ink to pay homage to the men we were before and to celebrate the men we are now. It's sort of a badge of honor to say, *hey we made it; we're still here.*"

For long moments she studied him as the sun grew closer to the horizon and turned the sky to the east the softest, most delicate pink. Then she offered her hand again and he didn't hesitate to shake it.

He *eagerly* shook it.

"I didn't like you when I first met you," she admitted with a teasing smirk. "But you're growing on me."

"Like a fungus," he quipped and felt regret when she dropped his hand.

She said only, "Goodbye, Sergeant Rollins."

He didn't like the finality of those words. And found himself blurting, "Odds are this isn't the last time we'll be seeing each other."

She made a face that looked slightly…*mischievous?* "Never tell me the odds."

He blinked, momentarily taken aback. Then it hit him. "Right. Han Solo. I got it this time." He tapped his temple.

"There's hope for you yet." She sent him an infectious grin before making her way around the vehicle.

He watched as she and her partner pulled down the road and told himself it was silly to be disappointed at her departure.

Manus poked his head out of the guardhouse window and, like a gunfighter, fired at him quick and from the hip. "You *like* her." The man's words found their mark.

Britt made sure to wipe the silly grin off his face as he turned back. "'Course I do." He shrugged with a nonchalance he didn't quite feel. "What's not to like? You saw her."

Manus shook his head. "To borrow one of your favorite phrases, don't piss on my boots and tell me it's raining. You *like* her like her. And not just because she's got a sweet face and a heart-shaped ass."

"Well, she's also smart and funny and trying to rid the world of criminals, so…yeah. I reckon she's pretty likable."

"Careful, brother," Manus warned. "Just because *some* feds are willing to keep their mouths shut when they find out what it is we really do here doesn't mean that *all* feds are."

The words crawled over Britt's skin like a line of ants. He wasn't offended by them. But neither were they welcome sounds in his ears.

Mostly because they were true.

CHAPTER 16

Fisher crossed his arms and leaned against the doorjamb of Eliza's bedroom as she disappeared into the bathroom. When she came back out, wearing nothing but those flimsy silk pajamas, his dick instantly went from six PM to midnight.

That's all it took now, apparently. Now that he knew what it was to hold her, to kiss her, to taste her skin on his lips and feel her heart thundering against the sweep of his tongue.

She crawled into bed and pulled the heavy covers up to her chin. He didn't know whether he wanted to sigh with relief or cry in disappointment that all that lovely, pale skin was now covered up.

Her dark eyes were captivating in the low glow of her bedside lamp as she studied him.

"What?" he asked when she'd been quiet for too long.

"Has anyone ever told you that you have a way of looking at a woman that's intoxicating? You make me feel like my face is the most fascinating thing you've ever seen." He opened his mouth to respond and tell her that her face *was* the most fascinating thing he'd ever seen. But she beat him to the punch. "And I might be fool enough to believe that except I've known you long enough to know that look—" she pointed at him "—isn't just for me."

He frowned. "Ya make it sound like I find women interchangeable."

"Don't you?" she quickly parried.

"No." He staunchly shook his head. "I know given my rather extensive datin' history that that might seem the case. But just 'cause I don't have *long* relationships that doesn't mean the ones I do have are meaningless or transposable." He frowned. "And surely ya don't count yourself amongst even those, right? What you and I have is…"

He stopped as he searched for the word.

What *was* it that they had? Chemistry, certainly. Admiration and respect and comradery and all the shared experiences of having lived and worked together for four long years. But none of that was quite what he was looking for.

He finally settled on, "*Different.* We're not two people who met at a bar. We live together. We work together. We're friends and colleagues and…" He grew more animated as he tried to adequately explain why she should *never* compare herself to the other women in his life. "And we're just *different*," he insisted with a determined jerk of his chin.

She made a face. "I guess that's something. Better than nothing."

He pushed away from the doorjamb so he could place his hands on his hips. "What's that supposed to mean?"

It kept feeling like she was trying to tell him something. But either she was being vague, or he was dumber than a stump, because no matter how hard he tried, he couldn't wrap his head around what she was alluding to.

"Nothing." She waved him off with a shooing motion.

He debated the advisability of continuing the conversation, then decided *to hell with it.*

"It's definitely *somethin'*. Earlier tonight ya said ya weren't the kind of woman to be another notch on my bedpost. And now when I tell ya that what I feel for ya as my friend and colleague is different from what I feel for the other women in my life, ya hit me with that look"—he pointed at her face—"and make a comment about that bein' better than nothin'."

She opened her mouth to respond, but he was on a roll. "So what does all that mean? 'Cause in my simple man-brain, I can't help thinkin' it means ya want somethin' from me that ya think I'm not willin' to give and—"

It was her turn to cut *him* off. "It's not that I *want* something from you. It's that I…I…" She faltered before squaring her shoulders. "It's that

I know that in a different universe, I could maybe, perhaps, perchance contemplate the possibility of starting something with you. But since we're in *this* universe, well…" She let the sentence dangle and punctuated it with a frustrated gesture.

And there it was. The truth he'd begun to suspect but hadn't dared believe might actually be a possibility. If he'd been capable of it, the agile-minded, attractive, admirable Eliza Meadows would have considered him for a partnership. A *relationship*.

It was too preposterous to fathom. Which was why the next word out of his mouth was, "Why?"

She blinked uncomprehendingly. "Why what?"

"Why would ya ever maybe, perhaps, perchance contemplate the possibility of startin' somethin' with me in *any* universe? You're educated and cultured and wealthy and beautiful. And I'm…" He threw exasperated hands in the air. "*Me.*"

Her mouth fell open as she stared at him. Then she shook her head. "We've already determined that education doesn't equal smarts. As for the culture and the wealth? Those are simply the consequences of having been raised the way I was raised."

She flattened her lips and skewered him with a look. "And you *know* you're beautiful. It's not just your charm and Southern drawl that draw women to you like moths to a flame. It's your face too." She pointed. "That movie star face that, annoyingly, only seems to be getting better with age."

He was about to feign shock and tease her about complimenting him again. *Twice in one day!* But she wasn't finished.

"Plus you're funny and you're kind and somehow, despite all the things I just listed, you're still humble. There's probably not a woman on the planet who wouldn't fall in love with you given the chance. But none of that matters, because you've made it clear you'll never give anyone a chance. So…" She shook her head in exasperation. "So *there*."

He tucked her words into a corner of his hard, stone heart. And there they stayed.

There had been plenty of times in his life when he'd wished things were different. When he'd wished *he* was different. But never more so than in that moment.

If he'd been anyone but Nash Wakefield's son, he'd have gone down on one knee and pledged his life to her. As it was, all he could do was give her the same truth he'd always given her.

"I can't be somethin' I'm not." His voice sounded rusty, like the old tools that had hung in the shed behind his parents' house. "And I can't feel somethin' I don't. The stuff they write about in the storybooks, the stuff we see here everyday between the original Knights and their partners? That stuff isn't for me."

She eyed him for a long while. Finally, she whispered, "Why? Can you at least tell me that much?"

"Just take my word for it," he assured her and stopped there even though he wanted to add, *But if I was goin' to be with anyone, if I was capable of pledgin' my life to anyone, it'd be you.* Because she was…everything. Everything that was good and beautiful and loyal and true.

He'd already said too much though.

Or…maybe he hadn't said enough.

Hellfire and damnation, she was making his head spin. It was time to change the subject. "How are ya feelin' after findin' out about the senator?"

He could tell by her expression she wasn't ready to switch topics. But she was too tired to keep bashing her head up against a brick wall, and so she shrugged.

"Sort of numb. I didn't know Bethany Chastain more than in passing. But if my dad liked her, then she must've been okay. You know, as far as politicians go."

"Speakin' of your dad. I wonder why he didn't phone ya when he heard of the senator's passin'?"

She blinked as if she found that strange too. Then she reached into her bedside table and pulled out her cell phone. The thick bedcovers slipped down to reveal her smooth, pale shoulders and her pajama top pulled toward the middle of her torso so he caught just the briefest glimpse of side-boob.

Six PM to midnight. Again.

It was becoming a problem. How was he supposed to get any work done if he was constantly slinging lumber?

After thumbing on her phone's screen, she grimaced. "He did call me." She turned the device to show him her home screen with all the alerts. "Three times. I had turned it off because I was…" She cleared her throat and shot him a shy glance from beneath her inky lashes. "Uh…otherwise occupied."

Liquid heat instantly flooded his veins.

The thought of her lying in bed touching herself or…better yet…using a toy on herself was nearly enough to make him get down on one knee and pledge to give her all she wanted, everything she could ever desire. And damn where he'd come from and *who* he'd come from and the danger that would bring them both.

Good sense won the day, however, and he simply asked with a flirtatious grin, "Anything you'd like to share?"

"Anything *you'd* like to share?" she countered.

With a self-deprecating sigh, he admitted, "You'd be disappointed."

"Why?" She cocked her head.

"Well, 'cause after holdin' ya and kissin' ya, and especially knowin' ya were next door touchin' yourself, I got off in about twelve strokes. So there's not much to talk about."

The blush that stole up her throat to stain her cheeks was the prettiest pink. When she bit her lip, it forced some color back into her mouth.

He could tell she wasn't comfortable entertaining him with tales of how she'd released her own steam. So as much as he wanted to press her, he relented and asked instead, "Ya goin' to call your pops back and tell him 'bout the feds wantin' to take ya to a safe house?"

"No." She shook her head. "He sounded exhausted. I hope he's in bed. I'll call him first thing in the morning."

"And what do ya think about Senator Chastain's death? Ya think it's nefarious or coincidence?"

"I have no idea." She pressed a finger to the temple that *wasn't* sporting a goose egg. "The only thing I know for sure is that this night is starting to blur. I feel like this entire experience is going to exist as more of an emotional scar than it will as an actual memory."

He knew about emotional scars. He had a big, honkin' one right down the center of his soul.

Which brought him back to their previous subject. "I wish I could be the kind of man ya want, Liza." His voice cracked on her name. "Not sure why that was so hard for me to say."

She smiled. And it was so sad that, had he *had* an actual heart, the damn thing would've snapped in two. "Probably the same reason it was so hard for me to hear."

He suddenly found the seam in the toes of his socks extremely interesting.

If he'd thought it had been hard to look at her and know she would never want him the way he wanted her, it was twice that hard to look at her and know she *would*. That she *could*.

If only he didn't have a cold stone for a heart.

If only there wasn't that venomous, prickly legged thing living inside him.

If only…

CHAPTER 17

Ohio House Motel, 600 N. La Salle Drive

Yang ignored the dubious stain on the carpet near the bathroom-side of the motel bed and tossed back the covers to look for bed bugs.

As far as lodgings went, he had stayed in nicer. *Much* nicer, as a matter of fact. But the squat little motel in the middle of downtown Chicago, flanked on all sides by high-rise buildings, was the only place he had found that had agreed to let him pay in cash.

He had checked in under one of his many aliases, so that was not an issue. But it was always nice not to leave a money trail behind him when he did wet work.

As good as he was, and as good as his team back home was, a credit card was always linked to a bank account. A bank account was always linked to the person or entity that opened it. And even though that person was swathed in pseudonyms and protected behind copious firewalls, a good forensic accountant matched with a good hacker could almost always find the source they were looking for.

The Americans have the saying "follow the money" for a reason.

He was relieved to find the sheets clean and the pillows fluffy. After toeing out of his shoes and placing them neatly beside the bed, he climbed atop the mattress.

The ceiling was freshly painted. He could see the roller streaks in a few places. And even though he had drawn the curtains, the sun rose to the east and its light seeped beneath the drapery to puddle on the floor.

It had been a long night. And depending on what Bishop decided to do about Eliza Meadows, it may yet prove to be a long day.

As if thinking of the man conjured him, Yang's burner buzzed in his pocket. He did not bother looking at the screen before answering. Only Bishop had the number.

Taking a page from Bishop's book, he skipped the pleasantries. "Well?" he asked.

"Hell if I know." Bishop sounded as tired as Yang felt. "My source has turned in for the night. I don't know what's happening in your neck of the woods or what, if anything, the agents on the case have to report."

"Surely after Senator Chastain's death they will be suspicious and want to move Eliza to a safe house. I can make my play when she is in transport."

"Maybe," Bishop allowed. "Or maybe they'll wait to move her until they're assured the Chastains didn't go naturally. How *did* you kill the senator, by the way?" Bishop asked.

Yang smiled. "We all have our secrets and our sources. You and I both know we live longer by not revealing them."

Bishop snorted. "Fair enough." Then he returned them to their previous subject. "My bet is the feds leave Eliza at BKI for as long as possible. They *hate* having to expend resources to house and guard witnesses. And besides, if they've been to that damned compound, they'll figure she's plenty safe there."

Yang had seen the Black Knights Incorporated property. The security was topnotch. A twenty-four-hour guard. Ten-foot-high brick walls topped by razor wire. More motion-sensor cameras than he could count. Plus… the men who worked there were armed to the teeth and trained within an inch of their lives in various and sundry ways to kill their enemies.

"Everything has a weakness," Yang assured Bishop. "Even that compound. If you ask me to find it, I will."

"I'll know more tomorrow once my source checks in," Bishop said with a weary sigh. Yang could hear the man turning on the shower. The spray through the phone sounded like rain on a tin roof. "In the meantime, I'll start working on phase two. Given the events of the night, we need to add a few more breadcrumbs to the trails that lead to Chuck Reynolds."

Bishop had determined Chuck Reynolds, the current senate minority leader, would be the obvious fall guy for the night's nefarious activities. For one thing, Reynold's was deep in the pockets of corporate lobbyists. For another thing, it'd been recently rumored he'd flown to a private island to rape an underage boy. But most importantly for *their* cause, John McClean had gotten his hands on the pièce de resistance, hard proof that Reynolds had made millions through insider trading.

Yes… if Bishop was good at anything, it was picking patsies.

Chuck Reynolds's days as a free man had been numbered the minute Bishop caught wind that John McClean might suspect Bishop for being the mole inside the federal government.

That was the *real* reason McClean had called together the night's guests. Not to share the proof he had on Reynolds, but to share his suspicions about Bishop.

Or at least that's what Bishop had told Yang. But it occurred to him he had never asked Bishop *how* he had come to know about McClean's suspicions.

Curiosity had him asking now, "How *did* you find out about tonight's gathering? Senator McClean strikes me as the kind of man who…plays his cards close to his vest, as you Americans like to say."

Yang heard his own words parroted back to him. "We all have our secrets and our sources, Yang. You and I both know we live longer by not revealing them."

With that, the line went dead.

Yang stared into the bathroom. He should probably shower as well. But sleep beckoned.

Murder was tiring work.

CHAPTER 18

There are two kinds of pain in the world. The kind that uses you, and the kind that you *use.*

It was her father's favorite saying. Eliza had never really taken it to heart until she'd woken up at noon to a throbbing head, an aching eye, and the memory of the carnage from the night before.

And then there's what happened with Fisher.

She wasn't sure if he was the cherry on top of a shitastic sundae or the only bright spot in an otherwise bleak and brutal night.

Maybe a little of both, she decided.

Because while he'd given her what she asked for, a taste of what could be, a distraction from all her grief and horror, he'd also hammered in the last nail on the coffin lid to her dreams.

Yes, despite telling herself he'd never love her the way she loved him, there'd been a part of her that had held out hope. That had thought... *maybe, someday.*

More fool me, she chastised herself now as she placed the sourdough in her favorite Dutch oven and popped on the lid.

Taking her dad's words to heart, all afternoon she'd used her pain to cross things off her to-do list. She'd called her father to bring him up-to-date on the visit from the feds while assuring him *again* that she was safer at Black Knights Inc. than anywhere else. She'd phoned Agent O'Toole to ask if she needed to come down to FBI headquarters to give an official statement, but the nice lady agent had allowed her to simply email her statement instead.

"Best if you stay inside those ten-foot walls until we determine if we need to move you," O'Toole had said. And when Eliza had asked if there was any new information on the Chastains' deaths, she'd heard the hesitation in O'Toole's voice. *"I usually don't share information about cases with witnesses, but given who your dad is, I'm sure you'll find out sooner rather than later. Especially since he was the one to actually give us this lead."*

Eliza's ears had pricked up. *"I'm listening."*

"Everyone at the party, at least all the members of congress, were working with Senator McClean on a joint committee that was investigating congressional malfeasance."

"So they were basically the congressional equivalent of Internal Affairs."

"Precisely." O'Toole hadn't been able to disguise her intrigue. Her partner had called her a dog with a bone, and it seemed, thanks to Eliza's father, she had picked up a scent.

"The question now becomes," Eliza had said, *"who were they investigating?"*

"And I'm looking into it as we speak. Can you recall any conversations you had about any government employees who weren't *at the party?"*

"I mean, that's pretty much all *that was talked about. I don't know if you've spent much time around politicians, Agent O'Toole, but they're the world's biggest gossips."*

"Anything specific spring to mind?" O'Toole had prompted and Eliza had cast her mind back to the party and the small talk she and Charlie had exchanged with others before he'd dragged her toward the back of the patio so he could propose.

"A lot of people asked about my father. There was the usual chatter about the president and her husband." The First Gentleman was a bit of a glory hound and was always appearing on the late shows and giving Washington *plenty* of material to buzz about. *"The usual chitchat about whichever recent congressional scandal was making headlines."*

"Include all of it in your statement," O'Toole had instructed.

"Will do," Eliza had assured her.

"No detail is too small," the agent had emphasized. *"No impression is too inconsequential. Once I've read it, I'll call you if I have further questions. In the meantime, stay inside the compound."*

After Eliza had gotten off the phone, she'd done inventory on the ammunition shed and had put in an order for more 5.56x45 mm NATO rounds. She'd answered the same question about Charlie a dozen times over, and her answer had always been the same. *No, she had not accepted his proposal.* Finally, she'd sat down to go through her cookbooks and pick out recipes for the next week.

Then she had started baking. And baking. And *baking*.

So far she'd used her pain to whip up two pans of banana bread—now that she knew Fisher loved it, she was determined to keep some on hand—two dozen red velvet cupcakes with homemade cream cheese frosting, one lemon tart, and she was on her second loaf of sourdough bread.

The sun had dipped below the buildings to the west. And it was way past time for everyone who no longer lived onsite to head home. But she found the kitchen full of the people she'd grown to know and love.

Boss and Becky sat at the center island taking turns feeding each other cupcakes like they were newlyweds instead of being old hats at the game. Boss looked like a giant next to his tiny wife. But Eliza had learned it was Becky who was the *real* big cheese. Her scowling, scarred behemoth of a husband was firmly wrapped around her pinky finger just like he was wrapped around the pinkie fingers of their two pigtailed girls who were currently upstairs playing pool with three of their honorary uncles: Graham, Britt, and Hewitt.

Michelle sat on the counter beside the sink with Snake standing between her spread knees. She filled him in on her day and when Eliza turned her ear that way, she caught a snippet of their conversation.

"I swear this practice was out in the middle of nowhere," Michelle said with exasperation. She was a pharmaceutical rep and spent her days visiting doctors' offices and talking about the latest wonder drugs to hit the market. "I got lost three times despite the help of my GPS. And then the universe decided I needed an additional challenge and gave me a flat tire."

"I'm sorry, babe." Snake slid his hands up his wife's linen-clad thighs and squeezed once he reached the bend in her hips. Eliza quickly turned back to her task because the gesture looked blatantly sexual. And right on cue, Snake added, "I'll make it all better once I get you home."

She didn't need to glance back to know Snake had swept Michelle's hair over her shoulder and leaned forward to kiss the woman's neck. Anytime she heard that note of innuendo in his voice—which was often—that's exactly what he did.

Ozzie and Samantha sat at the little bistro table in the corner play-arguing, which was one of their favorite pastimes. Eliza wasn't sure where the conversation had started, but she tuned-in in time to hear Samantha tell her husband, "Of course I know that. I'm not an idiot."

The look on Ozzie's face said he was prone to argue. But the way Samantha lifted a warning finger let him know that if he opened his mouth, she was liable to scratch his eyes out.

Ozzie simply leaned across the table, grabbed one of Samantha's riotous curls and let it spiral through his fingers. "Have I told you yet today just how adorable you are?" he asked with a wry grin.

Samantha told him where he could shove his charm using descriptive words that left no room for misunderstanding. But there was no heat in her voice while there *was* a definite twinkle in her eye.

As Eliza watched, Ozzie leaned forward to plant a long, lingering kiss on Samantha's lips. By the time he let the pretty investigative reporter up for air, Samantha looked breathless and dazed.

"Fine," she sighed. "You win."

"Yes!" Ozzie shot a fist in the air with enough force to have his mad-scientist hair bouncing. "Victory is its own reward!" He lowered his voice and lifted a seductive eyebrow. "But *you*, love of my life, will be the one to reap the benefits of my triumph once we get the baby to sleep tonight."

Eliza felt surrounded by love and affection. She usually drank it up. But this evening it only reminded her that *her* love would never feed her cupcakes or brush her hair back over her shoulder or tease her terribly before kissing her until her knees gave out.

Some of what she was feeling must have revealed itself in her expression because Becky reached across the large island with its soapstone countertop to pat her hand. "Hey, girl. I know intrusive thoughts when I see them. You okay?"

Becky had recently cut her long, blond hair into a flirty bob that suited her pixie face. Anyone looking at her would drop a jaw to learn she was the mother of two, because the haircut made her appear all of eighteen. But there was wisdom and understanding in her eyes as she let her gaze roam over Eliza's face.

"Yeah." Eliza nodded. "Thanks. I keep thinking if I just stay busy, I won't have time to *think*. But I forget that baking and thinking go hand-in-hand."

"It's perfectly normal to miss him even if you didn't want to marry him," Becky assured her. "I mean, you *liked* him, right? He was a good guy. So I don't blame you for replaying everything in your head. Just don't let that film roll on for too long, or it tends to get stuck in a loop."

Eliza felt like the world's biggest ass.

Of course Becky thought she was remembering Charlie and the horror of the shooting. Who *wouldn't* be remembering that?

Me, apparently, a lovesick fool and the world's biggest ass.

Embarrassed to admit the truth, she simply nodded. "Thanks. That's good advice." She glanced around the kitchen to find six sets of worried eyes fixed on her. "I know you're all hanging around because you're trying to distract me. And I appreciate it. But you have lives and kids and *bedrooms* to get back to." She pinned a meaningful look on Jake and Michelle and then transferred it to Ozzie and Samantha. Samantha had the good grace to blush. "Please go about your evenings. That's what's going to help me the most, I think. I just need everyone to keep on keeping on as usual and—"

Sam interrupted her when he walked into the room carrying Ozzie and Samantha's baby girl like one might carry an active grenade.

"She needs a diaper change." He quickly handed the baby off to Ozzie. "I'll do feedings and clean up puke. But when it comes to poopy diapers, I'm out."

"Coward," Ozzie accused.

Sam was unfazed. "Say what you will. But I'd rather face an armed assailant than a Pampers full of soft serve. And if the sounds that just came outta her are any indication, that's what's waiting for you." He gestured toward little Sophia Marie's bulging diaper with an offended curl of his upper lip.

The pitter-patter of little feet heralded the arrival of Charlotte and Hazel, Boss and Becky's two girls. And quick on their heels marched Britt, Hewitt, and Graham. Then Franklin and JJ, Snake and Michelle's two boys, pushed through the back door. Both of them wore baseball mitts.

Fisher sauntered in behind them, tossing a baseball in the air before easily catching it.

Just like that, the kitchen went from full to packed-to-the-gills.

The moment Fisher stopped by the back door to chuck the baseball in the cubby they kept for just such things, her mind flew back to the night before. To the way he'd kissed her. To the way he'd held her. To the way he'd told her under no circumstances would he ever love her the way she loved him.

They'd barely spoken two words to each other all day. Which, if she was being honest, was her doing.

She'd been avoiding him.

Or, rather, she'd been keeping herself so busy she hadn't afforded him any opportunity to talk to her. What was left to say? They'd said it all the night before.

Her lips burned from where she'd been biting them all afternoon. Her pulse thumped so hard it hurt. But she managed to offer him a small smile and a subtle nod when his gaze found hers.

It was the only olive branch she had to give. And she hoped he understood that just because he wasn't capable of giving her what she wanted, she wasn't upset with him. Sad? Sure. But not upset. *Never* upset.

How could I be mad at him when he's always told me the truth?

His chin dipped in response to her smile, but the rest of him was as still and as imposing as a mountain.

Good grief, why does he have to look so good?

His too-long hair was windblown from playing catch. His cheeks were tinged pink from the July heat. And the tan skin of his neck glistened with the faintest sheen of sweat.

All around her there was noise. The baby had started fussing. The two little girls were squealing and clapping their hands as their parents split a cupcake between them.

Hewitt and Sam were giving each other a hard time. "There are two things I don't like about you, Hew, and both are your face," Sam said.

To which Hewitt replied, "Oh, cry me a river, why doncha? And then go drown yourself in it."

Snake and Michelle were loading pieces of the lemon tart into Tupperware to take home with them while arguing with their boys about saving the dessert for tomorrow because, as Michelle was quick to point out, "You've both already had three slices each." And Peanut had followed the hoard into the kitchen and now wound himself around Eliza's ankles, meowing pitifully and begging her to drop a morsel of something, *anything*, onto the floor.

She barely registered any of it.

It was background noise. Unfocused. Seemingly far away. Every cell in her body was attuned to Fisher and the way his lips twisted into a wry smile at the chaos that was the kitchen.

She held her breath as he sauntered in her direction. It shuddered out of her when he slipped an arm around her shoulders.

The warmth and weight of his arm made everything better. Or worse?

She couldn't decide.

One thing she knew was that when he murmured her name or, rather, the nickname that sounded so right in his mouth, she was lost.

Lost in the gold glinting in his eyes. Lost in the way his expression held equal parts hunger and kindness—he wanted her, but mostly he wanted her to be happy. Lost in the way his hot skin smelled of sunshine and clean, healthy sweat, and just a hint of that smoky aftershave.

He gestured around the packed kitchen. "If ya ever needed proof of how much you're loved, it's all right here."

Every emotion she'd been keeping in, all the grief and guilt and loss, rose to the surface and there was no holding back the tears that filled her eyes.

He didn't hesitate to pull her into a hug. And she clung to him as what felt like the weight of the world, and certainly the weight of her wounded heart, bore down on her.

"I know." He whispered close to her ear. "You've been goin' ninety-to-nothin' all day. But now it's time to stop runnin' 'round like a chicken with your head cut off and feel all the things that need feelin'."

*Damnit! Why did he have to be so…*amazing?

Instead of stopping her tears, his words made them fall faster.

She wasn't sure how long they stood there like that, him holding her together even as she fell apart. By the time her tears were reduced to soft sniffles and she pushed out of his arms to grab a tea towel and wipe her runny nose, the kitchen had cleared out.

That was *another* way everyone at BKI showed her they loved her.

Because she'd said she wanted them to go about their evenings, and they'd taken her at her word.

They hadn't fawned or fussed. They'd seen she'd reached her wits end and they'd quietly and respectfully left her to it. Or, rather, they'd left Fisher to hold her through it.

She wasn't sure what family was supposed to look like. She'd been so young when her mother died, and her father had always felt more like a benevolent ruler than a relative. But if family was supposed to look like people who respected and supported you through thick and thin, who loved you and laughed with you through the good and bad, then what she'd found at Black Knights Inc. was family with a capital F.

"Who knew the easiest way to clear out a room was to burst into tears?" she said with a watery laugh as she continued to mop up her face. The swelling near her temple had disappeared. But the structures beneath were still sore. She was reminded of that when she got too aggressive with the tea towel and hissed.

"Have ya tried puttin' arnica on it?" Fisher asked.

"What?" She frowned at him.

"Arnica gel?" He cocked his head. "No one's ever told ya 'bout arnica gel?"

She shook her head, and he crossed the kitchen to rummage through the cabinet where they kept the Band-Aids, pain relievers, Icy Hot, and all the other things used by men whose jobs required them to put their bodies through the ringer on a regular basis.

After he found what he was looking for, he rounded the island and patted a barstool. "C'mere. Hop on up."

Her legs were a little wobbly—and Peanut's continued figure-eights around her ankles didn't help—but she did as instructed. The big tomcat hopped onto her lap and started making biscuits on her thighs as soon as she was situated atop the stool. She absently scratched between his eyes as she watched Fisher uncap the tube and squeeze onto his fingertip a good dollop of clear gel.

It didn't look like much. But it felt divine when he gently spread the gel over her injuries. He started with the bruise on her cheek—the thing had turned blueish in the center and sickly yellowish around the edges—before moving on to the sore spot near her temple.

The arnica was cool and smooth. But it was mostly the tenderness of his touch that brought relief.

"God, that feels good," she breathed.

"Mmm." He nodded, going back to add more gel atop her bruised cheek. "When you've spent the last fifteen years gettin' bruises, breakin' bones, and bein' shot, ya tend to learn all the tricks for takin' away the pain."

She'd seen him without his shirt plenty of times—the Black Knights weren't a bashful or a modest bunch. She knew about the puckered scar on his left shoulder.

Bullet wound, she'd guessed the first time she'd seen it.

He wasn't the only one to sport such a souvenir. *Most* of the Knights wore scars as easily as they wore their biker boots. And it was kind of an unspoken rule that they didn't talk about them.

Except…he'd piqued her curiosity. And she needed *something* to focus on other than his nearness. Other than his body heat that reached out to wrap around her.

"How many times *have* you been shot?" She winced and pulled out one of Peanut's claws when the cat got a little too zealous with the biscuits.

"Three."

"He said as if it's no big deal." She shook her head in disbelief.

"Comes with the job." He recapped the tube.

She couldn't decide if she was disappointed or relieved when he stepped back to study his handywork.

"The one on your left shoulder and…?" She let her question dangle.

"Right thigh." He sat on the stool next to her and patted the outer edge of his denim-clad leg. "And groin." He grimaced. "Two inches to the right and that one would've turned me from a bull into a steer."

She shuddered at the thought of all that pain. And despite having made a concerted effort *not* to think about it, the picture of Charlie's riddled body bloomed to life inside her head.

"Does it hurt?" she asked quietly and then made a face of self-disgust. "Sorry. That was a dumb question. Of *course* it hurts."

When tears threatened again, she looked up at the punched tin ceiling tiles. She'd always loved the kitchen at Black Knights Inc. It was huge and industrial, but the brick walls and the tin ceiling lent architectural interest and warmth.

"I was thinking about Charlie," she admitted hoarsely. "About how much he must've suffered."

"Honestly, for me the pain didn't come until later. In the moment it was more of a shock. I felt the impact and a sort of *burn*. But it wasn't excrutiatin' or anything. I'd bet, given what you've told me 'bout McClean and how many rounds he took, he didn't feel much of anything. The poor bastard was probably dead before the pain could set in."

I hope so, she wished silently.

Aloud she said, "Thank you, Fish. There's comfort in that." Then she looked around at the empty kitchen and the countertops strewn with dirty measuring cups, sticky mixing bowls, and the occasional dusting of flour.

She'd felt what needed feeling, as Fisher had said. It was time to get busy again. "Welp." She nodded firmly. "Guess I should clean up."

When she scooted Peanut off her lap, he meowed his dissatisfaction. But before she could stand, Fisher stopped her with a hand on her arm. "Why don't ya let me do that. You head upstairs and run yourself a bath."

She shook her head. "I need to bake that last loaf of sourdough and—"

"I got ya."

She lifted a dubious eyebrow. "In what world? You can't boil an egg without it turning into a rubber ball."

"But sourdough is easy. Ya bake it at 450 degrees for twenty-five minutes with the lid on. Then ya take the lid off and bake it for an additional fifteen minutes. And once ya take it out, ya set it on the coolin' rack." He pointed to where her first golden loaf of sourdough sat.

She blinked like he'd just revealed himself to be an alien wearing a Fisher skin suit. "How in the *world* do you know all that?"

"I've watched ya bake a hundred loaves of the stuff over the years. Reckon I learned through osmosis."

"You never cease to amaze me." She shook her head.

His expression was teasing. "I'm goin' to take that as a compliment." Then he stood and grabbed her hand to pull her up next to him. "Now, go on upstairs and hop in a bath."

A long, luxurious soak in a tub full of fragrant bubbles did sound wonderful. She'd been moving since the moment she woke up. But now that she'd stopped, she could feel the stiffness in her joints and the soreness in her muscles.

"Yes, sir. Sargeant Major, sir." She offered him a mock salute.

"Sassy." He smacked her ass when she turned to leave.

She jumped at the shock of it. He looked just as shocked when she slowly glanced over her shoulder.

"Hellfire and damnation." He shook his head. "I'm so sorry. I don't know where that came from. It just happened sort of automatically. But I never should've—"

"It's okay, Fish. What's a little ass-grabbing between friends?"

He still appeared apoplectic. But her words had his expression softening. "I'd be mighty honored if ya thought of me as a friend, Liza. Mighty honored, indeed."

She wasn't sure what came over her then. And later she'd want to kick her own ass for the words that tumbled out of her mouth. But blame it on grief or guilt or stress or…freaking PTSD, but in that moment she didn't give a rat's ass about continuing to disguise her feelings. "That's all you'll allow us to be. Right, Fish? So friends it is."

For the span of a few thundering heartbeats he stood there silently, his gaze searching hers. Then he said the most beautiful and heartbreaking words she'd ever heard. "I love ya too much not to love ya enough, Liza."

CHAPTER 19

Britt had seen Eliza walk by the television room headed for her bedroom nearly an hour earlier. He'd expected Fisher to find his way upstairs and had been all prepared to give his best friend a hard time for, you know, being all twitterpated and smitten. Annoyingly, though, Fisher had remained glaringly absent.

Since Britt couldn't stand to see his good material go to waste, he made his way downstairs in search of his quarry.

Should I start with a joke about how he can't stop staring at Eliza like she is an angel fallen straight from heaven? Or should I lead in by teasing him about how he'd been like a teenager debating whether he should throw his arm around his date at the movie theater when Eliza had started to break down in front of the feds last night?

The latter, he decided when he landed on the second floor and glanced expectantly around The War Room.

A forgotten mug sat on the conference table, its contents having gone cold hours before. Screen savers dipped and swirled on the various monitors, giving the space a club vibe—all that was missing was the *ootz-ootz* sound of a DJ spinning tracks and people waving around glow sticks. Peanut was curled in the cushioned rolling chair Ozzie preferred when he was balls-deep in the dark web. But...no Fisher.

On to the shop.

Britt made his way down to the first floor. Someone had switched off the large overhead lights. So it was only the ambient glow from upstairs that allowed him to see the row of custom choppers and the dull glint of the bike lifts topped with motorcycles in varying degrees of completion. Again…no Fisher.

Which meant his brother-from-another-mother was likely either in the outbuilding that held their gym equipment or in the kitchen making a mess of something that, to most, would seem impossible to screw up.

His nose told him it was the latter. He followed the acrid smell of smoke.

Stopping in the kitchen doorway, he saw Fisher standing over the sink. The former Delta Force Sergeant Major's hands were braced on the counter on either side of the deep bowl and his head hung between his broad shoulders in defeat.

"Why are you cooking when Eliza spent all day baking?" he asked as he made his way around the kitchen island. Once he stopped beside Fisher, he glanced down into the bottom of the sink at what looked to be a charbroiled football. Shaking his head, he sighed sadly. "Aw, man. You're the reason we can't have nice things."

Fisher's expression was miserable. "In my defense, I was left unsupervised."

Chuckling, Britt clapped a hand on Fisher's shoulder. "Well, then it's Eliza's fault for thinking just because you can install a V-twin engine, disassemble your primary weapon with your eyes closed, and recon a target space with a precision that still boggles my mind that you'd be able to accurately utilize the trickiest of manmade machines. That thing known as an oven."

"I did everything I was supposed to do." Fish gestured to the smoldering lump of blackened bread. "I don't get it." Glancing at Britt, he pulled a face. "She'll never let me hear the end of it if she finds it in the trash tomorrow. Reckon I better go throw it over the back wall and let the geese in the river have at it."

Britt picked up a fork and tapped the burned loaf. It was as hard as a rock and made a strangely hollow sound against the tines.

"That's a terrible idea. Instead of finding a blackened loaf of bread in the trash, she'll find a bunch of dead geese."

"Oh, ha ha." Fish snatched the fork from him. "It's not that bad. And surely it'll soften up once it's in the river." He tried stabbing the loaf but the fork just bounced off. Fish immediately changed his tune. "Maybe you're right. So then what do ya reckon I should do with it?"

"Send it into space where it can join the other objects orbiting Neptune in the Kuiper Belt."

Fisher scowled. "Is everything a joke to ya?"

"Only the funny stuff." Britt grinned. Then he forced a serious expression because Fish really did look wretched. "Maybe if we put it in the little garden by the back wall it'll blend in with the other landscape rocks and no one will be the wiser."

"Won't it start to rot and give itself away?"

"It's already been petrified. I think that means it's safe from rot."

Fisher cocked his head as if he saw the merit in the suggestion.

Britt used his best friend's distraction to get in his first dig. "While you think on that, how's about you tell me what's going on between you and Eliza. Because I swear, every time I've looked at you today, I've seen little hearts and flowers floating above your head. And I can't help wondering if the reason she wasn't quick to take McClean up on his proposal was because she's carrying a torch for you."

Fisher turned around so he could lean back against the countertop. "I had nothing to do with that last part. As for the hearts and flowers? Either you've been hallucinatin' or you're in desperate need of a trip to the optometrist. Ya *know* I'm allergic to romantic relationships."

"There's a first time for everything."

He closely watched his friend's face, expecting Fisher to continue to play it off. He was a little taken aback when, instead, Fish shook his head. "She's too good for me."

"Bullshit." Britt waved away the idea. "You're one of the best humans I know. Eliza would be lucky to have you."

Fisher's mouth twisted. "Thanks. But you're biased because I saved your life. *Twice.*"

Britt ignored that. "You really believe just because she grew up with heaps of money that she's somehow better than you?"

Cursing under his breath, Fish turned back to the sink and gripped the edge of the porcelain hard enough to make his knuckles go white.

Britt had been all prepared to pester and provoke, but he was getting the distinct impression that the situation between Fisher and Eliza was more complicated than he'd imagined.

"It's not just that she grew up spending summers in Europe and I grew up spending summers catching catfish on trotlines."

Britt waited for Fish to expand on that statement. He never did, which forced Britt to say, "O*kay.* So what else is there?"

"I'm not made to settle down with one woman."

Britt frowned. Fisher was a good-looking guy. He was wickedly funny, sharp as a tack, and wasn't embarrassed to quote poetry to women like some hero in a historical novel. So *of course* he'd had his choice of bed partners over the years. But Britt had always assumed Fisher's rather… *expansive*…dating profile was a temporary thing.

If anyone would make a good husband and father, it was Fish. The guy had more patience than Job, more compassion than Princess Diana, and more loyalty than a family dog.

"You mean to tell me that whole ladies' man schtick is legit? I guess I always figured you were biding your time and sowing your wild oats until you found the right one."

Fisher glanced over at him. "Is that what *you're* doin'?"

He blinked when he realized he'd never given it much thought.

"We aren't the same, Fish," he said. "You *like* it when we have downtime, and you get to hang around and be all domestic. I feel like I'm going to crawl out of my skin. You carry around babies as easily as I carry around rock climbing equipment. You joined the military because you *had* to. I joined because it was the only way I could get paid to jump out of planes and blow shit up."

The look on Fisher's face was forlorn and maybe just a little…wistful. "Believe me, bro, I wish that's all it took. But when it comes to a man having what it takes to be a good husband and father, it's more complicated than that."

"And you're convinced you don't have what it takes?"

"I *know* I don't. I don't know how to love the right way."

Britt narrowed his eyes. "And which way is that?"

"The calm, quiet, *healthy* way."

Britt's chin jerked back. "You're saying you only know how to love the violent, loud, *toxic* way?"

"Pretty much." Fisher shrugged.

"Bro, that's complete and total bullshit."

Fisher walked over to the liquor cabinet beside the back door. He opened the glass front and pulled down a bottle of bourbon from the top shelf. "How d'ya feel 'bout helpin' me drink this thing to the corners?" he asked.

Britt wanted to press the issue. But one look at Fisher's face told him it'd be a useless endeavor. Whatever fool notion Fisher had in his head wasn't going to be dislodged no matter *what* Britt said.

With a windy sigh, he muttered, "I feel like you're putting a period on *another* conversation. And once again I feel like arguing with you will get me nowhere and drinking with you will get me drunk. So…" He circled a finger in the air. "Get to pouring."

Fisher pulled two whiskey glasses down from the cabinet and dumped two fingers worth of the sweet, smoky bourbon into each. The overhead light glinted in the caramel color of the liquid, making it glow with warm streaks of gold.

"What are we drinking to?" Britt lifted the glass.

Fisher paused with his own glass raised. "How 'bout we drink to ya continuin' to find excitement and adventure wherever ya turn while I continue to whore my way through life until my cock stops workin'?"

Britt shook his head. "I guess that's as good as anything."

After they clinked glasses, Fisher braced himself against the countertop with one hand and threw back the glass of bourbon with the other, swallowing it like it was medicine.

In contrast, Britt took a slow sip, savoring the sweeter notes of butterscotch and custard before the *zing* of alcohol hit his palate.

To excitement and adventure, he thought and then immediately shoved away the image of Agent Julia O'Toole when it formed in his mind's eye.

CHAPTER 20

Eliza held the ring Charlie had given her up to the lamplight and appreciated the way the diamond sparkled with white fire.

She couldn't begin to guess what the thing had cost. But it was surely plenty. And if she'd needed another reason why she and Charlie had only been a good match on paper and not in person, it was the stone staring back at her.

She'd never been one to wear flashy jewelry. For one, she thought it was a classless show of wealth. For two, she viewed the entire diamond market with a jaundiced eye and was quite vocal about her beliefs.

Even if a person could be assured the stone they purchased wasn't a blood diamond, mined off the backs of the poor and desperate to finance regime change, insurgency, and genocide, then they still had to contend with the idea that the value of the gem was a construct.

De Beers held a monopoly on the market and hoarded their stash of the world's rough-cut diamonds to artificially create a shortage and push the idea that diamonds were rare and therefore expensive.

Yes. She definitely didn't believe diamonds were a girl's best friend despite what the ineffable Marilyn Monroe once sang. And she and Charlie had discussed this at length one evening over lobster bisque and crab legs.

So...either he'd forgotten their conversation, or he'd assumed it had simply been an intellectual exercise and not a personal belief she actually put into practice.

She sighed as she turned the ring again and watched the light reflect on the facets of the stone. *What the hell should I do with this now?*

She certainly couldn't keep it. It had never really been hers.

So, what? Donate it to one of his charities? Start a scholarship fund in his name at his alma mater? Sponsor some refugees from Nigeria where Charlie had spent so much time volunteering after the floods in 2018?

She would have to think about it and hope his memory would steer her in the right direction. But she was too emotionally wrung out for such an exercise tonight.

Fisher had been right. The hot bubble bath had worked wonders on her sore muscles and aching bones. But the soft, steamy water hadn't been able to touch the ache in her heart.

Good people had died in front of her eyes. People who, if Agent O'Toole was right, had been working to expose corruption within their own ranks. *Charlie* had died saving her. And then there was Fisher who loved her too much not to love her enough.

She rubbed at the pain behind her breastbone.

She knew grief. She'd been touched by it when she'd been far too young. And it felt the same now as it had back then. Like a canker on her heart. A sore spot that she could sometimes forget about and then *wham!* The pain would catch her unawares and she had to fight not to let it drag her to her knees.

She took a deep breath, forced her diaphragm to expand, and then let it out slowly.

Nope. Still there. Still feels like someone has stuck a hot poker through my aorta and—

The hard rap of knuckles on her door had her jumping. After gathering her wits, she carefully placed the ring back inside her nightstand, cinched her robe tight, and made sure the terry cloth covered her bare thighs.

"Come in," she called. Or at least she *tried*. The lump in her throat meant the words were barely a whisper. She cleared her voice and tried again. "Come in!"

The door opened and...*cue the butterflies.*

Fisher stood on the threshold and the hallway light haloed him in a golden glow. His grin was slightly provocative when he asked, "How was your bath?"

"Fine." She narrowed her eyes, trying to pinpoint what was off about him. Then she caught the faintest whiff of burned bread. "How'd the sourdough come out?" she asked with feigned innocence.

His grin slipped off his face. "I swear I did everything right. I think the cookin' gods have cursed me."

She snorted. "Given all the other ways you've been blessed, that's probably only fair. No one should be good at *everything*."

"Name one thing *you're* not good at," he challenged.

I'm terrible at not loving you.

She turned to stare briefly out the large window as she thought of an answer she could share aloud. There were no storm clouds to block out the stars tonight. And the sickle moon cut its white slice out of the black sky.

"I failed spectacularly at that pottery class I took last year," she finally admitted. "The walls on my bowls were always uneven. I have a terrible sense of direction. If I have to drive more than ten miles, I almost inevitably get lost. And I can't whistle to save me life."

To prove her point, she pursed her lips and winced when the air she pushed through her mouth sounded like a deflating rubber balloon.

He grabbed the casing above the door with both hands and leaned forward. As always, the move caused his shirt to ride up and reveal the trail of curly brown hair that started at his navel and disappeared into the frayed waistband of his jeans.

Desire bloomed at her center like a hot flower.

"Oh, yes." The light in his eyes turned teasing. "I stand corrected. Not sure how you've made it this far in life without bein' able to *whistle*."

Since she couldn't erect a physical barrier between them—after all, they lived and worked together—she decided she had to get good at erecting emotional barriers.

There's no time like the present.

"Is there something you needed, Fish?"

"Just reckoned I should check in on ya." He dropped his arms and stepped into the room. To her astonishment, he flopped down on the bed with his hands laced behind his head. As he stared at the ceiling, he added,

"Ya know, just in case ya needed someone to keep ya company until ya fell asleep. Like last night."

Former Eliza would've jumped at the opportunity to spend another evening held in his arms.

"I think the worst of the shock has passed," she assured him, proud that Current Eliza was able to ignore the temptation. "I'll be okay on my own."

"Ya sure?" He wiggled his eyebrows. "I'd be happy to offer a little more… *distraction.*"

She'd been sitting on the edge of the bed watching him over her shoulder, but that had her turning so she could fully face him. The flush on his cheeks, the overbright shine of his eyes, and the way his drawl seemed more pronounced had a lightbulb blazing to life above her head.

"Say *she sells seashells by the seashore,*" she demanded.

"What?" His dark eyebrows pinched together. "Why?"

"Humor me."

He shrugged indifferently. "She shells she shells by the she shore." He frowned and tried again. "She shells she shells by the she shore." Shaking his head he asked, "Was that right?"

"No." She pointed to his nose. "Are you drunk?"

He grinned impishly and held his thumb and his forefinger an inch apart. "Just enough to take the edge off."

"Take the edge off *what?*"

"Off knowin' I could have ya if I weren't me and you weren't you."

That canker on her heart was burning again. "Fish, we've been through all this. I guarantee the subject isn't going to improve with repetition."

"Hear me out." He lifted a finger in the air. She'd always loved how long and knobby-knuckled his fingers were. "The way I figure it, we've been lookin' at this thing all wrong."

"Have we?"

"Yeah." He nodded. "But the bourbon cleared my head."

"Mmm." She barely refrained from rolling her eyes. "Because that's usually how bourbon works."

"No, seriously. It gave me an epifoamy." He frowned and corrected. "I mean an epiphany. Hear me out."

She opened her mouth to tell him that nothing good ever came out of a bottle of bourbon, but he plowed ahead.

"See, ya don't want to be just another notch on my bedpost 'cause you're not a one-night stand kinda gal. And I can't give ya the great, big BKI love you're lookin' for. But there's something we haven't considered."

"Oh…kay," she allowed hesitantly.

"Friends with benefits." His grin was awash with self-satisfaction. "It's the perfect middle ground."

"Is it?" she challenged.

"Think about it. You'll have a ready and willin' bed partner while ya hunt for Mr. Right. And I'll get to scratch this itch that's been plaguin' me for four years."

Irritation had heat creeping up her throat to flame in her face. "From a notch on a bedpost to an itch that needs to be scratched. Wow, Fish. Way to make a woman feel *real* special."

He shook his head. "Maybe I didn't explain it right."

"Oh, I think you explained it just fine. And after much consideration"—the derision dripping off her lips was so thick, she was surprised she couldn't see it—"my answer is no."

"But why?" His expression was as petulant as his tone. "It's the perfect solution."

"It's not," she countered. "Because friends with benefits only works when neither party is…"

She stopped herself on a dime. She'd almost said *when neither party is in love with the other.*

Pressing a hand to her temple, she insisted instead, "It would be a mistake, Fish. Our situation, living and working together, would make it too complicated."

"What's life without a few mistakes, huh?" His grin was infectious. "If ya went back and erased all the mistakes you'd ever made, you'd be erasin' yourself. And yourself is pretty great if I do say so myself."

"Fisher—"

"If Britt has taught me anything," he cut her off, "it's that life is about takin' risks. Otherwise, it's just a string of mundane Mondays."

The more he talked, the more she wanted to say *to hell with it* and give in. He was just so tempting lying there with his thighs bulging against the denim of his jeans, with his pectoral muscles forming two near-perfect squares against the cotton of his T-shirt, with his beautiful mouth pursed into a moue of seduction.

Luckily, she was able to hold on to her good sense.

Unluckily, it was by a mere thread.

"I'm not sure you should be taking life lessons from the King of Carefree," she told him with a frown.

"Hey! No disparagin' my bestie."

She usually found drunks annoying. But Fisher just got more charming. All that golden retriever energy was multiplied ten-fold.

Or, the little voice that lived at the back of her head proposed, *you're just so smitten with him that you think everything he does is amazing.*

Gah. Seriously, sometimes that voice was a pain in the ass.

"Come on," he cajoled. "Let me help ya forget all your trials and troubles and tribilay…tribuh…" He blinked. "Tri-bew-lay-shuns."

"Oh, is *that* what this is all about?" She chuckled and shook her head. "You're doing me a favor?"

He grinned self-deprecatingly. "I should probably confess to finer feelings of friendship and compassion. But the truth is I've wanted to get ya naked since the second I clapped eyes on ya."

Later, she wouldn't be able to believe she'd done it. She'd never had a violent streak. Even as a little girl she'd always agreed to whatever game her friends wanted to play, avoiding any sort of controversy. But she flew across the mattress and pushed him off the side of the bed.

He hit the floorboards with a loud *thud*. And his hair was as wild as Ozzie's when his head poked over the side of the mattress once he sat up.

"For tit's sake." He scowled and moved his mouth like his lips weren't cooperating. "I mean, for *shit's* sake. Ya could've just said, *thanks but no thanks, Fish.* Ya didn't have to resort to violence."

"Blame it on the concussion."

"Oh, *now* you're goin' to use that as an excuse?"

She shrugged and watched him shove to an unsteady stand. He wiped imaginary dust off the seat of his jeans. "I take it that's a *no* to the friends with benefits idea?"

"Thanks but no thanks, Fish." Her tone was sugary sweet.

He sighed heavily. "Can't blame a guy for tryin' though, right?"

"Can't blame a guy for trying," she assured him, pasting on a soft grin to hide the grimace that threatened.

He suddenly looked far more sober. "We good? I mean, is there anything I can do or say to make things okay between us? 'Cause even without the benefits part, I'd still like it if we could have the friends part."

Why? Why does he have to be so damned wonderful?

"I think you said everything that needs saying, Fish." If her voice was a little hoarse, she hoped it wasn't enough for him to notice as he headed for the door.

Turning at the threshold, he proved that when it came to saying things that were as beautiful as they were awful, he was a champ. "Just so ya know, if it were possible for me to have a great, big BKI love, it would be with you."

He shrugged sadly before stepping into the hallway and softly closing the door behind him.

Five minutes later, she'd managed to crawl under the covers. The sound of his harmonica drifted softly through the brick wall. He played Nina Simone's "Wild is the Wind." And the sad sound of the tune perfectly matched the sorrow in her heart.

CHAPTER 21

Even in a metropolis as large as Chicago, there were corners of silence and solitude. Little enclaves of serenity that could make a person forget the city and its surrounding suburbs held more people than the states of Oklahoma, Kansas, Nebraska, South Dakota, and North Dakota combined.

The BKI compound on Goose Island was one such place. At five o'clock in the morning, silence cloaked the street that ran past the front of the property. The absolute stillness of nighttime slowly making way for the bustle of day was exquisite.

Not a horn or a siren could be heard. No tour buses or water taxis buzzed by with guides shouting through loudspeakers about the history of the city. The songbirds still slept. And the noisy, honking Canada geese that lived on the river were tucked away in their roosts.

Julia O'Toole was a city girl through and through. She was used to the clamor and the chaos. But she couldn't deny the peace she felt when she stumbled upon a pocket of tranquility.

Her window was rolled down and she breathed in the early morning air. Later, the entire city would be filled with the scents of hot concrete and acrid car exhaust. But right now, all she could smell was the cool wetness of Lake Michigan and the doughy, yeasty aroma coming from the bagel shop across the way.

Her stomach growled, but she ignored it to look at her reflection in the rearview mirror. Her hair was neatly pulled back in a slick ponytail and she'd donned her favorite gray pantsuit just in case she was forced to face reporters.

Her eyes were clear and bright. Her skin? Not so much. She had a zit brewing beneath the surface on the left side of her chin. But that was par for the course. Even at thirty-three years old, anytime she found herself under the gun she developed a raging case of adult acne.

She should be tired. She'd only managed a handful of hours of sleep since being assigned this case. But the adrenaline that had poured into her veins when the coroner called had burned away any fatigue.

She glanced over at Dillan. "You ready for this?"

"*No.*" He grimaced. "Babysitting a witness in a safe house is the worst part of this job. Why don't *you* do it and I'll be the one to work the case? You could use the girl-time anyway, right?"

She bared her teeth in a parody of a smile. "Careful, Dillan. Your misogyny is showing. Also, since I'm the lead agent"—his self-satisfied smirk faltered—"I get the privilege of picking my poison. And my poison is seeing this thing through until the end."

"We could call in someone," he cajoled. "It doesn't *have* to be me."

"But it *does*. Because whoever's behind this has a long reach. The fewer people who know where we're keeping Miss Meadows, the better. And by *few*, I mean you, me, and the director. Capeesh?"

He blew out a breath so blustery it caused his lips to flap.

Petulant. What is it about overgrown men and petulance?

She had pushed out of the vehicle and made her way around the hood by the time Dillan finally emerged from the passenger side. Still looking petulant.

The guard who had been on duty the night before was the same one on duty this morning. And he looked no happier to see them now than he had then.

Good grief! Is it my lot in life to be surrounded by sour-faced men?

"You're back," he said after he'd pulled open the little window on the side of the guardhouse.

"We are, indeed." She tried to win him over with a smile. It didn't work. He continued to scowl at her. "I know it's early, but we're here to see Miss Meadows."

The guy wanted to tell them to come back at a decent hour. The message was written across his freckled face as clearly as an assignment on a chalkboard. But he bit his tongue and made a phone call instead.

There was real regret in his voice when he said, "Sorry to bother you this early, Eliza. But those two FBI agents are back and asking to see you."

Julia couldn't hear what Miss Meadows said. It must've been an affirmative, because a second later the guard hit the button for the gate and the big wrought iron structure rattled open.

"She's gonna throw on some clothes. So you might be waiting by the front door for a minute or two," the ginger giant told them as he waved for them to enter the compound.

They quickly made their way across the blacktop expanse. But instead of having to wait for Miss Meadows to let them in, the door opened when they got within ten feet of it.

Ol' Blue Eyes stood on the threshold wearing another superhero T-shirt—this one had Thor printed on it. There was a steaming mug of coffee in his hand. And his Southern accent reached out like tickling fingers when he said, "You're back."

She quickly responded, "And once again you're awake at this ungodly hour. Do you *ever* sleep?"

He crossed his ankles as he leaned against the doorjamb. He was barefoot, and she noted as an aside that he had really nice feet. Pretty nail beds, high arches and, unlike a lot of guys, not too hairy.

Come off it, Jules, she admonished herself. *His feet? Seriously?*

"If I'm being honest, the answer to that is rarely."

"Huh?" She blinked at him as she dragged her eyes from his bare toes back to his face.

He lifted one dark, slashing eyebrow. "Sleep."

"Oh." She nodded. "Right." Then, feeling annoyingly discombobulated, she forced herself to get down to brass tacks. "We're here to talk with Miss Meadows. Your man out front phoned her and said she's headed down."

"Copy that." Sergeant Rollins held the door wide. "In the meantime, could I interest you folks in a cup of coffee?"

The smell coming from his mug was strong enough to burn her nose. Which had her answering eagerly. "Thank you. I'd appreciate that."

She'd been in too much of a hurry to pick up Dillan and get to Black

Knights Inc. to stop by a Peet's for a much-needed kick of caffeine. And now she gladly followed the former Army Ranger as he turned left instead of right after they entered the old factory building.

The row of custom motorcycles gleamed as brightly as she remembered. And she caught Dillan ogling the bikes with the same look of lust he usually reserved for leggy redheads. But it was Rollins's ass in his faded Levi's that held *her* attention.

Britt Rollins wasn't tall and lean like Fisher Wakefield, or huge and jacked like their coworker, Graham Coleburn. But he had a *very* nice body all the same. Broad shoulders. Lean hips. Enough muscle to make a woman take a second look but not so much to make her wonder if steroids had shrunk his testicles to the size of walnuts.

Yes, the more she was around Britt Rollins, the more attractive he became and—

Why aren't you thinking about the case? her brain screamed.

Right. Right. *The case.*

Two minutes later, she was sitting at a large island with a beautiful dark countertop. A piping-hot mug of thick, black coffee was clutched between her hands and after she took a tentative sip, careful not to burn her tongue, she hummed her approval.

Beside her, Dillan sputtered. "Christ on a crutch! Do you guys add water, or do you just grind the beans into a paste and serve them up?"

Rollins, who leaned casually against the countertop across from them, chuckled. "Little bit of A and a lot of B."

"I love it," Julia said around another appreciative sip.

"Says the woman who orders triple shot espressos." Dillan harrumphed as he eyed his coffee like it might try to crawl out of his mug and assault him.

Julia turned on the barstool when she heard footsteps behind her. It was Eliza Meadows. And she was looking far better than the last two times Julia had seen her.

The woman wore black slacks, a white button-down shirt, and comfortable-looking ballet flats. Her dark hair was pulled back into a low ponytail. And the swelling had gone down from her temple and cheek. Although the bruise was still there, still a painful-looking blue that faded to a sickly looking yellow around the edges.

"Good morning." Miss Meadows inclined her head and made a beeline for the coffeepot as Julia and Dillan returned her greeting.

Once Miss Meadows had a mug in hand, she crossed to the large, industrial-sized refrigerator and pulled out a gallon of milk. After adding a good dollop to her cup, she screwed on the lid and went to put it back in the fridge.

Dillan stopped her with, "Mind sharing some of that with me? It's the only way I'll be able to drink this stuff."

Miss Meadows made a face of commiseration as she slid the jug his way. "Ex-military types"—she waved to Rollins—"prefer their coffee to snarl and try to lurch out of the pot."

Rollins's laugh was so deep and rumbling, Julia felt it in her stomach. And then…*lower.*

Really, really, really *inconvenient!*

She ripped her gaze away from the dark-haired man and instead forced herself to watch the chief of staff's daughter as she returned the milk to the refrigerator. Miss Meadows came back to the island with a large, rectangular Tupperware dish. And after she took up a position opposite Julia, she popped the top and the smell of vanilla, sugar, and sweet cream filled the air.

Saliva instantly filled Julia's mouth as she stared at the decadent-looking red velvet cupcakes. Her stomach rumbled, reminding her she'd skipped breakfast.

"Would you like one?" Miss Meadows offered.

"No, thank you." Dillan shook his head. "Added sugar and fat leads to cardiovascular disease and obesity. I work too hard"—he patted his six-pack—"to sabotage myself."

Julia realized she was rolling her eyes when she caught Sergeant Rollins smirking at her. Quickly, she wiped her expression clean.

"I, on the other hand," she said to Miss Meadows, "would love a cupcake."

Sixty seconds later, she was rolling her eyes again. But this time they were rolling back in her head.

"Oh, my god," she breathed reverently as the moist cake and cream cheese frosting made slow, sensual love to her tastebuds. "These are heaven."

"The trick for the frosting is to make sure the butter is at room temperature before adding it to the cream cheese," Eliza told her while swiping a finger through the frosting on the cupcake she'd placed on a plate for herself. "It makes the blend light and fluffy."

"Whatever you say," Julia enthused as she took another healthy bite and tried not to let out an obscene-sounding moan.

Miss Meadows waited until she'd finished her cupcake before stating bluntly, "So you're here to take me to a safe house."

Julia had been pressing crumbs from the plate onto her finger and transferring them to her mouth, but that had her stopping with her hand in the air.

"How the hell do you know that?" Dillan demanded.

Julia answered for the woman. "Let me guess. Your father?"

Miss Meadows nodded. "He called right before you two showed up at the gate."

"I take it he gets updates from the director himself?" Julia didn't like the idea of the details of her case being shared with anyone, even the right-hand-man to the president. But what could she do? The director was her boss and she supposed, in a way, he probably considered the chief of staff *his* boss.

Plus, when her case directly involved Leonard Meadows's daughter, no doubt exceptions were made.

"Don't blame either of them." Eliza wrinkled her nose. "They're just trying to do what's best for me."

"Mmm," was all Julia allowed. Then a thought occurred. "Is your father onboard with our plan? Or would he prefer you fly to Washington?"

"You should *definitely* go to Washington," Dillan piped up. "That's a great idea."

Julia shot him a scathing glance and wasn't surprised when he offered up one of his patented shrugs.

Miss Meadows glanced back and forth between them before answering, "I mean, if that's what you think I *should* do, I will. But if I have a choice in the matter, I'd rather stay as close to Chicago as possible. That way, as soon as this is all over, I can come straight back home." A wrinkle appeared between her eyebrows when a thought occurred. "Unless your plan is to *not* stash me somewhere close."

"I don't like the idea of all the moving parts required to get you to

D.C.," Julia admitted. "Now that we know you're in danger, the quicker we can get you squirreled away, the better."

"And what's changed your mind about her being safe here?" Rollins interjected. His accent made the last word sound more like *hee-ah*.

Julia glanced at the large window behind the sink. There was a firepit in the courtyard surrounded by outdoor furniture. A smattering of small outbuildings stood in a neat row to the right of that. And beyond everything was the ten-foot-high brick wall topped by the razor wire.

To say the BKI compound was formidable was an understatement. But there was a difference between formidable and impenetrable.

"You guys have a great setup here," she admitted. "I'm sure it keeps out potential thieves and ne'er-do-wells. But now that we know someone is killing off our witnesses, I think it's better if we take Miss Meadows somewhere windowless and, most importantly, anonymous. All it takes is a quick internet search, and anyone can find out this is Eliza's known residence."

"Someone is murdering the witnesses? Does that mean—" Miss Meadows left the question dangling.

Julia frowned. "Didn't your father tell you?"

"No." The woman's inky-black ponytail swished over her shoulder when she shook her head. "Dad just said you two were coming to get me, and that I needed to decide whether I wanted to come to him or go with you."

"I got a call from the coroner a little over an hour ago. Neither Senator Chastain nor her husband died of natural causes."

For a beat, Miss Meadows remained silent, letting the information set in. And no doubt thinking about how she was now the lone survivor of the shooting. Then, she asked, "How were they killed?"

Once again, Julia balked at the idea of sharing information with a civilian. And once again, she reminded herself that there was no such thing as a *civilian* when it came to the chief of staff's one and only daughter.

"Traces of cyanide were found in the professor's lungs," she conceded. "We're assuming whoever got to him used the vaporized form of the poison."

Miss Meadows's hand jumped to cover her mouth. "And the senator?" Her voice was weak.

"Someone hacked her pacemaker," Dillan grumbled.

Tears welled in the woman's dark eyes but they didn't fall. "*Why?* Why is someone doing this?"

"That's what we're going to find out. But first, we need to make sure we get you somewhere safe."

"Wait a goddamn minute!"

Julia turned to the voice that boomed behind her. She found Mr. Movie Star, aka Fisher Wakefield, standing in the doorway.

If Miss Meadows was looking better than the last two times Julia had seen her, then Mr. Wakefield was looking decidedly worse. His hair stuck up in all directions. His five-o'clock shadow looked more like it was coming in at about midnight. And his pretty mouth was pulled into a thin line.

"I thought we agreed Liza is safe here." A muscle ticked in his square jaw.

"*There's* the scruffy-looking nerf herder I call my best friend," Rollins said, and Julia whipped around to find Ol' Blue Eyes smirking at her. "I'm catching on." He gave her a wink she would swear she felt down to her toes.

CHAPTER 22

Fisher listened to the reasons why the feds were now determined to move Eliza to a safe house, and he didn't like any of them. But what could he do? They were the FBI and he was simply a lowly motorcycle mechanic.

Supposedly.

"I'll go pack a bag," Eliza said.

"I'll pack one too." He'd been tentatively sucking on coffee in the hopes it would quiet the men operating large machinery inside his cranium. But now he set his mug aside and stepped around the kitchen island to follow in her footsteps.

"What?" She twirled on him. "Why?"

"Ya didn't think we'd let ya go without a bodyguard, did ya?" He lifted a challenging eyebrow. "The Knights stick together."

"I'm sorry, Mr. Wakefield." Agent O'Toole shook her head. "That's not protocol."

Adrenaline tore away the dusty cobwebs of his hangover at the same time the danger to Eliza snapped his hold on the violence that lived inside him.

He slowly turned to face the agent. It was the deliberateness of his move that should have warned everyone he'd let the affable Fisher Wakefield's mask slip to reveal the side of him that'd risen through the ranks of The Unit.

"I don't give a good goddamn about your protocol," he said bluntly.

"Hey now." Britt darted forward to give Fisher's shoulder a squeeze. It was meant both as a comfort and as a warning for Fisher to keep his shit together. "We all want the same thing here." The former Ranger's tone was overly convivial. "For Eliza to be safe. Surely there's a compromise."

"What did you have in mind?" O'Toole asked, coolly eyeing Fisher.

"We let you keep an eye on our girl, and you forget about your protocol and let Fisher go with you," Britt answered.

And this is why we're best friends, Fisher thought.

"There's no *let* when it comes to Miss Meadows coming with us." Like all asswads who'd never had their dicks knocked in the dirt, Agent Dillan Douglas met Fisher's anger with arrogance. "If we need to take her, we take her."

"Try it," Fisher challenged and felt Britt's grip tighten on his shoulder.

Fisher could barely believe his eyes when Agent Douchecanoe stood and whipped back his suit jacket to reveal his shoulder holster. The idiot went so far as to thumb open the snap on the leather sling.

Guess he never got the memo ya don't threaten a man with a bullet unless ya fully intend to make him eat it.

"I'm armed." Douglas grinned. "Are you?"

"My dick's in my hand." Fisher made a rude gesture toward his crotch. "Does that count?"

"Bruh," Britt whispered close to his ear. "There's a fine line between tenacity and stupidity. And I think you've crossed it."

"Oh, for the love of all that's holy!" Eliza rarely raised her voice. So hearing her shout knocked Fisher out of his bloodlust. "I'm *choosing* to go with the agents, Fish. And if they're saying it's better, *safer* for me to go on my own, then that's what I'll do."

He realized his gaze was a glittering knife blade that sliced into her when she stumbled back.

"Liza." He reached for her while mentally kicking his own ass for doing *anything* to make her look at him that way. With *fear*. "All ya got to do is say the word and your old man will insist one of us comes with ya. Then these two can forget their protocols and—"

"Fisher." She placed a hand on his arm. It was soft and cool and reminded him it'd been hard and harsh the night before when she'd shoved his ass out of her bed. Not that he hadn't deserved it. He *had*. What had he been thinking offering up friends with benefits? It was like a slap in the face considering what she really wanted was so, *so* much more. "I'll be fine. They know what they're doing. Besides, you're needed here."

The look she gave him was meaningful, and he was reminded he still needed to finish doing recon and analysis on their next mission.

"I hate the thought of ya out there without any protection," he growled, suddenly feeling like his skin was too tight for his body.

"She'll have Agent Douglas for protection," Agent O'Toole assured him.

Agent Douchecanoe?

The woman was bat-shit crazy if she thought that was a comfort. The idea of the pretty-boy fed locked up in a room with Eliza for hours, maybe *days*, made the venomous, prickly legged thing that lived in Fisher spring to life and hiss.

And *that*, that exact reaction, was enough to have him blowing out a windy breath and relenting. "I want hourly check-ins. Calls or texts or…hell…email us if ya have to. But I want reassurances she's okay every sixty minutes."

"Done," Agent O'Toole said at the same time Douglass grumbled, "Fuck off."

"It's the least we can do," O'Toole told her partner. "They're right to be concerned. And if hourly check-ins will keep everyone healthy and happy, that's what we'll do."

Agent Douglas whispered something unsavory about Fisher's parentage. But Fisher acted like he hadn't heard. Because acting like he *had* heard, and then feeding the cleft-chinned bastard his fist, would inevitably end with him in handcuffs. And the *last* place he needed to be while Eliza was in federal custody was behind bars.

Instead, he told her, "I'll keep ya company while ya pack."

"No need," she assured him.

"*I* need," he insisted and then turned to Britt. "Ya okay to hold down the fort?" He slid a speaking gaze toward the two agents.

"I'm sure I can keep Agent O'Toole occupied with another cupcake." Britt winked at the blond agent. "As for the other one." He tilted his head toward Douglas. "I'll try to hunt up a banana."

Fisher chuckled at the perturbed look on Douchcanoe's face before turning to follow Eliza upstairs.

"I need to grab something from my room," he told her after they'd reached the top floor.

Once he was in his room with the door shut behind him, he didn't hesitate to step to the side of his bed. He hadn't bothered to make it. When he'd heard her softly close her bedroom door, he'd snapped awake with cringe-inducing memories of what a dickhole he'd been the night before. Determined to apologize to her as soon as possible, he'd hopped out of bed.

Well, hopped *is a bit of an exaggeration.*

More like he'd stumbled out of bed, slouched to the bathroom where he'd spent some time washing his face, brushing his teeth, and castigating himself for being thirty-four years old and still being stupid enough to think he could drink that much bourbon without it making him feel like death warmed over.

By the time he'd slipped on the only pair of clean jeans he had—they were black denim with a hole in one knee and hems that were frayed—and the last T-shirt in his drawer, he'd been anxious to get downstairs and see how many ways Eliza had devised to kill him. Slowly. And *painfully.*

Now, here he was back upstairs without having had a moment to apologize. And it was all thanks to the feds' ill-timed arrival.

He wasn't sure *why* he felt the need to arm himself. But he never questioned his sixth sense. So he lifted his pillow and reached for his Glock.

It wasn't there.

A spurt of adrenaline fired in his blood as he threw back the top quilt and the flat sheet and—

There.

His sidearm sat atop the fitted sheet on the opposite side of the bed—he was always a restless sleeper after he'd had too much to drink.

Instead of taking the time to walk around the bed, he simply grabbed the fitted sheet and pulled. The gathered corners ripped out from under the mattress and his favorite pistol slid his way.

The grip was worn smooth in places from the palm of his hand. The familiar smell of gun cleaner tickled his nose. And the metal was cold as he slipped the barrel into the back of his waistband.

Eliza had left her door open, so he rapped his knuckles against the doorframe before leaning against the jamb. "I'm sorry 'bout last night," he said lowly. "I can be a real shit when I've been in the Wild Turkey."

"You're never a shit, Fish." As she loaded shirts and pants into a leather duffel, her tone matched her expression. Both were affectionate. And maybe a little sad. "And besides, like you said, can't blame a guy for trying, right?"

"You're too easy on me." He shook his head.

"Oh, I'd be happy to make a list of all your faults while I'm sequestered away under federal protection." The sun had risen over the horizon, and the pink light of morning filtered through her window to make her dark eyes glint like rich mahogany.

He was happy to see she'd packed a pair of frumpy, long-sleeved pajamas. If she'd packed the flimsy silk set he'd seen her in two nights ago, he might have had to shoot Agent Douchecanoe as a precaution.

"Not sure there's enough paper on the planet for that job," he teased.

The cold, hard stone that was his heart felt even colder and harder than usual at the thought of not being able to see her. Touch her. *Protect* her. And he planned to stay on Agent O'Toole's ass to get this entire thing solved so that she could come back where she belonged.

Back to BKI.

Back to him.

Except she doesn't belong to you, the better angels of his nature reminded him.

She could if you'd only let her, the lesser devils teased.

CHAPTER 23

Flour Power Bagel Shop, Goose Island, Chicago, Illinois

Yang's sniper rifle sat assembled beside him as he crouched on the roof of the bagel shop across the street from Black Knights Inc. He sighed when he felt his phone vibrate with life inside his jeans.

It promised to be a lovely morning. Too bad he would be spending it making a clandestine escape from the city.

He preferred stealth when it came to taking out a target. And all the better if he could take out a target from afar—like he had done with Senator Chastain. But Bishop had called him earlier to say he had gotten his hands on a summary of Eliza Meadows's official statement and people at the party had brought up Bishop's name—his *real* name—in conversation.

"I want her dead," Bishop had hissed. And for the first time, Yang had heard fear in the man's voice. *"And sooner rather than later. I've laid down all the crumbs needed to lead the feds to Reynolds. So that leaves only Eliza."*

Pulling his burner from his pocket, he thumbed on the device. "Yes?"

"Is it done?" There was always impatience in Bishop's voice. But it was emphasized this morning.

"Not yet. She is still inside the compound. But as soon as she emerges, I will finish it."

"Good. The car you requested is waiting for you two blocks west. It's a white Ford Fusion. Keys are on the front tire. Your destination is the northernmost airstrip at O'Hare. Your countrymen have secured a private jet that'll take you home. They've told me they plan to have you lay low for a while. Things have gotten too hot in this hemisphere."

Yang glanced over his shoulder at the metal fire escape and then turned to the west. The bagel shop afforded him a view of the surrounding streets and he spied the vehicle Bishop had provided.

It was the man's attention to detail—and his willingness to kill any and all who posed a threat to his position—that had kept him in his place of power for so long. It was also how he had managed to fly under the radar of the various American alphabet agencies while partnering with Yang's country to foment crisis and chaos in his own land.

Bishop was China's most valuable asset. Russia's too, if rumors were to be believed. There was even some gossip within the various spy communities that the man had ties to North Korea…although Bishop had his doubts about that one. The hermit kingdom eschewed all connections with the west, even when those connections might benefit them.

All that to say…if Bishop wanted Eliza Meadows dead, then Yang must do his best to make that happen, regardless of how harrowing the next hour might turn out to be for him.

Swinging back around, he studied the imposing edifice of the old factory. The brick walls looked thick and impenetrable, probably insulated with horsehair which had been the substance of choice back when the building was constructed. The windows were glazed and reflected the light, making it impossible to see inside. And the cameras mounted to the brick wall had red eyes that blinked to remind passersby they saw everything.

They would certainly see Eliza Meadows's last moments.

He pictured how he would line her up in his sights. He practiced how he would blow all the breath from his lungs before curling his finger around his trigger. He imagined what it would sound like when his bullet left his barrel.

One brief moment and five pounds of pressure was all that stood between him and a trip back home. Back to the little village where his grandmother still lived.

She would fill his belly with fried sauce noodles, and he would sit and smoke his grandfather's pipe and try to forget—at least for a while—that powerful men played powerful games that were slowly reshaping the world's geopolitical map.

A cog in the machine, he thought philosophically. *That is all I am.*

"So as soon as I finish today, we will say our goodbyes," he said into the phone as he loaded a 7.62mm round into his rifle.

"I'm sure your handlers will want you back here helping me poke holes in things again soon enough," Bishop assured him. "But for now, we go quiet. McClean got too close."

"I'll phone you when it is done."

"I'm looking forward to it."

Yang slipped the burner back into his pocket and watched as the tall, arrogant-looking FBI agent exited the factory building's front door and made his way across the grounds. Yang used the time to carefully get his rifle into position. And then gritted his teeth when he saw the agent jump into the driver's seat, start the engine on the big, black SUV, and begin navigating it past the open gate.

Fuck.

If they drove into the factory through one of those garage doors, he might not get a chance to take his shot. Which meant he would have to improvise.

Take out a tire as they leave? he wondered, his mind moving quickly through his options.

Riddle the vehicle with lead and hope a round finds Miss Meadows?

Follow them and make my move once they are on the road?

All were possibilities. None were ideal.

He would play it by ear, as the Americans liked to say.

CHAPTER 24

Fisher carried Eliza's duffel down the stairs even as the thought of turning her over into federal protection made him want to chew nails.

"Hold there," Agent O'Toole instructed once he and Eliza had stepped onto the concrete floor of the shop. "Wait until Agent Douglas pulls in."

"Copy that." He nodded as Britt hit the button for the garage door closest to them. The large metal structure peeled back to reveal night had made way for day.

The rising sun hit the skyscrapers to the east, casting long, dark shadows over the Black Knights Inc. compound. And something about the way the rest of the city sparkled with pale pink light while the expanse out front remained dusky and cool gave Fisher a terrible sense of foreboding.

He blamed his paranoia on the fact that he was moments away from waving goodbye to Eliza for…

Who knows how long?

Hours, if he was lucky. But it was more likely to be days or even weeks.

He wouldn't allow himself to consider the idea that it might turn into months.

The activity of the morning had finally awakened the rest of the Knights.

Sam, Hewitt, and Graham leaned over the balcony railing on the second-floor War Room, watching as Agent Douglas nosed the large SUV into the shop.

"Moving her into custody?" Sam called down and Fisher snapped him a salute as an affirmative. "Damn, man." Sam shook his head. "I hate that."

The look Fisher shot him said quite clearly, *You ain't the only one.*

"Careful," Graham called down as Agent Douglas continued to inch the big vehicle into the shop. "You break it, you buy it."

Agent O'Toole went a little green around the gills at the thought of that. And Fisher understood why. Her superiors wouldn't appreciate the six-figure line item that would show up on her budget report if her partner happened to destroy one of BKI's custom motorcycles.

Becky and Boss had been working hard to increase inventory on their spec-bikes—the ones Becky designed without any particular buyer in mind. Which meant the row of wheeled art took up more space the usual.

Agent Douglas had to be extra careful not to clip the front wheels on the first bike and he hung out the driver's side window so he could hear the instructions Britt gave him.

"Okay, Sergeant Rollins," Agent O'Toole said once her partner had pulled the back bumper past the outer edge of the building. "If you'll close the garage door, we'll get Miss Meadows loaded up and get this—"

Fisher stopped listening because a glint across the way caught his eye.

Had he been out in the desert or ghillie-suited in the woods somewhere, he'd have reacted immediately. But because it was the city, because there was glass everywhere that reflected the morning light, he hesitated.

That was a mistake.

He saw the orange glow of muzzle fire a split second before he heard the deafening *crack* of the report echoing through the open space separating the compound from the bagel shop.

"Shooter!" he yelled as the bullet lodged itself into the garage door motor with a loud *thwack* just as Britt hit the button on the brick wall to bring the big, metal door down.

No go.

The shooter's aim had been true. The motor whined and then exploded in a shower of sparks, leaving the garage gaping wide like a mouth frozen in shock.

Fuck, fuck, fuck!

Fisher's focus narrowed. And he automatically dropped Eliza's duffel to reach for the weapon in his waistband.

He'd just wrapped his fingers around the familiar grip when— *Crack!* Another shot echoed and he felt the air displaced by the bullet as it whizzed by his cheek and *pinged* into the metal staircase behind him.

He now understood why he'd felt the need to grab his gun and why the instant the garage door had rattled open he'd been stabbed in the gut with impending doom.

After more than a decade and a half of being out in the field, his sixth sense when it came to danger had been honed to a razor's edge. He cursed himself for having ignored it at the same time he threw himself down on Eliza, covering her head with his hands even as he lifted his chin to recon the area and see if there was more than the one shooter.

He noted three things in quick succession.

One, whichever Connelly brother was on duty had hit the switch to close the gate—and then, no doubt, taken cover beneath the guardhouse's console panel. The little building was reinforced with steel plating, so as long as the big redhead stayed low, he should be safe. Two, Agent O'Toole had taken cover against the brick wall next to Britt. And three, Agent Douglas had flung himself from the vehicle and had found shelter behind the SUV's big hood.

Glancing toward the hallway that led to the kitchen, he ran through his options. One, he could stay on the floor in front of the steps, protecting Eliza with his body. The gunman didn't have a clear shot. The angle was bad and the SUV was in the way. *But sometimes a bastard just gets lucky.* Or two, he could risk rising to a crouch to drag Eliza into the hallway. They'd be exposed for a few seconds, but then she'd be safe from—

Before he could spring into action, another shot rang out, fracturing the cool, calmness of the morning. He heard the bullet hit the floor in front of him a second before a chunk of concrete bounced up and sliced into his face.

He felt the sting as his flesh laid open. Felt the hot rush of blood down his cheek. But both things he noticed as an aside when, from the corner of his eye, he saw movement.

"Stay down, you fool!" Agent O'Toole yelled because Douglas had turkey-peeked his head above the vehicle's hood to take aim at the gunman.

"Damnit!" Fisher cursed aloud. Agent Douglas was an even bigger idiot than he'd given the guy credit for if he thought his Ruger was powerful enough to hit the assassin perched on the rooftop across the way.

Boom! Boom! Boom!

Agent Douglas fired three times in quick succession.

Crack!

The gunman fired once and his aim proved to be as precise as it had been when he'd taken out the garage door motor. Agent Douglas cried out as a hot slug found him. A puff of blood sprayed from his shoulder as the projectile blasted through his back.

It wasn't like they showed it in the movies. Even the big rounds snipers used weren't enough to send a body hurtling back through the air. Instead, Douglas simply fell backward, hitting the ground with a grunt before writhing in pain.

"Get Eliza to safety!" Agent O'Toole screamed, urgency lacing her voice as she bent her arm around the edge of the garage opening and began blindly spraying bullets.

It wasn't much as far as cover-fire went, but it was all Fisher was going to get. With swift, decisive movements, he scrambled to a crouch, grabbed Eliza by the wrist, and hauled her in the direction of the kitchen.

"Keep your head down!" he bellowed as they half-ran/half-stumbled down the short hallway. As soon as they made it to the large pantry with its brick walls and solid oak door, he unceremoniously shoved her inside. "Stay here," he instructed and impatiently wiped his forearm across his cheek to get rid of the blood he felt dripping from his chin.

Adrenaline had heightened his senses. He clocked the panic in Eliza's wide, dark eyes. Heard the fear in her voice when she said, "Jesus, Fish! You're hit!" And smelled the earthy scent coming from the basket of russet potatoes sitting beneath the shelf by the pantry door.

This was his element—the chaos, the danger. Instead of being overwhelmed by it, it focused him.

"I'm not," he assured her and gave his face another restless swipe so she could see he was sporting a cut and not a hole. "Got nicked by flyin' concrete and knocked a bit of bark off my face."

"Thank god!" Her face crumbled with relief as she threw her arms around him and hugged him so tight he struggled to breathe. "When you threw yourself on top of me, all I could think about was Charlie and—"

She couldn't finish. Her words caught on a harsh sob.

He allowed himself the space of two heartbeats to enjoy the feel of her in his arms. To savor her warmth and softness and spring rain scent. Then he gently unhooked her arms from around his neck and stepped back. "I have to help the others."

No more rounds had been exchanged. Which meant the shooter was watching. Waiting.

Tears stood in her eyes, but she nodded her understanding. He turned to leave, but she stopped him with a hand on his arm.

When he swung back, it was to see her chin quivering. "I won't be able to live with myself if any of you die trying to protect me." The tears that'd been standing in her eyes overflowed and spilled down her cheeks before she finished on a whisper. "One is enough." She immediately shook her head. "One is too much."

He didn't know what to say to that. So he simply leaned forward to press a quick kiss to her lips. Then he slammed the pantry door in her face and turned to sprint down the hallway.

"Britt!" he yelled after stopping at the corner. Britt had managed to grab Agent Douglas's ankle. And even though the former Ranger wasn't as big as some of the other Knights, the sonofabitch was strong. He was able to pull the moaning agent across the concrete floor until there was nothing left behind but a bloody trail. "How bad is it?" He darted across the expanse and took up a position against the brick wall beside Agent O'Toole, his sidearm out and at the ready.

"Through and through," Britt gritted from between clenched teeth. He was down on his knees, applying pressure to Douglas's shoulder. "But he's bleeding like a stuck pig. He needs an ambulance."

"Sam!" Fisher's voice was firm and commanding as he called up to the second floor. "You still up there?"

"He's already gone to get his rifle!" Hewitt called down. "We've got eyes on the shooter from here. Lone gunman. Roof of bagel shop."

"I have to call in backup," O'Toole whispered, her cheeks flushed with adrenaline.

"If I know Sam," Fisher told her, "it'll be too late by the time they get here. You'd be better served callin' in the paramedics to help your partner."

Her cell phone was in her hand, but she blinked at him. "What do you mean?"

"Sam was a Marine Raider."

"I know. I read his file," she said impatiently. "I read *all* your files."

"Did ya read the part where Sam has the most confirmed kills of any Marine sniper ever to walk the hallowed halls of Camp Pendelton? Once he's on the roof, the shooter is as good as dead. We just need to hang on until then."

His cut no longer openly wept. Blood now crusted on his face when he glanced down at Britt and Agent Douglas and grimaced.

The agent had been wearing a bulletproof vest. But the round had hit him beside the strap on his shoulder and had left behind a gaping hole.

Bzzzz. He pulled his cell phone from his pocket at the same time he heard O'Toole calling for an ambulance. Sam's number showed on his screen and he quickly thumbed on the device.

"You in position?" he asked without preamble.

"Affirmative." Sam's voice had taken on the calm, concise tone that told Fisher Sam had slowed his breathing and his heartrate and was in sniper-mode. "But the sonofabitch isn't on the roof anymore. I can't see— Wait."

Fisher did exactly that as O'Toole gave harried instructions to the 9-1-1 operator and Britt hissed at Agent Douglas to, "Stop moving, you dumb shit. You're just making yourself bleed faster."

"He's one block west and moving fast." Sam's voice came through the phone. "Do I take the shot?"

Fisher wanted to give the affirmative. That rat bastard had come here, to their *home*, to kill Eliza. But this wasn't a battlefield. The culprit was no longer actively shooting at them. And Sam wasn't a cop with a license to kill.

There were laws when it came to this sort of thing.

"Hold," he instructed as he turned to O'Toole. "The shooter is on the run. Sam has him in his sights but can't take a shot unless you give him the green light."

O'Toole didn't hesitate. "Do it. I'll take any heat that comes his way."

Fisher had liked her before, liked her smart, no-nonsense way of handling things. But now he respected her on top of liking her.

"End him, Sam," he relayed into the phone. "Take the shot."

Boom!

The familiar roar of Sam's sniper rifle sounded from above and Fisher held his breath waiting on confirmation of the kill.

It never came. Instead he heard shuffling as Sam picked his cell phone back up and relayed, "Missed. He bent down just as I pulled the trigger. He jumped into a white sedan. He's two blocks west and continuing west quickly. I don't dare take another shot. Too many buildings in the way and he's moving too fast."

"Fuck!" Fisher shoved his weapon back into his waistband and gave O'Toole the bad news. "Negative contact with the shooter. He's in a car and headed west." He walked over and punched the button on the wall that would roll up the second garage door. "I'm going after him."

"Wait! What?" O'Toole shouted but Fisher was already running toward Mardi Gras.

The purple, green, and gold chopper had been painted to remind him of his favorite time of the year when his mother had made king cake and his little town had thrown parades where all the citizens decked themselves out in shiny beads. But he felt no affinity for the machine now, other than it was what he needed to catch the sonofabitch who'd dared come for Eliza.

This ends now, he thought grimly as he hit the button that had Mardi Gras's engine rumbling to deep-throated life.

CHAPTER 25

"That man has no quit in him," Yang snarled as he took the exit at high speeds. He nearly lost control of the wheel and only managed to keep the vehicle on four wheels through grit and determination. Bishop had been on speakerphone when he had seen the massive motorcycle appear in his rearview mirror. And even though he did not have a close relationship with fear—they had parted ways long ago, because fear equaled death in his line of work—he could not deny the jolt of…*concern* he had experienced knowing one of the Black Knights had tracked him.

In the ten minutes since then, he had remained *concerned*. It had been an intense game of cat and mouse and tactical driving that had put all his training to the test. He had been on the median once. Had managed not to sideswipe a semi-truck trailer by the width of a hair. And had tried three times to run the black-clad rider off the road to no avail.

The man had stuck to the back of the bike with the tenacity of a tick clinging to a stray dog.

"The jet is fueled and waiting on the tarmac," Bishop yelled through the phone's speaker as it rattled in the cupholder. "Get there and get in the air. If they catch you, I won't be able to—"

"This man does not want to *catch* me," Yang snarled, his usually steady heart pounding like a war drum as the airport's perimeter loomed closer. The only thing that separated him from freedom and safety was the chain-link fence surrounding the area. "He wants to *kill* me!"

He knew it as surely as he knew his name was not Yang. As surely as he knew this was going to be a very close thing.

There it is!

The sleek-looking jet was parked precisely where Bishop said it would be. And the heat rippling around its engines in the cool morning air proved it was primed and ready to lift off into that big, beautiful sky.

There would be no driving around to the private entrance. It was now or never.

Without hesitation, Yang jerked the wheel. The sedan left the road and the tires immediately dug for purchase in the grassy space that separated the side street from the airport fence. He could feel the vibrations reverberating through his bones as the car bounced over the uneven terrain.

His breath whooshed out of him when he slammed his foot down on the accelerator as far as it would go. He gritted his teeth and winced the instant before the vehicle's front end contacted the chain-link.

He expected resistance.

There was none.

The car's momentum tore through the fencing as easily as a chopstick through fresh dumpling batter. Metal screeched against metal as he left nothing but a mangled mess of twisted vinyl-coated steel behind him.

He was not out of the woods yet, however. The terrain next to the tarmac was so uneven he was reminded of ski moguls. The sedan bounced and squeaked as joints were pushed to the breaking point, and the sniper rifle he had tossed into the passenger seat fell onto the floorboard. When the front tires finally hit the runway, they did so with a jerk so hard it threatened to send him hurtling through the windshield.

"Yang!" he heard Bishop yelling but did not dare respond. He could not. Not with his teeth clamped tight in concentration as he left rubber behind him while once more stomping on the gas pedal and hurtling down the runway.

Close. Close, he thought. *Get as close as I can!*

He chanced a glance over his shoulder and saw the Black Knight bent low over his handlebars. The man bounced over the lumpy earth beside the tarmac with enough force to make the motorcycle look like a seesaw. And yet, he was not catapulted over the handlebars or dumped sideways into the grass.

No quit. Absolutely no quit, Yang thought desperately, returning his attention to the expanse of runway in front of him.

He was near the jet now. Near enough to hear the loud *hum* of its engines. But even above that was the deafening thunder of the motorcycle as the man landed on the tarmac and laid on the throttle.

When Yang thought he might plow straight into the aircraft, he gripped the steering wheel with both hands and stood on the brakes. The sedan fishtailed to a chaotic, screeching stop that left the vehicle's engine ticking loudly and Yang cursing beneath his breath.

He was quick to unclip his seat belt and pocket his cell phone. But he did not dare reach for the sniper rifle in the passenger floorboard. There was no time—and he comforted himself knowing he had worn gloves and left no fingerprints behind. Instead, he flung open the door and leapt from the car as his heart roared right along with the plane's engines.

The smell of jet fuel was strong and tunneled up his nose. He barely noticed. His entire focus was the plane and the safety it promised. Because even above the noise of the airport, he could hear the big motorcycle careening closer. And atop it sat a relentless predator who was determined to make Yang his prey.

The private jet's door was open. The molded steps beckoned as he raced toward the waiting aircraft. And the pilot, the man his handlers had hired to spirit him away, stood at the top of the steps, beckoning him to run faster.

"Go!" Yang screamed as his foot hit the first tread. "Get us in the air!"

His shoulders hitched together to make the target on his back smaller. The Black Knight had a weapon. The man had used it twice while trying to blow out a tire on the sedan. And now Yang had no doubt it was aimed between his shoulder blades.

Pounding up the stairs, he ducked when he heard a shot and felt the air displaced by the round that flew by his head to embed itself in the cushion of the seat closest to the door. He hit the button that automatically retracted the stairs. And only turned when he could grab the handle of the door.

His heart clawed a frantic path into his throat when he caught sight of the man in black ditching his fantastical bike next to the abandoned sedan. The huge machine was still rolling when the big man leapt from its leather seat. Its front wheel plowed into the front fender of the rental car and then fell over to skid fifteen feet across the tarmac.

The soldier-turned-presidential-henchman didn't care. The giant sprinted toward Yang and time seemed to slow as they briefly locked eyes.

Rage. Revenge. Death.

Yang read all of it in the man's diamond-hard stare. And the Knight's jaw was set at a steely angle that matched the unforgiving metal of the weapon he aimed at Yang's chest.

The world seemed to hold its breath—or maybe that was just Yang. And then there was nothing. Yang was blind to everything as the door finally swung shut with an airtight *hiss* a split second before the *thunk* of a bullet lodged into the fuselage.

"Go! Go! Go!" he yelled at the pilot at the same time he tumbled back into the safety of the cabin.

The *relative* safety of the cabin.

Another *thunk* told him his pursuer wasn't finished. And it was only when the pilot hit the throttle and the jet lurched down the runway that Yang dared drag in a breath of relief.

Weaving unsteadily up the aisle, he slid into the closest seat. The powerful engines roared as the jet hurtled down the runway. Gripping the armrest with one hand and his cell phone with the other, he welcomed the G's that pressed him back into his seat as the swift, light aircraft quickly caught wind and lifted into the sky.

Finally safe from the man who had so relentlessly dogged him, Yang lifted his phone to his ear, shocked to find his hand shaking.

"Bishop? You still there?"

"I'm here. You in the air?"

"I am. Which means you are on your own."

"That's fine. It's done."

Yang frowned. "But Eliza Meadows—"

"Doesn't know anything," Bishop interrupted. "I was able to get my hands on her full statement. John McClean didn't share with her his suspicions about me. So my identity is still safe. Which means she'll live. For now."

Yang lifted an intrigued eyebrow. "And are you happy with this outcome?"

The sound of Bishop's snort echoed over the connection. "You know as well as I do there's no such thing as happiness when it comes to this business. There are only net-positive or net-negative outcomes. In this case, we have a net-positive. Have a safe trip home."

And then, as was his way, Bishop disconnected the call without saying farewell.

Yang pocketed the cell and his gaze alighted on the bag of White Rabbit candy stuffed into the seatback in front of him. He felt his lips quirk.

After twenty years, my handlers know me well.

Reaching for the treats, he was gratified to see his fingers steady.

It had been a while since he had faced an opponent that rattled his nerves. And he felt no shame in admitting he would be happy to finish his career without ever running into another Black Knight.

CHAPTER 26

Black Knights Inc.

Eliza's heart felt like it would explode from anticipation as she watched the TV screen mounted beside the front door. The real-time footage showed the outer gate sliding open and a familiar black SUV prowling onto the grounds.

"They're here!" she called over her shoulder and heard various acknowledgements from the Black Knights.

None of the original crew had made it into work. Not after Eliza had called Becky to tell her what was going down at BKI. For one, the OGs might be full-on civilians now, but they still avoided the authorities any chance they got. For another, it wasn't like any bikes could have been built in all the confusion. But mostly, the original crew often brought in their wives and children, and thanks to the threat to Eliza, Black Knights Inc. was no longer safe.

That was something she would struggle with for a long time to come. That *she* was the reason the people she'd grown to know and love were in danger if they stepped foot on BKI's grounds.

"We'll be right down!"

It was Sam who called from the second floor. He and the rest of the onsite crew had been going over BKI's security footage to see if any of the cameras had gotten a good picture of the shooter. She heard their heavy footsteps as they traipsed down the stairs to join her.

From the moment she'd emerged from the pantry to find Fisher had gone after the gunman on Mardi Gras, she'd been nothing but a bundle of nerves. Of course, it hadn't helped that soon after his departure, pandemonium had ensued.

The FBI had blazed onto the scene with tires screeching and sirens wailing, having responded to Agent O'Toole's call for backup. The paramedics hadn't been far behind, arriving in a flurry of flapping stethoscopes and a rattling gurney. They'd quickly carted away Agent Douglas, who'd been barely conscious at that point. And not two minutes after the ambulance disappeared past the gates to take the tall, handsome agent to the hospital, the press had appeared on the scene.

Like the reporters in most big cities, Chicago's newshounds kept their ears tuned to the police channels so they could be the first on site when it came to local stories. And if it hadn't been for Manus Connelly keeping the gate closed, the swarm of journalists would've busted down the front door.

Somewhere in the middle of all that, O'Toole had gotten a call from her superior informing her that Fisher had been arrested at O'Hare International Airport for trespassing, for destruction of property, and for discharging his firearm at a private jet as it had taxied down the runway. He was insisting to the local boys he was acting on FBI orders.

Which, according to O'Toole, wasn't entirely true. Apparently he'd taken it upon himself to give chase before the lady agent could green-light or red-light his plan.

"You have to tell them to let him out," Eliza had demanded of the little blond agent. *"You have to say he was working with you."*

"I'll take care of it," O'Toole had promised, although she'd appeared annoyed by the task. *"As soon as I talk to my director, make a statement to the press, check on my partner, and decide what the hell I'm supposed to do with you now."*

Eliza had wanted to argue. Heck, she'd wanted to demand the fed drop everything and go get Fisher *immediately*. But she'd known better.

For one thing, she wanted to stay in O'Toole's good graces. So far, the lady agent had been terribly accommodating, and she hoped to keep it that way until this thing was over. For another, if Fisher was in police custody, he was safe from doing something foolish like…oh…say…renting his own private jet and flying off to intercept the bagel shop shooter.

Honestly, what was he thinking taking off after the gunman on his own?

By the time O'Toole had dispatched the reporters and been informed her partner was in serious but not critical condition, hours had passed. Hours during which Eliza had been made to stay inside the windowless pantry with nothing to do but twiddle her thumbs and worry herself into a tizzy. Hours during which the Knights had worked to cover all the windows with tarps, aluminum foil and, in some cases, printer paper because Agent O'Toole had insisted it was the only way she would allow Eliza to stay at BKI—which Eliza was demanding because the one and only time she'd ever felt in danger since the night at Senator McClean's house was when she'd tried to *leave*.

Yes, the rooftop gunman might be 35,000 feet in the air. But that didn't mean there wasn't another assassin hiding around the corner, biding his time until her head lined up in his crosshairs.

Better to stay here at BKI where I'm surrounded by brick walls and my guys.

It was only after the final window had been covered, the busted garage door had been manually rolled down and locked, and after the remaining Knights had promised Agent O'Toole they would look after her, that Eliza had been allowed out of the pantry and O'Toole had finally gone to spring Fisher from CPD custody.

"I'll bring him home," the lady agent had vowed.

That had been…what?

Eliza checked her watch.

Two hours ago.

Since then, a million what-ifs had drifted through her head.

What if the police refuse to drop the charges?

What if Fisher ran into some sort of trouble while in custody?

What if another assassin took out Agent O'Toole before she could even get to *Fisher?*

But the most profound and agonizing what-ifs had been…*What if I lost him? What if he'd been killed trying to stop the man who came for me?*

The instant he'd thrown himself atop her at the bottom of the stairs, she'd been hurtled back in time to the cocktail party and the feel of Charlie knocking her to the ground. All she'd been able to think was…*No! Not Fisher too! Never Fisher!*

"We don't want you visible when they come in. Stand against the wall," Sam instructed now when the cameras showed the SUV coming to a stop outside the front door.

Eliza forced herself to blow out a calming breath. It did her little good. Her heart continued to race out of control, making her feel lightheaded.

Pressing her back against the rough bricks, she welcomed their solid presence.

Britt, Graham, and Hewitt arranged themselves in front of her. Human shields. Just in case. But that was the last thing she wanted. The thought of one more person sacrificing themselves for her was enough to—

All thoughts fell out of her when Sam grabbed the doorknob and peeked cautiously outside before moving back to hold the door wide.

She craned her head to see around Hewitt's broad shoulder and was disappointed when it wasn't Fisher, but Agent O'Toole who stepped into the building.

The poor woman looked like Eliza felt. Bedraggled, bone-tired, and surviving on adrenaline, caffeine, and stubbornness.

Of course, every ounce of tiredness weighing Eliza down melted away the instant Fisher walked into the shop.

He looked like he'd been through hell and back. His already ratty shirt was ripped at the collar. A result of him chasing the shooter or a result of what was likely a not-so-gentle arrest? His black jeans were smeared with something that looked like mud or blood—she wasn't sure which. And the cut on his cheek had been crudely closed with butterfly bandages.

Despite the weariness etched on his face, he cut an imposing figure when he turned to close the door behind him. Thanks to his military background, his mile-wide shoulders remained straight and true. His square jaw was held at a determined angle. And there was an impatient glint in his eyes when he swung back to let his gaze dart over the faces staring back at him.

Sam whistled. "Damn, man. Bet you took one helluva mugshot."

Always quick on the draw, Fisher quipped back, "*GQ* has already hit me up for the rights."

Sam shook his head. "You're proof that God has favorites, that's for sure."

"If I was his favorite, one of those shots I managed to squeeze off would've hit that sorry sonofabitch. Instead he's on his way to who knows where."

"Somewhere in East Asia say my sources in the bureau," O'Toole spoke up and all heads turned toward her.

"No way to intercept the plane before it touches down?" This from Britt.

O'Toole's expression was one of disgust. "Not in international airspace. And once that sorry sonofabitch is in sovereign airspace, we have no jurisdiction. He's lost to us."

"Any idea who the shooter was?" Britt asked.

Again, the tired-looking agent shook her head. Her blond ponytail got stuck over her shoulder. A few strands tangled with the top buttons on her white shirt.

"Not so far. But we're combing all the security footage and CCTV camera footage to try to get a good picture of him." She turned to Fisher then. "You *sure* you didn't see any identifying marks? Like a tattoo or a mole?"

Fisher made a face of regret. "Like I said, there wasn't a lot of time to be jottin' down notes. He was on the shorter side. Probably no taller than 5'8". He had improbable red hair and a long, hawkish nose that didn't match the shape of his eyes."

"You think he was in disguise."

Fisher nodded.

"Yeah." O'Toole absently brushed her ponytail over her shoulder. "That's what the techies back at headquarters are saying too. We finally got our hands on the hospital's ICU security footage. And in the minutes before Professor Chastain's vitals tanked, someone dressed as a doctor with reddish-orange hair can be seen entering his room. But the guy was good. He was careful to keep his face oriented away from the cameras. Plus, he was wearing a surgical mask. So there's no clear footage."

"And what about the hack on Senator Chastain's pacemaker?" Britt asked. "Any luck finding out where it originated?"

O'Toole shook her head. "It was well done, apparently. The closest the bureau has gotten to a point of origin is somewhere in East Asia."

"Where's Liza?" Fisher demanded, glancing around the shop.

"Here." She lifted her hand and waved it over Hewitt's shoulder.

Graham and Hewitt parted like the Red Sea—together they were about that big. And she sucked in a ragged breath when Fisher's eyes found her and remained fixed.

"Hey, darlin'," he breathed, his voice rough with relief at the sight of her. "Y'okay?"

"Thanks to you and your quick actions this morning."

Tension left his shoulders. "C'mere, then. Let me get my arms around ya so I can reassure myself you're all in one piece."

She didn't hesitate. And she didn't care who was watching or what they might think. With a cry of relief, she pushed past Hewitt and jumped directly into Fisher's embrace. Wrapping her arms around his neck and her legs around his waist, she hugged him tighter than she'd ever hugged anyone.

He grunted in surprise at her exuberance. But a second later, his arms came around her like a vice and they were as close as two people could get while still clothed.

"You fool," she breathed into his ear, loving the smell of him. Open road. Good, clean sweat. And that ineffable smoky aftershave that drove her wild. "Why did you go after him?"

"I want this thing over." His words came out slowly. Perfectly enunciated. As if he held onto his emotions by a thread. "If one more person aims a weapon your way, by god I'll—"

He didn't finish.

She didn't let him.

Instead, she framed his face with her hands—careful to avoid the cut and the butterfly bandages—and pressed her lips to his, kissing him unsparingly. Kissing him like nobody was watching.

He grunted in surprise again. But it quickly turned into a groan that had time standing still. When he canted her head so he could slide his thick, hot tongue into her mouth, the world faded away. There was nothing left but the taste of his luscious lips and feel of him against her, so tall and strong.

Reality returned in the form of Sam's voice. "Get a room, why doncha?"

Eliza reluctantly released Fisher's lips and pressed her forehead to his. "I'm glad you're home," she told him before loosening her hold.

Once she was on her feet, she expected him to step back, reclaim his space. He didn't. He kept an arm around her waist, his fingers firmly gripping her hip.

The fed's eyes were flinty as she glanced around the shop with a furrowed brow. When she turned back, she pinned each Knight with a hard gaze. "Now, you all have the dubious duty of making sure Miss Meadows stays safe. Although, something tells me you're all up to the task. But let me remind you that, despite your military backgrounds, you *are* now civilians. I can only vouch for any armed actions so many times before *my* ass will be on the line. So do me a favor, huh? Stow your weapons. And if you run into trouble or see anything suspicious, *call me* before you go sniping anyone from a rooftop or chasing them to the airport."

Fisher had the good graces to look chagrined. Sam only shrugged and said, "You can take the man outta the military, but you can't take the military outta the man."

O'Toole didn't look amused. But neither did she rise to the bait and respond. Instead, she said, "As for me? I have an assassin to track and *hopefully* identify, a mass murder to solve, and I'm down one partner for who knows how long." She touched a finger to her brow. "So I'll bid you all a good day."

O'Toole reached for the door handle, but Britt stopped her with, "Before you go, we have some footage that might be helpful." He waved her toward the stairs leading to the second floor. "Follow me."

Eliza and Fisher remained rooted to the spot as the rest of the crew marched up to the War Room. Once they were alone, Fisher cupped her chin. "How are ya *really* holdin' up, darlin'?"

She refused to rub at the ache behind her eyes. She didn't want him to know just how close she was to tears.

She had spent most of the day safely squirreled away while *he* had avoided taking a bullet to the face by mere inches, had participated in a highspeed chase, and had been arrested and confined to custody. If anyone deserved a good emotional breakdown, it was him. Not her.

"I'm tired," she admitted with a self-deprecating twist of her lips.

"Me too if I'm bein' honest," he admitted with a heavy sigh. "And my achin' bones are beggin' for a shower." The grin he shot her then was positively devilish. "I'd ask ya to join me. But part of my achin' bones can be blamed on you shovin' me off the bed. So I'll save myself the pain and misery."

She opened her mouth. But before she could say anything, Sam called down from the second floor. "Hey, Eliza? Mind bringing the coffeepot with you when you head this way?"

"Be right there!" she called and then made a face at Fisher. "All work and no play."

He chucked her under the chin. "That's what ya get for spoilin' us like ya do. We've come to expect it."

"I don't mind. I like feeling needed."

Something moved in his eyes. "We couldn't do what we do without ya, Liza. Ya know that, right? You're what makes this place a home."

Home. Family. Love.

It's what she'd yearned for since the day her mother died. And she might have lost it all today if that assassin's bullet had found its mark.

The tears she'd managed to hold at bay threatened to overcome her control. Before he could see, she turned away, throwing back over her shoulder, "Forget about me and go get that shower that's calling your name. You've earned it."

"Forget about ya?" he called to her back. "Not likely. If I had a flower for every time I thought of ya, I could walk in my garden forever."

She stopped and gave him her profile. "Alfred Lord Tennyson?"

He chuckled. "Woman, that settles it. You've been hangin' around me too much."

"Never," she whispered and then quickly resumed her trip to the kitchen because there was no more stopping the tears.

CHAPTER 27

Fisher stood beneath the showerhead, his hands pressed flat on the tile wall in front of him. He welcomed the steam that enveloped him like a warm embrace and was thankful for the force of the water that pummeled against his shoulders.

His whole body throbbed from the events of the day. Every muscle fiber he had had stayed flexed during the chase to the airport. He'd been slammed face-first onto the tarmac when the CPD had arrived with sirens blaring and guns drawn. And then he'd spent hours confined to the unforgiving hardness of a jail cell.

But it was the ache in the cold stone that was his heart that penetrated the deepest. The ache for Eliza.

If he thought he had yearned for her before, it was nothing compared to what he felt now. Now that he knew that were it not for the venomous, prickly legged thing inside him, then maybe…just maybe all those dreams he'd never dared to dream might actually have a chance of coming true.

"Fuck me," he whispered as the memory of her leaping into his arms and kissing him replayed itself in his mind.

It hadn't simply been a kiss of passion. It was as if every ounce of her being had been poured into that fleeting moment of intimacy.

A kiss of the heart.

A kiss of the soul.

A first kiss of its kind for him.

Which was strange to think about. Or maybe it wasn't.

He'd been careful with women from the start. Careful to keep things casual. To honor and cherish them without letting them get too close lest they be bitten by the monster.

But Eliza had spent four years worming her way past all his barriers. Four years flirting with him and arguing with him and working with him and feeding him. Four years being a colleague and a friend.

Was it any wonder kissing her was different from kissing anyone else?

As the water rained down on him, he continued to let the scene replay itself. Maybe because he was a glutton for punishment. Or maybe because he understood that it was as close as he'd ever come to having that big BKI love she talked about.

Last night, she shoved me out of bed.

Today, she kissed me within an inch of my life.

He might have thought she'd changed her mind and decided his friends-with-benefits offer was a good idea. But he figured that kiss downstairs had simply been a knee-jerk reaction to the danger of the day and her relief at seeing him alive and unharmed.

And I shouldn't read too much into it.

Satisfied he'd accurately assessed the situation, he turned his attention to carefully pulling off the butterfly bandages and letting the hot water rinse his cut. When he reckoned it was as clean as it was going to get, he reached for the faucet to shut off the water. Then froze at the sound of the shower curtain being drawn back.

Spinning around, he squeegeed the water from his eyes, and what met his gaze had his lungs collapsing.

It was a wonder his knees didn't follow suit.

Eliza was…*naked.*

No. Not naked. *Nude.* Her body was a work of art, all contours and curves. Her skin was pale and perfect. The little triangle of black hair at the top of her sex accentuated the feminine flare of her hips. And her breasts were high and round, the exact size to fit inside his hands.

For a moment, he was too stunned to speak. Definitely too stunned to move.

His fantasies about that kiss meant he'd already been semi-hard. Now his soldier stood at full attention and throbbed so painfully he only refrained from reaching down to rub away the ache by clenching his hands into fists.

"What are ya doin'?" he choked out.

Her dark, slanted eyes sparked with mischief and something deeper, something that had his balls pulling up tight against his body.

"Just thought I'd come check on you. You looked pretty wrecked downstairs. And this…" She winced as she gently brushed a finger across his cheek below his cut. "This needs better tending to than whatever they gave you down at the police station."

The wound still smarted. But her soft touch distracted him from any discomfort.

"Ya think I can't manage a couple new butterfly bandages?" It was a wonder he could talk, much less follow the conversation enough to form sentences that made sense.

Eliza is NAKED!

"I know you can. But I wanted to help. Well, that and I want to take you up on your offer."

Yes! All the lesser devils shot their fists in the air.

Not so fast, the better angels cautioned.

"Which offer?" His voice was so rough it sounded like he'd eaten a handful of a glass.

"Your offer to join you in the shower." A playful smile tugged at the corners of her delicious mouth. "And your offer to be friends with benefits."

His heart pounded in his chest and…lower, his body reacting to her proximity and her *nakedness—holy shit! Eliza is NAKED!*

He was tempted to pounce on her then and there, just shove her back against the tile wall and make all his fantasies come true, but…

He'd never forgive himself if she made a decision in the heat of the moment that would hurt her or haunt her in the future.

"Nothin' has changed for me, Liza." His words were a warning. "I can take ya to bed and give us both physical pleasure. But I can't feel the way ya want me to feel. I can't be what ya want me to be. It'll begin and end in the bedroom."

She stepped closer and he watched, mesmerized as a drop of water bounced off his shoulder to land on the upper curve of her breast. It dripped slowly, *slowly* down her smooth, pale skin until it caught on her erect nipple. There it stopped, dangling and sparkling like a delicious diamond.

He wanted to lap it up with his tongue. But he didn't dare move.

"If these past few days have taught me anything"—her hand cupped his jaw at the same time her dark gaze locked with his—"it's that we're never assured a tomorrow. So I want to live in the now. Revel in the now. And if I have to spend the rest of my life missing you for the privilege of getting to have you, that's a risk I'm willing to take."

He couldn't have scripted a better response if he'd tried. And yet…

"What about your abandonment issues? I don't want to set ya back on the progress you've made in therapy."

She hitched one pale, perfect shoulder. A shoulder he wanted to test with his teeth, taste with his tongue. "That's the beauty of friends with benefits, right? It's assumed there will come a time when the benefits cease, and we go back to just being friends. So there'd *be* no abandonment."

It sounded perfect to him. Too good to be true.

"And you'd be all right with that? Just bein' my friend after we've…" He let the sentence dangle as he gestured between them.

"How could I *not* be all right with it when I know that's what I'm agreein' to beforehand?"

He needed one last bit of reassurance. "You're positive?"

"I've never been more certain of anything in my life."

Even though the angels and devils warred inside him, fighting between desire and duty, he knew what the outcome would be.

He couldn't deny her this. Because this…*this* was what he'd wanted since he first saw her crossing the compound grounds the day she'd arrived at BKI. This was what he'd spent four years dreaming about. This was his moment. The closest he'd ever come to experiencing a big BKI love.

With a silent nod, he unfroze his muscles so he could pull her into his embrace.

Hellfire and damnation!

She was soft. Her skin was like silk and her lips like satin when he ducked his head to take a hungry taste. She was warm too. All that sensuous feminine heat radiated out from her lithe limbs and soft curves as she went up on tiptoe to press her length against him.

He could feel the rasp of her hard nipples through his chest hair. Feel the way her muscles quivered in anticipation. Feel how wanton she was in the way she undulated slightly, rubbing the hard column of his cock against the smooth flesh of her belly.

He let the water and liquid heat of his desire wash away all thoughts of what tomorrow might bring. For now, Eliza Meadows was his. And he was going to pack a lifetime's worth of love and passion into each second.

CHAPTER 28

What are you doing? What are you doing? the voice of reason demanded frantically when Fisher's perfect lips melded with hers, when his arms held her tight and his hands spanned her hips. *What happens when the loss of him is worse than never having him to begin with?*

Something is better than nothing, she argued back. *I might die tomorrow. If I do, I'd much rather go knowing what it is to truly be with him, to give him all of me, than to go being scared of the heartbreak the future holds.*

And when it all ends? Which he's assured you it will? What then? Don't you know how complicated it will be having to continue to live and work with him?

That's the domain of Future Eliza. All I care about is Current Eliza and finally knowing what it was to be loved by him.

She waited for the little voice to throw up another roadblock. But it was Fisher's low baritone she heard.

"You're so fuckin' beautiful." He pulled back from the kiss so his gaze could drift down her body. "You're the most beautiful woman I've ever seen."

She wanted to cover her breasts. Her boobs weren't large or perfectly round. And she'd always thought her nipples were too puffy. Like, the areola part wasn't flat. It was sort of raised.

That's not normal, is it?

"I'm glad you think so." She hoped she sounded coquettish instead of self-conscious as she tried to drag him back. Her lips missed his already. And if he was kissing her, he couldn't keep *looking* at her.

"I *do think* so." His tone was reverent as he resisted her tugging and kept his distance. "You have the most perfect skin." To prove his point, he slid a finger over her collarbone. Despite the heat of the shower, goose bumps rose to his touch. "The sweetest little waist." He used both hands to grip her there, his thumbs touching over her belly button. "The most feminine curve to your hips." He ran his hands over her hips and then around, until he could once again grip her ass, his long, callused fingers fitting firmly around the bottom curves.

"You forget I've seen some of the woman you've been with, Fish," she whispered, her lack of body confidence warring with the lovely sensation of having his big, hard hands roaming over her flesh. "I know what I am and what I'm not."

He stood to his full height to frown down at her. With the shower hitting him on the back and steam rising above his head, he looked like a god. Some ethereal supernatural sprung from the water and the waves, more beautiful than Aquaman and more impressive than Poseidon.

"Why do ya insist on makin' it hard for me to compliment ya?"

Since today she was in the business of admitting truths, she told him, "Because if I made it easy for you, you might stop."

He brushed her loose hair back over her shoulder. The steam from the shower had dampened the strands and one stuck to the side of her breast, forcing him to run a finger under the wet ribbon of hair.

Her nipple pinched painfully at the proximity of his touch. And she nearly moaned in disappointment when he didn't cup her breast. Instead he gently brushed that recalcitrant lock of hair behind her ear.

"I'll never stop complimentin' ya, darlin'." His voice was low and deep and seemed to come up from the broad expanse of his chest. "Because no matter what crazy notions ya got in your head"—he tapped her uninjured temple—"I know the truth. The truth that your form matches your heart. And both are so beautiful I can't imagine how I got so lucky as to have ya here with me."

"Kiss me again, Fish," she begged, hating the distance between them.

Hating that she could see all that lovely, crinkly hair smattered across his chest but not feel it abrading her nipples. Hating that, from the corner of her eyes, she could see the long, solid length of his erection standing tall and proud between them but couldn't feel it cushioned against the curve of her belly.

"Stop talking and kiss me breathless," she added desperately.

"Oh, I plan to do that and more." Confidence was in his tone, teasing was in his eyes. "But first let me look at ya. I've been dreamin' of this day for years. Don't rush me now."

She twisted her hands together, feeling unsure. But he grabbed them in one of his hands and whispered, "Trust me."

All the tension drained out of her. So did all the uncertainty.

She *did* trust him.

Trusted him more than she'd ever trusted anyone because he'd only ever been good and true.

When he saw her acceptance, he stepped back farther so the water rained down over his shoulders and ran in thick rivulets through the hair on his chest, over the rippling muscles of his stomach, and seemed to make love to the thick rod of flesh that sprung unrepentantly from between his legs.

For mercy's sake!

She'd peeked before. But it had been quick and only from her periphery. Fisher was…wow.

There weren't words. Or maybe there were, because while she'd always thought his body was perfectly proportioned—Ryan Reynolds only *wished* he could be so physically superlative—and while she'd always thought his face was exquisite, neither his body nor his god-like jawline could compare to the sheer flawlessness of his erection.

He was long and straight and thick. His skin there was two shades darker than the flesh on his body. And his mushroom cap head was plump and promised untold pleasure. Thick veins snarled up and around, pulsing with every beat of his heart. And when he caught her staring and…drooling? Was she drooling? His entire cock wagged as if to welcome her perusal.

To her utter delight, he grabbed his wide base and squeezed. Seeing him touch himself after years of *fantasizing* about him touching himself made her throat go as dry as the desert wind despite the thick humidity in the shower.

"This is what happens when I look at ya, Liza." His voice was gruff.

"When I see those pale, perfect breasts topped by those cotton candy nipples. When I see the inky softness of your pubic hair coverin' your sweet pussy. When I see how long and luscious your legs are and how"—he pressed a hand on her hip, turning her slightly—"full and firm your ass is, I'm so hard I feel like I might split my own skin."

She took a page from Hannah Blue's alien books and didn't give in to self-consciousness. Instead, she reached forward and took him in hand.

"That would be a shame," she whispered, shocked at the heat of him, the steely hardness of him, the…*thickness* of him. Her fingers struggled to wrap around the entirety of his girth.

He hissed and threw his head back. His Adam's apple invited the nip of her teeth, and she didn't deny herself the pleasure.

That was all it took to break the hold he had over himself. She suddenly found her back pressed against the back wall. The tiles were warm from the steam. But nothing was as hot as Fisher pressing his entire length against her front.

His chest was solid. His mouth was ravenous. But the best part?

Oh, the best part was the way his hands roamed over her skin, igniting flames of desire wherever he touched. And she couldn't deny his practiced skill, how he was both gentle and commanding.

He gripped her hip, holding her firmly against him. Then his rough calluses skated up her side, coming to a stop just beneath her breast. His tongue had been eagerly exploring her mouth, but when his thumb bumped the underside of her boob, he pulled back.

She blinked bleary eyes but closed them again on a groan when he cupped her breast and plumped it high. "Yes," she encouraged.

"My favorite word," he rumbled as his thumb passed over her nipple once, twice, three times. It was as if a string was attached from her breast to her womb, and his soft caresses awakened a hunger deep inside her core.

"Take me to bed, Fish," she whispered as his thumb continued to circle the painful point.

"In due time," he promised, and she opened her eyes to find his gaze glued to what his hand was doing. His nostrils flared and his cock pulsed against her lower belly like the sight of her body's reaction to his touch was the sexiest thing he'd ever seen. "For now, I want ya to relax and let me learn ya, darlin'. Let me learn all the things that make ya moan and pant. All the things that make ya cum and scream my name while doin' it."

Dear. God.

She moaned as his words fanned the flames of her desire.

"Just like that," he whispered as he leaned forward to reclaim her lips. "Now I know ya like it when I talk dirty."

And he did. For long moments as his hands worked wonders on her skin and his lips and tongue made magic in her mouth, he told her how sexy she was, how much she turned him on, teased her with all the things he planned to do to her.

With each touch, each kiss, he erased the future, leaving her lost in the now, lost in *him.*

When his fingers brushed through the silky hair at the top of her sex, her eyes flew open, but they were blind with pleasure. She knew he watched her for her reactions, but his face was blurry, seeming to look down on her as if from a dream.

"How do ya want to be touched?" he breathed against her neck as he left a string of hot kisses down her throat. "Ya want it soft or hard? Fast or slow?"

She couldn't think, much less talk or make decisions. She simply whimpered and shook her head.

He chuckled. Or maybe it was a growl. "That's okay, darlin'. I'll figure it out."

Slipping a finger between her slippery folds, he found her clit swollen and oh-so achy. Circling it softly with the tip of his finger, he rubbed a groan out of her.

"Good girl," he praised, reclaiming her lips at the same time he sank one thick finger inside her, softly slid it out, and then returned with two. In and out. In and out. Slow and steady as he gently explored her.

"Fisher," she breathed, feeling full and tight. Each thrust of his fingers stretched her. Each retreat left her empty and needy. She placed her foot on the lip of the tub to give him better access.

His touch was intuitive as he changed angle and pressure and speed until he found what worked best. He knew how to pay homage to a woman's body. To *her* body. And just as he'd said he would, he discovered the perfect pace to make her moan and pant.

The entirety of her focus, all of her consciousness, zeroed in on the place where his fingers worked. And it wasn't long before she felt the telltale ache of quickly building orgasm.

"Yes!" she cried out, shamelessly riding his hand. Bucking her hips against his ministrations as she climbed higher, higher, higher still.

So close. So close. So—

When he dipped his head to suck her nipple into the hot haven of his mouth, everything inside her broke apart. It was as if she shattered at the cellular level and what was left of her were shimmering incandescent pieces of pleasure.

She wasn't sure how long she remained that way, broken apart and yet fulfilled in a way she'd never been before. It could have been seconds or minutes.

Hours?

Eventually, however, all the pieces of herself coalesced into a whole. And her mind, which had blanked with ecstasy, returned.

The first thing she noticed was him nuzzling her throat, leaving soft, suctioning kisses over her pulse points. The second thing was the slick feel of his cock notched against her hip. Pre-ejaculate had oozed from his head to leave a delicious trail of desire above her belly button. And the last thing was that his hand still cupped her. He'd removed his fingers from inside her body, but he still palmed her sex as if he couldn't help himself. As if, now that he'd finally gotten his hands on it, he didn't want to let go.

There was something wonderfully erotic about that.

"So fuckin' sexy," he whispered against her throat. "I love how hard ya cum, darlin'. Feelin' your hot pussy clamp down on my fingers like that damn near had me shootin' against your belly."

"That's sexy," she groaned, snaking her hand between them so she could fist his hard, pulsing length.

"No." He grabbed her wrist. "I can't have ya touchin' me."

"Why not?" She arched a challenging eyebrow. "What's good for the goose is good for the gander."

"'Cause the first time I cum, I want to be inside ya. And I'm so close to the edge, I can't guarantee I'll be able to hold off if ya keep touchin' me."

"Put yourself inside me then," she invited provocatively and watched all the muscles in his jaw flex at the same time his nostrils flared.

"You're a goddamn temptress," he growled.

"Only with you."

He stared at her long and hard, as if he was trying to decide if he believed her. In the end, she wasn't sure what conclusion he settled on, because he turned to switch off the shower.

"I'm takin' ya to bed," he told her after he'd climbed over the lip of the tub and offered her a clean, fluffy towel. "There's still lots I want to do to ya. And most of it is better accomplished while horizontal."

"Do tell," she teased.

And he did. As they dried their bodies, as she helped him apply new bandages to his cut, as he continued to tease and torment her by softly brushing and squeezing and kissing her all over, he told her in no uncertain terms, and in deliberate, scorching detail, all the fantasies he'd ever had about her.

By the time they fell into bed, she was hot and achy and more than ready for another orgasm.

CHAPTER 29

Watching Eliza come apart in his arms was the most erotic sight Fisher had ever seen.

And hearing her scream his name had changed something inside him. He wasn't sure what. All he knew was that there was the Fisher who had existed before. And there was the Fisher who existed now.

And *this* Fisher? Oh, this Fisher had big plans.

Plans that started with him kissing every bit of her decadent body until he'd learned each curve with his lips and explored every dip with his tongue. Plans to learn her with his mouth the way he'd learned her with his hands in the shower.

Laid out naked atop his sheets, she looked like a goddess. All pale skin and black hair and exotic eyes that sparkled with desire in the low glow given off by his lone bedside lamp. And the way she responded to him, to his every whispered word, every stroking touch, made him feel like a god.

He realized he was staring, letting his gaze drink in every luscious inch of her, when she cupped his jaw and whispered, "I want to make love with you now, Fisher."

Make love.

Not screw or fuck or bone or bang. But *make love.*

Had he ever made love to a woman? He racked his brain and came up empty. He'd fucked slowly and sensually. He'd screwed desperately and passionately. But never had he slept with a woman for whom he had feelings beyond a general appreciation and fondness.

He had feelings for Eliza.

Lots of them.

He might not have the one she wished for. But he sure as shit had all the others. Respect, admiration, acceptance, trust, connection… The list went on.

So yeah. We'll make love.

"Soon," he promised, watching the way her nipple puckered when he gently cupped her breast and ran his thumb over the tip. He loved her puffy areolas, how they crinkled up like discarded holiday wrapping paper anytime her nipples tightened. "But first I want to taste ya, darlin'. Taste every sweet inch of ya. Is that okay?"

She caught her bottom lip between her teeth. "Oh." She waved a hand and feigned indifference. "I suppose so. If you must."

He squeezed her nipple between his thumb and forefinger. A tiny rebuke. She gasped and he watched delightedly as a blush stole up from her chest to stain her cheeks.

Ahhhh, he thought. *One more item to add to my growin' list of things Eliza likes.*

"Should I start now?" he whispered against her skin as he skated kisses from her arched neck down to her breast.

"Yes." Her fingers curled into his hair when he sucked her nipple between his lips and tongued the hard little nubbin to the top of his mouth.

He set about implementing his plan. There wasn't an inch of her that didn't receive the attention of his teeth, lips, and tongue. Sometimes he licked. Sometimes he laved. And sometimes he sucked. Her breasts, her belly, the jut of her hip bones were mapped by his appreciative mouth.

She held her breath when his face hovered above her sex. He dragged in the smell of hot, healthy woman. But he didn't put his mouth on her. Oh, no. He still had her legs to explore. The turn of her ankles. The delicate skin behind her knees. The soft flesh on the inside of her thighs.

By the time he settled his broad shoulders between her spread legs, she was whimpering and mewling. Sweat dewed her delicate skin, and her sex was overripe and melting in front of his eyes.

Goddess…

"Put your mouth on me, Fish." Her hips arched impatiently. "I can't stand it a second longer."

"I've had my mouth all over ya, darlin'."

"You know what I mean." She pumped her hips again. "Please."

"Lemme hear ya say it."

She lifted her chin. Her lids were lowered to half-mast, the definition of bedroom eyes. And when she spoke, her words were the definition of seduction. "Lick my pussy, Fisher. Tongue my clit until I cream."

He growled, the sound seeming to come up from the depths of his soul. "With pleasure, darlin'."

Her feminine flesh was pink and slick with desire. Her little clit was swollen and peeking from beneath its hood. Lowering his mouth to her most delicate flesh, he set about torturing it with his tongue.

Her voice was rough as her nails bit into his scalp. "God, yes, Fish. Just like that."

He settled in to truly feast, watching the way she threw her head back against the pillows, paying attention to how she unconsciously played with her own breasts, tweaking her nipples and rubbing them between her fingers.

Is there anything sexier than a woman who participates in her own pleasure? he wondered. *If so, I've yet to find it.*

Time and space had no meaning as he flicked and sucked and paid special attention to what made her catch her breath and writhe beneath him. It wasn't long before she began to make the climb.

She caught his hair in her hands to press his mouth harder against her, to aid herself in rubbing her delicious sex against his happily working tongue.

Her smell was tart and clean.

Her taste was tangy and sweet.

When he glanced up to check her progress, the lamplight bathed her breasts and belly in a golden glow. And he was reminded of a poem he'd recently read by Pablo Neruda. *"I want to eat the sunbeam flaring in your body."*

She was a sunbeam. And he was ravenous. Not to mention the way she was riding his face in abandon was so unbearably erotic that he had to press his dick into the top sheet to keep himself from humping his way to orgasm.

He was so swollen and achy, his balls so hard and needy. It wouldn't take much to send him over the edge.

"Fisher," she gasped when he slid two fingers inside her and set up a steady rhythm. "God, yes. I'm so close."

She blindly thrust her hips to meet his fucking fingers. And when she finally flew over the edge, he held still inside her, marveling at the hard, quick contractions of her vaginal walls. Loving the way she screamed his name until it ended on a shattering moan. Breathing deeply the smell of her arousal until it'd coated the inside of his nose the way the taste of her coated the inside of his mouth.

She shuddered against him over and over, her thighs clamped tight around his ears, her legs shaking as wave after wave of pleasure continued to roll through her. And then…

She collapsed.

Her hands fell away from his hair to lay palm-up on the bed. Her thighs let go of their vice grip around his head. And her breath shuddered out of her on one long, windy sigh.

He crawled up to lay beside her.

Her raven hair was a wild tumble across his pillow. Her chest rose and fell in quick succession. And her face was absolutely glowing.

Petting her softly, he ran a single finger over her collarbones, her ribs, briefly delving into her belly button as she slowly returned from the heavenly heights of orgasm and once more inhabited the earthy plane.

When her eyes blinked open, he noted they were still unfocused. "Ya—" She had to stop, clear her throat, and try again. "You're quite good at that."

He nuzzled her neck because he loved how warm her skin was there, how it held on to that ephemeral bergamia tree scent that was uniquely Eliza. "So are you, darlin'."

She chuckled. "Only with you."

"That's the second time you've said that." He pulled back and watched her eyes find his and focus. "But ya don't have to pander to my ego. I know you've had lovers before."

She cocked her head on the pillow. Her tone was the one she used when they tiffed.

"Since when have you *ever* known me to pander to your ego?" He opened his mouth to respond, but she raced ahead. "When you tell me I'm a temptress, I can assure you, it's only with you. Because no one before you has ever given me the opportunity to play the role."

"What do ya mean?" He frowned.

"I mean, my previous lovers"—just the thought of her with another man was enough to have the prickly legged thing growling with murderous intent—"didn't really give me a chance to be…" She trailed off as she wrinkled her nose. "*Sexy*, I guess. It's always been so fast and furious that I just sort of went along for the ride." Now she grimaced. "No pun intended."

He was still confused. *Is she sayin' she's gotten to the ripe old age of thirty without ever havin' good sex?*

Her next sentence confirmed it.

"As for being good at having orgasms, I'll admit to having perfected the art when I'm alone. But with a partner? I can count on one hand the number of times I've been able to finish with a man."

"Bullshit." The two syllables were out of his mouth before he could stop them. He added more diplomatically, "I can't believe it. Your body is so responsive."

She made a face. "No one has ever…*paid attention* the way you do. Until today, it's been my experience that men go through the motions of foreplay as quickly as possible to get to the ol' in-and-out." She made a rude gesture with her fingers that had his lips twitching. "Then I'd just…" She waved a hand.

"Just what?"

"Finish myself off whenever they left the room."

The thought of her having to give herself her own pleasure when she was so easy to please left him dumbfounded.

He side-eyed her. "How many partners have ya had?"

It couldn't have been many. Because men couldn't be *that* selfish and unskilled, could they? Surely his gender was better than that at knowing what women liked.

She blushed to the roots of her hair. Considering what he'd just been doing to her, he found it adorable that such a simple question might embarrass her.

"How many partners have *you* had?" she countered.

"Dunno." He shrugged. "I stopped countin' 'bout a decade back."

She blanched. "You're not serious."

"Promiscuity and military service go hand-in-hand. I'm not proud of it. But I'm not *not* proud of it, either. It just is."

Her upper lip curled. "So you're saying I should've made you get an STI panel before I decided to take you up on this whole FWB thing?"

He shook his head. "You've seen my most recent physical. Ya know I'm clean."

She harrumphed. And the way her bottom lip stuck out was impossible to resist.

He leaned down to rub a soft kiss against her mouth, got caught up in the way she tried to resist him and couldn't, and realized they were once again making out like horny teenagers when, minutes later, she fisted his hair in her hands and pulled back with a gasp.

"See?" She panted, licking her kiss-swollen lips. "It's *you*. *You're* the one with all the skill and expertise. And no wonder since you've had *so* much practice."

He probably shouldn't like the note of jealousy in her voice. He did.

"Ya want to keep talkin' 'bout this? Or ya want me to finally get around to makin' love to ya like I promised?"

She touched a finger to the side of her pursed mouth and pretended to ponder his question. Then she sighed. "The second, I suppose. Because the former makes me want to clamp your balls in a vice until you beg for mercy."

He chuckled. "Considerin' I plan to use my balls, let's not do that." Then he set about working her back into a frenzy. In doing so, he worked *himself* into a frenzy. Because despite what she claimed, she *was* a sexy temptress.

She met him kiss for kiss, ran her hands all over his body, squeezed here and rubbed there, used her own body in a sensual, undulating way as if she'd been in the business of seducing men for decades.

"Please, Fisher," she begged when he laved one nipple with his tongue and rubbed the other in a slow circle with his thumb. "I can't stand it anymore. I need you in me."

Thank the lord.

He needed to be in her too. He'd needed to be in her since the moment she stepped into the shower.

Rolling away, he delved into his bedside table and yanked out a condom.

He had it open and fisted down his swollen length in under three seconds.

When he turned back to her, it was to find her skin hot and damp from desire. Her eyes glittered with passion. And her thighs spread so he could see her pussy was ripe and open, ready for him.

He was so hard, he stood almost vertical. And when he positioned his hips between her legs, he though he might cum just looking at her lying there, a willing offering.

Grabbing her hand, he guided it to his throbbing cock. "Put me inside ya now, darlin'."

She whimpered when her fingers wrapped around his thick base. Then she worked her hand up his length, following every pulsing vein, exploring the crest around his swollen head before firmly fisting him and pumping twice. *He* was the one doing the whimpering then.

He fucked into the clasp of her hand. He couldn't help himself. It felt so damn good. But he quickly stopped because, as much as he wanted to let her flex her sexual siren's muscles, he couldn't hold back much longer.

"Have mercy, Liza," he begged, feeling a bead of sweat slip from his temple down to his jaw.

Her lopsided smile was one-hundred-percent pure enchantress as she slowly guided him to her entrance. He wanted to kiss her. He wanted to play with her breasts. He wanted to do all the things he knew he was supposed to do in that moment. But all he could do was watch as she placed his swollen tip against the opening of her vagina.

Where she was pale, he was tan. Where she was soft, he was unbearably hard. While her pubic hair was inky black, his was medium brown.

The contrasts alone were erotic enough to have his eyes threatening to roll back in his head. And then she slowly, subtly raised her hips until his meaty head disappeared inside her and he realized *that* was the definition of erotic.

Tight.

Hot.

Slick.

He gasped at the same time she did and lifted his chin just enough to see that she was watching too. Watching the place where they were joined. Enjoying the view of his thick, purple dick being welcomed into the glistening pink folds of her body.

"That's…" She didn't finish, simply shook her head in awe.

"Yeah," he agreed, his muscles quaking as he held himself back from slamming into her—which was what his body begged him to do. Just rut and fuck and stroke in a hurried, frenzied rush that would send him over the edge in mere minutes and relieve the terrible ache in his testicles. But that sort of satisfaction would be fleeting. And what he wanted was something long-lasting.

He hadn't allowed himself to think about it but, just as she'd said, friends with benefits implied an ending. At some point, they would stop the benefits and go back to being simply friends. When that happened, he wanted a million-and-one fantasies to look back on, to take out and enjoy on the nights when he was quiet and alone, to cherish for…well…very likely the rest of his life.

With that future in mind, he ignored his baser instincts and instead focused on memorizing every single detail of their joining. The way her body welcomed him, inch by slow, delicious inch. The way she fisted the sheets into knots in her hands and groaned once he was halfway home. The way she pressed her heels into the mattress and humped her hips up at him until he was seated to the hilt, the head of his dick mashing hard against her cervix.

They both hissed then. With sweet relief. With hot pleasure.

It took everything he had to remain still. To give her time to adjust.

Sweat beaded his brow. His voice was like gravel when he asked, "Y'okay?"

She opened her eyes and framed his face with her hands. Her expression was full of desire. "You feel amazing." She wiggled her hips, stirring him inside her. "And that feels even better."

Understatement.

It felt fan-fucking-tastic.

"And what about this?" he teased, slowly sliding out an inch before firmly reseating himself.

Her eyes rolled back in her head. Her feet found purchase on his calves, her heels tucking themselves into the bend of his knees.

"Yes, Fish," she murmured, catching her bottom lip between her teeth. "Just like that."

It was all the encouragement he needed.

Claiming her lips, he used his tongue to mate with her mouth in rhythm to the stroke of his hips. With each withdrawal, she moaned. With each return, she sucked in a ragged breath.

Eliza was tight and hot and soft and wet. Everything a man dreamed of. Everything a woman was meant to be.

He found the tempo that had her pussy milking him. Found the angle that rubbed his pubic bone against her swollen clit. And soon they were both panting.

"Fisher!" Her fingers clung to the divot in his back where his muscles bracketed his spine. "Yes."

There was that word again.

Favorite word in the English language.

He could feel the tension in his balls, his ejaculate begging for release. But Eliza wasn't ready. The two orgasms she'd already had meant he'd need to work for this one.

Releasing her mouth, he ducked his head to suck her breasts, rolling her nipples with his tongue, reveling in the way her core tightened.

Pressing up on his arms, he looked down to the place they were joined. Saw the way her juices glistened on his dick when he pulled out. Took great pleasure in the way his balls slapped her ass on each downstroke.

"You're so fuckin' sexy," he breathed, fixing his mouth to her throat so he could feel the hammer of her pulse against his tongue.

"I want to feel you cum in me, Fish," she panted. "I want you to fill me up."

Fuck me, he thought. Hearing classy, elegant Eliza talk dirty *did* things to him.

He lengthened his strokes. Strengthened his thrusts. And that did it because she went from panting to mewling. She went from running her hands across his nipples and down his abs to gripping his shoulders desperately as her legs clamped around his waist.

"Come on, darlin'," he gritted into her ear. "Fight for it and it'll happen."

Their sweat-slick bodies worked desperately, each giving and receiving pleasure. And it was everything he had ever wanted—only more.

Her hips went wild, humping like crazy, grinding desperately.

He could feel the strength of what was building inside her. Hear the harsh sound of her breath. Smell her growing arousal perfuming the air around them.

She was driving herself to the brink and taking him with her. And when he went he knew his was going to be blown to dust, reduced to atoms. When he went it was going to be unlike anything he'd experienced before.

"Fisher!" Her cry was one of frustration.

He knew what to do.

Snaking a hand between their bodies, he found her hard little clit and pressed it with his thumb, worked it in a delicate circle.

Her hands fell from his shoulders to gather up the sheets at her sides. He pulled back slightly to check her progress and saw her whole body was pink and her nipples were so hard they looked like little stones.

She chanted *yes* over and over, her head thrashing against the pillow, her lashes fluttering frantically. Then it hit.

Her sweet pussy grabbed his dick so hard he thought he'd lose the condom on his retreat. And when he slammed back into her, he felt each hard spasm that rippled through her sheath.

She didn't scream his name this time. It sort of sighed out of her as her body convulsed around his. And that's when his own release found him.

He gritted her name between his teeth as he drove home one final time, pouring himself into her. Endless jets of ejaculate ripped up from his balls to explode from his pulsing dick.

It was heaven.

It was hell.

It was a pleasure so intense it bordered on pain.

And it seemed to last forever. Just when he thought he was finished, her womanhood would ripple around him and another spurt of semen erupted from the tender head of his cock. But eventually, *finally*, they lay still. And the rasp of their ragged breathing was the only sound that filled the room.

If that's not makin' love, he thought when his synapses started firing again, *then it's the closest I'll ever get.*

CHAPTER 30

Fisher had given Eliza more than she'd ever known she could take.

So much passion. So much pleasure. So much…*love.*

Except that last bit is only me, she thought sadly as she lightly ran a finger up and down the sweaty divot of his spine.

She forced herself to mentally shake off any sorrow. She refused to focus on what she *didn't* have when what she *did* have was so, so much.

She had Fisher. She had his lust and admiration and respect. She had his affection and his friendship. She had his lovely weight pressing her into the mattress and his long, thick cock buried inside her.

He'd shoved his hands beneath her, cupping her ass when he drove into her as his orgasm hit. And he squeezed each cheek now as if, despite his satisfaction, he couldn't help continuing to tease her and, by extension, himself.

His head was beside hers on the pillow, his nose buried in her throat. Which meant his voice was muffled when he asked, "Am I crushin' ya?"

"No." She wrapped her arms and legs around him. "Don't you dare move."

"Mmm," he hummed contentedly, kissing her pulse point. "So I take it you're satisfied? Don't need me to leave the room so ya can finish yourself off?"

She smacked his shoulder. "If this is your way of asking, *Was it good for you?* I think you already know the answer. But I'll bolster your ego if you need me to."

"You've spent most of the four years we've known each other cuttin' my ego down to size, so I think it's only fair if ya give it a pat on the back now."

She dutifully patted his back. "Good boy. Job well done. Best orgasms ever."

He pushed up on his elbows to stare down at her. She loved seeing him from that vantage. She'd *dreamed* of seeing him from that vantage.

"I'm not sure I like the note of sarcasm I'm detectin'."

She tenderly pushed a whorl of hair back from his forehead—he really did need to go see his barber. Then she cupped his cheek. "Best orgasm ever," she told him softly, sincerely.

"Yes!" He shot a fist in the air. "Score one for Fisher!"

"And score three for Eliza," she was quick to add. "Which makes me the real winner."

He dropped his hand. His expression turned serious. "That you actually believe that between the two of us *you* are the real winner is the best compliment ya could've given me."

She shook her head. "You're amazing, Fisher. And not just in bed. In *life*. You don't give yourself enough credit. You should work on that."

"I'd rather work on *you* some more." He wiggled his eyebrows and reclaimed her lips. When his tongue delved into her mouth, mimicking the recent motion of his body, she felt her vagina clamp around him.

"Lord almighty, that's hot." He sighed as he pressed his forehead to hers. "But it reminds me I need to vacate the premises. I don't want the condom to leak."

I do.

The thought buzzed through her head before she had time to catch it and throw it away.

If she got pregnant with his baby then maybe…

No. I'd never trap him.

Even if the idea of having a little boy or girl with her dark hair and his pirate's eyes filled her with a longing she'd never experienced before—she'd always said she wasn't sure she even wanted kids—she could *never* use that as a reason to make Fisher stay when leaving was all he'd promised.

Hoping none of what she was thinking showed on her face, she patted his shoulder. "I'm ready."

They both hissed when he slid out of her. It felt delicious. And also a little sad. Because she'd been complete before and now…she wasn't.

Turning onto her side, she pressed up on one elbow so she could watch him walk to the bathroom. His ass was so high and round and tight, his back so wide and muscled and tan. He truly was The. Most. Beautiful. Man.

And *thoughtful* too. Because he returned from the bathroom with a towel and a glass of water. Both of which he handed to her before climbing into bed and pulling the covers over them.

After she'd taken a drink—more like gulped down the entire glass—and used the towel, she snuggled in beside him. With her leg thrown over his hard, hairy thigh and her head nestled on his chest, she could hear the solid, steady beat of his heart.

Solid and steady. That's Fisher.

Had he always been that way, she wondered? So dependable? So loyal and true? Or had the Army taken the amorphous lump of clay that was eighteen-year-old Fisher Wakefield and molded him into the man she knew today?

"If you could redo any moment of your life," she asked, "which would it be?"

She felt him duck his chin to look at her. But she didn't return the gesture. Instead, she played with the swirling hair over his chest and stared at the window that was covered with a blue tarp.

"Wow. Your pillow talk is really…uh…serious."

"Considering we've known each other for four years and considering what we just did together"—she gestured between them—"I figured I'd skip the small talk and get to the good stuff."

"Ya consider *regrets* the good stuff?"

"No." She moved her thumb over his flat, brown nipple and watched delightedly as it hardened. "I consider having conversations that *mean* something to be the good stuff."

"How 'bout ya go first, then. If *you* could redo any moment of your life, which would it be?"

"That's easy." She closed her eyes and immediately regretted the decision when the image of Charlie's bullet-filled body projected itself across the backs of her eyelids. Opening her eyes, she forced herself to focus on the opposite wall, on the festive-looking Mardi Gras masks Fisher had hung on the bricks. "I'd decline Charlie's invitation to attend his father's cocktail party. I knew he was more serious than I was. And I knew I wanted to pump the brakes because, as much as I liked him, I'd already resigned myself that I was never going to fall in love with him. If I'd told him *any* of that, we wouldn't have gone to that party, he wouldn't have sacrificed himself to save me, and he'd still be alive today."

"Charles McClean's death is not your fault, Eliza."

Even though he couldn't see her, she made a face of regret. "Maybe it wasn't my *fault*, but I'm the reason he's dead."

"No." Fisher hooked a thumb under her chin and forced her to look at him. There was such kindness in his eyes that she felt tears tickle the back of her nose. "If ya hadn't gone to that party, who's to say he wouldn't have gone without ya? And even if he *hadn't* used his body to shield yours, chances are more than good he'd still be dead anyway. That chef managed to kill most everyone."

That was true, she supposed.

She opened her mouth to admit as much, but Fisher wasn't finished. "Charles is the reason you're alive. But you're not the reason he's dead."

She hadn't realized how badly she'd needed to hear that logic until he spoke it. The tears that'd tickled her nose rushed to her eyes and spilled over onto her cheeks. She tried to duck her head, but he wouldn't let her.

"Nod and tell me ya know that what I just said is true." He used his thumb to brush away her tears.

She nodded and found herself caught up in his arms. And that's when the tears *really* came.

He held her through the storm of sorrow and regret, petting her back, murmuring sweet nothings. When her sobs were reduced to sniffles, he pulled a tissue from the box on his bedside table and chuckled when she noisily blew her nose.

Afterward, she released a tired breath and once more lowered her cheek to his chest. There was something infinitely soothing about the hard, rhythmic *thud* of his heart.

She counted the beats for a minute or two before saying into the quiet of the room, "Your turn."

She could tell by the hitch in his gentle stroking he'd hoped she'd forgotten he hadn't answered her question. And when he was quiet for the span of a dozen heartbeats, she thought perhaps he'd choose not to answer at all. But finally…

"I'd go back to the day my mom died." There was regret in his voice. When she pushed up on her elbow to look at him, she saw the same in his face.

"The day my mom died is one of the worst days of my life." Her confusion was evident in her tone. "Why would you ever want to go back to that day?"

"Because I might've been able to save her."

Oh, Fisher. Sweet, wonderful, wrong Fisher.

She shook her head. "How? You weren't even there."

His Adam's apple worked over a swallow before he hoarsely admitted, "But I was."

Now it was *her* turn to swallow.

He seemed to be holding his breath. She was certainly holding hers. When she finally spoke, she did so carefully, choosing her words deliberately. "If you'd rather not tell me, I understand."

"Ya showed me yours. It's only right I show ya mine."

"No." She shook her head. "You don't have to—"

"Shh." He pressed a finger over her mouth. She placed a gentle kiss on it that made him smile. "For the first time in my life, I *do* have to. 'Cause I want to. I want ya to know why I am the way I am."

She nodded hesitantly. "O-okay."

He started talking then. Haltingly at first, and then with more certainty. By the time he finished telling her about the afternoon he'd come home from school to find his father beating and raping his mother, more tears had spilled down her cheeks. Inexplicably, she felt her love for him grow.

He'd witnessed the unthinkable. The un*speak*able. And yet…somehow… he wasn't broken by it. Somehow, despite the horror and trauma of that awful, *awful* day, he was still good and generous and true.

And he's mine, she thought as she hugged him close, willing him to *feel* her love for him even if she couldn't speak of it. *For as long as he'll let me keep him, he's mine.*

CHAPTER 31

Two weeks later...

*T*he Fisher and Eliza era sure didn't last long, Britt thought as he helped Hewitt drop a shiny, new V-twin engine into the frame of one of Becky's spec bikes.

Hewitt must have been thinking along similar lines because he muttered, "Is it my imagination, or are they even worse than before?"

Britt shot him a look of agreement that ended with a grimace.

For over a week, Fisher and Eliza had been on each other like white on rice. One night, Britt had gone to get cereal from the pantry for a midnight snack and had caught Eliza down on her knees…uh…*polishing Fisher's chrome,* so to speak. Just FYI, there wasn't enough brain bleach in all the world to erase that memory from his mind. Hewitt had complained he'd found them half-dressed and making out like high schoolers on the sofa in the TV room after everyone had gone to bed one evening—the couch they *all* had to sit on, mind you. *Gross.* And Graham had admitted he'd walked in on them in the kitchen early one morning and, even though Graham had refused to give details, he'd alluded there'd been whipped cream involved.

That last incident had prompted Britt to corner Fisher in the shop and have a talk with him about keeping his exploits with Eliza in the bedroom.

Because while *Fish* might think Eliza was the sexiest thing on earth, the rest of them thought of her as a sister and…

No. Just…no.

But Fisher had simply scowled and said, *"Ya don't have to worry, bruh. We're done. Back to bein' friends* without *the benefits."*

That had been five days ago. And in that time, Fisher and Eliza had returned to bickering like they were getting paid to do it. Except previously it was like they'd been making a buck per word and now they were making a cool G.

They never stopped sniping and snapping at each other. And even now, with Ozzie's music blaring from the second floor, they could be heard above Guns N' Roses welcoming folks to the jungle.

It was getting out of hand. It was keeping everyone on edge. And it was starting to worry Britt because he wasn't sure how this new dynamic would ultimately affect their band of merry men.

I think I preferred it when they were doing it in the pantry.

"I love to shop, but I'm not buying your bullshit." Eliza stood over Fish with her hands on her hips and her jaw thrust out at an angry angle.

Fisher was crouched in front of his motorcycle, hand-painting details on the front fender.

Poor Mardi Gras had suffered some serious wear and tear when Fish had gone after the bagel shop shooter. Ever since it'd been delivered to the shop the day after the debacle, Fisher had been working to get it back in shape.

Although, it was safe to say he'd redoubled his efforts since he and Eliza had called it quits. In fact, Britt figured his wingman for life was now using Mardi Gras as an excuse to avoid their girl Friday as much as possible.

"It's not bullshit," Fish countered, not looking up from his work. "I said I'll get to it, and I will. I'm just goin' to get to it on my own schedule and not yours."

"It's *our* schedule," Eliza emphasized. "As in BKI's schedule. I can't get clearance for the next op until you finish your report. And I take *issue* with you acting like I'm asking you for the moon and stars."

Now Fisher deigned to glance up at her. "I could've sworn I canceled my subscription to your issues."

"Oh, no." Hewitt muttered from the side of his mouth. He and Britt were no longer pretending to work. Instead, they unabashedly watched the train wreck that was Fisher and Eliza's exchange. "How much you wanna bet she grabs that lug wrench and brains him with it?"

"My money's on the tire iron," Britt deadpanned. The smell of axel grease was strong in the shop this morning, but not as strong as the coffee Eliza held in her hand. He could see the steam rising from the mug and rethought his response. "Scratch that. Ten to one she dumps her coffee over his head."

"I hear Northwestern Memorial has a decent burn unit."

"Question is, do we call an ambulance or pull the child seats out of Becky's car, load him up, and drive him ourselves?"

Before Hewitt could answer, Eliza took a step closer to Fisher. Hewitt and Britt both held their breath, waiting to see what violence would follow.

"My father is expecting my summary tomorrow," she growled menacingly but, thankfully, didn't resort to death-by-scalding coffee. "The *president* is expecting it too. And here I am stuck between a rock and someone I'd like to hit with it!"

"I'll finish it this afternoon," Fisher assured her cooly, refusing to match her animation and only pissing her off more because of it. "Until then, have a nice day…somewhere *else*."

Eliza threw a hand in the air. "I can't have a nice day when I'm going out of my mind. I haven't left this stinking factory in *two weeks*. I haven't even seen the sun! Oooohhh!" She stomped her foot, then turned on her heel to march angrily toward the kitchen.

To keep from committing homicide, no doubt. Smart girl.

She stopped in her tracks, however, when her phone chimed in her pocket. Lifting the device to her ear, she barked, "What?" Her tone was instantly contrite when she quickly added, "Sorry, Geralt. I didn't mean to bite your head off. But I've got the worst case of cabin fever you can imagine, and *Fisher* isn't helping matters by—"

She quit talking and walked over to the television screen hung next to the front door. "Really?" Now there was curiosity and maybe a bit of excitement in her voice. "Are they coming to tell me this is all over and I can go back to having a life instead of hiding in this sunless hovel? A hovel that's home to the world's most frustrating troll, I might add."

Britt felt a little kick of adrenaline. Tilting his head around the bike frame, he saw on the monitor that Agents O'Toole and Douglas stood at the front gate.

Julia…

He'd made it a point not to think of her for the past two weeks.

Had he rewatched every *Star Wars* movie and TV series ever made in the interim? Sure. But he had *not* thought about her.

And dreams don't count because I don't have any control over them.

He wiped his hands on his jeans. His palms were suddenly sweaty. So was his brow. He dashed his forearm across it.

"What's with you all of a sudden?" Hewitt lifted a bushy eyebrow. "You coming down with something?"

"Nah." Britt shook his head. "It's just hot in here."

Hewitt narrowed his eyes but refrained from calling bullshit.

Hewitt could be counted on to keep his mouth shut, and Britt decided he'd never given the man enough credit for that particular trait.

He watched on the television monitor as Julia and her partner made their way across the grounds after Geralt opened the gate. Her pantsuit was black. Her shirt was gray. But instead of her usual ponytail, she'd piled her long, blond hair atop her head in a sloppy bun.

It suited her.

But maybe he thought that because it gave him an idea of how she'd look postcoitus, hair all tousled and messy.

Before he could stop them, his feet had skirted the bike lift and were taking him across the shop to the front door. "Ozzie!" he called. "Cut the music, man! The feds are here!"

Night Ranger, who'd been in the middle of singing about Sister Christian, immediately switched off. In the sudden silence, the *clacking* of Ozzie's fingers on a keyboard sounded as loud as gunfire.

Britt nodded to Eliza. Ever-dutiful, she pressed her back against the brick wall beneath the TV screen so she didn't present a target should someone nefarious be on any of the surrounding rooftops. Once he was assured of her safety, and before the FBI agents had time to knock, he threw the door wide.

The day was sunny and bright. And *hot.*

Heat mirages waved atop the blacktop. But he noticed them as an aside. Because his eyes were instantly glued to Julia O'Toole.

Her brow was dewy-looking. Her button-down shirt was damp and wrinkled from the humidity. And she whipped off her wayfarer-style sunglasses when he said without preamble, "We meet again. At last. When I left you I was but the learner; now I am the master."

Just as he'd hoped, her pale, pink lips quirked up in a smile. "Darth Vader's famous line when he meets up with Obi-Wan in *A New Hope*." She cocked her head. "Is this a thing with us now?"

He experienced a frisson of delight at the thought of them being an *us*, much less having *a thing*. Then he castigated himself for feeling anything.

"Just trying to make up for my poor showing of *Star Wars* knowledge the first time we met. I wouldn't want you thinking I'm slow on the uptake."

"I just assumed you were a superhero fan instead of a space opera fan." When he frowned, she nodded to his T-shirt. Printed on the front was a picture of Groot holding a cassette tape. "Marvel movies, right?" she asked.

He shrugged. "What can I say? I like a good antihero."

"*Deadpool* must be your favorite then."

He blinked at her accuracy. Although, he didn't know why he was surprised. He'd never met anyone as observant as Julia O'Toole. Which, undoubtedly, was why she was already a senior agent at the tender age of… what? Thirty? Thirty-one?

It was hard to guess since her diminutive stature made her appear younger than her years. And the smattering of freckles across the bridge of her nose screamed preteen.

"Not that I'm not enjoying this little tête-à-tête," Agent Douglas spoke up. "But the heat coming off this blacktop could fry an egg. And it's making my shoulder ache like a bad tooth."

"Right." Britt stepped back to admit the feds.

Did he notice Agent O'Toole smelled festive and warm, like cherries and almonds and sweet vanilla, as she breezed by him?

No he did not.

Okay, so maybe he did. But he didn't let it sink in. Because if he let it sink in, he'd have to concentrate on not thinking about her fragrance like he'd had to concentrate on not thinking about *her*.

Five minutes later, the two FBI agents had been shown to the conference table in the War Room. And all the current Black Knights, as well as Boss, Becky, and Ozzie, had gathered around.

In typical Eliza fashion, carafes of coffee had been provided along with a tray of fresh chocolate croissants, blueberry muffins, and bite-sized goat cheese quiches.

Fisher had been using Mardi Gras as a distraction. Eliza? She'd been baking like her life depended on it.

Not that Britt was complaining. He'd enjoyed three muffins with his coffee earlier.

Agent Douglas—who looked a little pale and drawn thanks to his recent stint in the hospital—had shaken his head when the tray passed his way. But Julia? She'd loaded her napkin with two croissants and three mini quiches.

She was busy chewing a quiche now as she turned to Eliza to say around a mouthful, "I'm sure your father will call soon to tell you we have our man. Or, rather we *will* have our man here in…" The little blond checked her watch and swallowed. "About fifteen minutes. Once our colleagues in Washington make the arrest. But I wanted to stop by and give you the news in person. Figured after everything you've been through, you deserve it."

"So who was it?" Fisher demanded, ignoring the irritated look Eliza shot him when he didn't wait for her to speak first.

"Chuck Reynolds," O'Toole answered before popping another quiche into her mouth.

For such a little thing, she could really put away the food.

"Why does that name ring a bell?" Boss asked at the same time Becky slid him a root beer-flavored Dum Dum.

"He's the minority senate leader," O'Toole said around the goat cheese pastry.

"And he's made headlines recently," Douglas added. "He was accused of flying to a private island to sexually assault an underage boy."

Britt blanched at the foul notion. All those around the table cursed in disgust or shifted uncomfortably. Agent O'Toole dropped her third quiche and pushed the napkin away like she'd suddenly lost her appetite.

"Is that why John McClean called together those folks on the committee?" Eliza was finally able to get a word in edgewise. "To talk about Senator Reynolds's depravity?"

"That's what we thought." O'Toole nodded. "When we first suspected it might be Reynolds behind the plot. But come to find out—and I won't bore you with the long, convoluted details on *how* we found this out—Senator McClean actually had proof Chuck Reynolds has been doing a little insider trading. And by *a little*, I mean *a lot*. The man has enriched himself to the tune of twenty million dollars through illegal investments over the last ten years. McClean found the proof, and it appeared he had every intention of sharing that proof with the committee at the cocktail party."

"Why share it at a cocktail party?" This from Becky. She had her own Dum Dum shoved into her cheek. "Why not call a committee meeting the next time congress is in session and make it official?"

"From what we can gather, McClean caught wind that someone in his office was slipping information to someone working in Reynolds's office. So he threw the cocktail party as a way to hold a committee meeting without, you know, actually holding a committee meeting. It was too late, though. Reynolds had already discovered what McClean had planned, and he decided to kill all the birds with one stone. Or…one gunman, as it turns out."

"Yeah." Britt frowned. "What the hell—excuse my French—did Reynolds have over on McClean's chef that would make the guy commit mass murder?"

"It's not what he had over on Peter Sullivan," Douglas answered, shifting his slinged arm into a more comfortable position. "It's what he promised him. Sullivan was dying of pancreatic cancer. He was leaving behind a wife and two small boys, and he needed the money. Not to mention, his recent psych eval showed some cognitive decline. His doctors suspected his cancer had metastasized to his brain. Which made him the perfect target for Reynolds. The poor man was desperate and not thinking straight."

"How did you link the two?" Eliza asked. "Reynolds and Sullivan, I mean."

"Couple of ways," O'Toole said, pulling the napkin back toward her and tearing into a croissant. "The day after the shooter at the bagel shop tried to take out Miss Meadows, a scheduled post popped up on Peter Sullivan's Facebook page. It was a long-winded, fanatical rant about the evils of our government. What you would expect from a guy who'd just killed a bunch of officials. But his wife *assured* us the post didn't sound anything like her husband. I had our Cybersecurity and Technology Division take a look at it. They determined Peter Sullivan's account had been hacked. They traced that hack back to the office of Chuck Reynolds."

"And the other way?" Eliza prodded.

"Once we made that initial connection, we put Reynolds's entire life under a microscope. The forensic accountants at the bureau noticed some recent activity in one of ol' Chuck's Swiss bank accounts."

"Because *all* folks on the up and up bank with the Swiss," Britt said sarcastically.

"Well, right." O'Toole nodded. "Anyway, on the night of the cocktail party massacre, Reynolds transferred three million dollars out of his account."

"Transferred it where?"

"We didn't know for the longest time. In fact, it took our accountants these entire two weeks to trace all the dark web wire transfers that money went through. But come to find out, it landed in an account at a bank in the Cayman Islands."

"*Another* place where all the folks on the financial up-and-up bank." Britt shook his head.

"Guess whose name was on that account?" When everyone blinked at her expectantly, Agent O'Toole answered her own questions. "Debra Sullivan. The account was scheduled to begin paying her five thousand dollars a month at the start of next year. And the *monthly donation*"—she made air quotes—"was going to look like it'd come from an anonymous source, some angel philanthropist who was sympathetic to the plight of Debra and her boys."

After that pronouncement, there was a moment of silence as everyone mentally assembled the puzzle pieces.

"So let me see if I have all this straight." Eliza rubbed her temple. She was no longer sporting a goose egg or bruised to high heaven. She was back to looking sleek and cool with her raven hair pulled into a ponytail, her lips painted her signature dusty-rose hue, and her black eyes enhanced with kohl eyeliner. "John McClean got the dirt on Chuck Reynolds and planned to share that dirt with the members of the newly-formed committee investigating congressional malfeasance. But Chuck found out about it somehow and paid Peter Sullivan, who was dying and desperate for money, to off the entire committee in one fell swoop before they could bring John's evidence to light."

"That pretty much sums it up." O'Toole nodded and then shoved a bite of chocolate croissant into her mouth.

Britt didn't notice how her lovely throat worked when she swallowed it. Nor did he have a brief fantasy of what it might be like to kiss that lovely throat.

"But then there were survivors." Becky spoke up. "And Reynolds feared Senator McClean might have already shared his evidence. So Reynolds… what? Hired some rando mercenary out of Asia to finish the job the chef started? How does one even go about finding someone like that?"

Britt had to bite the inside of his cheek. As if Becky didn't know *precisely* how that was done. If the woman hadn't gone into custom bike building, she'd have made an excellent actress.

"Oh, believe me, there are ways," O'Toole muttered. "And no doubt a man in Reynolds's position knows those ways. But to be honest, we haven't determined how he found this particular man. And we don't know if this man or any of his potential cohorts were the ones responsible for the hack on Senator Chastain's pacemaker. Those are mysteries we may never solve. Unless, of course, Chuck Reynolds tries to use that information to cut himself a deal. *Then* we might know how it all went down."

Britt could tell by her expression it rankled to leave a question unanswered.

"Which means you don't know *who* the bagel shop shooter was," Ozzie concluded. Their onsite tech wizard had made sure the various computer monitors showed nothing but highly detailed CAD drawings of fantastical motorcycles.

Britt hoped it was enough to convince the overly perceptive Agent O'Toole they kept all these computers for their work. Because the night two weeks ago when he and the others had taken her to the second floor to show her what little security footage they had of the shooter, she'd glanced around at the technology with an analytical eye.

She hadn't questioned why a bunch of motorcycle designers would *need* so much high-quality equipment. But he'd seen the speculation in her eagle-eyed gaze.

"Nope." O'Toole shook her head now, and it caused her messy bun to wiggle in the most delightful way.

Not that he noticed.

Okay, maybe he noticed *a little.*

"We know from the CCTV footage we pulled, the security camera video taken at Northwestern's ICU, and the images you guys supplied us that it was the same man at both sites. But he was wearing a prosthetic nose and forehead and, obviously, his hair was dyed. Our facial recognition software failed to find a match on his identity."

"Where did the plane land?" Fisher was the one to ask this question, and Britt couldn't help but admire the easy way Agent O'Toole handled the inquiries being lobbed at her from all directions.

"China." She grimaced. "Beijing to be precise."

"Right. So then that's a dead end." Ozzie ran a hand through his out-of-control hair. The man avoided the barber like most guys avoided talking about their feelings.

"We had our ambassador to China make inquiries with his contacts in the NPC but, as you can imagine, everyone over there is claiming to know nothing about a mysterious private plane jetting an orange-haired passenger from Chicago to mainland China." She shrugged resignedly. "If the assassin Reynolds hired *is* Chinese, or if the Chinese government was tied up with Reynolds in some way, you can bet your ass they're not going to admit it."

"So that leaves only one question." Again, it was Boss who spoke up. He gestured with his sucker, which looked tiny and incongruous in his big, work-worn mitt. "Why did McClean include his son and Eliza on the guest list? *They* weren't on the committee."

O'Toole wrinkled her nose and glanced with sympathy toward Eliza. "If I had to guess, it was Miss Meadows whom Senator McClean *really* wanted present that night. As powerful as Chuck Reynolds is, he's still not as powerful as the chief of staff. McClean probably hoped the information he planned to share would get passed along to the White House through unofficial channels."

"Makes sense." Boss nodded. "We *are* talking politics and politicians here, and the bastards are always working some angle." His wife smacked him on the arm—which was the equivalent of a fly bumping into an elephant. Even still, Boss feigned a wince. "Ow. What was that for?"

Becky widened her eyes and hitched her chin toward Eliza.

"Oh." Boss looked chagrined. Or...as chagrined as a middle-aged man with a buzzcut and facial scars could look. "Sorry, Eliza. No offense to your dad."

"None taken." She shrugged. "You're right. He *is* always working an angle."

"Yes, well…" O'Toole wrapped her last croissant in her napkin and slipped it into her pocket. "That's the long and short of it. But I think it's safe to say you all are free to start taking down your window dressings." She checked her watch again. "I expect to be getting the call any minute now that Reynolds is in custody. And with him locked up, I seriously doubt there will be any more attempts on Miss Meadows's life."

"Hallelujah!" Eliza threw her hands in the air. "Sweet sunshine, here I come!"

The group disbursed. Ozzie and Becky went over to the computer bank and started playing around with the CAD drawings. Boss retired to his office. And the rest of the Knights headed down to the shop to work on the five spec bikes that were in various stages of completion.

We're just your regular ol' custom motorcycle mechanics, after all.

Britt and Eliza escorted the feds to the front door. And when Eliza pulled Agent Douglas aside to thank him for his service on the day of the shooting, Britt crossed his arms and smiled down at O'Toole.

"I reckon this is goodbye, then." Was there a note of dissatisfaction in his voice? *Nah.* That was just his imagination.

"I suppose so." She tilted her head. "Unless you plan to commit a felony anytime soon. And then you might find me knocking on your door."

"Commit a crime? Me?" He lifted his hands. "I'm as pure as the driven snow."

She chuckled. "Somehow I doubt that." She was still grinning when she added, "You know, the first time I met you, I thought you were the world's biggest dickhole. And I'm not usually wrong about people. But I'm glad to find out I was wrong about you."

He grimaced. "I wasn't my best self that night. I'd like to blame it on the circumstances. But the truth is, I'm usually shitty to law enforcement."

She blinked. "Why is that?"

"Tough childhood. And the cops getting involved always tended to make a bad situation worse."

"Well, I hope I've given you reason to rethink your stance on those of us who carry a badge."

He hesitated, wondering if he should say what was on the tip of his tongue. Then he thought, *screw it*. "You've changed my mind about *you*, specifically. But law enforcement in general? Not so much. Still feel like too often y'all hurt more than you help."

She grunted. "You don't believe in bullshit for the sake of bullshit, do you, Sergeant Rollins?"

"Call me Britt. And actually, I can bullshit with the best of them. But when someone asks me an honest question I try to respond with an honest answer."

"Hmm." She nodded. "I like that. In fact, I think maybe, despite first impressions, I kinda like *you*."

His breath strangled in his lungs. His heart thundered like it did every time he jumped out of a plane. And the lovely, familiar spurt of adrenaline he felt had him scrubbing a hand over the top of his head.

Adrenaline was his crack. He sought it with a single-mindedness that probably warranted a trip to a good psychiatrist.

Which meant Julia O'Toole was dangerous to him in ways that went beyond her nose for rooting out the truth which stood in direct opposition to his position there at Black Knights Inc. where he had to keep most things about himself a secret.

There *was* a bit of honesty he could give her though. "I like you too, Agent O'Toole."

"Julia," she corrected. And the smile she wore was so genuine he felt another little spurt of adrenaline. "You can call me Julia now that I'm no longer working a case that involves you. Or…involves one of your coworkers and you by proxy, rather."

"Julia it is then." He liked the sound of her name when he spoke it out loud.

She opened her mouth to respond, but the buzz of his phone had her closing it again.

Pulling the device from his pocket, he frowned when he saw it was his brother calling. *Again.* It was the third time this morning. He'd ignored the first two. He didn't dare ignore the third.

"Sorry." He winced. "I really should get this." He was never sure what might come out of Knox's mouth, so it was best if the call wasn't overhead by a federal agent. "I'll just take it in the kitchen."

"Of course." She nodded her acquiescence.

"Hey, brother," he answered once he'd reached the hallway because his phone was about to switch over to voicemail. "What's up?"

He didn't hear what Knox said because, glancing over his shoulder, he saw Julia O'Toole slip through the front door. She took any further discussion about them liking each other with her.

It's for the best, he told himself and blamed the hard punch of disappointment that landed in his gut on indigestion from eating one too many blueberry muffins.

CHAPTER 32

Fisher squatted in Mardi Gras's shadow, pretending to fiddle with his exhaust pipe. But really his eyes were fixed on Eliza as she spoke animatedly with the tall, handsome FBI agent.

When Douglas reached out to touch her arm, jealousy twisted in Fisher's gut and had the prickly legged thing rising and gnashing its teeth.

It wasn't just that she was talking to another man—she talked to other men all day. She *lived* with other men too. It was the way she laughed, the way she leaned closer, the way her eyes lit up with interest.

He wanted to march over there, slap Douglas's hand off her, and bare his teeth at the bastard. He wanted to pull her next to his side and snarl, *"She's mine."*

But she wasn't.

She never had been even though, for awhile there, it had *felt* like she was and, as a consequence, he'd been happier than he'd ever been in his whole sorry life.

I had to end it, he reminded himself. *She'd gotten in too deep.*

In the long, lonely days since he'd pulled the plug on things, he'd been miserable. Even though he'd done the right thing. Even though it would be better in the long run. Even though he felt like the cold, hard stone of his heart had been ripped from his chest.

He closed his eyes and remembered how it had all gone down…

They'd been in her bed, dozing after another lusty round of lovemaking. Or, *he'd* been dozing. Then he'd felt her reach for him. Felt her run her thin fingers through his chest hair. And he'd been instantly awake.

Awake and gettin' harder with every pass of her fingers.

Except he hadn't let on he'd come out of sleep. He'd kept his breathing low and steady, added in the occasional snore, hadn't moved a muscle. He'd wanted to see what she would do.

It had been wildly exciting to watch Eliza hone her skills as a seductress, to see her grow more confident in her ability to tempt and beguile. And he'd been eager to learn how she'd go about rousing him that time.

Would she tongue his nipple like she'd done the night before? Duck beneath the covers and take his cock in her mouth like she'd done two mornings past? Or would she come up with something even more erotic and wonderful?

He'd continued to feign sleep when she'd whispered his name. He'd continued to feign sleep when she'd said, *"I love you."*

Even now, days later, remembering her confession made him want to curl into a ball and cry. Made him want to curse fate or the universe or whichever god was responsible for making him in the image of his father.

If she had stopped there, he might have allowed their little tryst to continue for a few more days. He'd have figured she mistook their wild physical chemistry for something more. He'd have figured she was mistaking limerence for love. But she hadn't stopped there.

"I love you like secrets are loved, in the shadows of the soul. I love you like sunshine is loved, in the warm, wide-open spaces of the heart. I love you simply, without artifice or ego. I love you elaborately, with all the weight and complexity of my life's experiences. I love you without knowing how or when or from where it comes. I love you because I know no other way to exist."

She'd kissed him softly. A warm, gentle press of her lips against his jaw. Then she'd snuggled into his side where she'd promptly fallen asleep.

As for him? He'd lain awake all night replaying her words, over and over until he'd had them memorized. By the time morning had rolled around, he'd known three things.

One, he might be able to quote others' poetry, but Eliza had a way with words that could compete with Plath or Poe. Two, the way she spoke of her love, so surely, so completely was how his mother used to speak of her love for his father, as if she had no control over it. And three, he'd die before he ever let history repeat itself.

Over coffee in the kitchen, he'd told her, *"I think we should go back to the way things were before."*

She'd been in the middle of biting into a lemon poppyseed muffin. His words had had her dropping it onto her plate. *"What do you mean?"*

"I mean, we've scratched our itch. We've lived for the day. But it's my experience that the quicker these things end, the easier it is to slip right back into our old roles. And the less likely it'll be that anyone gets their feelings hurt."

He'd felt pieces of himself breaking in two with each word out of his mouth. And the look on her face? If he'd had a heart, her expression would've broken it.

She hadn't argued though. She'd had more pride than that. She'd simply picked up her muffin and her coffee and disappeared upstairs.

When she'd come back down, her head had been held high and her back had been straight. The next time she'd spoken to him, her tone had been cool and professional with just the smallest hint of scorn.

He'd jumped on the scorn, figuring the best way to make her fall out of love with him—and her little speech had convinced him it *was* love and not simply limerence—was to show her the nasty, sarcastic side of himself.

He'd been making sure that side of himself stayed at the forefront ever since.

If their increasingly bitter exchanges were anything to go by, his plan was working.

When she laughed at something Agent Douglas said, he found himself longing for his next mission. The Knights were due to fly out in three days, which couldn't come quickly enough to suit him. And when she patted the fed on the chest, he felt possessiveness slice into him like a blade made from volcanic glass. Which proved just how toxic he was.

Possession is about ownership, remember? Love is about freedom.

She deserved better than what he had to offer her. She deserved better than *him*. But when she reached up to brush a stray strand of hair behind her ear, he couldn't help recalling how she'd done that *exact thing* as she'd gone down on her knees in the pantry.

She was so damn sexy. So damn beautiful. So damn *wonderful*.

The angels and demons waged war inside him again. The demons told him to go to her, to tell her he'd been wrong to put a period on their affair so soon, to rip her away from that square-jawed asshat. The angels shouted for him to stay away, to save her from himself, to be a better man than his father had ever been.

He listened to the angels…

CHAPTER 33

Ten days later...

Eliza paced back and forth across the shop floor, her heart firmly lodged in her throat.

At some point, the damn thing had grown spikes that dug into her trachea, making it difficult to breathe. But that wasn't the only part of her body that had turned traitor. Her hand shook as she clutched at her locket. Her lips burned where she'd bitten them.

It had been two hours since the Black Knights had landed at O'Hare. Two hours since they'd returned from a mission that had gone sideways from the start. Britt's injury weighed heavily on her, along with knowing they hadn't reached their objective.

What in the world went wrong out there? Human error? Faulty intel? What?

Anxiety gnawed at her stomach. Impatience poked at her brain.

Because Britt had been hurt, instead of letting them make their way home via cab, Uber, or train, Boss had rented a van to pick them up. Which meant they should've pulled into the compound an hour ago.

What is taking so long?

Although...if she was being honest, she could no longer rely on her ability to measure the passing of time. The seven days her guys had been

OUTCONUS—military speak for *outside the continental U.S.*—had felt like seven years.

She was always a little bored and lonely when they were away. But this time, she'd been bored and lonely and *heartbroken*. And apparently that last thing caused the hours to trudge by at a snail's pace.

She still wasn't sure what had happened to make Fisher call it quits on their arrangement. Had she said something to drive him away? Done something to push him to end it?

She'd replayed every interaction in her mind—most of which were so steamy she'd found herself sweating. But no matter how many times she'd gone through it, an answer eluded her.

She might have thought the reason behind his decision could be blamed on her confessing her love for him. But it wasn't like he'd heard. He'd been sawing logs like a lumberjack, and she'd been careful to keep her voice barely above a whisper.

The voice of reason that lived in the back of her head demanded, *Why did you have to go and confess? Why didn't you keep things to yourself?*

The answer was simple. She'd been unable to sleep that night because her feelings had been too big to hold in. She would have burst open like a human piñata if she hadn't spoken her love aloud, just once.

She'd waited until she was sure he was deep asleep before letting her feelings out. She'd said to the unconscious man all the things she'd promised herself she'd never say to the conscious man. And then she'd fallen into a deep, peaceful slumber.

If she'd known what the next morning would bring, she might have pulled a Rip Van Winkle and just *stayed* asleep for the next twenty years. Instead, she'd woken up with a heart full of love and a head full of ridiculous ideas that maybe…just maybe, if she played her cards right, she could convince Fisher he didn't want to Hugh Hefner his way through life. That what he *really* wanted was to experience a big BKI love. With *her*. Because they were so, so good together, and he had to see that, right?

What an idiot I turned out to be.

I warned you the loss of him might be worse than never having him to begin with, the voice taunted.

But it's not, she argued back. She had no regrets about becoming his lover. She'd loved every moment of being with him and she'd learned so much about him and about herself.

However, her worry that things would get complicated *after* they'd been together. Well, *that* had turned out to be justified. Because Fisher was—

Before she could finish her thought, movement on the security feed caught her eye. Her breath strangled in her throat as she watched the heavy wrought-iron gate roll open, revealing the sight of a white van as it pulled into the compound grounds.

Relief flooded her veins, momentarily washing away her heartache and worry.

They're home!

My guys are home!

She smashed the button on the wall that activated the garage door. Snake had replaced the shot-up motor. And this new one was quieter than the original as it rolled back the metal panels.

The summer sun had baked the blacktop outside until it looked shiny and slick. The smell of new seal coat tunneled up her nose and left an acrid taste in her mouth. And the heat was nearly enough to steal her breath.

She didn't care.

After two weeks of living in what had come to feel like a cave, she welcomed the intensity of the sun and the chemical smell of the blacktop. Since they'd removed the various window treatments they'd hung, she'd watched the dawn of each new day from her bedroom window, promising herself she'd never again take that view for granted.

"Are they home?" Ozzie called from the War Room. He was spinning his usual hair band playlist. Currently, Mötley Crüe was telling the girls to *kickstart my heart.*

"Ten-four!" She shouted. And, speaking of hearts, hers raced with anticipation as the van pulled up next to the factory building and Boss cut the engine.

It seemed to take forever for someone to open the sliding door. But it eventually rolled back to reveal Britt looking wan and weary. His entire left leg was encased in a blue cast.

"My god." She rushed forward. "Hewitt called and said you broke your leg. But I didn't realize how bad."

"Femur," Britt grunted as he accepted her help out of the vehicle.

"Throw your arm around me," she told him. "I'll help you inside."

"How's 'bout you let someone more Britt's size do the heavy lifting?" Sam hopped out after Britt and took up a position on Britt's other side.

Graham tapped her on the shoulder. He didn't have to say anything. In fact, he *rarely* said anything. She understood what he wanted her to do, though, simply from the look on his face.

Moving out of the way, she allowed Graham and Sam to haul Britt inside.

"What took you guys so long?" she asked Boss once he'd rounded the front of the van with three duffel bags in hand.

"Britt insisted we stop by Taco Bell on the way home."

"Painkillers make me hungry for cheap, fast-food Mexican!" Britt called over his shoulder. "Think outside the bun, baby! Live mas!"

Boss chuckled. "Don't mind him. He's high on morphine."

Hunter and Hewitt were at the back of the van, pulling out their go-bags. Fisher remained in the passenger seat, his phone in his hands and the screen lighting his face.

It was so good to see him and the butterflies he always managed to excite in her belly agreed. But she wondered if he was pretending to text in the hopes she'd wander off and he could avoid talking to her.

She hated the thought of that. Especially because she'd missed him like crazy.

Once again she racked her brain for what she'd done to change his mind and start acting like a bona fide jackass. And once again she came up with a big ol' handful of nada.

"Did they tell you what went wrong?" she asked Boss, forcing her mind to latch onto a topic that *wasn't* Fisher.

No easy task.

"Nope." Boss shook his head. "Just said the whole damn thing was pear-shaped from the beginning."

"That's the second time that's happened." She felt a crease appear between her eyebrows. "I'm starting to wonder if the guy inside the D.O.D. who's been dropping intel to Dad knows what the hell he's doing."

"That's a question for another day." Boss shifted all three duffels to one hand so his giant paw could grip her shoulder and give it a comforting squeeze. "For now, let's be glad they're home and give them time for some R and R."

"Right." She nodded.

When Hewitt and Hunter lumbered past her, their shoulders weighed down with all their gear and Britt's crutches, she told them, "I made spaghetti and lasagna. There's tiramisu for dessert. If you're not full of Taco Bell, of course."

"I'll take you up on that, thanks," Hunter said over his shoulder as his foot landed on the metal staircase's first tread. "In high school, I got a case of Montezuma's revenge from Taco Hell and haven't been able to touch the stuff since. Mind if I load some up in Tupperware to take home to Grace?"

"Not at all." She shook her head. "Everything is on the stove. Help yourself whenever you're ready."

"Has Becky eaten yet?" Boss glanced at his wife who was in the shop welding some framework. Becky wore pink bib overalls over a white tank top, and her thin, muscular biceps bulged as she worked. Becky had always given Eliza arm-envy.

"Not yet. She was waiting on you."

"Excellent." He smiled broadly. "I was hoping you'd say that."

"You avoided Taco Bell too?"

"Nah. I ate two burritos. But you know me. That was just an appetizer."

She chuckled and watched him saunter up the stairs to deliver her guy's gear to their rooms. After he disappeared onto the second floor, she turned to see if Fisher was still sequestered in the van.

She nearly fell over backward when she realized he was standing directly behind her, his own duffel thrown over his shoulder.

Her hand automatically clutched at her locket. When she realized what she was doing—a dead giveaway that she was nervous—she hastily dropped it.

"Welcome home," she said. Or, rather, whispered because her throat had suddenly closed up.

Welcome home? Seriously? That's the best you could come up with?

"Thanks." He dipped his chin and then brushed by her.

She opened her mouth to say…what? She had a million things she wanted to tell him and yet she couldn't think of a single one of them. In desperation, she reached for the one topic she knew he wouldn't avoid. "What happened out there?"

He swung back around. She tried to read his expression and couldn't.

"Simple. Either they knew we were comin' or they just got really, *really* lucky."

She blinked uncomprehendingly. "No way they knew you were coming. If they knew that, you'd all be dead."

"Oh, they tried. Believe me. And once they realized we were getting the best of 'em, they figured out a way to hurt Britt."

"Hurt him? Not kill him?"

"A dead soldier reduces a force comin' against ya by one. But a wounded man puts a strain on the *entire* force. They were good." A muscle ticked in his jaw. "Too good."

"Well, I'm glad you're all okay."

"Thanks."

There was that word again. She was beginning to hate it.

"Is there anything I can do for Britt? Should I run to the pharmacy or—"

"He's got everything he needs. And the only thing that'll heal that leg is time."

"Right." She nodded. When he went to turn around again, she felt desperate to keep talking to him. To keep looking at him. To keep breathing the same air. "So what about you? Is there anything I can do for you?"

God, you're an idiot. And you sound as desperate as you feel.

He lifted an eyebrow. "What exactly is it you're offerin'?"

She felt her cheeks flame red. "Well, not *that*. You made it clear we wouldn't be doing *that* anymore. I just feel like maybe we got off on the wrong foot once we ended things, and I feel like if we just—"

"People feel things all the time that are inconvenient. It sucks. But it happens."

Blood rushed to her head. The roar of her heart in her ears was enough to give her a headache. "What are you talking about?"

"You're tellin' me how ya feel like we got off on the wrong foot. And I'm tellin' ya that I'm not sure what the right one would be." When all she could do was shake her head and blink at him, he sighed. "Look, I'm dog-tired. And I'm not sure why we're standin' here havin' this conversation."

"Because standing here in awkward silence would be worse?" she offered, trying to lighten the mood.

It didn't work.

"This is worse than awkward silence. This is an awkward conversation."

"I'm just trying to show I care, Fish."

"Stop trying, Eliza." She swallowed when he used her full name. He hadn't done that since she'd told him she liked it when he called her *Liza*. "It just makes it worse."

Tears threatened. But only for a second. Because she reminded herself he was being a dick and she didn't deserve it.

Squaring her shoulders, she snarled, "Do you have a heart in your chest or is there just an empty space where you keep your wallet?"

Instead of answering, he asked a question of his own. "Are we done here?"

"Yeah." She nodded, her hands curling into fists so tight her nails bit into her palms. "We're done. Because you might not currently be the biggest asshat in the world, but you better hope the guy who is doesn't die."

Instead of coming back with a quick quip, he simply headed for the stairs.

She shot his broad back a venomous look. But when she saw Becky walking over to her—she had to have overhead everything—Eliza was careful to wipe her face clean and offer a smile.

"You're right," Becky said from the side of her mouth once Fisher disappeared onto the second floor. "He *is* being an asshat. I hope you're not letting it get to you. I know you…have feelings for him."

Eliza's shoulders drooped. "Is it that obvious?"

"Only to anyone with eyes," Becky affirmed unhelpfully.

"Well, damn it." *Like, seriously, DAMNIT!*

"But don't worry." Becky nodded decisively. "You'll get over it." She pulled a Dum Dum from the front pocket of her overalls. "You're beautiful and kind and smart, and there's plenty of fish in the sea."

Eliza would've *loved* to share Becky's optimism, but… "Yeah. There's lots of toxic trash too."

Becky winced. "So what say we go crack open some beers and enjoy your Italian spread? Did you make that yummy garlic bread I like so much?"

"I did." Eliza nodded. "But don't you and Boss need to pick up your girls?"

"Nope." Becky shook her head. "They're having a sleepover at Aunt Michelle and Uncle Snake's house. We try to take turns one weekend a month looking after each other's kids, so we get some adult alone time."

Boss came bounding down the stairs then. He didn't hesitate to pull his wife into his arms and smile down at her. "I missed you."

"You were only gone two hours."

"All the same." He wiggled his eyebrows before planting a smacking kiss on her mouth.

"Fine. Yes. I'll share a beer with you guys." Eliza was glad to have a distraction from Fisher, from her thoughts of Fisher, from her *love* for Fisher. "If it'll make you stop rubbing your sickeningly *wonderful* relationship in my face, I'll share ten beers with you."

"Challenge accepted. I've been needing a good, ol' fashioned, adults-only house party. " Becky laughed and grabbed Boss by the hand to pull him toward the kitchen.

Eliza took a more leisurely journey down the hall, marveling she was still functioning when she felt as fragile as glass and as sad as a person could get. She still talked and walked like normal. Still got up in the morning, brushed her teeth twice a day, washed her makeup off before climbing into bed at night.

The human heart is stronger than I ever imagined, she admitted. *Even broken into a million shards, mine still manages to pump blood.*

CHAPTER 34

Fisher cracked open one eyelid and stared at the digital display on his alarm clock.

Two AM. Who the hell is still up and carryin' on?

He could hear music coming from the courtyard out back. There was also a lot of laughter and the occasional shout.

He sniffed the air. Someone had built a fire in the firepit despite it having been ninety-five degrees when they landed at O'Hare.

Chicago summers were usually beautiful, so much more pleasant than the brutal, cloying heat of the South. But this summer had been particularly warm in the City of Broad Shoulders. Even at night, it was rare for the temps to drop low enough to make an outdoor fire enjoyable.

He tried going back to sleep. The last op had been awful. He'd probably only slept fifteen hours in seven days and every muscle in his body ached from having spent a trans-Atlantic flight crammed into the cargo hold on a military transport. The instant he heard Eliza's delighted giggle, however, he knew he was more likely to sprout a second dick than get back to sleep. Especially when a responding male chuckle reached his ears.

Who the fuck is out there with her? And don't they know we need rest?

After throwing back the covers and tugging on jeans—he skipped the boxer briefs; there was no time—he jerked open his bedroom door and took the stairs to the second floor two at a time. By the time he'd landed on the first floor and had made his way down the hall to the kitchen, his blood was at a full boil.

He told himself it was because the music was too damn loud. He told himself it was because Eliza and company were being rude as hell. But the truth was, he was mad because he was miserable.

He was miserable and it sounded like Eliza was having the time of her life and—

All thoughts screeched to a halt when he yanked open the back door and saw Boss, Becky, Hewitt, Graham, Eliza and Britt sitting around the firepit.

The sky was clear and bright, the stars managing to compete with the city lights. There was a slight breeze blowing in from the direction of Lake Michigan. It was cool and pleasant. There were bags of chips, empty bottles of beer, and a few of Eliza's homemade desserts strewn around the mixed-matched end tables next to each Adirondack chair.

In short, it was a party.

"Did my invitation get lost in the mail?" He stepped onto the wide, gray flagstones. Everyone currently in residence was outside enjoying the night—Sam had adiosed himself over to Hannah's apartment as soon as he'd stowed his gear, and Hunter had loaded up some of Eliza's dinner and then quickly raced home to his wife, Grace.

Everyone but me, apparently.

"Sorry," Becky winced. "Were we being too loud?"

Her phone was face-down on the arm of her chair. But she quickly turned it over and started swiping. Within three seconds, the volume coming through the Bluetooth speakers lowered from club levels to more appropriate backyard barbeque levels.

"Somethin' like that," he admitted, frowning at Graham as he walked over to an empty seat. "Aren't ya exhausted, G-man?" Fisher accepted the longneck Hewitt handed him. "Ya been humpin' yours *and* Britt's gear for two days now."

In typical Graham-fashion, he said succinctly, "Never too tired to drink with friends."

"And what about you?" Fisher turned to Britt while popping the top on his Goose Island IPA. His wingman's busted leg was propped on a stool, his bare toes glowing pink in the firelight. "You shouldn't be drinkin' when you're takin' scheduled narcotics."

"Don't worry, Mom." Britt picked up a water bottle from beside his chair. "All I'm doing is hydrating"—he pulled a prescription bottle from the pocket of his robe and shook it—"and staying high." His grin was toothy.

Becky and Boss sat next to each other, holding hands and looking like newlyweds even though they were decidedly *not* and had two kids to prove it. "Where are the girls?" he asked them with a curious cant of his chin.

"With their aunt and uncle." It wasn't Boss or Becky who answered. It was Eliza. Her words were slurred and one eyelid hung lower than the other. And her grin? It wasn't just a little lopsided. It was a *lot* lopsided.

He couldn't remember the last time he'd seen her tipsy. In fact, he wasn't sure he'd *ever* seen her that way.

"Did you rouse yourshelf—" She stopped and blinked. "*Yourself* out of bed just to come down here and harsh everyone's mellow?"

Despite his foul mood, he found his lips twitching. "Have you been dippin' into Britt's pain meds?"

"Oh, ha ha." She gave him an irritated look. He reckoned that was what she was aiming for anyway. In truth, she looked sort of…constipated. "That's what we've been missing tonight; your unparalleled wit."

For whatever reason, her drunkenness made it impossible for him to maintain the dickish disposition he'd donned since the morning he told her there would be no more benefits. "I'm thinkin' ya might want to slow down on that stuff." He tilted the neck of his own beer toward the one she held in her left hand. "You're startin' to sound like Ozzie."

"Can you recall when I asked for your opinion?" she snapped back. "Neither can I."

To prove her point, she took a long slug of her beer. After she'd drained it, she slammed the empty bottle down on the arm of her chair and belched loudly.

He blinked. Then he blinked again when she stood and walked— wobbled?—over to him to point a finger at his nose.

"I don't like this pershun—" She stopped and moved her lips like they might be numb. "*Personality* you've recently acquired," she managed. "Being a bitter butthead doesn't make you prettier, in case no one's told you."

She turned, stumbled a little, and announced to the group, "Thanks for the fun, everyone. But since Sir Sourface has arrived"—she gestured to Fisher—"I'm calling it a night."

She weaved her way to the back door and Fisher called after her. "Don't let me ruin your fun!"

"Too late!" She stabbed a finger in the air before disappearing inside.

"Yeah." Britt slapped the arms of his chair. "She's right. It's late. Time to turn in. Who's carrying me upstairs?"

"I'm your huckleberry," Hewitt raised a hand.

Graham simply drained the last of his beer and stood to assist Hewitt in getting Britt out of the Adirondack.

"Wait. What?" Fisher frowned. "I show up and suddenly everyone's turnin' in?"

"You snooze, you lose, brother," Britt grinned.

Graham and Hewitt acted as human crutches and escorted him into the old factory building.

Fisher looked expectantly at Becky and Bossy. "And then there were three."

"Two," Becky corrected. "I'm headed to the cottage to brush my teeth. They feel like they're wearing fuzzy sweaters."

"Y'all are spendin' the night?"

She winked at him. "We figured we'd take advantage of bein' child-free and relive a bit of our past."

Before they'd had children, Boss and Becky had lived in the little foreman's cottage out front. Now it sat empty most days.

"I'll be right behind you." Boss smacked Becky's ass when she stood. "Just lemme finish this last beer."

"Don't keep me waiting too long." She bent to kiss his lips. "You know I get impatient."

"One of my favorite things about you," Boss grumbled, and the light in his eyes as he looked at his wife was so hot and intimate Fisher feigned sudden interest in the dancing fire.

After Becky disappeared around the side of the building, Fisher made a face at Boss. "Didn't mean to run everyone off."

"Nah." Boss dismissed his comment with a wave of his big mitt. "You just reminded us we're not twenty-five anymore. If we don't call it quits now, we'll be paying for it tomorrow."

"I think Eliza is going to be payin' for it regardless."

Boss eyed him curiously. "Sometimes the only way a person can hide their hurt is to drown it."

Shifting uncomfortably, Fisher returned his attention to the flickering flames.

Boss wasn't deterred. "You gonna tell me what happened between you two?"

Being put on the spot by Boss made him feel like a twelve-year-old who was seconds away from getting into trouble.

Taking a slow sip of beer, he tried to find the right words. Then he decided there were none. There was only the truth.

"We want different things, that's all." He shrugged and tried to act nonchalant even though talking about it caused his throat to go dry. He took another drink and welcomed the harsh taste of the hops. It matched the bitterness in his cold stone heart. "She wants a big BKI love like all you originals have, like Hunter and Grace have, like Sam and Hannah have. And I…" He trailed off, unsure of how to finish.

"You what?" Boss prodded.

"I can't."

Boss stared hard at him. Which was sort of like being stared down by a silverback gorilla. When it became clear Fisher wasn't about to go on, Boss forced the issue. "Can't or won't?"

Fisher sighed. "If I'm being honest? Both."

Boss took a slow sip of his beer, eyeing Fisher over the end of his bottle. Once he swallowed, he said, "You're gonna need to give me more than that."

Fisher debated the advisability of airing the piles of dirty laundry from his past. But eventually decided, *Fuck it. If anyone will understand, it's Boss. Boss who knows* exactly *how dangerous guys like me can be even when we aren't saddled with hereditary jealousy.*

He told Boss the same story he'd told Eliza about his parents. He went on to admit the way he was programmed to love wasn't healthy. And he ended with, "I knew right from the start Eliza was dangerous for me. Because I liked her and respected her and thought she was the most beautiful woman on the planet. And the first time I saw her with another man, I wanted to walk over and gouge the sonofabitch's eyes out. When she seemed to be gettin' serious about Charles McClean, it took everything I had not to punch the bastard's teeth in each time he opened his damn mouth around me."

He ran a hand through his hair. "Lord, when I saw that ring on her finger? Before I found out how it all went down at that cocktail party and how she hadn't actually accepted McClean's proposal? Ya know, when I thought she was goin' to be *Mrs.* McClean?" He took a sip of his beer because his voice had gone hoarse. Likely due to the lump suddenly lodged in his throat. "Man, I tell ya what. I wanted to break the world into a hundred pieces and then bury it where no one would ever find it. And if that isn't fucked up, I don't know what is."

For a while after that pronouncement, they both sat in silence. Both staring into the orange and yellow flames. A knot in a log popped and sparks erupted into the air above the firepit like lightning bugs.

When Boss finally spoke, his deep voice was quiet. So quiet Fisher had to lean forward, elbows planted on his knees, to hear the big man.

"So what I'm hearing is you broke things off with Eliza *not* because you were scared she isn't the one. But because you're absolutely terrified she is."

Fisher swallowed. The damn lump in his throat kept growing.

"She told me she loves me. She thought I was asleep, but I was fakin' it. And she said…"

He couldn't repeat what she'd said. It'd been too beautiful. Too painful. If he spoke those words aloud, he'd lose it, and the last thing he wanted was to break down and cry like a baby in front of Boss.

Shaking his head resolutely, he declared instead, "I had to end it. If I could love her the way she deserves, free of jealousy, free of obsession, free of all that toxic shit that runs in my blood, believe you me, brother, I'd have gone down on one knee then and there. But I can't promise her that. No matter how much I wish I could."

"Ah." Boss nodded. "I think I'm starting to understand. But let me ask you this. Why *didn't* you walk over and gouge that man's eyes out? Why *didn't* you punch Charlie McClean's teeth in?"

Fisher's chin jerked back. "Because, despite my most recent behavior, I try *not* to be an asshole and take my frustrations out on innocent folks."

Boss nodded again. "You know, one of the interesting things about us humans is we tend to judge ourselves by our intentions and everyone else by their actions." When Fisher frowned, he continued. "If we hurt someone, especially someone we love, we always say to ourselves, *but that wasn't my intention.* Whereas if someone hurts us, especially if that someone is supposed to love us, we don't care what their intention was. All we care about is that their action *did* hurt, and we don't want it to happen again."

Fisher lifted his eyebrows. "Yeah. I reckon you're right about that."

"Which means we usually go easier on ourselves than others," Boss went on. "We give ourselves a pass if we didn't *intend* to do something. But you? You're harder on yourself."

"How so?" Fisher felt his eyebrows form a V.

"You thought about gouging that guy's eyes out but didn't. You considered punching McClean's teeth in but didn't. And yet here you sit, castigating yourself as if you'd actually followed through."

"The fact that I even had the thoughts—"

"Proves nothing," Boss interrupted before he could finish his sentence. "You think I don't want to break legs and bash heads when some asshole ogles Becky? You think I don't get jealous when Graham walks by her without a shirt on? The bastard's built like Alan Ritchson. Of *course* I get jealous."

"You're built like Alan Ritchson too, Boss."

The big man made a rude sound. "I used to be. But I'm middle-aged and enjoying the good life as a civilian now. My six-pack is long gone, and I'd likely have a stroke if I tried to hump eighty pounds of gear more than a hundred yards."

Sighing, Boss added, "My point is, jealousy is a human condition. We *all* suffer from it. And obsession? You think I'm not completely obsessed with my wife? She's the first thing I think of in the morning and the last thing I want to see before closing my eyes at night. My love for that woman is all-consuming."

"Yeah, I know. But—"

"No buts." Boss cut him off again. "You're not your father. You're not a monster. Because you *can* be obsessed, you *can* be jealous, and yet you don't act on those baser instincts."

Fisher's nostrils flared as he fought to keep his emotions in check.

Is Boss right? Is what I feel normal? Is it possible I can love the right way? The real *way?*

"I've known you for four years now, Fish. I've seen the way you treat people. You're a good man. And if anyone can break unhealthy cycles, it's you."

The back of Fisher's eyes burned. Hearing Boss, someone he'd grown to respect and admire, call him a *good man* healed something in him. Maybe that something was the little boy who'd sought the approval of his own father but had never gotten it.

Boss chuckled. "But don't get me wrong. If you decide to give in and give love a try, don't be thinking it's all gumdrops and gladiolus. There are times it's hard. Times when you'll be so mad at your woman you can't see straight. Times when you doubt *yourself* and wonder if you're enough. But news flash, she'll feel all those ways too. Loving someone is incredible and awful and then incredible again." Boss's teeth flashed white when he smiled at the slowly dying fire. The embers glowed and danced in that magical way only embers could. "And in-between the incredible and awful is the boring, routine, ordinary parts of living a life together."

Boss held Fisher's gaze then as he finished. "So you revel in the incredible. You make sure to be gentle with each other through the awful. And you relax and enjoy the comfort of the routine. That's what it means to truly know incredible, awful, ordinary love."

Fisher couldn't speak past the lump in his throat. It had grown to the size of a watermelon. And he hastily dashed away a tear that had slipped past his barriers to roll down his cheek.

"Welp." Boss slapped the arms of his chair before pushing to a stand. "I don't dare keep my wife waiting a minute longer." He looked around at the mess. "Don't bother cleaning up. Becky and I will get to it in the morning. Just be sure to douse the fire before you turn in."

Fisher nodded because that's all he could manage.

Boss turned once he'd made it to the corner of the building. "Hey, Fish?"

Fisher dashed another tear from his cheek before swinging around in his chair to face the older man. "Yeah?"

"I know it might not feel like it given how all us original Knights are partnered up with our soulmates, but real love, *true* love doesn't just fall out of the sky like frozen airplane toilet water."

Fisher fell back on his humor because it was the only thing that wouldn't end with him in tears. Or...*more* tears. "Wow, Boss. And they call *me* the poet."

Boss chuckled, shook his head, and disappeared around the corner, leaving Fisher to stare into the flames and ponder the big man's words...

CHAPTER 35

Eliza's head felt like a battlefield where a thousand tiny soldiers waged war.

Groaning, she attempted to pry open her eyes only to be met with a searing pain that made her regret the attempt.

Too bright.

The morning sunlight streaming into her room was *so* damn bright it made her miss the time her window had been covered by a tarp.

Her tongue was sandpaper. Her stomach was a cauldron of sloshing foulness. And she had the absolute *worst* taste in her mouth.

The memories of the night's indulgence flooded back, how she'd cracked open a third, fourth, and *fifth* beer despite knowing better.

You idiot, the voice of reason chastised. *What were you thinking?*

The answer was simple. She'd been thinking she needed oblivion, just a few minutes of not feeling like she would shatter if someone looked at her the wrong way. Just a few hours of being numb instead of raw and exposed.

And now I'm paying for it. I feel just as raw and exposed as ever. Plus, I have the world's worst hangover.

Brilliant plan, Eliza! Top-notch decision making!

Through the haze of her hangover, she heard the familiar sound of Fisher's harmonica drifting in from the room next door. A Taylor Swift melody trilled through the air, all happy and upbeat. Which was a stark contrast to the way she felt.

Seriously, Fisher? she thought with annoyance that quickly morphed into anger. *You're over there as happy as a clam while I'm over here with a heart broken into a million irreparable pieces?*

Well, fuck you very much!

With a furious growl, she grabbed the nearest pillow and buried her head beneath it, attempting to drown out the noise and, simultaneously, her spiraling thoughts. She wanted to scream into the pillow, thinking it might help release some of her pent-up anguish and frustration. Her already aching head kept her quiet.

Eventually, the futility of hiding became unbearable. It wasn't helping anyway. She could still hear the music.

With a heavy sigh, she threw back the covers and climbed unsteadily out of bed, her limbs protesting every movement.

First order of business, toilet. Second order of business, toothbrush. Third order of business…maybe death.

She wobbled her way to the bathroom and only realized she'd failed to change out of her clothes and into her pajamas when she had to work the zipper on the fly of her jeans. She sat on the toilet with a groan and then closed her eyes when the room began to spin.

She kept her eyes closed while washing her hands and running a makeup wipe under her eyes where her mascara had smudged two black stripes that made her look like she was trying out for the NFL. And when she brushed her teeth—or, more specifically, her tongue—she found herself bent over the toilet depositing what was left of the night's tomfoolery into the porcelain bowl.

She was shaking by the time she'd emptied her stomach. But when she straightened to make a second attempt at brushing her teeth, she was gratified to find the room no longer doing its best impression of a whirligig.

After popping two Tylenol, she made the return trip to bed while cursing the weakness of her limbs and the incessant throbbing of her head. She'd just pulled the covers back over her head in an attempt to block out the light when Fisher switched from "Love Story" to "You Belong with Me," and she'd had enough.

Was he intentionally torturing her?

"Sonofabitch!" she hissed as she tossed back the covers and clambered out of bed. She was across the room, down the hall, and pounding on Fisher's door six seconds later. Each time her fist made contact with his door felt like a cathartic release.

The music cut off immediately. A handful of heartbeats later, the door swung open and Eliza was momentarily struck my Fisher's tousled hair and soft eyes. Memories of the handful of mornings she'd woken up to find him in bed beside her, looking just like this came crashing back and tried to soften her resolve.

Cue the butterflies.

Then she remembered the pain he'd caused her when he'd unceremoniously called it quits, and the hurt he'd been inflicting ever since by becoming the world's biggest ball-bag. And she mentally pictured taking a BB gun and shooting the damn butterflies one by one.

With a glare she felt could have cut through steel, she demanded, "What the hell are you so happy about?"

He cocked his head. Humor tugged at the corners of his mouth. That mouth that was too pretty to look at. That mouth that she now knew was too talented for his own good.

She wanted to punch it.

She also wanted to kiss it.

But mostly punch it.

"Good mornin' to ya, too, Liza." His deep drawl was smoother and more melodical than his harmonica playing had been. And the fact he'd used her nickname made her knees wobble.

She staunchly firmed them up and continued to glare at him.

"What makes ya think I'm happy?" he asked, his tone far too cordial for her liking.

"Taylor Swift. You play Taylor when you're happy," she declared, hands on hips. "And you're doubling down today, which means you must be doubly happy. But I can't figure out *why* that should be because you just got back from a failed mission and your best friend is in a cast."

He shrugged and stepped back to swing an arm wide. "Would ya like to come in? Or do ya prefer to keep havin' this conversation in the hall?"

She blinked. They hadn't stepped foot in each other's rooms since the breakup—or whatever one called it when one person in a FWB scenario decided to end things.

Hesitantly, she crossed the threshold and turned to frown at him when he closed the door behind her.

"Take a seat." He motioned to his bed. It was unmade. And a flurry of images of what the two of them had done atop those very sheets flipped through her mind.

She took a tentative step in that direction and then stopped. "You know what? I think I'd rather stand."

She already felt vulnerable. She didn't want him towering over her to exacerbate the situation.

"Suit yourself." He breezed by her and sat on the edge of the bed.

She hated the way he nonchalantly leaned back on his hands. She hated worse the way he let his eyes roam over her face.

When confronting an ex-lover, she figured it was pretty normal to want to look amazing. But she knew she looked as bad as she felt.

He confirmed it by asking, "How are ya feelin' this mornin'?"

"About like you'd expect," she snapped back, her fingers automatically seeking the comfort of her locket.

When his gaze tracked the move, she immediately dropped the necklace.

His expression turned sympathetic then. He glanced slowly around the room before returning those golden eyes to her face. "Ya sure ya don't want to sit?" He patted the space next to him.

"Nope." She crossed her arms. "I'm happy where I am."

"Okay." He nodded. "So, ya asked why I'm so happy this mornin'. And I reckon my answer is I'm happy because I realized last night after talkin' to Boss that all the reasons I've been denyin' my love for you all these years don't hold water."

Her knees wobbled again. This time there was no firming them up.

Fisher hopped off the bed and caught her before she could crumble to the floor. He gently escorted her to the bed and only resumed his seat once he was assured she was settled.

Her heart raced. The air in the room was still and warm and smelled faintly of his smoky aftershave. It all combined to have her head spinning as his words echoed in her mind.

Had she heard him correctly?

Nah. Couldn't have, she told herself. Her hangover had caused her to hallucinate.

"I'm sorry." She shook her head, her voice straining to rise above a whisper. "I'm not sure I caught that last part." She lifted a trembling hand to her temple. "I think my hangover is screwing with my auditory processing."

He took her hand into his and she marveled at how small her fingers looked in comparison to his. How pale her skin was next to his.

His callused fingertips brushed her palm and she realized just how much she'd missed his touch. How much she'd been craving it.

"Which part?" he asked. "The part where I said I had a conversation with Boss last night? Or the part where I confessed to lovin' ya?"

His grip tightened when she swayed.

"Whoa there." He pulled her close so he could throw an arm around her waist and keep her upright.

His confession hung in the air like a fragile promise. But she still couldn't make herself believe she'd heard him correctly.

It was obvious he read her bewilderment because he said patiently, "Let me put it in no uncertain terms. I love you, Eliza Meadows. The first time I saw ya, my heart stumbled. The second time I saw ya, it fell right at your feet. And there it's stayed for four years."

Her breath caught. Her heart stopped beating. And despite feeling as dehydrated as a raisin, she burst into tears.

"All right." He pulled her into his lap and held her as she tucked her face into the warm crook of his shoulder and wetted the collar of his T-shirt.

Why am I crying? she wondered when the tidal wave of emotions had finished washing over her, leaving her limp and drained.

It was the voice of reason that answered. *Because when dreams come true, sometimes tears are the only way to express the enormity of one's euphoria, one's relief, one's gratitude.*

Right.

She pushed back so she could look into Fisher's beautiful, beloved face. "Why did it take you so long to admit it?"

"Well…" He twisted his lips. "For one thing, I didn't think I was worthy of ya. I mean, you're *you*, and I'm *me*. I figured ya wouldn't look twice at a murder's son from Nowhere, Louisiana."

"Fish—"

"No." He shook his head. "I know how ya feel 'bout that. I still think you're too good for me. But somehow ya don't see things that way. So I'm goin' to stop questionin' my good fortune and just enjoy the fact that ya seem to have real dubious taste when it comes to who ya decide to go and love."

Her breath caught again, and he smiled that smile of his that had always made her heart skip a beat. "Yeah." He nodded. "I know ya love me. I heard your confession that night."

She shook her head. "But you were sound asleep."

"I was fakin'." He winked and then smiled even wider when she slapped his arm.

In her head, the puzzle pieces fell into place. "So *that's* why you broke it off the next morning."

"I was scared." He nodded.

"Of me?" She blinked in disbelief.

"Of myself." When two lines appeared between her eyebrows, he explained. "My father ended up killin' my mother for the very things that drew her to him. For her beauty, for her laugh, for her soft manner. She was desirable in every way, and he knew if he wanted her, other men did too. He couldn't stand the thought of that. And the only way he could truly keep her to himself was to destroy her."

She nodded. Then shook her head. "But what does that have to do with you?"

"I was never crazy 'bout anyone 'til I met you, Liza. I never felt possessive of a woman or jealous of the other men who talked to her or touched her until you came along. And then *bam!*" He snapped his fingers. "Suddenly all those things I'd hoped I hadn't inherited showed up and that *terrified* me. I didn't want to be like my dad."

"You're nothing like your father," she declared staunchly.

"I realized that last night. Or, rather, Boss talked me around to the idea. He told me it's normal to feel the way I do 'bout ya. Normal to want to *break the legs and bash the heads*, as Boss puts it, of the men I see lustin' after ya. But what matters is the way I act when I'm feelin' that way. I would *never* think to try to isolate ya from the world the way my father did with my mother. I would never be so afraid of losin' ya that I'd..." He shook his head, unable to even say the words aloud.

"I know you wouldn't, Fisher." She framed his face as the air hung heavy with the meaning of all he'd shared.

His words were more than she'd ever dared dream of. He'd laid his heart bare before her, and she'd spend her life safeguarding it.

"I'd like to give ya that great, big BKI love ya been dreamin' about, darlin'." His deep voice was filled with quiet determination. "If you'll let me."

If I'll let him?

If I'll let him?!?

Was he crazy? It was a dream come true!

"I'll let you." She nodded, thinking of Charlie and the opportunity he'd given her. Because of him, she was going to have a chance at something amazing. A great, big BKI love, as Fisher called it.

I promise to love with everything in me, Charlie, she swore. *I promise to live a life big enough that it'll make what you did for me worth it. I promise to be happy enough for both of us.*

When the tears standing in her eyes slipped over her lower lids and trailed down her cheeks, Fisher thumbed them away. He searched her gaze before his attention drifted down to her trembling lips.

"Tell me again that ya love me, darlin'. I want to hear the words when I'm not havin' to pretend *not* to hear them."

"I love you, Fisher."

His Adam's apple worked in the tan column of his throat.

"I've never been the best at anything," she continued, her voice shaking with the weight of her emotions. "There has always been someone smarter, someone prettier, someone funnier. But when it comes to loving you? There's no one better than me."

He kissed her then. Kissed her like she was his whole world. And it dawned on her she'd found in him more than just that great, big BKI love she'd been looking for. In him, she'd found her person.

Finally...

CHAPTER 36

Fisher smiled when he heard Eliza's soft snore.

They'd spent the day making love and making up for lost time. Now they were both exhausted. But he couldn't sleep. Mostly because he didn't want to miss one minute of his time with her.

Didn't want to miss the way her head was made to fit under his chin. Didn't want to miss the way her smooth thigh felt perfect thrown over his. Didn't want to miss one breath or one heartbeat or one…snore.

It was all suddenly important because life was no longer about surviving, it was about living. And he wanted to revel in it all because…

She's mine.

Eliza Meadows is really and truly mine.

It was mindboggling. Unbelievable. Too good to be true, and yet…

He placed a soft kiss on the crown of her head, dragging in the scent of her.

I guess the rich girl and the poor boy do *sometimes fall in love outside of sappy rom-coms and cheesy romance novels*, he admitted with a silent chuckle, feeling warm and light in ways he hadn't in…well…forever.

A snippet from the Persian poet Hafez ran through his mind.

"The sun never says to the earth, you owe me. Look what happens with a love like that. It lights up the whole sky."

That's how he was going to love Eliza. Not like his father had loved his mother, but wholly, freely, without artifice or selfishness.

And the best part? He would get to build an incredible, awful, amazing, ordinary life with her.

How extraordinary is that?

EPILOGUE

Washington D.C.

Bishop crossed the room and grabbed the television remote from the coffee table. He thumbed up the volume and then sat on the edge of the sofa, blinking in astonishment at the news anchor as she reported on a breaking story.

"The senate minority leader, Chuck Reynolds, was found dead inside his jail cell this morning. Senator Reynolds was recently arrested on charges of insider trading and murder-for-hire. He was denied bail because the prosecutor insisted he was a flight risk. Authorities are saying the cause of Senator Reynolds's death is a suspected heart attack, but they will know more once they have the coroner's report."

"Convenient he's dead," the president said from beside him and he lowered the television's volume.

The president. What a strange idea.

He had known Sandra J. Stevens since she was eighteen years old and went by the name Sandy Waterhouse. It was incongruous to think she was the leader of the free world, the most powerful person on the planet. Especially because he knew she cried at Hallmark movies and ate entire sleeves of Oreo cookies dunked in milk when she got overstressed.

The president.

It was a position that should have been his. But the world had been turned on its ear since his younger days in politics. Men like him, men who preferred the status-quo, who liked the idea of an America run by powerful men and populated by nuclear families, had fallen out of fashion.

Now the voters wanted politicians who looked like them. They wanted their leaders to reflect the actual populace of the country which meant all three branches were chock-full of women, people of color, and those who wanted to raise the minimum wage until the person flipping hamburgers full-time could actually make a reasonable living.

The woke mob, he thought with derision. *They're taking this country to hell in a handbasket.*

By god, he wasn't going down without a fight. It wasn't possible to turn back time, but history repeated itself.

That's what he was after.

A repeat of history.

The Roman republic fell when Julius Caesar's adopted son, Augustus, became ruler of Rome. Augustus shifted power away from a representative democracy and claimed imperial authority for himself. And what happened after that?

The fucking Roman empire, that's what. Nearly 500 years of global authority and dominance.

That's what Bishop was after. Power. Dominance. An American ruler who would crush all progressive thought regarding workers' rights, racial justice, and equality between the sexes. A like-minded autocrat who would make the country what it was always meant to be.

All-powerful. Ferocious. FEARED.

"Convenient in that it means we will all be spared the spectacle of his trial," he said now, waving away the water bottle the president offered him. "But inconvenient in that he got away scot-free."

"What happened to innocent until proven guilty?"

He snorted. "Please. You and I both know Chuck was as dirty as day-old dishwater. He killed John McClean and the others on that committee even if he wasn't the one to pull the trigger. Not to mention he's been using his position to enrich himself for decades."

"Like so many others," the president countered with a troubled frown.

"Yeah. But others use their positions to enrich themselves the legal way.

Chuck got greedy. And besides, we all know those *other* rumors about him are true."

"We don't *know*. We just suspect."

He laughed. "Good ol' Sandy, always giving people the benefit of the doubt."

She made a face and then checked her watch. "Damnit. I'm late for a meeting with the Joint Chiefs."

"Good luck with that," he called to her back and then increased the volume on the television after she'd closed the door behind her.

The reporter, a dark-eyed woman with a voice made for radio, continued, "In related news, congress has voted to award Senator John McClean the Congressional Gold Medal for—"

Bishop turned off the television. He didn't care what posthumous awards McClean would be given. He only cared that one more thorn in his side had been removed.

No, two more, he reminded himself. *Chuck Reynolds is gone too.*

He'd considered having the senate minority leader killed in prison—it's not like he hadn't done it before—but he'd ultimately decided against the plan.

Despite Reynolds having denied hiring Peter Sullivan, hacking Sullivan's Facebook, and wiring money to the account in the Cayman's as well, all the evidence Bishop had planted had been iron-clad. So Reynolds had posed no real threat to him.

Still, it's good he's dead, he decided. *Now, it's all tied up in a neat bow.*

Which meant, after a brief period of laying low, Bishop could start planning the ultimate coup de grâce.

AUTHOR'S NOTE

As time and society progress, we become aware certain words and phrases that are part of our everyday lexicon actually have problematic origins or can be used to further marginalize already vulnerable readers.

As a writer and a lover of language, I strive every day to educate myself on outdated, offensive terms and stereotypes, and work to eliminate them from my novels. (We're not talking swear words here, people.) But I'm still learning. And if I screw up, I'd love to be educated and allowed the opportunity to correct any mistakes. Because I truly believe the pen is mightier than the sword.

Or, in simpler terms, *words matter*.

ACKNOWLEDGMENTS

Major thanks to "The Asheville Crew" for keeping me hiking, laughing, and karaokeing. You all save me from atrophying behind the keyboard by forcing me (sometimes unwillingly) out of my pajamas and into the real world. Glad to be on this part of the journey with all of you.

As always, kudos to the people who do the unsung work of getting a book into readers' hands: Marlene Roberts-Vitale, proofer extraordinaire, Jennifer Johnson, formatter for the stars, and Erin Dameron-Hill for the beautiful cover.

And last but certainly not least, thank YOU, dear readers, for coming back for more Black Knights Inc. I hope you all had as much fun jumping back into the world of motorcycles and mayhem as I did.

OTHER BOOKS BY JULIE ANN WALKER

Black Knights Inc.

Hell on Wheels
In Rides Trouble
Rev It Up
Thrill Ride
Born Wild
Hell for Leather
Full Throttle
Too Hard to Handle
Wild Ride
Fuel for Fire
Hot Pursuit
Built to Last

Black Knights Inc: Reloaded

Back in Black
Black Hearted

Deep Six

Hell or High Water
Devil and the Deep
Ride the Tide
Deeper than the Ocean
Shot Across the Bow
Dead in the Water

In Moonlight and Memories

In Moonlight and Memories: Volume One
In Moonlight and Memories: Volume Two
In Moonlight and Memories: Volume Three